I0615916

SYNDICATE FISTS

SYNDICATE NEXT GENERATION

KIRA STANLEY

AUTHORS NOTE

If you didn't read SYNDICATE PRINCESS....

The world has changed as you know it. The veil which has kept the land of Faerie and the Hellscape underneath separate from the human realm grew weak, and the supernatural lands have been slowly shrinking over time. Fairy folk and demons crossing over into the human realm became more prevalent, causing the mages, vampires, and werewolves to come out of hiding. This forced the Awakening to happen.

Humans and supernaturals fought until the leaders of each side met and made a treaty. In America, five families rose up, the descendants of the firsts of each supernatural species, tasked to keep the supe communities in line. They were told to do this however they saw fit, as long as humans didn't get hurt in the process.

The Syndicate was born, with each family having a pivotal job in the supernatural mafia geared toward a specialty of theirs.

The Rossey werewolf clan was in charge of the recruitment and training of soldiers, the muscle of the organization. Being masters of illusion magic, excellent crafters of making your wildest dreams come true, the Glovefox fairy clan was a natural choice to lead the skin trade. The Winstale mages, being in control of elemental magic and the ones most used to human mechanics, took up the mantle of weapons and innovation, blending magic with technology. The Devil demons were in charge of the darker side, their shadow magic making them tailor fit as assassins for hire and handing the deadly clean-up always needed. The Desmond vampires took over the head seat, putting them in charge of the financials and laundering for the Syndicate as a whole.

Although there were originally some rifts between the families, Rayla Desmond's mating of Ax Rossey, Avery Glovefox, Falcon Winstale, Lex Devil, and Cosmo Desmond, blended the Syndicate into one cohesive family. They became stronger, unstoppable, but the rules still applied.

In order to keep the treaty with the American human government intact, they agreed to have five children, one to take up the mantle of power and leadership for each of the five different sectors of the Syndicate, but there was one major change. No longer would the next boss be determined by their species, but by the talent and passion they possessed. Each child was allowed to carve their own path as long as they still kept everyone in line and the human tragedies were kept to a minimum.

This is the story of the next generation of leaders, the ones who're forging new paths and making the Syndicate their own in the bloody, savage way they were taught.

CONTENT WARNING

This is a dark themed urban paranormal RH romance, in which the main female character doesn't have to choose a love interest. This book is about morally grey characters/villains who only care about themselves and their family, NOT the greater good.

It has dark themes around underground mafia dealings, graphic gore and torture, death, blood play, rough sex, sex with multiple partners.

This book has graphic sex scenes between consenting supernatural beings with magical bodies that are not able to get STD's or bacterial infections. Please do not think humans can make the same sexual choices without consequences.

There are scenes in this book that were heavily influenced by music, and as such, you will see a music list below. I have also added footnotes as to what scenes have been influenced by what songs throughout the book.

If this is something you find <u>distracting, don't like the genre of music, isn't something you enjoy</u> - PLEASE IGNORE IT.

This feature is for those readers that really want to be fully immersed in the process of making this book and is ONLY HERE to enhance the readers' experience. This DOES NOT MEAN you need to listen to these songs to understand what is going on.

Scan QR code below for Playlist:

DEDICATION

To Tiff. Someone who came into my family later in life, but is so engrained that you're a sister to me. This characters hard exterior, need to be strong, but on the inside is full of deep emotions was inspired by you.

1

NOVA

Swaying my hips to the pounding beat, I closed my eyes and tried to just *feel*. Tried to let the bass smooth over the sharp edges of the sounds clamoring for my attention. The clicking of heels from an overdressed patron downstairs, a woman demanding a free drink, the soft moans of a couple tangled up in the corner. I let all of it blur into the background until all I could hear was the music thumping through my skin, syncing with my pulse.

For just a moment, I didn't feel the pressure in my chest from being the Rossey heir. I didn't hear my dad, Ax, in my head, telling me to go harder, to be tougher. Didn't hear the muttered doubts and or see the forced smiles that followed me into every room. I was just a body in motion, hands raised overhead, letting the beat carry me.

"Damn, Nova! Girl out here being all sexy! Get it, girl!"

Cracking one eye open, I glanced down at my little sister. Aniyah. The birthday girl was twenty-one tonight. All of us siblings were here to celebrate her, but today was also the end of an era and the beginning of another—one we'd spent years preparing for.

Now that she was of age, and Calix, the oldest, was pushing twenty-seven, it was time for us to step into power. For years, we'd been the bosses-in-training—grilled, tested, taught how to manage our clans, our territories, and our duties to the Syndicate and our family. The lieutenants were watching, waiting to see which of us would rise and who might crack, but I knew none of us would. Failure was *not* an option.

Change always ruffled feathers, and in the Rossey clan, you didn't get handed power. You earned it, fought for it, or bled trying.

"Come *on*! Look at those two over there." Aniyah's grin widened. "You think either of them has the birthday dick I'm looking for?"

I followed her gaze to the bar, where two men were eyeing her with open interest. One was a werewolf, the other a vampire. Both tall, both attractive, both clearly clocking Aniyah in her glittering excuse of a top and barely there white mini skirt with slits up the sides. She looked like some kind of ready-for-sex club Barbie—flawless skin, full glam, and wild confidence to boot.

No wonder they were staring.

Looking down at myself, I internally grimaced. The ripped black jeans, thick-heeled boots, and cropped black tee I wore under my worn leather jacket didn't exactly scream "sex kitten" like Aniyah. I let the self-conscious twinge fall away, like I usually do, and grabbed two shots from a passing waitress, shoving one into her hand with a smirk.

"Go find out, girl. Can't know what they're packing unless you cop a feel. And, hey… what if he's a grower?"

I wiggled my brows teasingly, knowing damn well she didn't need a push.

She grinned and tossed back the shot. I downed mine to match, savoring the way the Hellfire liquor burned all the way down. Smoke and spice hit my throat, and when it hit my stomach, a cold rush spread through my body, making me shiver.

"Damn!" she gasped, shaking her head. "That shit's *harsh* going down, but once it settles? My veins are *buzzing.*"

I shrugged. "That's Hellfire for you. It figures out what your body craves, then drowns you in it."

Ezra was a genius for sourcing and producing an alcohol that worked for supes. The only downside? It gave your body what it wanted most, which, in turn, made it slightly addictive. For a werewolf like me, who ran extra hot, it created the cool chill that my body craved. If you weren't strong of body and mind, able to control your urges, you might end up broke and at the bottom of the bottle, begging for more.

That was why we were the only ones who sold it. Hellfire was a Syndicate exclusive with a high price tag and heavy consequences for those who abused it. Only we were in possession of a quick fix antidote to counter its magic, and our establishments kept it on hand as insurance to make sure the supes didn't get out of line too quickly. If you got sloppy, not only would we hit you with the antidote, but we would leave you broke, bruised, and blacklisted from our establishments. A heavy price for a supe, one that no one wanted to mess around with.

Aniyah shook out her body like she was shedding all restraint, casting a quick glance back toward the booth. Ezra and Calix were deep in another one of their intense debates. Riot, true to form, stalked the perimeter like a bloodhound, scanning faces while pretending she was dancing with us. That girl *needed* a good dicking more than anyone I knew, just to knock the edge off.

"Come on," Aniyah said, grabbing my arm and tugging me along.

I resisted half-heartedly. "Nah, girl, looks like they both want *you* to take them for a ride, and why not? It's your birthday— call it a two-for-one deal."

She rolled her eyes. "No, Nova. I need a wingwoman." She nodded toward the werewolf. "I've got my eye on the blond with the *come-fuck-me-in-the-forest* eyes."

She blew him a kiss. His pupils dilated, and he unashamedly adjusted himself, which made her giggle.

We stopped at the bar opposite them, and before we could even flag anyone down, the bartender slid two drinks in front of us.

Aniyah took a slow sip, then leaned toward me, her voice completely sinful. "And if he plays his cards right? Might be a little fuck in the bathroom. Start the night off right, you know what I mean."

I shrugged and drank. My eyes never left the werewolf and his vampire friend as they peeled away from the bar and started making their way toward us. Aniyah leaned forward, hiding a smile behind her glass.

"He just got a point for taking the bait. Men have to come to me, *especially* in a club. If I have to go to him, that's the first red flag."

I laughed into my drink. "Now, why is it a red flag *on him* if *you're* the one who walked over and said something?" I genuinely wanted to know, so the question was only a half-joke.

Aniyah rolled her eyes like I was the slowest person alive. "Because, Nova, if they're not willing to get their asses up and chase me, they're not gonna be willing to do all the things I want in bed. It's about reading the situation, and if you can't do what I want, then you're just wasting my time."

She tilted to peek around me, then straightened. "And by the look of it, that vampire's not the one. He's yours."

I choked on my drink, sputtering. "W-what?"

She casually set her glass down, fluffing her hair and smoothing a hand down the few inches of fabric pretending to be a skirt.

"I can just tell," she said with a shrug. "He looks like the type who wants to hear *you* moan for *him*. I'm looking for someone who'll moan for *me* tonight."

What the fuck did that even mean? In my experience, moaning was usually a good sign—regardless of who was doing it.

Before I could respond, the wolf leaned in, bracing both hands on the bar to box Aniyah in, his voice eager. "Now, I *know* me and my buddy are out of our league here," he said, practically inhaling her scent, "and you can shoot me down if you want, but even your rejection would make my night."

Resisting the urge to roll my eyes, I took another sip. Aniyah, of course, giggled at the line and fired back without missing a beat.

"You're right. We *are* far above the likes of you, *but* it's my birthday. I'm feeling generous, so I'll give you a once-in-a-lifetime shot... if you're a good boy."

I turned away, took another drink, and found myself locking eyes with a pair of deep orange ones.

The vampire.

He was watching me now, but he threw his chin toward his friend and my sister. "Looks like those two hit it off. Guess our job's done."

Job? I blinked. *Wasn't he eyeing Aniyah, too?*

Keeping it light, I gave a small, amused smile and shrugged. "Right? Who would've guessed." The sarcasm came out a little strong as I gestured over my shoulder. The wet sounds they were making got louder. "Definitely didn't have *that* on my bingo card tonight."

He chuckled, finishing the rest of his drink. His broad chest was on display in a tight black T-shirt that strained across thick arms, and his gray slacks hugged muscular thighs that looked strong enough to choke a fighter out all on their own. My brain immediately went into recruitment mode, wanting to ask him where he worked out and what his profession was. Aniyah moaned behind me, snapping me out of it, the sound a reminder that tonight was *not* for work. Tonight was for fun.

"There's a bingo card?" His orange eyes lit up, lips stretching into a grin that flashed the tips of his fangs. "Knew this place had more going on than drinking and dancing. I always miss the good stuff."

"Oh, yeah." I nodded toward the doorman, who looked like he'd rather be strangled than listen to the music that was blaring. "Just ask Mr. Sunshine over there. He'll hand you a little sheet."

I chuckled, finishing off my drink before lifting the empty glass in a salute. "I've already got 'drink two drinks' and 'shake your ass on the dance floor' marked off."

A loud thud hit behind me. No need to look. I already knew those two had moved from *making out* to *mounting* each other on the bar.

I smirked, tipping my head toward the chaos. "Looks like Aniyah just scored 'make out with a stranger' and 'make the bartender nervous' in one go."

He laughed, full and genuine. My stomach fluttered. I leaned on the bar and waved at the bartender. "Another," I said, pointing to my empty glass. "Actually, make it two!"

"Is there a square for 'get a drink from a beautiful woman'? Because I think I just scored it."

I laughed for real that time and rolled my eyes. "Oooh, smooth."

The drinks landed between us, perfectly timed. We lifted our glasses to each other, eyes meeting over the rims as we drank.

Something about him put me at ease. He didn't feel like someone I had to keep a wall up with. I could breathe around him. Maybe even have a little fun.

"What's your name?"

He leaned in, still smiling. "Liam."

"Nova," I replied.

"Oh, I know. I don't think there's a single supe in Las Vegas who *doesn't* know the Syndicate heirs. You're in line to take over the Rossey clan, right?"

I nodded and took a gulp of my drink. "And now you're going to run for the hills, right?" My voice was light, teasing, and a laugh even tumbled out, but deep down, I was bracing myself.

It always happened. Once a guy figured out who I was and what I could do, they bailed. The kind of woman who could pulverize a man with her fists wasn't exactly top-tier fantasy material—at least, not for the ones who needed to feel bigger than me. I was too strong, too dangerous, too emasculating.

"Why would I run?" Liam asked, back against the bar with his head cocked in question.

Skeptical, I arched a brow, but he tilted his head, earnest and calm. "You're different than I imagined. A *good* different. You're... fun. Inviting."

Caught off guard, all I could do was blink at him. I couldn't remember the last time a man didn't bolt or treat me like some access pass to my dad or the Syndicate fortune after finding out who I was, but Liam just sat there—steady, warm, and a tad bold.

Taking my silence as an invitation, he stepped closer slowly, giving me every chance to back away before his lips brushed mine, gentle at first. The taste of Hellfire mixed with something sweeter drew me in deeper as my eyes closed.

His hand slid behind my neck, thumb gliding along my jaw, tilting my head just right. My hands found their way under his shirt, gripping his sides and pulling him closer like I'd forgotten why I wasn't supposed to want this.

This thing between us wasn't ravenous, not like Aniyah and her wolf behind us. It was slow, teasing, dizzying, and I wanted *more* of it.

"Come on, guys! Dance floor!" Aniyah's voice rang out, and we broke apart just in time for her to snatch my wrist and tug me with her.

Lifting my head, I glanced toward Ezra, who tipped her glass in a wordless check-in from the booth where she sat beside Calix. I gave her a nod back—*all good here.*

Aniyah leaned in as we pushed through a crush of bodies. "I need to see what this wolf's stamina looks like *before* I take him for a ride." Her eyes flicked to Liam behind me. "But *you* look like you're having a real good time."

She winked, then opened her mouth and mimed a blowjob.

Groaning, I shook my head. "Aniyah, I'm *not* about to suck a dick in the middle of the dance floor. That's your lane."

With a cackle, she released my arm and spun toward her wolf, grinding against him without hesitation.

The beat dropped, pulsing hard in my chest. I raised my hands, swaying into it, letting the rhythm guide my body instead of my brain. For once, I stopped thinking. I just *moved.*

A hand slid around my waist.

I jerked, instincts flaring, but the hard chest behind me didn't shove, didn't trap. He just moved with me. Slow, steady.

"Is there a square for 'dancing with someone who tried to ditch you'?"

A laugh escaped before I could stop it. His grip firmed just slightly on my waist, grounding me. I could've broken out of it easily.

I turned my head, catching sight of Aniyah in full seduction mode. She was folded over, shaking her ass against wolf boy as he grinned down at her like he had already won. A pang hit my chest. She could just *let go*. She never cared what anyone thought. Didn't have to prove herself every damn second. Aniyah was chaos and charm and impulsive pleasure. I loved that about her, but I envied it too.

Me? As the leader of a rough group of fighters, I had to stay hard. Sharp. Ready to swing, ready to hold the line.

Just once, I wanted to do what *my body* wanted. To live a little… or maybe a lot.

I glanced at her again, my decision firming up as I let go. It was a special occasion. I deserved a little indulgence. My hips rolled back, grinding against Liam, and heat flashed through me as his cool body met mine.

The song changed. Lights dimmed. A deep red pulse lit the air, slow and steady, like a heartbeat in Hell. I leaned back, resting my head on his shoulder. His hands slid up my sides, mapping me, and I sighed, my hand drifting up behind me to trace the back of his neck.

His nose ran along my throat, drawing a full-body shiver from me. The scent of heat and something darker curled around me… and then his fingers drifted lower, pulling at buttons.

Slipping past the waistband of my pants, he brushed my clit with wicked precision. I gasped, heart stuttering, and he kissed the side of my neck with enthusiasm that said he was barely holding himself together.

"I can't help it," he whispered, his voice rough, breath shaking. His other hand cupped my breast as his thumb brushed over my nipple. I had no bra to hide the way it peaked under his touch.

"Oh, fuck," I exhaled. The words were soft and breathless, something I rarely let anyone hear.

He chuckled against my skin, running his fangs teasingly along my neck. I growled, deep and low.

My wolf stirred—awake now. She only ever came out when we were about to fight or fuck, and right now, she wanted both. I could feel her circling around in my mind, the urge to go farther hitting home.

"You know," he hissed against my ear, his hand sliding lower, "I'm just getting started, and look how wet you're getting."

Without warning, he shoved two fingers inside me. I bit down on my lip so hard I tasted blood.

"Fuck," he breathed, his nose coming right up to my lips, "you just *had* to tease me."

His other hand drifted up, fingers curling under my chin, forcing me to turn my head. He licked the blood from my lips and pumped his fingers harder, deeper, over and over until I could barely breathe. My wolf fangs slid out, creating a fresh slice across my mouth before I retracted them. He groaned at the sight of the ruby red liquid running down the side of my mouth.

Smiling up at him, lips smeared crimson, I counted the seconds. He stared for one long breath then lunged, devouring me in a kiss so hungry I thought he might swallow me whole. Tongues tangled. Lips bruised.

His thumb found my clit just as he pushed a third finger inside my soaking cunt. I whimpered, grinding against his hand. The way he moved, relentless, claiming, made it nearly impossible to think.

I wanted more. *Needed* more.

Reaching behind me, I found his cock, already hard and twitching. I stroked him once, then positioned it between my ass cheeks, thrusting back in rhythm with his hand. He growled. His teeth caught my bottom lip as he sucked at the closing wound, drinking me in.

That was all it took. My core clenched around his fingers, and I moaned, loud, guttural, as I gushed around him.

"Oh, fuck, Nova," he rasped. "I can smell your arousal from here. It's *so* sweet."

He pulled his hand from my pants and licked each finger clean with a satisfied sigh. "I have so much more I want to do to you."

My legs trembled as I leaned into him.

"Let's take this somewhere else," he whispered, voice thick with promise. "Somewhere we can enjoy each other to the fullest."

My mind clouded with lust, I nodded, needing more of *everything*. More orgasms. More of him taking control. I didn't want to think. I just wanted to feel.

Just as he took my hand and led me off the dance floor, my phone buzzed. Reluctantly, I pulled it from my pants. My calendar alarm rang, reminding me the fight was starting in twenty minutes.

Shit. Fucking *shit.*

I yanked back on Liam's hand, grimacing. Of course, duty would call *now*.

"I'm sorry," I panted, motioning to my phone. His gaze became confused.

"I need to go." I leaned in to kiss his lips one last time, dragging my tongue across the last trace of my blood on his mouth before pulling away. This was always meant to be just fun, and now it was time for work. He could understand that, right?

As I turned, buttoning my pants and scanning the crowd for Aniyah, Liam reappeared in front of me, holding up his phone.

"Is there a square that says 'stood up by the woman of your dreams'?"

My heart flopped as I replayed 'woman of your dreams' over and over in my head. No one, not a single person had ever even *hinted* at me being the woman of their dreams. I didn't know how to react to that. "I'm sorry." I winced, knowing how that sounded. "I already had this planned, and now I'm late. It's... something I can't miss."

He lifted his phone again, sounding a little desperate now. "What about after? Or tomorrow? I'd really like to see you again."

I had to admit, I wanted that too... but this *was* supposed to be a one-time thing. No strings. No attachments.

Still... the way he looked at me wasn't like the others. The men who glared with annoyance, others with rage, the older ones whose eyes were filled with pity or doubt. Liam looked at me like I was *wanted*... and I liked it.

Snatching his phone before I could overthink it, I punched in my number and handed it back.

"I don't know *when* I'll have time," I said, "but I'll let you know. Okay?"

He nodded, smiling wide enough to flash fang. *Damn*, he was cute.

Nodding goodbye, I made my way toward the bar where Aniyah was downing a drink... alone.

"Hey." I tapped her shoulder, and she turned around, grinning.

"*Hey!* I saw you with the vampire," she said, brows wiggling. "Very nice. Very nice."

I glanced around her, not acknowledging what she said. "Where's your wolf?"

She rolled her eyes so hard I thought they might get stuck. "That motherfucker! Took him to the bathroom to get our fuck on, and when he pulled it out—" She mimed pulling a dick from pants, then flung her hands up in frustration.

"—it was an *average* dick!" She huffed. "Like fucking *this!*"

She held her palms about six inches apart, glaring at the space between them like it was offensive before she looked up and pointed a finger at me.

"That's not *birthday* dick," she snapped. "That's need-this-in-a-pinch dick. And tonight, that's unacceptable."

She rubbed her palms together like she was washing him off her hands. "So I sent him packing."

Grabbing her drink, she knocked it back in one go and swiped her arm across her mouth with a dramatic flair. "I'm gonna find me some birthday dick," she grumbled, "and when I do, I'm riding it so fucking hard—"

I almost felt bad for whoever that poor bastard was. She was on a mission now. Vengeance in heels and glitter.

Patting her on the shoulder, I sighed. "I gotta split. Got a fight I can't miss."

Her bottom lip jutted out in a pout, but she nodded. She knew the drill, and I'd warned her I might need to dip early.

"All right. I get it."

I knew she understood that the Syndicate was always first. Always. Still... I couldn't pretend I wasn't bummed. I was actually enjoying myself.

Pulling her in for a hug, I leaned down and whispered, "Happy birthday, baby sis. Hope all your birthday dick dreams come true."

She grinned up at me, wicked as ever. "Thanks, Nova. And I hope you catch that fine-ass fighter you've been chasing."

I leaned back, frowning, and she cackled like she'd cracked the best joke in history.

"Oh, come on, Nova." She wiped a tear from her eye. "You know fighters have bodies on them. Built like fucking mountains, and you're around them *all the time*." She sighed wistfully. "I wouldn't mind the rigorous climb if I knew for sure their milk would pour down on me... or *in* me, like an avalanche."

I winced, full body. Her analogies had a talent for scarring the soul. Immediately, my brain betrayed me with a vivid image of some meathead fighter jerking off on a cliff while Aniyah cheered him on like it was the main event. Hell no. Banish. Delete forever.

I turned to say goodbye to the others, but Aniyah called out, "They already bounced." She lifted her glass again, a little shrug in her shoulder. "Ezra's got an important meeting, Calix is being a whooped little bitch, and Riot's got a late job tonight or this morning. She wanted to make sure she got back in time for family dinner."

Guilt must've been written all over my face because her smile turned soft, and a hand flicked through the air as if she could shoo the emotion off me.

"No hard feelings. I'm just glad you guys came out. Really. It means a lot."

She looked down into her cup, swaying a little. Something about it tugged at me—just enough to make me want to stay, but I knew I needed to go.

"I'm sorr—"

"Nope." She cut me off and stood up, full power mode again. "Not doing that. I'll see you at dinner tomorrow. Okay? Love you. Bye bye."

She grabbed my shoulders and spun me toward the exit, giving me a little push. "Go on. You've got a job to do, and I've got a birthday dick to hunt."

I blew her a kiss and slipped out of the club, leaving the guilt and the ache behind.

Tonight was a work night.

2

NOVA

"What is that damn kid doing?" Old Man Vic grumbled beside me. "He's going to get himself hurt doing all this fancy work."

With a chuckle, I shrugged, eyes still locked on the last prelim fight of the night. "Hey, it's his choice to go in the ring." Old Man Vic was a human gangster back when my parents were just getting together. He stayed out of their way and his groups stayed out of ours, but now he was retired and liked to watch supe fights. He was good at spotting talent, and his grumpy attitude made me laugh.

In the ring, the werewolf tried for a right hook, but, surprisingly, the fairy dodged, holding his own.

Against all odds, the fairy lasted until the final bell—black eye, clawed up, but still standing. The werewolf won by decision, as he had more hits and more damage, but the fairy? He'd gotten in some solid licks, and most importantly, he'd *earned* some respect tonight.

Putting my hand into my pocket, I fingered the card I gave out when I wanted to recruit someone.

Technique? I could train him, molding his natural instinct into something lethal. But that grit? The unrelenting will to keep swinging even when your face was half-caved in? That was rare. That couldn't be taught.

Sliding my boots along the floor, I was about to get up when Vic whispered, "Wait until you see the last fight before you go scooping up fighters. Make them think you don't need 'em."

I lifted a brow at him, and his hands went up in immediate surrender. "Sometimes the first fruit isn't always the sweetest. All I'm saying, lady boss."

Rock music pumped out of the rickety speaker system in the old boxing gym. A large troll came out, lugging around his tree trunk arms, giving me a nod right before he got into the ring. Rabid had been in the local scene for years and made a name for himself.

If it wasn't for his anger issues, he'd have had a spot in the supe fighting league he so coveted. While the underground fights drew in the crowds for the bloodthirsty nature, the fighting league brought in the money thanks to sponsorships. If you weren't a part of the official league, all that was left to you was the underground fight scene.

All in all, he just wasn't a good listener, which made it a no go. The supe fighting league had so many rules of conduct that it was a little boring for those of us that enjoyed the brutality of a good fight.

What if I made something to combine both?

A young wolf came out, bouncing around as he got into the ring. He seemed newer to the scene, looking around more than paying attention to his opponent. Leaning back, I realized this fight was easy to predict from the first few seconds.

The two fighters strutted around the ring, full of swagger, showboating as they worked the crowd into a frenzy. I scanned the room, spotting a few familiar faces. A bunch of local gamblers called out numbers while a couple of our bookies wrote all of it down. There were also some human gangsters that liked to say they went to supe events to bolster their street cred.

As expected, this match didn't last long. First round, Rabid won by knockout. The young wolf was left sprawled on the mat, face bruised and bleeding, ribs likely broken. Judging by how slow his regeneration was, he wasn't too powerful, which meant he likely wouldn't be healed until the morning. At least he'd have the experience under his belt for the next fight.

It wasn't long before they cleared out the fighters and wiped up the mat to prepare for the main fight. Straightening up in my seat, I kept my eyes open. The guy I'd originally come here to watch was fighting next.

I'd been told to keep an eye on the mage, that he was something special, but when I saw the first fighter, a thick-necked, broad-shouldered, vampire that looked like a one-man wrecking crew, I started to doubt the intel I'd gotten. When I saw the strong but lean mage climb into the ring, it didn't look like a fair match-up.

In any regulated setting, like the supe fighting league, mages had strict thresholds on their magic. No launching opponents across the ring with wind spells, no fireballs, no waterboarding them with their own saliva, no boulders slamming down on them from thin air. If they wanted to fight, they had to do it with minimal magic, relying mainly on body contact, a sharp mind, and maybe a little healing magic on the back end. That naturally made mages the underdogs against vampires, werewolves, or the bulkier fae breeds like trolls.

You usually saw them in featherweight or lightweight classes, pitted against fairies—magic vs. illusion, wings vs. speed. This fight was different. A mage going toe-to-toe with a bulky vampire brawler? Definitely not standard.

The bell rang, and everything exploded into motion.

The mage darted forward and *cracked* the vampire across the face.

"Red shorts has a killer right hook," Vic mumbled, leaning forward like the fight was pulling him in.

Couldn't argue. The way the vamp's head snapped back, you knew he wasn't expecting that kind of heat, especially from the get go.

The vampire recovered fast, feinting with a left blow before swinging a hard right uppercut. The mage ducked just in time, but it was a close call. He had been milliseconds from kissing that jawline goodbye.

Then I noticed it… his feet. There was a subtle gap between the soles and the mat, not even a full centimeter. He was using gentle air magic, making sure to follow the rules, but just enough to float, to keep light on his feet. Smart. Very smart.

I leaned back, arms crossed, forcing myself to look unim-pressed. At these lower-tier matches, you never knew who was watching, so I couldn't let on that I was interested. Not yet. Fighters like him, quiet, clever, underestimated, I liked bringing those types into the Rossey fold and watching them rise.

The crowd erupted again as the mage ducked another hammer swing and landed a jab to the vampire's side. That one *cracked*, a clean, hollow sound that made my veins race. The sound of hits, the smell of blood in the air. It was the only thing that made me feel alive.

My phone buzzed.

It was a text in the sibling group chat. Aniyah. I smiled when I saw it: a video of her dancing in the club, tossing a kiss to the camera before flipping us all off.

I felt a twinge of guilt for leaving her birthday party early, but judging from that clip, she was doing just fine.

Lifting up my phone, I took a quick video of the bloody, sweat-slicked males trading blows in the ring and sent it to the sibling group chat.

Nov: *Someone still has to do the dirty work around here.*

The buzz came instantly.

Cal: *Sorry. I refuse to get my hands dirty.*

I rolled my eyes. Bold-faced lie, and he knew it.

Ri: *They'd look good on a meat hook.*

I squinted at that one, rereading it before huffing out a quiet laugh. Riot never failed to bring it to a weird place, but I loved it. She was unpredictable.

While the typing bubbles from Aniyah danced on my screen, I braced for whatever madness she was about to drop.

Niyah: *I mean, red shorts? I would take that for a RIDE!!!!!*

Niyah: *Do you want to see a picture of my DIRTY WORK?*

Not even a second passed before Cal launched into his usual big-brother meltdown.

Cal: *If you send a pic of a dick, I will fucking murder it!*

Cal: *Then lock you up.*

Cal: *Then tell the fathers.*

Cal: *And the grandfathers.*

Cal:

Niyah: *Fucking snitch!*

I bit the inside of my lip to keep from laughing out loud. This was going to go on for a while.

My phone buzzed again. And again. And again.

Cal: *Not snitching if it's to family.*

Cal: *That's called informing.*

Niyah: *Aaaaand it's called my foot up your ASS.*

Cal: *Aww, that's not nice, baby sis.*

Cal:

Oooooh…. He did *not* just hit her with the baby emoji. I was bracing myself for the incoming storm of all-caps rage texts when the voice of reason finally stepped in.

E: *Enough.*

E: *Aniyah. You provoked him.*

E: *Calix. Quit it.*

E: *Nova. Don't let him slip away. But don't go over what we discussed. Worst case, apply pressure.*

I leaned back, smirking at the screen. Ezra. Even though she was second-born, it had always been obvious she'd take the Desmond seat. Cool, calculated, and impossible to rattle. Nothing like our mom or Tata Ternin, both of whom could burn down a room if they were pissed. Ezra was the opposite. Strategic. Patient. The kind of leader who'd wait *years* for the perfect opening then strike without mercy.

Me: *Got it, Captain.*

Just as I hit send, a gust of air brushed past me. The distinct sweet scent of cherries, mixed with the sharp, smoky flavor of tobacco. I knew that smell. I knew that smell so well that I thought I'd smelled it a million times in the past year.

Don't look, Nova. Don't you dare fucking look. Just keep your gaze straight. Don't let him get to you.

The rapid thumps in my chest were so hard and loud I prayed he couldn't hear it. Keeping my eyes on the ring, I watched the mage dodge another hit, but all I could think about was the man sitting next to me. The one who disappeared and broke my heart a year ago.

"You got your eye on the mage, huh?"

Even his voice was the same. Light and just a bit husky.

I took a few seconds, gulping down a couple breaths before I shrugged. "I'm always looking for men to strengthen the Rossey clan. You know that." I couldn't help turning toward him, but I made sure to keep my face devoid of any feeling—

even when a wavy caramel lock slipped into his eye. My instinct was to brush it back, but I balled my fist up instead.

His striking turquoise eyes were locked on me, crinkling in the corner as his lips tipped up. He smiled at me like he hadn't disappeared for a year, like he was easily slipping back into the best friend role again.

A spike of rage hit me, and my hands tightened so hard the tips of my claws poked my palm. My wolf turned her attention to him, and a flood of emotions ran through me. Excitement. Longing. Heartbreak. Hope. Everything she was feeling for him came at full force. It was unfair, really, especially when I wanted to throw him into the wall as much as I wanted to hug him.

"What are you doing here?" I swallowed hard, trying to keep my cool. Pretending I didn't care that my best friend and first love was sitting next to me. The same man I shared a passionate kiss with and then the next day disappeared on me. Sure, I was told he was undergoing special training with my grandpa Manic but that it was something he requested. He wanted to leave.

"You're not glad to see me, Nov?"

Hearing the nickname he used to call me caused my body to shudder. In my head, my wolf howled that her mate was back. That he didn't reject her. I just wanted to roll my eyes at the claims.

How could he reject you when we never told him that you picked him as your mate? How could anything happen between us after he left once I finally hinted at my feelings for him?

With a whine, she settled into the background. She remembered how I'd felt when he left without a word. She remembered what I'd told myself.

Never again.

I would never again be put in that kind of a position. To be hurt so completely.

The crowd roared as the mage got in a round of jabs and hooks that made a bloody mess before dodging the vampire's counterattacks with the wind below his feet. Only thirty seconds left of the third round, and this vampire had yet to do any real damage. The mage had a shot.

"What are you doing here, Zeth? I'm working." I kept my tone sharp and clipped, letting him know he was treading on thin ice with me.

He leaned over, getting too close for comfort. "Aniyah had her twenty-first birthday, right?"

Tearing my eyes away from the ring, I wanted to yell. *Why the fuck does he care? He left! He has no reason to be here.* Before the words came out, those sea green eyes captured mine, luring me into their depths before I could get an angry word out.

His breath skated across my skin, eyes shining bright. "You're going to be Boss Rossey soon, right?" He paused, and his tongue swiped along his lips before he said, "I'm ready to take my place beside you. Be your second. Like I was always meant to be."

The bell rang just as I shot up out of my seat, the crowd roaring in the background, but my focus was on the insufferable man next to me. *Now* he wanted to be by my side, right when I was about to take my seat?

I grabbed him by the arm, yanking him up with all my might as I growled, "Locker room. Now."

His eyes flicked to where my fingers were digging into his bicep. His muscles flexed, and I let go like he'd burned me. "Of course, Boss Rossey."

We easily made our way to the back since everyone was paying close attention to the judges, waiting for the final verdict. I was pretty sure the mage won, purely based on how many hits he had landed versus the vampire. He was just too quick for him.

He propped open the door for me, and I went in. No one was in there, but there was a dark section off to the side, so I went in that direction.

The door clicked shut, and I spun around, grabbing him by the neck and slamming him into the lockers. Longing and rage warred within me.

I wanted him as my second. I missed him as my best friend, but the pain was still raw.

Getting in his face, I could feel my body vibrating with the warring emotions, and my voice clipped out, "You think it's just that easy? You disappear on me for a year, no reason, no explanation, and then bam, you're back! You think you deserve your spot again?!"

Not trying to get out of my grip, his eyes narrowed. "It's my spot, rightfully. Our dads worked together. I've trained by your side. I know what to do and what is expected of me. I'm a good fit for the job."

My fingers dug into his neck harder, the anger edging out. "It's. Your. Spot. Only. If. I. Say. It. Is."

I could feel his muscles move as he swallowed, taking short, shallow breaths. Still, there was no hint of fighting back. "You're right," he said, his voice barely a whisper. "Can't we… move on?"

Move on? He thought rejecting me and running away was something we just needed to move past? Did that kiss mean nothing to him?

Taking a step away from him, I let him go, and he bent over, gasping for air.

My wolf was teetering between being upset and wanting to rage. Her feelings of rejection and pain threatened to take over, but I pulled up that strength and control from my training and shoved it all down into a deep black box inside of me, never to be brought up again. He would never know that my wolf had picked him as my mate.

Rubbing my hands over my face, I shoved down all the feelings and looked at this logically. He was one of the only people that knew me inside and out. I'd built a rapport with him, and I knew he would follow my directions to a T. He also knew the inner workings of the Rossey clan dealings and how to get stuff done the Syndicate way. He was a legacy, so he already had his own connections and network he could tap into.

All of those reasons said it made sense to keep him at my side, but those nagging, hurt feelings built up in the background until I felt the pressure of it all against my skull.

"Look, Zeth," I sighed, tired of keeping all these emotions at bay, "I just don't—"

Footsteps echoed outside. I caught Zeth's arm, yanking him

into the dark shadows of the corner before this conversation ended up as locker room gossip.

"Don't worry about it, man. The decision went your way anyway."

A familiar voice carried in as the metal door slammed open. Since this was the locker room, I assumed it was one of the fighters.

I shot Zeth a look that said *shut it*. He gave a small, tight nod, and I was again reminded that he would be a great second... if it wasn't for my damn heart.

"Fucking mage! I just couldn't catch the slimy asshole." The voice was a low snarl, each word dragged over fangs. "What the hell do you know? You didn't even show up until the last thirty seconds! Some cousin I have."

"I'm sorry!" The other voice was smoother, lighter, and although the speaker was attempting to sound sorry, his words tasted of arrogance. I knew that voice but couldn't place it. It tugged at my memory like a burr in fur.

The growly voice kept griping about the mage and the decision. This was the vampire that had fought the mage. He was favored to win by a landslide, but apparently, that didn't happen. The mage must've lasted the full fight. Impressive. I'd need to find him later.

"But don't worry," the slick voice reassured, puffed with smugness, "I think I solved all our problems."

I moved toward the edge, needing to see them. Zeth's grip clamped on my arm, but I shook him off.

"Oh, yeah? How?"

"I met one of the Syndicate heirs tonight!"

That made me freeze. Zeth's face darkened like a storm cloud.

I pressed a finger to my lips.

"No, you didn't. Someone tricked you," the growly voice scoffed, then metal slammed as a locker shut.

"Yes, I did. Got her number, too."

The laugh that followed was a knife scrape. "I wanted the younger one, she *so* fucking hot, but my friend got her. So I took the other. Bit manly for my taste, but desperate. I threw her some attention, and she swallowed it whole. Guess who?"

The slow boil in my gut hit my lungs. My stomach clenched tight, the knot twisting and twisting until it felt like it would choke me.

"It was Nova fucking Rossey. I bet if I fuck her a few times, she'll be putty in my hands. I could get you into prime-time fights, and we'll rake in the cash."

Everything inside me went ice-cold. Not rage. Not yet. Just that familiar, splintering ache I thought I'd buried.

I hadn't been expecting forever with Liam, far from it, but I *had* thought, maybe, for a heartbeat, that someone wanted me. That someone saw me as a woman, not just an heir to a dangerous name. That maybe I could be... enough.

Stupid.

All of it was stupid. I should've known better. I did know better.

This wasn't just rejection. It was mockery, a slap in the face wrapped in smug arrogance. A reminder that, to some people, I'd always be "the Rossey sister," the one you settled for.

"Get out of here," a growly voice tried, but Liam's mouth was still running, digging his grave further and further.

"For real! Smell my fingers. Got her to come on the dance floor. She was so fucking easy." A pause, then a chuckle followed. "For a manly woman, she tasted sweet."

The sound of their laughter wasn't just noise. It was every whispered comparison, every sideways look, every smirk from someone who thought I didn't notice. It was the sting of years pressed into a single moment, a sharp, cutting reminder that the hurt had never really gone away.

This was why Zeth didn't want me, why he put distance between us until now. He didn't feel that way for me, how a man feels for a woman. Being the loyal second he was, he just didn't want to hurt my feelings or embarrass me.

Piping hot anger splintered up my spine. Anger at myself, at Zeth, at my beautiful sister, but most of all, at the man in front of me.

My dad's voice echoed in my skull. *We can't let disrespect go unpunished.*

I straightened my back, took a calm breath, and focused on the two men talking in front of us.

No. We can't.

*"Lock the door." The clipped order was powered by quiet fury. I was holding it all back until I was ready.

As soon as I heard the lock slide into place, I lunged. My

---

* Nightmare by Halsey

body broke and reformed mid-air. Bones shifted, fur bursting over skin. My jaws lengthened into a predator's snarl before my paws hit the ground, the change happening in record speed.

Liam went down under me with a grunt, my fangs an inch from his face. His scent—blood, arrogance, citrus cologne—hit the back of my throat and made my lips curl. He shoved, but my claws sank into his shoulders, and the sound that ripped from him was music.

The other vampire stepped forward. Without looking away from Liam, I let my shift melt back through my limbs, leaving my claws hooked deep. It was my speciality, after all, to shift any piece of my body with precision and control.

"You want to lose your life and your career? For him?" My voice a growl layered over human words.

He faltered.

"Try me." I wrenched one claw free and slowly licked the blood off, letting my tongue drag over each drop.

His eyes flew wide, backing away step by step until the door shut, and he was gone.

"No loyalty," I rasped, staring down at Liam. "Must run in the family."

"N–Nova, I-I didn't—" His voice broke when I twisted my claws deeper, his flesh and tendons breaking beneath my grip.

"No, you didn't." My other hand clenched into a fist. "But you fucking will." For once, I let all that control go.

Pound. *Crunch.* Slice. *Splat.*

Over and over, fist, claws, fist, claws. His face, his ribs, his chest, I made a mess of everything I could get to. Warm blood spattered up my arms, slicking my palms and matting my fur. He stopped trying to block when he realized he couldn't keep up.

His cries died down as his jaw broke, becoming little whimpers of pain that fueled my soul. *This was what you expected, right? The savage, beastly Nova Rossey.*

I almost said those words out loud before Zeth's arms locked around my waist, hauling me back. My claws scraped the ground before leaving him.

"It's enough," he whispered in my ear, all calm and levelheaded. "He'll remember. They'll all remember. You did good, Nov. You're so strong, and no one will doubt that. Never again."

Liam was barely breathing, his jaw hanging wrong, his skin torn in deep red lines. I stared down at him and felt... nothing.

Something inside me slid shut. A lock turned. *Never again. I will not be affected like this again.*

"You're lucky he stopped me." I blew out a breath. "A girl like me could kill you so easily." Liam whimpered, curling up into himself.

I crouched down, voice empty and cold. "Next time I see you will be your last." He slowly nodded, curling away from me.

Getting up, I turned away, ready to let go of this disgrace, of this mistake I let happen. "I'm done with him."

Zeth followed, his footsteps almost silent behind mine, and I hardened my heart. "I'll take you as my second. Nothing more, nothing less. Understand?"

"Yes."

I didn't look at him, couldn't. Instead, I closed my eyes. This was the most logical decision, so it made the most sense. And when the time came, I would let him go. I had to. For my own sanity.

THE NEXT DAY, our parents set us up to save them, to beat out this rival gang that had tried to make a name for itself using supes as slaves. After we beat them, proving ourselves to the community, we had Aniyah's family birthday dinner.

It was business as usual—Tata Ternin making jabs at our dads, praising my mom, praising us. In my mom's toast, she shared that they'd be announcing our official takeover as the new bosses the following day.

All of that was fine and dandy, but the looks on my siblings' faces worried me. Aniyah stared at her plate, looking oddly determined. Riot, who normally didn't show much emotion, seemed entirely devoid, like she was numb to everything. Calix, looking utterly depressed, barely touched his blood burger, which was his favorite food. But the one who scared me the most was Ezra. Her eyes blazed with fury and a thirst for vengeance that could not be quelled.

By the end of dinner, a plan had been set in motion. At our mother's encouragement, us siblings were going to get tattoos to commemorate the occasion. Ezra grabbed the keys from her, and we all followed her out and peeled off in our own cars, heading toward the nearest shop.

Bright lights blurred past my window, and my throat tightened. I was going to miss Vegas. This city wasn't just home, it was *mine*. Every shadow, every glint of neon, every corner had my fingerprints on it. It felt safe.

I'd just have to make Montana my new home. It would be a fresh start, and I had a whole lot of reasons to stay focused on work. I had a fighting destination to build.

When I pulled into the parking lot, Ezra had beaten me there. She was unlocking the shop with a small woman at her side. I got out, eyeing the stranger. What was Ezra planning?

"Who's that?"

I jumped, hand halfway up, before I realized Riot had materialized beside me.

"Quit doing that shit, fuck." I rubbed my chest, trying to keep my heart from bolting. "No clue who she is, but you know Ezra. She'll loop us in when we're supposed to know."

Riot scanned the street, eyes sharp, air knife ready, then she nodded. Even though something was up with her, Riot still did her job. She was still too focused, but that was how I needed to be. Leave behind everything in the past and focus on the future.

Inside, Ezra was waiting. Aniyah breezed in a minute later, practically vibrating with excitement, then Calix came through the door, looking like shit. Shoulders slumped, eyes unfocused, hair a mess. A heavy knot of worry coiled in my gut.

What the hell happened to him? Did that bitch Valentina start something? I'd kill her. We all hated her anyway, so it'd be no sweat off my back.

My wolf growled her agreement, that vicious, protective monster already sharpening her teeth. Nobody hurt my siblings and walked away whole.

"I know the past few days have been rough," Ezra said, looking around at us, but her eyes lingered on Calix. *Did something happen that I didn't know about?* "But this is it. Our time. We're taking the throne and building something so big, so terrifying, no one will dare cross us."

She introduced the woman, a mage named Greta, who made special tattoos, then she told us that she was getting one to block mate connections.

My eyes nearly popped out of my head as I tried to wrap my brain around what she'd just said. A mate-blocker tattoo? Unheard of.

Why do you care? the voice in my head sniped. *It's not like you're ever going to find one anyway.... Your wolf picked someone who doesn't see you like that. It's over for you.*

I wanted to say it was wrong, shove the words back down its throat, but after everything with Liam... with the pain I shoved down from Zeth's unintended rejection... I couldn't exactly argue. Maybe removing this option completely would help me focus on what was real. What I could have in this life.

Ezra's calm voice caught my attention. "I need to focus on the Syndicate, on protecting all of you and what our parents built, while also expanding. I want to build something bigger, more powerful, and I... can't afford distractions."

Her expression eased when she looked at all of us. "This is my choice, but I wanted to offer it to you."

Like it was a goddam race, Riot blurted, "I'll do it."

I wasn't the only one staring at her like she'd just said the last thing any of us could imagine. On the outside, she was a stone-faced killer, but deep, deep, *deep* inside, she was a romantic. The kind who'd always dreamed of finding her mate... her flame.

"How long does it last?" The question fell out of my mouth before I put any thought to it.

"I'm in," Calix snapped. "Fuck mates. Fuck love. Just give me my lab and my family. I'll survive."

Watching him stomp past us and drop into the chair, I felt a strange mix of sadness and relief. Something must've gone down with Valentina.

He slapped at his neck. "Right here. I want everyone to see it."

The tattooist looked at Ezra. "Blocator de mate, da?"

Ezra nodded. The woman turned back to Calix. "Nu-ți face griji. Va fi invizibil."

"What'd she say?" he asked.

"Invisible, the tattoo will be invisible after she places the magic into it," Ezra replied. Invisible so no one knew the grave sin we were committing. That was interesting. This was getting more and more enticing.

Calix slumped, mumbling under his breath, "Then how will she know I've moved on?"

Leaning into Ezra, knowing that she would have the answer, I asked, "What's going on with him?"

"Valentina and Calix... broke up. For good."

I nodded, a pang twisting in my chest for my brother. He'd never cared whether she was his mate or not. He'd believed their love could survive anything, but now it laid shattered at his feet.

"The spell is ancient," Ezra explained, moving on. "She couldn't give me a solid answer as to how long it lasts. Maybe around... ten to twenty years."

Ten to twenty years. Not forever.

I prodded at my wolf, asking if she cared about it, but she didn't even acknowledge me.

Zeth and Liam had proved that my instincts about men were shit, and if she didn't care, then why should I? Why waste time? Better to keep things clean. Fuck whoever I wanted while keeping my focus where it mattered: the Syndicate. I would make the doubters listen. Everyone would see that I was more dedicated to the Rossey clan than anyone else alive. I was meant for the position, even if I was a woman.

The more I turned it over in my head, the better it sounded.

"I'll do it."

Ezra stepped up, squeezed my arm, and nodded in solidarity.

This was the right call. No distractions. I'd prove to my men, to the whole fucking world, that Nova Rossey wasn't someone to fuck with. Not now. Not ever.

3

NICK

FIVE YEARS LATER

My old truck rattled like it might shake apart as I bumped down the rutted dirt road my lieutenant swore was the right one. Dust swirled in the headlights. The air inside the cab was thick with the smell of old coffee and motor oil, and the chicken-scratch map in my lap was more scribble than sense. I fought the urge to tear it in half.

My wolf growled in my head, hot, sharp, the sound vibrating through my chest. Anger. Distrust. My grip on the wheel tightened until the leather bit into my palms.

"Get the fuck back down."

He didn't retreat right away. I could feel him staring at me from somewhere deep, his presence heavy. Hot breath ghosted the inside of my ribs before he huffed and sank away.

Six weeks, and the bastard still felt like an intruder under my skin. He could yank my emotions, my body, in any direction he wanted. It was like living with a loaded gun pressed against my spine.

You never should have saved her. You ruined your life for nothing, and now you're this... this thing.

The voice slithered through my skull, cold and bitter. I clamped down on it, shoving it into the deepest, darkest crevices. I had a job to focus on, one only I could do.

Light bled through the trees ahead. I pressed the gas, the hum of the engine turning into a growl under my feet. The road curved, and floodlights slammed into my eyes, searing my retinas.

A steel gate loomed out of the dark. I slowed, gravel crunching under the tires. The lights stayed locked on me as a big, bald guy with an AK-47 slung across his chest stepped up, boots thudding against the packed dirt. He motioned for the window.

I drew a slow breath, lungs straining against the weight in my chest, before rolling it down. Hopefully, he couldn't hear the hammering of my heart.

The scent hit first, feral, wild, tinged with wet earth and magic. My wolf stirred, rumbling low. *Werewolf.*

"Lost?" he growled. His voice was deep enough to feel in my bones. "Don't think I've seen you before."

I shook my head, forcing a lazy, cocky smile onto my face.

"Nah. Jesse sent me." I pulled the wad of cash from my pocket, the bills warm and soft from my body heat, and flashed it. "Said there's good action here."

His eyes lit like a matchhead at the sight of money. "Jessie Logan? He coming tonight?"

He leaned in, and that overpowering smell of wildness and fur assaulted my senses. My mind scrambled for an answer, and the beast inside lunged forward. I blinked, and the cab seemed to sharpen. Shadows snapped into focus, every pore on his skin visible, then it was gone. Back to normal.

"Just... me tonight."

The man's frown shifted into a smirk. "Sure. Pull up and park. See Raven to place your bet." His eyes flashed bright yellow before dulling again, his beast retreating like mine had earlier.

With a casual wave, he motioned for the gate. My gut dropped.

I didn't know who the hell he was talking about, but a name was something. I'd start digging, see what kind of dirt clung to this Zeth.

Past the lights, a large building squatted low against the night, surrounded by cars, their metal shining underneath the moonlit night.

I rolled in and found a spot, the engine ticking as I cut it.

Be likable. Make connections. Show strength. Supes only respect strength.

The moment I opened the door, sounds hit me—cheers, shouts, the *thud* of flesh on flesh. The metallic tang of blood rode the humid night air. My wolf bristled, hackles prickling under my skin, and excitement bloomed from my chest.

Behave, I told him. I didn't want anyone to know I was freshly made. Supes were naturally suspicious, and I didn't want to spook them.

Too many mothers had been pounding on my captain's door, swearing their kids were being dragged into these fights, coming home bruised and broken. Supes didn't have cops, just the Syndicate, a crime family that played by its own rules.

So the captain sent me, said keeping me after the change was "for the betterment of humanity."

My wolf growled at that, but the captain was right. When it came to supes, you used whatever weapons you had. They were untouchable by law, protected by that damn federal treaty. In Flathead County, if we didn't handle them ourselves, no one would, which meant we had to use whatever means possible—even a human cop who had recently turned because he was in the wrong place at the wrong time.

Being useful was all I had left. No human cop wanted to be paired with a monster. They had made that *painfully* clear.

The hate notes left on my desk. The way they parted around me in the hallway, backs stiff, eyes flicking anywhere but my face. The whispers, the dry hiss of my name like a curse. Their fear clung to me the way damp clothes stick to skin— heavy, cold, impossible to shake.

Even Faith, my girlfriend of two years—now *ex*-girlfriend— couldn't stand it. Couldn't stand *me.*

The memory of her recoiling when I touched her, pupils blown wide with panic, still gutted me. She had looked at me like I was a monster. I didn't blame her for moving out that first week after my change, but, fuck, it still ripped something out of me.

Flexing my hands, I experienced the ghostly sensation of claws shimmering just beneath the skin, ready to pop out. I could almost *feel* the weight of them, the sharp bite of air they'd slice through if I lost control.

This job was my only shot to prove I was worth something, that I wasn't just a savage beast hidden beneath human skin. I could feel it in my bones. I could protect. I could save. That was all I'd ever wanted. To pull people out of the dark even if I had to stand in it to do so.

That thought was a steel rod down my spine as I walked toward the building looming in the night. The wood was too clean, too strong, smelling faintly of fresh-cut lumber instead of rot. The massive doors were thrown wide, spilling warm, golden light that bled into the gravel outside as if daring me to come closer.

Crossing the threshold was like stepping into a storm. Noise slammed into me—shouting, stamping feet, the metallic screech of bleachers shifting under restless bodies. The air was thick with heat and sweat, a humid press of flesh and magic. Metal stands were packed in tight rows holding countless bodies whose attention was pointed toward the dirt ring below.

I shoved my way through, the scrape of coats and rough fabric dragging across my arms, the invading breath of strangers brushing my cheek. Two fighters circled each other in the ring, their feet stirring dust into the air as the crowd howled for blood.

"Bite him, you big lug!"

"Dodge! Don't let that right hook in!"

"Quit dancing! Give us blood!"

The beast under my skin jolted, ears pricking, eager as an unchained pup. My senses fractured under the weight of the room. A cold, stale scent like damp soil packed into a grave slid into my nose. I turned, tracking it, and found a pale man

45

glaring at the fight, his jaw tight enough to snap, his knuckles white from grasping crumpled betting slips.

Vampire, my wolf murmured, the word curling in my head with the invasive and inescapable nature of smoke.

Then... flowers. Wild and sun-warmed, tangled with something like secrets. My gaze jerked upward. A man floated above the crowd, wings outstretched, beating the air in time with his shouted encouragement.

Fairy, my wolf added.

No shit, I thought. *I can see the wings.*

I moved sideways through the press of bodies, every shift of air against my skin telling me where people were, how close they stood. A caged-off corner reeked of human sweat and cheap cologne. A human bookie called out numbers, his voice cracking with greed, while hands shoved money through the bars. Humans here, in *this*? Risking their lives for a payout?

We told them to stay away, to live in their own neighborhoods, shop at human-owned stores, and keep a healthy distance from anyone with magic in their blood. Flicking my eyes around, I could see that either our warnings meant nothing... or money and a magical high were worth more than survival.

A sharp, smoky burn scraped down my throat. The scent curled in my lungs, a gasp that tasted like a bonfire came out, and I coughed. A woman with black hair turned toward me, her eyes spilling into tendrils of smoke before snapping back to normal. She winked, laughter spilling from her mouth like sweet poison.

Demon.

Yeah, I thought, *I figured that one out, too.*

The room pressed in. My wolf rumbled, expressing his desire to roll around in all these new sights and sounds, and the sound vibrated through my ribs. My fingertips tingled with the urge to shift. I spotted an empty row at the top of the stands and climbed, every step easing the pressure a fraction.

From above, the chaos sharpened into something almost orderly. In the center ring, a fairy female with hair like orange flames crumpled under a banshee's scream, clutching her head as fists rained down. Blood splattered the dirt, copper-sharp and hot in the air.

At first, I flinched, prepared to cover my ears, but every time she screamed, a ripple of magic shone around the ring. A barrier.

Bruised and battered, the fairy pulled herself up and flew off. Once the announcer claimed the banshee as the winner, a set of males came out, boasted a bit, then shifted into wolves. Their snarls rattled the metal rails before they charged at each other.

They slammed together, all claws and teeth, in a battle for dominance. After a few minutes, the brown one clamped onto the black wolf's throat until the wet *crack* of bone snapped, echoing against the barn doors. As the black wolf slumped to the floor, the brown wolf shifted back, human skin slick with blood, howling at the ceiling as if he could claim the night itself. The black wolf laid broken in a scarlet pool of its own blood, but his soft whimpers meant he was still alive. Supes didn't die easy. You had to crush their heart to finish the job. It was the only way.

The air shifted again, clean, crisp, with an electric buzz that stung my nose and crackled against my tongue. I looked around. Off to the side was a female who flicked her fingers toward the wolf. Air curled under him like invisible hands, lifting him off the ground.

Mage.

Yes. They were born into this world like humans, but inside them laid a power to control the elements. Those beings were just as dangerous as the ones who were monstrous in appearance.

The mic squealed overhead, and the whole room froze. Even the air knew to hold still.

"Aaaaare yyyyyou rrrrready?!"

The crowd's answer hit like a physical wave. Hot breath, stamping feet, and raw animal hunger for violence rolled over me in one deafening roar.

Grinding my teeth, I shut my eyes and hummed under my breath, trying to drown out the deafening mix of voices, footsteps, and pounding heartbeats, but it was no use. My ears rattled. My body shook. My breath caught as the magic in the air rolled over my skin in shimmering waves, making every nerve spark.

Was being around other supes always going to be like this? Or was it just because there were so damn many packed into one place?

Then a tantalizing scent found me, slicing through the tangled knot of stimuli.

Cool, clean air. Crisp as the first breath at sunrise. Beneath it, a thread of wildflowers, delicate but unshakable, wove through the chaos until it reached me. Then came the last note, honeysuckle—sweet, lingering, curling into my lungs slow and sure like it belonged there.

I froze mid-breath, holding it in as though exhaling might make it vanish. It didn't. It grew, subtle and relentless, spilling warmth into my chest until my heartbeat shifted, slower, heavier, hungrier. Every inhale pulled it deeper so that it settled in my bones, seeping into hollow places I didn't know were empty until that moment.

The noise of the crowd dulled to nothing. The thrum of magic faded. It was just that scent, steady and certain, pulling me toward its source like it had my name written in it.

Then I looked up.

*The crowd parted, and she stepped through, a woman with a wild, wavy mane of white hair and a smile that made my beast slam into the bars of his cage in my chest.

"It's now our faaavvvvoooorrrite time of the night!" the announcer bellowed, gesturing to a fighter off to the right. "Our challenger, Brutus Hamersmith, is looking to take a shot at claiming the top spot of the Rossey clan leader!"

The beast inside me lunged to the surface, his focus zeroed in on her. Her head tilted toward the man walking beside her. His face was pinched, brows drawn tight, a stark contrast to her wide, careless smile.

A deep growl crawled up my throat.

Mate. Mate. Mate.

My heartbeat slammed into a harder, faster rhythm. Primal. Hungry. Absolute. I had the sudden, nearly uncontrollable

---

* Big Dawgs by Hanumankind &Kalmi

urge to vault over the seats, storm down there, wrap her in my arms, and never let go.

I crushed my grip on the metal seat until it bent, forcing myself to stay put. She shrugged off her jacket, handed it to the man beside her, and turned back to the crowd, arms thrown wide as they roared for her.

She motioned to the announcer, who threw her his mic, then her voice, light, teasing, slid into every corner of the room.

"As you all know, I'm Nova Rossey, the current head of the Rossey clan."

The name snagged in my mind, followed by a flash of her file, the grainy photo I'd seen at my desk. I'd always stayed out of supe business, but after becoming a cop, the Syndicate's reach became impossible to ignore, along with the Rossey clan's role in it.

The crowd erupted at her introduction. She leaned against the ring wall, that hundred-watt smile making the beast inside me salivate. I clenched my jaw.

"Now, I see a couple new faces..." She shielded her eyes, scanning the crowd. Her gaze caught mine for a heartbeat, and my wolf threw himself against my skull, begging to see her, talk to her, shift with her.

No. Not happening. I locked him down. I was in control.

"So, I'll explain," she continued. "The last fight is usually for the best-known fighters, but here? The last fight is for anyone who wants a shot at leading the Rossey clan." Her smile sharpened into something dangerous. "You just have to get through *me* to take it."

She whirled around to point at a mountain of a man vaulting into the ring. He glared at her like he was already planning to rip her apart. He was three times her size—illegal, if there were any justice in the laws of physics. Even if she was fit and skilled, this guy could snap her in half.

Big wolf. Protect mate.

For once, I agreed with the intruder inside of me.

She was toned in all the right places, her crop top revealing sculpted abs and taut arms. That grin—cocky, playful—made me want in on the joke. Made me want to be in other places.

Wait. She's a supe. What the hell am I thinking?

"I've accepted a challenge from little old Smitty here," she told the crowd, jerking a thumb at him before pointing outward. "And all of you are witnesses."

She tossed the mic back to the announcer, cracked her neck, and nodded.

"Alllll riiiigggghhht! On the count of three, the fight begins!"

Panic prickled up my chest as she started swinging her arms loose.

"One!"

The beast paced inside me, back and forth, eyes locked on her.

"Two!"

Her opponent didn't move, just glared at her with laser-focused hatred.

"Three!"

The first moments were chaos. Both of them shifted in a blink, lunging at each other like missiles. The collision was all teeth and claws. The impact was so hard I could feel a gentle breeze all the way up here.

He became a hulking, black-furred monstrosity, night given form. She was his opposite, pristine moonlight-white fur that was so soft-looking I wanted to know what it felt like under my hands.

In a flash, a splash of crimson slashed across that perfect white fur, and the beast inside me locked up in fear. Then, like a dam bursting, his thoughts flooded into mine. He wanted to take control, rip out the black wolf's throat, and lay it at her feet as an offering. A plea. A *see-me-choose-me* gesture to win our mate.

I shook him off and forced him back down, telling him we needed to watch the fight rather than daydream.

As the fight carried on, I realized the black wolf had the size, but her smaller frame gave her speed. She didn't charge head-on. She went for pain points, darting in and out. Smart. It made me think she just might keep her position, though I still couldn't figure out why she'd risk it at all. Especially for a woman, it seemed needlessly dangerous.

One second, they were trading blows, her white wolf raking his belly before spinning out of reach, but the next, his stance shifted. Something was coming.

He swiped short with one claw, baiting her, and when she dodged, his other came down fast. She twisted and rolled, avoiding massive damage, but his claws clipped her leg. She turned to hide the injury from him, but that was all it took, just a second, for him to pounce.

The beast in my chest howled, slamming against my self-control, demanding I let him help her. *She's ours.*

I gripped the seat harder, staying still. I was here to do a job, not rescue beautiful... I mean, supe females.

I glanced at the man holding her jacket, expecting him to intervene, but he didn't move. Didn't blink. Just kept glaring at her like this was all her fault.

Back in the ring, things were shifting in her opponent's direction fast. She wasn't going to last long like this. I told the beast she'd brought this on herself, trying to convince him that wolfing out at this moment was not a good idea, then a breeze stirred, and I blinked. Somehow, it took only a split-second for her back legs to become human. She kicked him off, shifting back mid-movement.

The crowd roared, voices calling for her to shift again. The black wolf staggered, eyes fixed on what he'd just seen, giving her time to shift one hand human then slam her fist into his snout.

"Wow!" a young she-wolf in front of me exclaimed, turning to the older male werewolf beside her. "Dad! How do I do that?"

"Nah, baby, that's her special power," he replied. "All the Syndicate leaders have special abilities or insane strength. That's how they run things. Don't let their smiles fool you. They're vicious, and they always win. That's why there's no betting this round. It's just for show—hers and ours."

It was at that moment I realized how little we actually knew about the Syndicate leaders' powers. We knew their species and had heard vague rumors, but a werewolf who could shift body parts on demand? Dangerous. Impressive.

The beast inside puffed out his chest. *Perfect mate.*

I told him to shut it. This was a job, not a love story.

Then Nova fully shifted to human and stalked toward the dazed black wolf, naked as the day she was born. My neck grew hot, but my eyes followed her toned, muscular body as she moved with pure confidence, my heart pounding harder than it should.

She glared down at him. "I was trying to go easy on you, but if you wanted hard mode, you could've just asked." Then she kicked him hard enough to rattle his teeth. "Get the fuck up. Let's finish this. Give me everything you've got." Her golden-pink eyes blazed.

She gave him space. He staggered upright, wounds stitching back together, breathing like a freight train. He nodded. She smiled.

"Go!"

They clashed again. He was fully human now, but she shifted her fingers into wolf claws, moving faster, sharper, bloodier. Her strikes were surgical, relentless. That was when I saw it, the enjoyment in her eyes each time she landed a hit. The crowd fed on it, hungry for more, willing her to tear him apart.

When she slashed deep across his belly, spilling his guts, he dropped to his knees, scrambling to shove them back in before regeneration took over.

The bell rang. She lifted her wolf fists in victory, still naked and mostly human, smiling like this was all casual fun. The crowd went feral, chanting her name as she made a lap around the ring, slapping hands.

Then jacket-man appeared, holding all her clothes, telling her to get out.

Who the hell was he to order her around? The beast inside growled his agreement as she laughed, slipped on her top and bottoms, and waved to the crowd before leaving *with him*.

I shoved the thought away, forcing my focus toward the human section. *Job, remember?* They were filing out a side entrance, separate from the supes. I caught a few familiar faces leaving, young punks with worried mothers waiting at home, and made a mental note.

Hands in my jacket pockets, I climbed down the bleachers and headed back to my truck. I was going to need to write a report tonight and submit it to the captain.

Why were the kids here? Why were any humans here? What could they possibly gain that outweighed the risks?

From what I'd seen tonight, I wasn't going to get any answers by just sitting in the bleachers. I needed to get involved. Go deep undercover. Maybe I could get some of these humans to stay away if I got in deep.

Even though I tried to think about work, I couldn't shake the image of her white waves of hair, eyes like pink-gold jewels, those bloody claws, and that savage smile. She was one hell of a female.

4

NOVA

"Stop sulking," I growled over my shoulder before driving a spinning back kick into the punching bag. "It makes wrinkles on your forehead."

Brown-gold hair swung into view first, then those jewel-toned, blue-green eyes found me. They narrowed in my direction, but I kept my gaze locked on the bag. I'd spent years training myself not to fall into those eyes, not to drown there, and I wasn't about to slip today.

"I'm not sulking."

His clipped tone almost made me laugh. Instead, I lifted a brow and popped off a one-two jab, deliberately close to his head.

"Yes, you are. You always get pissy after fight night."

I pivoted, swinging hard—punch, punch, elbow—hammering the bag until he finally grunted. "They're getting bigger. Stronger. The ones challenging you... they're coming from all over the continent for a shot."

I stilled, tilting my head at him. "And you're worried I'll lose?"

He shrugged. Those blue-green eyes that usually cut like glass suddenly looked too soft, and my fingers itched with the urge to hook under his chin and make him meet me head-on. Instead, I shoved the heat in my chest into my fists and drove one brutal punch into the bag. The canvas split, sand bursting out in a cloud around him.

He didn't flinch. Just glared through the storm of grit, jaw tight.

I smirked at the mess at his feet, then pointed toward the spare. He muttered under his breath but hauled it over anyway, muscles flexing as he slung it into place. For just a second too long, I watched the corded strength in his forearms, the easy roll of his shoulders. When he caught me looking, I went back to lacing up my wrist tape like it hadn't happened.

The others in the gym were staring, wide-eyed. Perfect. I gave them my best unhinged grin and a finger-wiggling wave, the kind of thing my grandfather would've done just to keep everyone guessing.

"All right." Zeth's tone was resigned but not beaten. He rubbed the back of his neck, eyes flicking to mine with something rawer than he probably meant to show. "You made your point. I just... don't want the impossible to happen."

I stepped forward, moving close enough to feel the heat of him. "I'll always win. Losing's not an option. Even if they get a shot in, I'll prevail. So, quit sulking and have a little faith in your best friend."

His eyes flicked over my mouth before he grunted, that rough sound low enough to crawl down my spine. Then, with a wicked twist of his wrist, he yanked the bag out of my range, smug bastard that he was.

I narrowed my eyes, then snapped a vicious kick that sent the bag swinging back. My punch landed dead-center, the chain rattling overhead. "Careful, Z. Keep teasing me, and you might be the one I take down next."

His grin was slow, sharp. "Maybe I'm counting on it."

My fists drove harder into the bag, each blow cracking the air, the impact shoving him back a step. A clear warning. I wasn't someone to be toyed with; I was the Rossey boss. *His* fucking boss.

The bag swung wide, rattling on the chain, and for a flicker of a second, I caught the gleam in his eyes, something warmer than mischief. Heat prickled up my spine before I slammed it back down with another strike.

"Okay. Okay!" His laugh tripped out, a little too quick, and I stilled. My chest rose with sharp breaths, sweat damp on my temples, eyes locked on him.

He raised his hands, palms out, a grin tugging at his mouth. "You proved your point."

Hands on my hips, I tilted my head and gave a short laugh. "Really? Zeth Carter, surrendering that easily? I don't buy it."

That grin widened, cocky as ever, though I didn't miss the way he looked at me like I'd just knocked the wind out of him. "Only if it's for Nova Rossey. No point fighting with a brick wall."

My heart thumped hard in my chest. That demon smile of his was meant to disarm people, to make others feel at ease, but that only made me hyperaware of what it did to me and how it made me feel.

I reminded myself to rein it in. I'd done a great job hiding my feelings from him and his powers for this long. It would be a shame to be caught now, but that was impossible. I'd kept it all bottled up inside, locked down tight. I had to combat these momentary feelings by thinking of all the things he did that annoyed me, and fast.

He smiles at everyone like that. He never throws his drinks away, so they're scattered around his apartment. He thinks he knows what's good for me and always makes it known. He's always ten minutes late, and it's usually because he's fucking with his hair.

Then there was the big one.

He's your best friend and your work partner, and that's all he'll ever be. He had made that clear years ago in the old training hall in Vegas, and it almost broke me, so I was *not* going there again.

Grinning wide enough to hide the crack in my chest, I jabbed a finger at him. "You better back off and be nice to me. I'm the one who signs your paychecks."

He laughed, and I turned away, bending over to fish my phone from my gym bag. Scrolling through, I saw a few texts from my captains. Updates, requests, the usual. *I'll just forward those to Zeth.* I had my hands full with starting this fight club channel, and with the launch date only a week away, I was in double-check mode. Then I saw the time.

"Shit. We gotta go." I slung my bag over my shoulder and strode toward the door. Zeth fell in step behind me. Ezra was already twitchy because Aniyah was growing habitually late, and when she was late, the rest of us suffered for it. *Damn mated bitch.*

"What was that?" Zeth asked.

Oh, hell. Did I say that out loud? Fuck.

I shook my head and tossed him my keys before he could push. The Jeep chirped as he lifted the fob, and my eyes snagged on his tattooed arms. Tan, toned muscle wrapped in inky lines of dark smoke. A wolf etched into the smoke like it was emerging from it, the smoke weaving into the Syndicate mark on his hand.

The day I was crowned the Rossey boss and announced I was moving to Montana, he got those sleeves. Standing next to me as my second, he showed the world that he might be a demon, but he was a wolf at heart.

I threw my bag in the back and climbed into the passenger seat. "Think you can make it in seven minutes?"

He slid behind the wheel, revved the engine, and grinned. "Hells yeah! Wave goodbye to the gym, Nov. We're blasting off!"

The jeep shot forward, pressing me into the seat as we whipped out of the lot and onto the road skirting around Whitefish Lake. My ponytail snapped against my face, but even that couldn't stop me from drinking in the crisp air. Vegas would always be home, but this—trees, earth, wild green—was in my blood.

I closed my eyes, spread my arms wide, and drew in a deep breath. My wolf stirred faintly, warmth flickering in my chest, content.

The jeep lurched. My eyes snapped open, a glare locked on Zeth. He wouldn't meet my gaze, but his neck was getting all red. I bet he nearly hit another deer. Idiot.

"Need me to drive?" I shouted into the whipping wind.

He shook his head, hair flying around his face, wild and boyish. "No! Just didn't want to hit a rabbit!"

Biting back a laugh, I turned away. He was such a softie when it came to animals. You'd never guess he was a demon if you didn't feel his aura.

He veered sharply onto a dirt path, and I grabbed the bar overhead to keep from sliding out. My own fault since I told him to go fast.

Glancing at my watch, I muttered, "We're cutting it close."

"I'll get you there, Nov. Don't worry your pretty little head."

I choked. "Little?! There's nothing little about what's in this head!"

His grin slid sideways. "Exactly my point. Big head, big ego, dangerous combo."

I smacked his arm, and he barked out a laugh, which only made the jeep fishtail harder. Those bright turquoise eyes twinkled at the corners like they'd caught starlight, and he said, "I just meant, I got you. *Always.*"

Butterflies erupted in my stomach, but I strangled them quickly. Nope! No, stomach. He meant as a friend. Ally. Confidant. Nothing more.

The forest broke into a clearing where my Calix-upgraded cabin-mansion rose, luxury dressed up in rustic charm. A mixture of dark, rich wood, glass walls, and steel accents with magic carved into them. Calix even installed a sliding wolf door just for me.

I checked the time. No second to spare. As Zeth steered toward the garage, I leapt out, shifting into my wolf form mid-air.

Behind me, his voice called, "I'll park it and toss your clothes in the wash! I'll be in the casita if you need me!"

Running on all fours, I dodged through the deadly traps that lined the way up to the patio—Calix's extra security after what happened with Aniyah.

The wolf door scanned my fur and eyes before beeping green and sliding open. I bounded up the stairs and smashed into my office, shifting back just in time to snatch the robe hanging on my door. No way in hell was I giving my siblings a free show. I wasn't like Aniyah and her damn honeymoon phase.

Dropping into my chair, I slammed on the conference button. Holograms of Calix, Ezra, and Riot flickered to life, all of them sitting and looking at me, but no Aniyah. *Yes! Beat her.*

"Nova!" Calix gasped, clutching his chest in mock horror. "We don't care what you do with your personal time, but did you really need to show up in a robe?"

He slammed his hands over his eyes like I was blinding him.

I breathed in, counted to three, and let my voice drip sweet and sharp. "Some of us actually step outside and do things. Unlike *you*." My gaze dropped to the dark stain on his shirt. I arched a brow. "Is that day-old blood I see, dear brother?"

He glanced down and grimaced. My grin went feral. "Mom taught you better than that."

"Nah," he chuckled. "Mom would've laughed at the mess. It'd be Papa Avery giving me shit, demanding I take a shower and look like a decent member of society." He rolled his eyes, and I swore I could hear his voice in my head saying exactly that.

I missed my parents. For almost five years, they'd been traipsing across the globe, leaving us to solidify our place as leaders. It was long enough.

A soft, sweet giggle drifted from the speaker as Aniyah's hologram flickered to life. Head down at her desk, she murmured something in a hushed tone before looking up, trying to school her expression.

"How nice of you to grace us with your presence, Boss Glovefox."

Ezra's tone was dark, disappointed. Aniyah swallowed.

"Sorry," she peeped, eyes flicking nervously. Her body jerked. Something was happening.

Before I could signal for her to stop, Calix groaned. "Please, dear god almighty," he whined, rubbing his face like he could erase the moment from existence. "Tell me one of your mates isn't under your desk giving you a... a happy ending! Please. Please tell me I'm losing my mind!"

Aniyah's face flamed as black wavy hair and red horns peeked out from beneath the desk. Red eyes, sharp and furious, glared at us like we were the source of all evil—Rasmus. Should've known. Aniyah's demon mate almost never left her side.

"I haven't even started, my star," he said, his voice teasing, "But I agree with you, Calix. You *definitely* need to get your head checked."

Calix nearly lost it. "Why, you little—"

"Enough!" Ezra's voice cut through, firm and final. Rubbing at her temples, she sighed. "Aniyah, I told you. These are closed meetings. Even to mates."

Aniyah's guilty gaze flicked to us, then she whispered to the mate still kneeling before her. "See what you did? You got me in trouble! I told you this wouldn't work."

Rasmus took her hand, kissed it, and flipped it over, pressing a slow, sensual kiss to her palm. His tongue traced her finger before drawing it into his mouth. Her eyes stayed locked on him, lips parted in a soft gasp.

"I *do not* want to see your personal porno, Niyah! Meeting!" Calix barked, shattering the spell.

I looked away, heat rising to my cheeks. I was happy for Aniyah—truly—but seeing them reminded me of what I didn't have. What I couldn't have.

A gnawing pit twisted in my gut, but I shoved it down. I was fine. I didn't need a mate. I had the clan. Laughing inwardly, I reminded myself that being the Rossey boss came with its own trials. I couldn't afford to look weak. Couldn't afford weak knees for anyone, not even for a mate.

Red eyes full of demon fire squinted at Calix. "If I wanted to give you a porno, I would've. Keep your nose out of my business with my mate."

"Rasmus!" Aniyah gasped, trying to rein in her wild mate, but it was too late.

"Rasmus Nefter, do you have a death wish?" Ezra's words were cold, precise, lethal. Shoulders relaxed, one leg crossed over the other, her posture gave off a sense of ease, but her eyes bored into him like twin bullseyes. Swift and exacting.

Rasmus bowed instantly. Smart boy. Aniyah's eyes darted between him and Ezra, trying to navigate impossible waters. I felt for her. Having to balance us and time with her mates was probably hectic.

"I apologize for my rudeness, Boss Winstale," Rasmus said, bowing again but more theatrically.

With a scoff, Calix waved it off. "Yeah, yeah. Just… keep it PG. Too early for my corneas to burn."

Being the one who'd hired the tech genius to work at our little sister's sex club, the Winged Palace, I could tell Calix had a soft spot for the demon.

Aniyah quickly shoved him out of the room, her whispered promise far less discreet than she probably thought. "Wait for me right here, my sexy stalker, and we'll finish what we started." A hungry moan rumbled through the space just before the door clicked shut, then she reappeared as if nothing had happened.

"So…" She shuffled a few documents around her desk, giving herself the illusion of composure before lifting her gaze. "What are we talking about?"

A sharp laugh slipped out of me, somewhere between amusement and disbelief. Across the table, Calix slumped into his chair with a dramatic sigh, clearly done with the theatrics before things even started. Riot sat straight-backed and unblinking, looking like a soldier carved from stone, not a ripple of reaction disturbing her mask. Ezra, though—

she closed her eyes for a slow, measured breath, and when they opened again, a storm was building behind them. She didn't need to speak for us to feel the weight of her restraint.

"I'll keep this short," she began, her voice clipped but steady. "You all sent over your finances earlier, and they look good. Everyone's on track. The legitimate side of our businesses is expanding steadily, which is fueling the illegitimate side with even greater returns."

"Nova," she called out, and I straightened up. "Do you need any last-minute help with the launch of your fight channel? Advertising? Tech issues? Need bodies in seats?"

I shook my head. "No. I have everything lined up. Testing happened yesterday with all the networks, and it all passed. The fighters are lined up and ready. I think we've had a lot of online buzz about the event. A lot of humans have already pre-ordered the channel for opening fight night, and I've already had the spells for the crowd's safety put in place with mages at the ready. It just needs to launch."

For the past year, I'd worked my ass off trying to get this channel up and running. A fight channel for supe fights that took bets through an app. These fights were a lot less stringent with the rules than the supe league. They'd be more of an all-out cage fight between two supes, going as far over the line as the networks would let me.

"Your connection with the heads of the networks helped to get them all on board for something like this." I nodded at Ezra, knowing that she was the real reason I was able to get this televised.

"That's what I'm here for." She threw the words out like it didn't matter, but her smug smile said she knew how much her help meant and she loved that she was the one to get it done. Older sibling reaction at its finest.

"Let us know if you need anything else." She flipped open a file, the edge of the paper snapping with more force than necessary, and faced Aniyah. "Now, about the group that went after you, Niyah. I won't lie, I've been hitting walls. Every lead I chase either ends up dead, disappears, or the trail runs cold before I can grab anything." She exhaled, the harsh breath laced with frustration, and her shoulders tightened with the weight of the failures she refused to accept.

I wanted to tell her it was okay, to not take the failure to heart, that we didn't blame her for anything, but I knew from experience that it would be like talking to a rock. An immovable, stone-cold rock.

I kept my mouth shut.

When she leaned forward, her gaze speared into each of us in turn, her vow burning in her eyes before the words even left her mouth. "I'm not giving up on this. These people, this group, this man, will pay tenfold for what they've done. With. Fucking. Interest."

Her words slammed into me, pounding in my chest like a second heartbeat. Judging by the sharp grins that spread across the room, the same was true for the others. Bloodlust pooled between us, an unspoken pact, a shared hunger.

This was why Ezra sat at the head of the table—not just her ruthless patience or her razor-wire planning, but her refusal to bend once she set her mind. She carried her promises like iron chains, and none of us doubted her ability to drag an enemy straight to hell with them. Whoever had made the mistake of touching what was ours was already dead. They just didn't know it yet.

"Until then," she went on, her jaw tightening, "keep your eyes wide open. Anything out of the ordinary, you chase it. I don't want another situation like Aniyah's happening again."

The way her teeth ground on Niyah's name made it clear that Ezra took the attack as a personal insult, a challenge she intended to answer in blood.

We nodded as one, and the tension in the room softened when she gave us one of her rare, precious smiles. Ezra's real smiles weren't the polished kind she gave to outsiders; they were raw, private things. The kind that said *you're mine, I'm proud of you,* or *I got this.*

"Now," she said, the steel never leaving her tone, "one last thing." Her attention landed squarely on me. "With everything you've got going on, I hate to put this on your shoulders, but I got word from one of my legitimate branches. They need help finding someone who's gone missing. The last place he was seen was at one of your fight nights in Montana. Can you handle this?"

"Of course." I straightened, my voice steady with the conviction she deserved. I'd never deny her, not when she asked like that.

"I'll send you the information in the next few minutes. Keep me updated."

"You got it," I said. Needing something to distract me from my own nerves, I was already anticipating the hunt. "After I review the details, I'll handle it myself."

Ezra gave a single sharp nod of approval before leaning back in her chair. "Good." Her gaze swept over the rest of the table. "Anything else to add?"

Silence answered her. One by one, we shook our heads, falling back under her command. She laid out the time for the next meeting, precise as always, then dismissed us.

The moment the call cut, an email chimed. Ezra's name lit across my screen, and I didn't waste a second before diving in. She had chosen the right woman for this job. If anyone could sniff out the missing, it was me, and I would not disappoint her.

5

NOVA

"Reece Walton. Twenty-nine. Turned werewolf five years ago. Blond hair, brown eyes, medium build. Works for Rathvan, a wayward house for newly turned wolves." Zeth paused, then read more. "Last seen Friday the seventeenth at eleven p.m., Whitefish fight night. Wearing a brown leather jacket, denim jeans, and black steel-toed boots."

Zeth skimmed the file and let out a low whistle. "Turned wolves who actually live past their first change aren't exactly thick on the ground. He should stand out."

Werewolves, like vampires, weren't some ancient race carved out of myth. They were mutations. A demon's deal in the wrong hands, a mage's spell layered on top, and humanity suddenly had a new branch on the tree. One that could be passed down through bloodlines or forced onto a body when the supe DNA mixed into a human's bloodstream.

Being born with it was easier; your body adapted from the start, and you had a lot more support on how to control yourself and your urges. Being turned was different, like jamming a new operating system into hardware that wasn't built for it. Most crashed and burned before they ever made it through the transition. That was why turned wolves and vamps were rare.

Those who survived carried a mark all their own. You could sense it in the aura they put off, the smell in the air around them. Like a human skin was stretched over a wild and restless wolf body, just waiting for its moment to bust out.

"If he was that easy to find," I muttered, tightening my grip on the wheel, "Ezra would've already had him."

His job at Rathvan set alarms buzzing in the back of my mind, and I finally understood the connection to Ezra. It fit her recruitment playbook to a T.

She was always planting roots in projects that looked noble on the surface—orphans, shelters, scholarship programs, training centers. On paper, they were lifelines. In practice, they were hooks. People ate because of her, slept under her roof, and learned skills on her dime. Gratitude turned into loyalty, and loyalty made good foot soldiers. By the time the Syndicate asked for payback, you were already in too deep to walk away.

"Does it say why he was here?" I asked, flicking a glance at the file. "Last I saw, he was based in San Diego."

Zeth flipped a few pages. "Came for the brother of a dead friend. Robert Delton—human, got strung out, OD'd. His brother Jeremy hit the bottle hard one night and wandered into the wrong woods, wrong night, ended up under someone's claws, and was turned. Reece lived with him for a while, helped him get on his feet, then Jeremy found work here in Montana. Looks like Reece just kept tabs on him... until about a week ago when he finally showed up."

I nodded, trying to wrap my head around the situation. "We got a work-up on Jeremy?"

One question kept circling in my skull. Why had Reece needed to come all the way here to check on him? A phone call could've done it. Hell, a damn video call would've been better, but no, he flew out, showed up in person, then vanished. That reeked of something wrong, and the only one who could possibly have the answers was Jeremy.

Zeth tapped at his phone, exhaling sharply. "Not yet. He kept himself off the radar, cash only. Everything under the table, nothing that left a trail. I've got guys digging, but he's slippery."

I ran my tongue along my teeth. The more I heard about Jeremy, the more I was convinced that he was the pin in the grenade. Find him, and we'd find Reece.

"Fine. Just tell me the second you've got a lead." I swung the wheel hard, shifted into all-terrain, and took the jeep up the rocky incline.

"You got it, Boss."

I almost rolled my eyes at that but let it go. Zeth only used the boss card when optics mattered. Most of the time, he was the one pulling strings I didn't have time for. That, and he was my only friend, the only person by my side at the end of the day.

We worked out, ate together, and wasted hours on dumb movies or video games, but the second it got late, he was gone like clockwork. Off to some woman's bed, no doubt. I never asked. Never wanted to see it. The thought of watching him walk away into someone's arms, giving her everything I wanted, would've hollowed me out worse than I already was.

I always reminded myself I didn't have the luxury. I could barely keep the plates spinning as it was. Captains across the Rossey clan who needed wrangling, Ezra breathing down my neck for weekly numbers, siblings who were allergic to asking for help but needed me anyway. My life wasn't mine. It was the Syndicate's, and there wasn't room left over for anyone else.

So, when the itch clawed too deep, I gave in to the wolf. I'd slip into the woods, find a stranger, and let the moonlight erase me for a while. Just a night. Just a body. Wolves were wired to crave it, to take whoever was there under the silver glow. That was the law of instinct. At least until you found your mate. Then it was different. Once that happened, nothing else would ever touch that hunger unless it was them.

I clenched my jaw, refusing to look at my wrist. The invisible ink there was a promise I'd made to myself, as binding as any chain. No mate. No weakness. My choice. No regrets.

Except... Aniyah. She'd shattered the rules, torn straight through the same spell we'd resigned ourselves to, and now she had *five* mates. Five mates who adored her, worshipped her, would bleed, burn, and die for her. She was wrapped in the kind of love I didn't even let myself dream about anymore.

Some people got everything, while the rest of us? We watched. We kept moving. We swallowed it down and pretended it didn't hurt. It was my duty, and strength and control were my gift, so I was built to handle it.

Grinding my teeth, I shoved the thought back into its cage and focused on the trail. The truck bounced down the far side of the hill, carving its own path toward the pits. That was what we called the Rossey training center, where every supe who wanted into the clan came to prove themselves. I liked to get a look at the goods before Hime got the pleasure of tossing them out.

I just wasn't able to pass up on good potential.

About a half-mile out, the one-story building came into view, looking more like a warehouse than the state-of-the-art fight gym it was. Exactly how I liked it, remote, tucked deep in the forest, where I could clock outsiders before they even thought about knocking.

The Rossey training center was meant to bring all of our potentials together in one place and train them. From there, we'd see if they were meant for the main stage, our legal security work, or Syndicate muscle. Everyone had a place and their own worth; it just depended on what your strengths were and where you could make us the most money.

As we rolled up to the gate, I leaned out the window and whistled at the two bird-shifter brothers, Rax and Rumble, perched on guard duty today.

Soon the chains clinked, the gate dragging open at its usual glacial pace. I eased forward and through just as the iron jaws snapped shut, a beat after my back tires cleared.

"Fuck, they almost clipped us!" Zeth screeched. Half out the window, he flipped the finger toward the trees.

I sighed. "They're just doing their job." He flopped back into his seat with a huff, arms crossed like a brat who'd been denied dessert.

Rax and Rumble were oddballs, sure, but they were loyal. Efficient. I could live with quirks. My family was so full of eccentricities that nothing fazed me anymore. Anyway, I wasn't here for them. Hime had flagged a few new fighters as being worth my attention, and while I was at it, I'd press the crew about Reece and Jeremy.

We pulled up to the front. I cut the engine and climbed out. Taking a second to stuff my key into my back pocket, I went for the door to the facility, only for Zeth to suddenly dart ahead and hold it open for me with his smooth, practiced smile.

I froze mid-step. What the actual fuck? Zeth Carter, playing the gentleman? With *me*? Why?

My eyes narrowed. I closed the distance, standing so close his warmth brushed against mine, and studied his face like I could peel back skin and bone with a single look. His smile faltered, unease flashing in his eyes as I leaned even closer, moving slowly and deliberately. His breath hitched, and for one reckless second, I could feel how easy it would be to just... tilt forward.

"What, Nov?" His voice cracked slightly, his gaze flicking down to my mouth before darting away. "W–what're you staring at?"

I straightened at last and folded my arms like armor, keeping my emotions in check even though my pulse was still quick. "Trying to figure out if you got body snatched. Usually, the eyes give it away. Nothing's screaming 'I'm not the real Zeth'... yet."

His easy grin shattered. Jaw tight, he growled through his teeth and threw his hand behind him like he was flicking at a fly. "All right, all right. Just get your ass inside, then."

Pointing at him as I crossed the threshold, I laughed, covering the little spark of heat in my chest with mockery. "There he is. That's the Zeth I know."

"Haha, hilarious." Shoulders loosening, he rolled his eyes, but the slip of disappointment didn't escape me. I almost asked about it when Hime's booming Brazilian accent thundered across the room.

"Aw! *La princesa!*" Hime threw his arms out wide like he was wrangling lions, his grin cutting bright under the lights. "Come, come! The *torneio de luta* has begun!"

Only Hime could look like a walking mountain and still play the gregarious entertainer. My dad, Ax, and Hime had been my first teachers, training me since I was a teen. We'd broken bones together as he taught me to fight, taught me how to walk into a testosterone-choked room and own it. Built me up to be the best fighter I could be while teaching Zeth beside me, too. That was why I pulled him out of Vegas, family and all, to run my training facility here in Montana.

He didn't just train fighters. He could read them. Give him three minutes, and he knew whether they had lungs for five rounds and the swagger to draw a crowd or if they were just alley brawlers with nothing but grit. I trusted his judgment... most days.

He bent down, voice quick with excitement. "Glad you could make some time for us with your busy TV schedule." I glared at him. Wanting to rip out that cocoa-colored man bun and stab him in those dimpled cheeks. His smile widened. "Got a couple of strong contenders today. I'm buzzing to see what they've got. You came at a good time."

Zeth slid in at my side, leaning on the bar like he'd been here all along.

"These two?" He flicked his fingers at the pit, where a vampire clutched at his guts to keep them from falling out while a werewolf bled from the throat like a broken hydrant. "Worthless."

"Not every fight's about the prize," Hime said, his voice loud enough for the pit to hear. "Throw the rabble in with the talent, and everybody gets sharper." He waved at the ref. "Call it. Win goes to the wolf."

Blowing the whistle, the ref scrambled over to the tournament board and erased the vampire's name. The guy limped his way over, begging for another shot, but was shooed away. Behind him, hungry eyes shifted, salivating at the chance to step in and show what they got.

"Don't dismiss the rabble yet," I said. "The desperate ones always bite hardest, and those princesses look like they're ready to get eaten." I pointed to the few fighters off to the side that were laughing and pointing at some of the others. The tone of their bulked-up bodies screamed that they were professionals, but their eyes were filled with more dollar signs than instinct.

Hime folded his arms, lips twitching in that stubborn way that said we weren't on the same page. He wanted proof of what a fighter already was. I wanted proof of what they could be. I liked the gamble, the thought of the diamond in the rough. It was part of the Desmond DNA inside of me I could never shake.

"Come on! This isn't just-for-TV fighting." And there was another shot at my project.

When I came up with this televised cage match idea, some of the captains of the Rossey clan were skeptical. My dad, Ax, ran a tight ship. Real clean fights were held in Vegas in front of a stadium of people, while the bloody side of things was kept to the underground that only supes could see.

I had a different vision. I wanted to make a channel that not only made recurring business but also showed the world how vicious and brutal supe fights could be. It would also announce to the world how powerful the Syndicate was. That had made Ezra almost giddy when I told her.

"You think one of these strays could take down a *real* fighter?" he asked, sweeping his hand across the crowd before his eyes lit with mischief.

"Fine, Boss Rossey. You pick your hungry dog. I'll pick one of my killers. Let them tear each other apart. Winner makes their point."

"And the loser?" I asked.

He scratched his jaw, searching for a prize both of us would be good with, but rewards didn't mean much to people like us. Punishment, now *that* stuck with a person.

"Loser calls Tata Ternin and begs for a good-ol'-days story," I said.

Zeth jerked his head in our direction so fast he nearly dropped his sunglasses. "No. No, no, no. Don't take that bet, Hime." His eyes went wide, and he shook his head like he could somehow ward off the challenge.

Seven hours. That was how long Tata had held him hostage last time, talking about his first kill, finding his mate and winning her hand, then a good long rant about how he didn't see his daughter or grandchildren enough. That night, Zeth walked away a hollow man.

Hime's eyes flicked between Zeth and me, weighing whether to take the bait. I shoved my hand out, a smug smirk curving my lips.

"It's fine if you don't take the bet. I know how much you hate losing."

That lit the fuse.

His eyes narrowed, Zeth groaned under his breath, and Hime's grip closed around my hand, hot and unyielding, pulling me a step further into his space. His mate Jasmine's honeysuckle scent clung to him, but I caught the sharp edge of his own hunger bleeding through.

"I wouldn't be running your mouth, *princessa*. This is my pit. My rules. I know who'll stand and who'll crawl out of here, so yeah, I'll take your bet. I won't lose."

I squeezed back, my smirk sharpening. "We'll see, Hime. We'll see."

He let go first, growling his frustration straight into the dirt before snapping at the fighters, "Tournament's on pause! The great Nova Rossey has decided to join us. Line up. Five rows of ten. Now!"

His face softened when he turned back, drill sergeant air replaced with an almost theatrical sweep of his arm. "I'm still a gentleman. Ladies first."

"Don't lie. You're a gentleman because Jasmine would kill you otherwise." I knew who wore the pants in that relationship. His mate had a firm grasp on those huevos.

He had the decency to rub the back of his neck and look away as I laughed. "You don't need to bring my mate into this. She'll skin me alive if she hears I'm betting again."

I dipped my chin in agreement before scanning the crowd, cataloging my choices. Suddenly, my gaze locked onto molten gold eyes, and the world... shifted.

Heat curled low in my belly, and my pulse thrummed in my veins. Heart pounding so hard it was about to break out, skin prickling, I couldn't look away. It wasn't just eye contact. There was some kind of invisible tether tugging at me. My wolf stirred uneasily, half-curious, half-ready to bare her teeth. Both of us were confused as to why we were feeling this way.

I forced myself to keep moving, dragging my eyes across the other fighters like he hadn't just stolen every ounce of air out of my lungs. I held him in my periphery, though, like my body refused to let him go.

"Nova?"

Zeth's hand brushed my elbow, grounding and infuriating at the same time. My head snapped toward him, his clenched jaw and those worried Caribbean-tide eyes seeing far too much. I yanked my arm free with a tight smile, covering the slip.

"Just taking my time. Don't want my ears bleeding later because I chose the wrong one."

I spun back fast, as if I could outrun his suspicion, only to collide with those golden eyes again. They weren't just on me; they were *in* me. The words left my lips before I thought better of it. Chin lifted, I pointed.

"That one."

Shading his eyes with his hand, Hime squinted. "You want to stake a bet on a turned wolf?"

His disbelief wasn't unfounded. Turned wolves were slower, weaker, fragile in comparison to bloodline-born, but those eyes—gods, those eyes—held a determination that dared me not to trust it. He had pain buried deep, but it was burning hot enough to ignite and win. That man would survive if he wanted to... and that seemed like the best bet for me. High risk but high reward.

"Yep." I popped my hip and turned to Hime, arching my brow in practiced defiance. "So, really, you have no excuse not to win, right?"

The look Hime shot me said he knew I was pulling something, but he didn't know exactly what.

"Nash! Nick! Get in the pit!" he barked. Eyeing me again, he huffed, "We'll see, Boss. We'll see."

Those piercing, molten yellow eyes—*Nick's* eyes—never left mine. Even as he moved forward, even as a lock of raven-black hair slid into his face. My breath caught when he dragged off his dark grey shirt, the fabric clinging until the last second before baring a body cut from years of training and control.

If I were anyone else, I'd be fanning myself. If Niyah were here, she'd be hooting and demanding he strip off the rest.

Nick. So, that's his name. I'll remember that.

The same chill from before ran down my spine, electric and unsettling, and I couldn't tell if it was from the thrill of the fight about to start... or because of *him*.

I forced my gaze off him and onto his opponent, the vampire, and gripped my arms hard. He looked like he'd crawled straight out of a war zone. Scars webbed across his face and body, catching the light in jagged slashes. That alone told me something. Vampires weren't supposed to keep scars unless they deliberately stunted their healing, which meant this male carried his damage like a badge.

His muscles swelled under his skin as if they wanted to break free, his dark eyes narrow, head shaved clean. Grim Reaper, that was the vibe. For half a second, I almost worried for Nick. *Almost.* Then the ref's whistle blew.

The scarred vampire lunged, slamming his shoulder into Nick's face. The crack of bone made me wince, and the thud of his body hitting the floor shook through me. The vampire straddled him and started hammering blows with no hesitation. Nick covered his face, weathering it like a shield wall, but it wasn't a good look.

I nearly opened my mouth to call it, to tell Hime he won and to end it, but something stopped me cold. The air shifted. Down in the pit, the vampire started showboating, throwing in unnecessary flourishes between strikes. That arrogance was his mistake.

Nick had been waiting for his perfect time to strike. One second, the vampire was pointing to another fighter, and the next, Nick's legs snaked around the vampire's ankles, twisting with sharp, brutal efficiency, and rolling him to the side. In a blink, he had the upper hand. My chest jolted so hard I thought it might crack my ribs. He shifted his hands into claws, slowly, deliberately, then raked them across the vampire's face. Flesh tore. Blood sprayed, but not once did Nick hesitate. He just kept going.

Nick was measured and steady, almost restrained, and obviously trained in combat... until he struck like lightning. It was the stuff of nightmares and dreams. I'd owned plenty of gyms all over the United States, but I'd never seen a supe male fight like this before. Elusive. Controlled. Under that calm, the killer was alive and hunting.

The vampire managed to buck him off eventually, but it didn't matter. The damage was done. His body slowed, but not in a calculating way, more like he was unraveling.

"What the fuck?" Zeth barked, his voice cracking. Beside me, Hime's arms were folded taut, eyes locked on the pit, and I saw it. He finally recognized the potential I'd spotted from the start.

The vampire fought like any other supe, using raw speed and brute strength. Nick fought like something else entirely. His dodges were slick, his footwork deceptive, like the way he slid behind an opponent like smoke then punished them with precision.

When the final countdown hit, he unleashed. Kicks, strikes, every blow landed, every dodge clean, and when the whistle blew, he finished with a savage uppercut that rattled the vampire's teeth. The body hit the ground hard. The crowd along the edges roared, fighters pounding his back. The winner was obvious.

I turned to Hime, arms crossed, a sharp smile cutting across my face. I flicked my tongue over a fang I'd let slide out, long and thin, a flash of my savage side. "Told you."

"Fucking fine," Hime grumbled. "You win. Don't get a big head about it."

Too late. That giddy rush burned through me, hot and electric. I glanced back down at Nick, who was already looking up at me. Our eyes caught, held, before I blew him a kiss and winked. A promise. He'd be mine.

"Good job, Hime," I said briskly, looking down at my watch to see whether we needed to head out to the next spot. "We've got to split, but make sure Nick's name is on my winners roster tonight."

"You got it, princesa," he muttered, trying for good sportsmanship.

I hugged him quickly, but my eyes betrayed me, darting back to that wide, sweat-slick, toned back in the pit. My lip caught between my teeth before I could stop it, a thought burning hot in my mind. What would it feel like to touch him? To dig my nails into that muscle and feel it flex beneath me?

"Nova!" Zeth's bark snapped me back, pulling me toward the door.

I scrambled to catch up, but the truth stayed under my skin, burning. Eventually, I'd get him alone. I'd figure out what it was about Nick that pulled me in, making me restless and hungry.

I couldn't wait.

6

ZETH

The jeep rattled over potholes, kicking up dust against the windows as my thoughts ricocheted like loose parts in the engine.

What the fuck was that? What the flying fuck was that?

My hand tore through my hair, tugging hard until sparks of pain danced across my scalp—anything to shove away the burn of what I'd just witnessed. Anything to drown out what I'd just felt.

I should've looked away the moment Nova's eyes snapped open at the sight of that turned wolf, but I couldn't. I should've pretended I didn't see, didn't care. Instead, I leaned in, heart hammering as golden-pink flecks ignited in her pupils like embers fanned to life.

I saw the way her knuckles whitened around her leather sleeve the moment his fist smashed into flesh, the snap of bone echoing in her widened gaze. My chest felt aflame with questions I had no right to ask yet couldn't stop myself from wondering. What did she feel when his eyes met hers? Why had she hesitated when I called her name?

Not knowing was as irritating as angry ants crawling all over me. I *had* to know, had to find out the truth. I had the power to do that at my fingertips... even if something inside told me not to cross that line. I'd never seen her eyes shine like that for anyone but me all those years ago.

Against my better judgment, I'd reached for my demon power, letting the invisible tendrils of my magic brush against her so softly she didn't notice, so focused on the fight in front of her. As soon as her feelings flooded me, I regretted it.

The first thing that hit me was attraction. No big deal. She'd been attracted to other men before, and while it was annoying, it never went further than that. Nothing more than a flicker she'd never let catch. Not worth my time or effort when I was the one by her side.

Ever since the situation with Liam five years ago, attraction was something she'd feel but snuff out before it grew into anything more. She had cracked open that door, peeked through, then slammed it shut before the air could change.

Staring out the window, I reminded myself that even her urges were mechanical. I knew about the pack nights, the faceless bodies, a release she needed so she wouldn't explode. Those nights, I drank myself to sleep, but I understood it. It was an itch she needed to scratch. Once that wolfish urge had been relieved, she would shut the door in their faces. No repeats. No names. They meant nothing to her. *They were nothing.*

And that was exactly how I liked it because *I* was the one who mattered. I was the one she actually trusted and laughed with. The one she leaned on when the weight of the world pressed too heavily. I was her anchor, her sounding board, her safe choice. *Me.*

Which was more important than a warm body for a few worthless minutes of animal aggression.

At least that was what I kept telling myself.

Just the thought of her eyes on him had my nails biting into my palms, but it wasn't enough to cut through the pain and despair clawing in the back of my mind because I knew the truth. I'd *felt* it.

It was interest. Real fucking *interest.* This wasn't a door creaking open; it felt like a crack in the lock, the kind that would grow if you let it.

It started small. A spark when their eyes met. But with every move he made, every second of that fight, it grew, while I just sat there, feeling like someone was driving a knife straight through my chest.

If I were a wolf, I'd have growled so loudly the entire place would've heard. Maybe I would've leapt down and ripped him apart right there in front of her, just to remind him who he was looking at, or more like who he was *not* allowed to look at.

I didn't. I stayed frozen, choking on the sweet taste of her interest while fury gnawed at me from the inside out.

"You good, Z?" Her voice cut through my spiral. She turned in her seat, hair drifting free of its braid, eyes soft with concern. It nearly eased the pain in my chest—nearly.

Those gold-threaded, rose-hued eyes searched mine, soft with concern for *me.* It almost made me smile. Almost made me forget the knife still twisting in my chest. I loved it when she looked at me like that, giving me all her attention. In those soft moments, she let me in. Looked at me the same way she did before I left, before my power got ahold of her.

"Uh—yeah," I rasped, yanking my hand away and rubbing at my chest as if to smother the ache.

Think. Cover. Say something.

"Just… indigestion?" The words came out half-question, half-stammer. *Idiot.*

Her eyes narrowed on me, and when I didn't back down, she rolled her eyes, a playful smirk tugging at her lips. "Zeth, don't tell me you ate another bag of flaming hot Cheetos. I told you not to eat the whole bag."

I shrugged and played the guilty card, hoping she bought it.

She laughed, and just like that, the knots in my gut came undone. Her laugh always did that, smoothed me out, quieted the chaos. She only laughed like that with *me*. Only let her guard down with *me*.

Even with her laughter softening me, the truth scraped me raw.

That wolf was nothing but a shiny new toy with a couple of good moves and a face easy enough to stare at. He didn't have the years we had. He didn't have the scars we shared. All the late-night training, the blood, sweat, and regret I'd poured into her. He hadn't held her when she broke or watched her pull herself together, determined to prove her strength to the world.

He also didn't make your mistakes. Gritting my teeth, I told that voice to go fuck itself. I knew I'd fucked up, and I was paying my penance for it. Every. Fucking. Day.

But still... she looked at him differently, and I hated him for it.

My hands curled at my sides, nails biting into my palms as memory bled through. Chalk-dust air, the echo of our bodies hitting the mat, power ripping loose where it shouldn't have.

Six years ago. Both my best and worst memory. Finally feeling like she saw me as a man, feeling my horns poking through my skull, growing, just when I saw those eyes glaze over, the shine of magic rippling through them. Then everything came crumbling down.

One moment of loss, one failure to hold the reins. I had to go before it got worse. Before she realized she just felt that way because of my magic then hated me.

If I'd been stronger... if I'd tried to learn how far my magic could go before that night—

The jeep jostled me as she veered off the dirt road and into town. "Hopefully, it'll go away soon. Want me to drop you off? I can do this on my own if I need to." She kept her gaze split between the road and the rearview, her voice too casual, too certain.

Her words gutted me.

She doesn't need you anymore. She can do this all by herself. She doesn't want you around. Serves you right for pushing her away. She's going to find someone better.

Panic clawed at my chest. It didn't help that I was already on edge because of that fucking turned wolf, but now my mind was falling off the deep end because she mentioned doing something without me. *Fuck. I need to get a grip.*

I bit the inside of my cheek until I tasted blood, forcing clarity through the haze before I spoke. "It's not so bad. Just a little blip." My tone was light, but she kept eyeing me like she wasn't sure. Before she could press, I redirected. "Where're you taking us? Did someone text you with a lead?"

Her head shook, those pale strands of hair slipping loose to frame the glow of her skin. My fingers twitched uselessly at my sides. All I wanted was to tuck them back, just one touch. Help her brush back those unruly strands.

"No," she said, voice steady, sharp with purpose. "I thought about what you said. He was working under the table, always in cash, right? That limits him. Places that pay in cash, that let you slide under the radar…" She flicked her blinker and turned into a strip mall shrouded in shadows. A neon purple sign shined bright against the dark, spelling out *Moon Runner.*

She pointed. "Here. Best cash rates for work under the table, and anyone who pays with cash is untaxed. If he's been running this long, he's either worked here or at least come through."

The jeep settled into a spot. She leaned toward me before sliding out, her voice dropping into something smug and certain. "I may have only been here five years, but I make it my job to know my territory."

She winked and gave me a wolfish grin.

My heart flopped, ugly and desperate. If it had arms and legs, it would've busted out of my chest to chase her down like a mangy stray begging for scraps.

Why did it feel like both home and hell to be near her? Soft comfort twisted with hunger, rightness tangled with regret? For a year, I worked so hard to learn how to control it so she wouldn't be under the influence of my magic again, and we could build something naturally. Eventually, I'd tell her that she was my mate, and it didn't matter to me if I wasn't hers. I would prove to her wolf that I was the right one for her. But as soon as I came back, she'd closed that door and put me in the friendzone. *Fucking idiot!*

Before I could smack myself in the head, I reminded myself about her secret pact with her siblings.

That mate-blocker tattoo of hers was my only solace. It meant I had time. I just needed to get her to see me as a mate candidate, then everything would be okay. It would all work out. I just needed patience. She said Ezra told her it should last ten to twenty years. I could wait for that.

Climbing out after her, I shoved my hands into my pockets, locking every reckless urge in a cage. If I slipped, she would turtle up so fast, I'd lose the scraps I still had. That risk was not one I was willing to take.

Once I got to her side, she kept her voice low and level. "When we get in there, I need you to read everyone in the room. Find out who feels guilty or nervous and flag them for me. If need be, we'll track every single one later with fewer eyes."

"You got it, Nov." She didn't even look up at me any more to make sure I understood. She knew me so well that she never had to explain beyond the basics of what she needed. That ultimate trust burned a longing in my heart worse than her earlier wink had.

No matter how badly I wanted her, my first duty was the same as it always had been, to be at her side, to use what I was to make her stronger, to remind every supe in this city that the Syndicate had eyes everywhere, and the Rossey clan was not to be messed with.

It was the only way I still mattered in her life. *For now.*

Stepping in front of her, I opened the door and went in first. I held it wide as I released my magic, feeling out the crowd before she even crossed the threshold.

No one inside immediately registered as a threat, but that didn't mean anything. Danger didn't always show itself until it looked straight at her. When she stepped in behind me, all the eyes in the room fell on her. The shift in their emotions hit me like static.

Fear. Agitation. Exhaustion. Excitement. Hesitation.

When I was younger, the flood of all those emotions would've knocked me sideways, leaving me drowning in everyone else's noise. My father had been useless, his demon power more connected with levitation and moving objects, but Ax—Nova's dad—he'd seen me unraveling and took pity on me. He'd asked his dad, Manic Rossey, to train me.

Manic was ruthless when it came to controlling one's powers, and Nova had naturally inherited an effortless control over her powers that others could only dream of. Her wolf and core self were so in tune that she could transform a single fingernail if she wanted. For me, it was blood, sweat, and years of clawing my way up to the kind of stillness I needed to be an asset.

Now, as the flood of emotions poured through me, I filtered it without a second thought. Rather than getting lost in the river of emotions, I grounded my stance and plucked at each pulse of emotion, following it back to its source and cataloging it. Most of them were fleeting—admiration, envy, fear. Nothing was sharp enough to signal real danger.

"You're good," I murmured, signaling that she could step in without worry.

She glanced at the booth in the back and threw her chin at it before making her way down the walkway. I almost told her we needed more cover, but I could already hear her answer in my head. *Do you really think anyone would take me out here? No one touches the Syndicate and lives.*

Her arrogance should've irritated me, and sometimes it did, but other times? It dragged heat through my chest, something that was equal parts pride and hunger. The only ones who completely understood that edge of hers were her siblings, each of whom were unhinged in their own right. Out of them all, Nova was the sanest one.

We slid into the back booth, her claiming the corner seat that put her back to the wall and left her facing the door. That was how we worked. She called the shots, and I executed them. Clean, simple. Except for the fact that I noticed the way heads tilted toward her, their eyes following. She was in a room full of predators, and although she made it seem like she didn't notice, she really just didn't care. She could slice up this whole room, tearing out hearts before they knew what was happening.

It took a few minutes for the bartender to finally come over, wearing a permanent fuck-you scowl, except her emotions radiated excitement, even admiration.

My lips turned down, but Nova, cheerful as ever, asked for a vodka tonic with extra lime, winking at her like they were best friends. I ordered a local beer under my breath, though it felt like an afterthought.

As the bartender left, Nova pulled out her phone and started up some game, feigning nonchalance. Like she'd said, no one wanted to fuck with the Syndicate, so she had to try to make herself look approachable.

The drinks came fast. The server nearly managed a smile when she set Nova's glass down. Nova murmured her thanks as my beer was set down in front of me. I took a sip first, letting that initial jolt of alcohol tingle across my tongue before the effect wore off a second later. The curse of being a supe. Our bodies processed human alcohol in an instant.

The woman turned to leave, but Nova's voice cut through the noise.

"Hey. Do you know anyone who goes by the name Jeremy Delton?"

The server froze mid-step, every muscle locking tight. "I—I don't know who that is."

Nova leaned forward, her untouched drink gleaming under the dim light. Her smile turned sharp, a warning in her eyes. "That didn't sound convincing. Why don't you sit down and tell me everything you know before I get angry?"

Whatever admiration the woman had for Nova bled out in an instant, replaced by raw, sour fear that settled deep in my bones. Sifting through the emotion, I could tell it was tangled up with more than just Nova's presence. She knew something.

Nova slid a magic-forged gun from her side and laid it on the table. Her finger traced along the barrel, tongue flicking over her lip. "Now, I don't want to use this on you. You were sweet enough to get me a drink, but I need the information in your head. We can do this the easy way or the hard way. Up to you, sweetheart."

Oh, shit. She was pissed. "Sweetheart" only came out when she was done playing games.

A man's voice suddenly cut in. "Why don't you leave the poor girl alone? Jemma, get to the other customers. I'll talk to Miss Rossey."

I turned to see a dark-haired werewolf, late fifties maybe, scowling at us like we'd pissed in his beer. No fear came off him, just a weighted acceptance for what was to come, like a man who'd survived too many fights to ever be scared of violence. He was probably the owner since he slid into our booth with the air of someone who belonged there. "What do you want with Jeremy? He's a good boy."

My fingers flexed, wanting to scratch that itch and introduce his face to the table for even thinking he could be eye-to-eye with her, but Nova lifted her hand, telling me to stop, and sipped her drink instead. "I never said he wasn't. He was last seen with someone else, and that someone's family wants him back."

The wolf's mouth split open in a hollow laugh. "Since when has the Syndicate ever cared about missing family members and lost boys?"

The urge to smash in his teeth burned hot, but Nova didn't rise to the bait.

"We care plenty." Her calm, carefree voice gave off the illusion that she was just talking about the weather, but when her eyes flashed, you could see the lethal beast just under the surface. "As long as they're part of our Syndicate family, we care a whole hell of a lot."

"Jeremy isn't one of yours." His arms crossed, his glare screaming he wasn't afraid of her, but I caught the tremor in his hand and the nervousness behind his bravado. I gave Nova the nod. She smiled, took another slow drink, and pulled up her phone.

"Maybe not, but Reece Walton *is*." She slid the screen across the table with his picture on it. "Now, tell me... did Jeremy come in with his new friend?"

The wolf hesitated.

Nova sighed, her patience snapping. In one smooth flash, she pulled out her pocket knife and drove it straight through his hand. His howl tore through the bar, the sound almost comical for a man his size. A few people stood up, but I pulled out my gun and aimed it at them, warning them not to get involved.

Her smile was razor-sharp. "I'll ask again, *good sir*. Did you see Reece Walton with him or not?"

He nodded frantically, eyes locked on the silver knife still jutting from his flesh. The skin around the blade shriveled as the smell of burnt flesh filled the room. Nova smiled and lifted her glass to him in salute. "This is quite good."

The bar had gone silent. Every head turned our way, their breath held at bay when she stood up and scanned the room's occupants.

"Now that you know what I'm after...." She fingered the handle of the knife, twisting it until the old wolf gave a groan. "And that I'm serious, let's add some incentive." Her whole face lit up, and she took her hand away from the knife.

"Whoever coughs up information first gets a thousand dollars cash. Right here, right now."

It didn't take the room more than a few seconds before they started moving. Half the room surged forward, waving for her attention, eager to spill whatever they knew.

While all that commotion happened, the wolf was desperately trying to yank the knife out, but it was useless. Nova laughed at him. "It's spelled, sweetheart. Only I can pull it free." His eyes went wide, despair creeping in.

Her fingers elongated, nails hardening into claws as she slowly raked them down his hand. Thin red lines bubbled along her path as her tone became almost soothing. "Now, your job is to sit tight. Let's hope these people you were willing to defend will tell the truth. The sooner I get what I want, the sooner this will be pulled out."

Some individuals in the crowd recoiled. A bunch of eyes flicking to his hand, burning with a blade shaped hole, before looking at her, reconsidering their odds of survival.

Some red-haired fae lifted his head and pushed his way forward. "I saw them a few days ago."

The closer he got, the easier it was to take in his appearance. The fairy kid looked like he was fresh out of school and struggling to make it on his own. His worn-out hoodie and jeans had obvious holes, and his shoes looked like they were barely hanging on. Not to mention, that glowing skin fairies had when they were regularly fed life essence was vacant. It was obvious what side of the tracks this kid was from.

"So, you saw them? *Both* of them?" Nova asked.

The kid nodded. "Yeah. About two days ago. They came in and had a few beers. Looked like they were in a heated conversation, but it stopped the second the human boy showed up."

Nova's eye twitched, and I forced my expression into something neutral, not wanting either of them to see my shock. A human was mixed up in this? That was bad.

"How long did they stay after he got here?"

Nova placed her hand on the hilt of the knife and spoke the incantation, letting the old wolf go now that we had someone who was talking. The fairy boy tilted his head, searching his memory, then snapped his fingers. "They left once they finished their beers. I guess they didn't want to stick around long."

"Where did they go after that?" she asked, a bloodhound locked on the trail.

Trembling under her gaze, the fairy blurted, "The human underground fights! I heard Reece telling Jeremy it was wrong, that they didn't need to do it, but Jeremy said they had to. He was meeting someone to make a bunch of money, so they all went." I pulled out a wad of cash and handed it to the fairy boy, whose eyes went so wide you would think they might pop out.

"One last question." He looked at her, nodding. "How old was the boy who showed up?"

The kid squinted, thinking. "Probably seven or eight."

Nova's eyes snapped to mine. Fuck. That changed everything. A human child in the middle of this made the entire situation a hell of a lot messier.

7

NOVA

A kid? Why the hell would anyone bring a human kid into this world? Especially as a turned wolf. Who knew what kind of control he really had and whether he could keep the kid out of harm's way. This situation already reeked of disaster, and it soured my mood.

Staring out the window with my arms folded, I couldn't shake the feeling that I was missing something. The fairy kid at the bar had been generous with information, his eyes growing double in size when Zeth handed him a wad of hundreds, but all he left me with was more questions.

Why had Jeremy gone to a human fight club? Sure, being a turned wolf meant he might still have ties to the human world, but he'd left his home and moved here. Most turned wolves or vampires did so in an effort to distance themselves from those they loved or hide from the world and themselves. Also, what did Reece have to do with all of this?

Was he just playing the part of the concerned surrogate big

brother, or was this something more? Did he know about the kid? Did he bring the kid here?

I pulled out my phone and typed out a message to my tech guy, asking him to find out if Reece had purchased an extra ticket when he flew out.

"Thoughts?"

I glanced at Zeth in the window's reflection, blowing out a frustrated breath. "All I was supposed to do was find Reece Walton."

He let out a heavy sigh. "Yeah. It's feeling like a goose chase, but I'm sure we'll find him once we know where Jeremy went, and this human fight club is the next step to finding him."

"And the kid," I reminded him. The kid, since he was human, was now my number one priority. "Now that a human's involved, there's more pressure to bring them back alive. A dead human trailing after turned wolves spells nothing but trouble for us—trouble we've worked too hard to avoid."

If the U.S. government got even a whiff of a human being killed by supernatural means, they'd be up our asses, and we'd be screwed. The treaty between the human government and our family, one that we'd kept alive for decades, would shatter, which could lead to all-out war with the humans. That was a hassle none of us needed, especially with all the work Ezra had put into making part of our business legitimate. She'd put a lot of time and effort into convincing the humans and their leaders that we were people to work *with*, not against.

Even worse than all-out war was the thought of facing my parents' disapproving stares and the grandfathers lecturing us about how we'd disgraced the family name, dragging the Syndicate, and everything we stood for, through the mud.

People could say what they wanted about us being villains or a family of thugs with no law to take us down, but they couldn't deny we kept the supe community in line and under a firm thumb. Our rule was fierce, bloody, and absolute, but it was simple: follow the damn rules, pay your dues, and you were left alone. It was easy if you let it be.

"We can't let that happen," I muttered under my breath, envisioning Tata and Papu circling me, yelling in my ear for all eternity. A cold shiver ran down my spine.

"Don't worry, Nov. We'll find them, and we'll make sure the kid gets back home. I bet his parents are worried sick."

I winced inwardly. I'd only been thinking about the fallout *I* would face if the human died. Shit. That was a little heartless, right? Still, what he said snagged in my mind. *Parents.* A lightbulb went off. The kid had to have parents, ones who would report him missing and give us more information to help find him.

"You're a genius, Z!"

I texted my IT guy, telling him to hack into the human police network and send me reports for any children that had been reported missing in the past few days. I was sure that I could narrow down the options by cross referencing some of the other information we had. Maybe we could take some pictures back to that fairy kid to see if he could ID him.

"I mean, I know I'm a genius, but... for what exactly?"

The look Zeth was giving me nearly broke me. His uneasy eyes darted between the road and me, his hesitant crooked smile stretching wider when I met it. All of it was like he was screaming, *tell me what I did right!*

Not a next second later, I folded over, laughing so loud and hard my stomach hurt. Maybe it was because of the stressful situation, or perhaps I just needed a release, but I couldn't stop.

"I was kinda serious," he mumbled, which only made me laugh harder. It took a few minutes for me to catch my breath.

Wiping a tear from my eye, I chuckled. "Man, I needed that. Thanks, Z."

His eyes flicked toward me, lingering, waiting. I let the silence stretch before finally giving him his answer. "The parents. You gave me the idea to check the database for missing human kids. I've got Mac on it now."

The grin that lit up his face was contagious, and I felt my chest tighten. My wolf let out a small whine in the back of my mind, her yearning for the mate she'd chosen rising in my gut.

Like an addict, I drank in his scent, sweet cherries and creamy almonds with a spicy end note of tobacco. That rich sweetness filled my lungs, and memories rushed through my head.

When our fathers introduced us, and I kicked him in the shin; when he made a trap in the spot I usually shifted, and I fell in; how I'd pretended to cry until he rushed over in a panic and hauled me out, apologizing over and over like the world had ended.

As much as Zeth had grown into a hardened man I could trust with my life, he was still my best friend. He had this gooey center that made me feel… comfortable. Around him, I was safe; I didn't have to be the Syndicate boss. I could just be me.

It was why my wolf and I loved him, not to mention why she'd picked him as our mate.

But thinking about the past didn't bring only good memories.

Pain cut deep as those old memories of rejection resurfaced. The training room. My confession. His disappearance the next day, a clear rejection of me. That day, I started to build the walls around my heart. That day, my wolf became lifeless, only stirring at the need for pain and the scent of blood, or on rare nights when the moon called, and she was compelled to answer.

Until she scented that fighter, Nick. I still didn't know what that meant.

"That'll help us find him faster, especially if there's a photo. Send it to me when you get it. I'll push it through the grapevine."

I nodded, shaking off the shadows of the past. The old feelings sank back to where they always lived, lying heavy in the pit of my stomach. Maybe it would always be like this, yearning for a man I couldn't have, especially not now.

Absently, I traced my fingers over my wrist, reminding myself that this had been my choice. No one had forced me. Aniyah's mates had shattered the spell binding her, but only because they craved her with a hunger that went bone-deep, needed her so completely they wouldn't leave, even when she pushed them away. Maybe it took that kind of devotion to break it?

Ezra was still digging for answers, but progress was slow. The woman who had inked the tattoos was killed a year later by a jilted lover, which meant finding the truth about this spell was going to be a damn near impossible task.

We slid down Highway 93, black and endless beneath the wheels, heading for Kings Point. Underground human fights weren't usually my playground since I left it to their human gangsters and/or billionaires to duke it out, but this was still my territory. Every shadow in my state belonged to me, whether the humans knew it or not. That was why I kept an undercover man everywhere. It had taken me a couple years to do it, but now there was nothing I couldn't get into if I wanted to. Tonight, my guy handed us a key to a very private door.

Vegas had once been the heart of bloodsport, the cathedral of violence, but since I'd moved the Rossey head base into Montana, I'd been chiseling out a new crown jewel. Whitefish and the surrounding cities were becoming the hub for supe fighting.

Fighters, both supes and humans, followed the scent of opportunity north, and the money followed with them, particularly from humans who loved to watch the bloodsport. Hedge fund brats, thrill-seekers, men and women with more cash than conscience, all of them wanted that slice of violence and brutality that the professionals couldn't give you. So, it didn't surprise me that some rich human had purchased a secluded plot of land and built his own arena. Everyone wanted to play at being king; it was just time to bring him back to reality.

The road twisted like a serpent until my watch blinked eleven thirty. An hour and a half gone, but there was still time to catch blood on the canvas. The rough dirt road turned into smooth, pale concrete in an instant, and I knew we were getting close.

The light grey river led us to a mansion that rose like a fairy-tale rewritten in greed. The three-story concrete monstrosity, with its blackout windows and shadowed balconies, was surrounded by silence but humming with power.

Luxury cars glittered along the drive like jeweled offerings. Bentleys, Lamborghinis, and Jaguars lined the house, leading into a large hangar big enough to fit them all. We circled the fountain, its water spilling silver in the moonlight. A valet was already waiting, posture crisp, eyes sharp.

"Miss Rossey?" he asked as I let the window slowly roll down.

I gave him a nod, savoring the pause. "Yes."

"Mr. Mecariee was expecting you. Keys, please. My colleague will escort you inside."

I flicked my gaze to Zeth, who side-eyed the man, acting like he was going to pull a knife on me, but I wasn't nervous about being around a bunch of rich humans. They bled and broke so easily.

Pushing the door open, I took the outstretched hand of the valet and got out. Zeth left the keys in the ignition and joined me. Another tux-wearing man approached, gloved hands folded, bowing with theatrical precision.

"This way."

The air inside was rich with perfume and aged liquor, every surface gleaming. I leaned toward Zeth, whispering with a curl of my lips, "Humans like their underground draped in diamonds."

He smirked. "Supes are too messy for all this. Hard to scrub blood out of silk."

True enough. Where humans had rules, we had appetites.

The butler guided us to the living room, where a marble fireplace dominated the space. Pale stone with a faint blush, two mermaids were carved into the sides, their figures twisting free from the block. Their torsos arched, lips parted, tails curled like dancers caught mid-pose. It was decadent, obscene, and perfectly on brand.

For the first time, the butler's mask cracked with a smile. "Imported from an Irish castle. Mr. Mecariee insists his guests feel transported into an old world."

I tilted my head, lips curving. "Then, congratulations. He's succeeded."

"Downstairs, to the left," he said, pressing something behind the left statue's head. The marble shivered and split, revealing a stairwell of dark stone.

The stairwell was cool and narrow, lit by thin torches that made the shadows cling. Zeth muttered, "Humans and the fortunes they burn."

I shrugged. "We spend just as much on compounds and training halls."

"Yeah, but we're professionals."

I stopped, letting my boots echo on the stone. One hand on my hip, I pinned him with a look sharp enough to cut glass.

"Zeth, we're criminals. We don't need to dress it up. We write the rules, then we break them. Money's just the smoke we throw over the bloodstains."

He scoffed, eyes gleaming. "And you think any of these rich humans don't cheat, steal, and kill to keep this circus? To keep what it is they have in their tight little grasp?"

"Of course, they do." My smile became feral as I hooked my arm through his. "But they're little fish in the massive ocean, while we're the great white sharks. They mean nothing in the grand scheme of things."

His chuckle rumbled low, his grip tightening around me as if he liked the sound of that. "Come on. Let's see the show."

The staircase spiraled forever until the thunder of voices rose to meet us. A few more steps, and the dark gave way to a golden hue.

The cage spread wide at the heart of the room, the fighting ring gleaming under spotlights, circled by around sixty golden chairs. Every one was filled. Men in designer suits barking bets, women in dresses like the fabric was poured over them, gemstones draped over their arms, diamonds dripping from their throats. The air smelled of money, lust, and champagne fizz.

And me? In ripped jeans, boots, and a crop top under a moto jacket, I was the wolf that had walked into their glittering smoky parlor. Understated. Dangerous. Exactly how I liked it.

Two more butlers in tuxedos stepped forward, offering seats and cocktails. My eyes slid to the bar at the side, all gleam and glass. I slipped free of Zeth's arm.

"Go on," I told him, my voice velvet. "I'll get my own drink. You know I'm particular."

He didn't argue. He knew I wasn't after the liquor. I was after the pulse of the room, the secrets humming under the bright lights and bubbly.

I made my way toward the bar in the back, watching as Zeth was led to a pair of golden seats right up front, close enough to catch sweat and blood. Two chairs, empty and waiting. That told me all I needed to know. Mecariee not only knew who I was, but he'd placed me among the important ones, and at the last minute, no less.

This was going to be interesting.

Sliding onto a stool, I ordered a lemon drop. If I wasn't going to get drunk, I might as well sip something that went down like lemonade. The bartender nodded and went to work. I leaned back against the bar, eyes drifting to the fighters in the ring.

They weren't bad. One had decent footwork. If he'd only follow through on his left jab, he might even have a career. Show fighters only had two ways to make money: winning consistently or working the crowd hard enough to fill every seat. Otherwise, you were nothing but a punching bag with limbs.

"Miss," the bartender called, sliding over a martini glass that belonged in a mixology lounge, complete with a flair of lemon garnish. It was almost too pretty to drink. I plucked it by the delicate stem and lifted it, the sugared rim on my lips, right as a smooth, cocky voice slipped in beside me.

"Now, isn't that a sight? A gorgeous woman in boots and leather, drinking from a fragile martini glass."

My eyes flicked toward him. I gave him the once-over without bothering to turn my body.

"And you," I muttered over the rim of my glass, "looking like a hobo who stumbled into a billionaire's mansion."

His laugh was a velvet baritone that sank into my skin with the inevitability of smoke. It made my wolf bristle. That was the laugh of a man who had money and knew exactly how to use it. This kind of man always had a beauty draped on his arm, which made it strange that he was alone.

Like my words were an invitation, he slid in closer, ordered the same drink with a flick of his hand, and leaned against the bar in perfect mimicry of me. It was equal parts irritating and disarming.

I hated it.

"So," he asked, "are you here for the fights, or are you with someone?" The end had a bite to it, like he hated saying it.

I gave him the truth. "I like fights. I came here with someone, but that's not why I'm here."

The bartender set down his drink. He downed half of it in one go then turned to face me fully, his back to the spectacle behind him. "Now, *that's* intriguing. Tell me more."

I almost told him to get lost, that men like him weren't my type, but then I caught those eyes for the first time. A deep green, framed by burnt red-brown hair that looked messy in the best of ways. Words dried up in my throat.

My mind whispered, *"Go, this man is trouble."*

My wolf argued, *"Fall deep into those eyes and never let go."*

I wanted to step back, give myself some space to get a grip, but I refused to give him that kind of ground. To look that weak. Instead, I stepped closer, though unease crawled over me like static.

I inhaled openly, not caring if this human thought it was rude. It was simply how us wolves gathered information quickly. His scent hit me like a wall. Nothing. Blank. Humans always smelled like sweat, blood, fear—something. This man reeked of absence. Somehow, his very essence was locked away.

A growl rattled low in my throat. My grip tightened on the stem of my glass as I glared at him. No one masked their scent among humans, not unless they weren't one, and I did not like being deceived.

He lifted his hands in surrender, but his eyes told a different story. They weren't afraid. They were ravenous with hunger.

Warning bells screamed inside me. His sneakers-and-slacks combo. The long tan coat in the middle of summer. Every inch of him was wrong for a full-of-himself human billionaire with money to burn, and I couldn't look away.

"I'm not going to harm you," he said, reaching a hand toward me.

He thinks I'm scared of him? Me? Fuck that! With my pulse beating in my ears, muscles constricting, I told myself I needed to teach him a lesson.

I caught it, twisted his arm behind his back, and slammed his face into the bar before he could blink. Black-suited men surged toward me, but he spoke fast against the marble slab he was pinned to.

"Okay, it's okay. I can see we started on the wrong foot."

I flicked my gaze toward Zeth. He was already up, ready to go to war. He was a damn good second.

"Let me up, and I'll wave them off. We don't want a spectacle in front of all these humans, now, do we?"

From the way the men circled, trying to stay discreet so as not to drag the humans' attention from the fight, it dawned on me. This man wasn't a guest. He owned this place.

Heat surged through me as if I'd grabbed fire itself, and I released him. Moving back to my spot, I picked up my drink and downed the rest in one swallow, wishing for supe-grade alcohol to take the edge off. At this point, my mind and body were warring between killing him and fucking him. Neither extreme would help me at the moment.

Taking a deep breath, I pulled up that iron control of mine and squashed both instincts, nodding at him.

He straightened, waving off his men, and I motioned Zeth back with a shake of my head. If Mecariee leashed his dogs, I'd leash mine.

He tapped his watch, and the air around him shifted like a barrier had melted away. The rich metallic sting of blood, the weight of hollow ground, the stillness only vampires carried. All that was missing was the slightly sweet note that born vampires had, which meant he was made. A turned vampire.

His lips curved, flashing fang as if it was the last piece of evidence I needed. It was so darn cute, giving him a boyish charm that made me bite the inside of my lip. I hated it.

The crowd behind him erupted at the end of the fight, the timing uncanny. I rolled my eyes, hands tightening at my sides.

"Mr. Mecariee," I said, jaw tight, focusing on what I was here for. "I'm going to be straight with you, even if you're not giving me the same."

Instead of arrogance, his eyes softened, tilting down like I'd just bruised him. I didn't buy this wounded-puppy act. Not for a second.

"Look, I just need—"

"This isn't how I pictured our meeting," he said smoothly, tapping his glass. The bartender refilled it instantly. He took a sip, smiling. "That's good. A sweet tooth. Just another thing you and I have in common." His laugh followed, a soft sound, and I eyed him like I was waiting for the other shoe to drop. "I told you, I'm not here to hurt you. Relax." He motioned to the stool beside him.

Crossing my arms, I lifted a brow and puffed out my chest in disbelief. "I'd like to see you try. Even with your goons— which I *could* handle—you'd still die in a puddle of the blood you guzzled tonight."

His laugh burst free again, rich and genuine, and I'd be damned if my stomach didn't clench at the sound. It was beautiful, magical, reminding me of moonlit trysts and seductive whispers. I hated it. *Maybe if I repeat that enough, I'll start to believe it.*

"How about this," he said, green eyes fixed on me. Despite the crowd bustling around us, his stare said I was the only one in the room who mattered. "Tell me what you need, and I'll help you get it. Deal?"

8

CONRAD

"Pssh. What the fuck are you playing at?"

The way her luscious pink orbs sparked for a second before icing over with mistrust sent a rush of heat through me. Something about her staring me down like I was some gutter-level hustler, a nobody, dumb enough to think I could con her, nearly made me laugh out loud.

But I knew she wasn't the one being tested. I was.

She was the one I should've been afraid of, the Syndicate's legendary fists, a woman who could tear me in two and walk away with blood glistening on her hands, her name still untouchable. And yet... I couldn't summon the fear I should be feeling. All I could think about was how gorgeous this ballbuster of a woman was. How just hearing her rich timbre did something to my insides.

Throwing my hand out, I tried to steady the air between us and build a fragile bridge since she clearly hated that I'd hidden my species. "How about we start with you calling me Conrad?"

She didn't so much as twitch. Her arms stayed crossed, her tone sharp as an executioner's blade. "You can call me Boss Rossey."

My jaw ached from holding back the grin that wanted to spread across my face. She thought she was putting me in my place. Instead, every clipped word, every bite of ice in her voice only made me want to taste the heat I knew was simmering underneath.

First and foremost, I was a businessman, but none of my previous business deals had ever made me this hard.

Well, if it was over seven figures, I got a bit of a chub.

I'd built my empire by staying in control and picking the right untouched markets, like the turned supes market. Everyone knew the Syndicate had a firm hold on the supe community as a whole, but there were always cracks when you made a fist. Always a small minority group that was being left out, and that was the turned supes.

Partnering that untapped market with the elite humans that wanted the thrill of being right in the face of a beast, experiencing it up close and personal, I had found myself a little gold mine.

It wasn't easy being a turned vampire who was trying to court fancy humans. I had to claw my way up the ladder, going from making back-alley trades all the way up to boardroom contracts where the big boys took me seriously, but I wanted more freedom. I wanted to enjoy myself instead of always working for the next deal.

To do that, I needed a solid partner, one who had the manpower and knew what they were doing. It was just my luck that one of her men showed up, trying to be sneaky about needing tickets for a high-value client.

*The second I caught her leaning on the bar, all that carefully crafted control right in front of me, I was transfixed. Something in my veins pulsed for her, hard and relentless. Gravity somehow bent around her, dragging me across the floor.

The room fell away. All I saw was *her*. Hot and warm temptation sculpted by the gods and wrapped in feminine discipline. Liquid denim jeans hugging every muscle, a short white top stretched across her breasts, and a cropped jacket covering her arms. She was a statue of strength softened by the mouthwatering swell of her hips and chest.

I told myself to lock it down, to swagger over like this was just another business move, an opportunity to capitalize on, but the moment her scent hit me, my plans detonated.

Floral honeysuckle, sweet and decadent, crashed through my lungs, tearing my careful chains apart. My fangs ached. My vision sharpened. My mouth watered. Every inch of me screamed to devour her, blood, body, and soul.

Need rippled through me, hot and urgent, muddling my mind. My instincts clawed to sink into her veins, to drag her against me and make her mine. I tried to play it cool, not letting her continued rejections of my advances deter me. It only made me want her more.

Even when she grabbed me by the back of the head and slammed me against the bar, all I thought about was how her body felt pressed against mine. Her hard curves molded perfectly to my frame, and my cock jerked in my pants, my body not caring that we were locked in a battle for domi-

---

* Weak by AJR

nance. I wanted her under me. Over me. Wrapped around me. Inside of me. Her threats only made me harder.

My hands shook from holding myself back, from caging in the part of me that wanted to rip into her neck and drink until she screamed my name. To claim her over and over.

Never before had I felt this magnetizing pull that I couldn't ignore or pass off. I'd never been this attracted to anyone before, let alone a woman who radiated so much lethal control she could break my life apart with her pinky. Nova Rossey was dangerous and would probably kill me, but, for some reason, my survival instincts were turned off while my risk-taking ones were turned on.

"Okay, Boss Rossey." She stiffened as her title dripped from my tongue like sin. I'd play her game... for now. Games always ended with a winner, and I didn't plan to lose.

Twenty minutes ago, I would've told you I wanted power, respect, and a seat at the table with the born supes who thought turned vampires like me were trash. Meeting Nova Rossey tonight was the opportunity of a lifetime. It was a gamble, too, for sure, one that could help me achieve what I'd always dreamed of, but the second I saw her, all of that was put on the back burner. Now, all I wanted was to bury myself so deep inside her she'd never forget my name.

The crowd roared as someone hit the mat, and her jeweled eyes flicked toward the noise. The sight of her attention drifting elsewhere burned me raw. My teeth clenched as I forced myself not to snarl. This place was too loud, too distracting. I wanted her attention on me and only me.

She let me go, and I leaned in, lowering my voice to a husk meant for only her ears. "Let's move this somewhere private. You can tell me *everything* you need from me."

Not giving her the chance to reject me, I slid past the bartender and tapped the fake brick. A keypad appeared, and I punched in the numbers. A concealed door swung open, revealing the darkened space that was my backroom parlor. I motioned her inside, my voice silky and inviting. "Ladies first."

She looked back at Zeth, her second, who was standing up again, ready to follow her. My teeth ground together when I caught the way his eyes clung to her. *Pathetic*. The glare I sent his way promised I'd cut him down if he followed us. "I'd be more comfortable if it was just you and me," I said roughly. "I won't bring anyone either. Unless you're... afraid?"

She tilted her head, studying me the way a predator would prey. Thirty long seconds ticked by before she strode toward me, her chin tilted high, her mouth curled into something sharp. She brushed so close her scent nearly undid me, her growl vibrating against my chest. "You don't bother me in the least, Mr. Conrad."

The way she wrapped my name in that venomous purr made my lips split into a feral grin. She thought she was still in control, but with how her eyes were eating me up, it seemed like we were both on edge. I just hoped it was the same sexy edge, not the rip-my-chest-apart edge.

Her head turned back to Zeth, and with just a slight shake of her head, he stopped in his tracks. She lifted her hand, tapped her watch, and gave him a look. Panic flashed in his wide eyes before his training snapped back into place. He forced himself to nod. *What a good little puppy.*

Then she turned her back on him and glared at me before stepping into the room as though she owned every inch of it. When she didn't look back, expecting her silent orders to be obeyed without question, I licked my lips and gave him a wink.

With his back straight and his face getting all red, his gaze followed her as closely as a shadow. He only tore his eyes away once she was gone, then he turned them on me. Pure venomous hate seared into my skin. He flicked his eyes toward where she'd vanished, then back to me as he dragged his thumb across his throat. If she got hurt, I was dead.

Lucky for him, hurting her was the furthest thing from my mind. In fact, even the business deals and plans I *should* be thinking about weren't anywhere near my thoughts. All I wanted was more of her and that intoxicating honeysuckle scent that made my veins pound like war drums. I was never much of a warrior type guy, but I'd be damned if she didn't make me want to sign up for the damn Rossey clan.

Walking up to the threshold, I turned around and saluted Zeth just before the door slid shut in his face. The way his whole body coiled into fight mode was deliciously satisfying.

"You said you'd tell me anything I wanted to know, didn't you?"

Her voice cracked through the silence, crisp, commanding, wrapped in heat I couldn't ignore. She was already across the room, sitting in my high-backed chair at the desk, legs crossed with the grace and power of a queen on her throne. She'd left me the smaller seat across from her. *Message received.*

To her, I was just another underling being brought to heel.

Damn. She was good.

If she thought that was enough to put me in my place, she was dead wrong. This little game only made me harder.

Adjusting my pants, I sauntered over, but instead of sitting where she wanted, I prowled around the desk. Facing her, I casually perched on the edge right next to her, sitting close enough to feel the heat radiating off her. Her narrowed eyes sliced into me, and I would be lying if I said sweat didn't bead along my spine.

For a split second, her lips moved in the faintest twitch. It was so quick you could've missed it, but I didn't. She liked me. She just didn't want to admit it yet.

Leaning back, letting my leg brush against the chair, I nodded. "I'm a man of my word. Tell me what you came here for."

She folded her hands together and leaned back, cool as a glacier. "Do you know Jeremy Delton? He was last seen on his way to one of your fights. Do you know why he was here?"

Jeremy? What the hell does she want with him?

My fingers curled against the desk, my face schooled into indifference even though something tugged in my chest. Jeremy wasn't a friend, not really, but I'd listened to his story and recognized too much of my own reflection in it—a turned supe with a broken past and no family to turn to. His desperation had cut too close to mine.

"I'll take your silence as a yes," she said, her sharp tone slicing deeper than I expected. For a second, I almost lost my cool and rubbed at my chest. "I need to know where he is."

Her voice left no room for negotiation. The words bit at me with an authority that should've rattled me. Instead, I found myself fighting the urge to grin. God, she was magnificent when she was demanding.

Memories of the night before, of Jeremy's face etched in desperation when I couldn't help, came to my mind. After that, a frantic need had taken over, and I told him he was making a bad decision.

"He came by a few nights ago," I admitted, my fist clenched uncontrollably. "Wanted to find an acquaintance we shared before I severed ties with them long ago."

Feeling restless, I pushed up from the desk and crossed the room to the decanter set. *He's a big boy. He made his bed, and now he has to lay in it.* At least that was what I told myself.

Pouring two glasses, I forced my mind off Jeremy and back onto the goddess sitting behind me.

"Who's the acquaintance, and what did Jeremy want with him?" Her voice sharpened, but I caught the faintest thread of curiosity winding through it. Carrying the glasses back, I set one in front of her before taking a sip of mine.

"Donnie Leman. A turned werewolf." Rolling my eyes, I chastised myself for ever getting involved with him. "For years, Donnie's been desperate to claw his way into the supe league fighting ring. Willing to take any job, any fight, always looking for a quick buck and an award-winning fight." I shook my head, knowing his impulsivity and lack of foresight would be his undoing. "Always playing with risk for a big payout."

I threw my chin at the untouched drink in front of her, my meaning clear. *If you want more from me, you'll have to drink with me.*

She let out a husky little chuckle, like she found me ridiculous but maybe amusing enough to play along, and lifted the glass.

The moment the liquor touched her lips, her eyes flared bright with demon magic. Watching the shimmer of it light up her gaze, a ripple of heat swept through me.

Before she could tear into me about how I'd gotten my hands on Syndicate-exclusive stock, I leaned closer and let my mouth curve. "I cashed in a favor with one of your lieutenants." I winked.

Her body went taut, eyes blazing with the kind of fiery rage that demanded blood the second it was roused. Nowadays, we just called it the Desmond rage, something that only those white-haired, pink-eyed beings were capable of.

I cut in quickly, my voice coaxing. "Relax. I saved his mate from an unfortunate situation, and he simply repaid me with the bottle you gifted them for Christmas."

The flicker of fury on her face warred with intrigue, and all I could think was how badly I wanted to taste that fire on my tongue.

Her lips pursed like she was dragging a memory out of the dark, and when she glanced down, her hand had already transformed into a vicious claw, the equivalent of a loaded gun aimed squarely at me.

My blood thundered, eyes locked on the lethal length and shine of those claws, wondering, against every survival instinct, what they would feel like pressed against my throat or dragged down my chest. Intrusive thoughts whispered that maybe I was into being dominated, but survival beat that craving back... barely.

"They'd have to be idiots to steal from you or your family," I muttered, tossing back another swallow of liquor. Her claws retracted, smooth skin reforming like nothing had happened.

Her shoulders loosened. She took another drink, slower this time, savoring it, and exhaled. "You'd be surprised."

Something about the way she said it had layers. Power, bitterness... exhaustion. I'd be damned if that didn't intrigue me more. The small possibility of cracks in her armor, even small ones, made me want to press closer.

"Look, Conrad—" The way my name rolled off her tongue set my soul ablaze, her voice cutting right through me like she owned it, like she owned *me*. "I don't know if this is some kind of 'turned alliance' or loyalty stunt you're running, but I need to find Jeremy."

She dragged her fingers through her hair, frustration breaking her cool exterior before she admitted, almost begrudgingly, "Actually, I'm after Reece Walton. He came here to see Jeremy. Reece is the target, but since Jeremy has a human kid with him now, I need to find him, too. Make sure the kid doesn't end up dead."

Trouncing around with a human kid? What the hell was Jeremy thinking?

Her lips tilted, sharp and dangerous, more kingpin than queen, though she probably hadn't meant it that way. "We can't have humans getting hurt around supes. But you already know that, don't you?"

I dragged in a heavy breath, forcing my gaze away from her before my hunger betrayed me. "He came by yesterday looking for fast cash."

Her brow arched, and I knew I had to spill before she carved the truth out of me. "Sometimes..." I hesitated, praying she wouldn't sprout claws again. "Let's say I *sometimes* pay turned supes to take the fall against human fighters."

Her eyes widened. I downed the rest of my glass.

"I make sure it's safe," I said defensively, even though the argument sounded weak. I didn't want her to think I was putting the Syndicate in hot water with the humans.

"Humans get off on the fantasy that maybe they can take down a supe. I give them that glimmer of hope now and then. One night like that pulls in around three hundred to five hundred thousand without breaking a sweat."

She tilted her head, appreciation flashing on her face until she snapped, "That still doesn't explain where Jeremy is."

Damn. I'd expected her to demand a cut or shut me down. Instead, she was relentless. She knew my throat was already caught between her teeth, and she wasn't letting me go anytime soon.

"When he came in and I told him I had nothing, he mumbled that he would just go see Donnie instead." My jaw ticked at the memory of Jeremy's twitchy nerves, the desperation rolling off him. "I told him Donnie would only drag him into shit deeper than quicksand, but he didn't care."

"Fuck." She slammed her palm into my leather chair, and I could hear it crack. Well, that was ten grand down the drain, but I wasn't about to say that.

"So, you don't know where to find him either." She downed her glass and folded forward, elbows on her knees, hands clasped, staring into nothing. For a second, that damn ache to take care of her clawed up my chest, and I blurted out the last thing I wanted to do.

"I could take you to Donnie's place."

Her head lifted, white hair slipping back like a curtain. The beginning of a smile tugged at her lips, only to vanish behind a scowl when suspicion snapped back into place.

"Why? What's in it for you?"

I wanted to say *'time with you.'* I wanted to tell her I craved every second of her voice, her scent, her fire, but that would send her bolting. No, I had to be useful. Indispensable.

In a flash of vampire speed, I brushed her hair back behind her ear before she could react, letting my fingers graze that warm skin that burned like wildfire against my cool fingertips. "Because I'd rather not end up with my chest split open, my heart ripped out, and my blood burned in a ritual for the Syndicate gods."

Her eyes cut to the side where I'd tucked her hair, then slowly came back to me. The screeching sound of the chair dragging along the hardwood echoed in the room as she stood up.

Every nerve in me lit up when her hands slammed down on either side of me, boxing me against my own desk, her breath sharp and hot against my lips. "If you try anything—*anything* —I don't like," she whispered, each word laced with venom and promise, "you won't have to worry about gods or death."

Her lips parted in a wicked smile, teeth flashing. "I'll chain you upside down over my tub. Your new job will be to fill it with your blood. Every. Damn. Day." Her finger traced my throat in a mocking caress. "I'll slit you open again and again until my whole body is covered in crimson stains, then leave you there until the next day and the next, until you're used up, old husk of a body has nothing left to spare."

I should have flinched, should have felt fear, but something dark and primal inside me broke loose, and I wasn't in control anymore.

A growl ripped out of me as I snapped, arms locking around her waist to yank her flush against me. My cool collided with her heat, my lips barely an inch from hers. "If that's your idea of an invitation," I rasped, "you could've just asked. I'd love to get you naked and paint your skin with my blood."

Her breath hitched, her jewel-pink eyes dropping to my mouth for one heavy heartbeat, then her fist cracked across my face. Pain exploded, and I doubled over.

She stalked back to the door, boots thudding her victory as her satisfied huff echoed in the air.

Fuck. No, no, no. I blew it. She'd never speak to me again if I left it like that.

Unexpectedly, her steps stopped. "You may heal slower because you're a turned, but I didn't touch your legs. Let's go."

At the sound of her steady, commanding voice, I glanced up. Arms crossed, hip cocked, but her lips... there was the faintest traitorous curve. Maybe I imagined it, but... maybe not.

Either way, I wasn't about to waste this chance. I hauled myself up off the floor.

9

NOVA

Conrad Mecariee. That was a name I was going to remember.

It had taken far too much of my self-control not to answer his incessant invitations. It wasn't the first time someone had flirted with me to get something in return, but it was the first time I almost responded. With the ravenous urge to put him in his place... to pin him underneath me... I almost took him right there on his desk.

It was just a blip of a thought, but before I knew it, I was pressed against him, his arms circling me tight, the heat from my body transferring to his, spiraling out of control. Getting this close, I could see the way his deep evergreen eyes burned with carnal desire. When he licked his lips, my whole body tensed, ready to climb on top and ride him hard and fast.

Then I came to my senses and punched him.

Gulping down some air, I forced myself to walk away from that sophisticated grapefruit-crisp scent, laced with warm sandalwood and a cozy bite of nutmeg. His scent called me to stay, to sink into his space and see where this could lead us. My wolf let out a small whine at the loss, purposely making my steps louder to drown her out.

I tried to steady myself by thinking about Reece and that human kid, praying Jeremy hadn't done anything stupid enough to get either of them killed. That thought sobered me up fast. I turned to ask for Donnie's address, only to realize Conrad hadn't moved off the floor. He was staring into space with a stricken look on his face.

What the fuck was he doing? Twiddling his thumbs? He might've been a turned vampire, making him weaker than someone who'd been born that way, but I hadn't hit him *that* hard.

"You may heal slower," I snapped, glaring over my shoulder, "but I didn't touch your damn legs."

His head swiveled around in a flash, eyes lit with hope at my words. My wolf all but wagged her tail.

I. Hated. It.

"Let's go," I growled, turning away before he saw the heat in my cheeks.

The door had no button or lever to open it, so I stood there, waiting. Even without looking, I felt him approach, that broad, cool chest hovering behind me. When he leaned forward, his chest brushed my back, making me very aware of where we were touching as his arm curled around me to tap against the wooden wall twice. A panel slid aside, revealing a keypad.

He entered the code slowly, deliberately, his body pressing harder against me with every number he keyed in. With the way his heavy breath ghosted over my neck, I wasn't even paying attention to the code he was putting in. His presence pulled me in like a siren's spell, daring me to lean back and let myself be enveloped by him and that delicious scent.

Grinding my teeth, I steeled my spine, refusing to bend. *Hold, Nova. Don't break. Show him how little he affects you.* This was just another power play, one *I* was going to win.

"I'll say this…" his voice slid against my ear, quiet and full of sin, "knowing you'll probably hit me again for saying it, but you have the most intoxicating scent. Drives me half-mad. No one has ever affected me like this." His ending words were breathless, like he didn't even know what he was saying, and my heart thumped.

Oh, he's good. That damn male is gooooood.

The door slid open before I could respond, but I was glad since I needed a break from all this… heat. Instead, I came face-to-face with heat of a different kind. Zeth stood on the other side, hair disheveled, eyes wild, as though he was one heartbeat from tearing down the wall.

"Zeth—" I breathed, ready to step toward him, but Conrad's voice coiled right behind me, dragging me back into his gravity.

"Oh, Zeth," Conrad purred, "just in time. We were about to head out."

I elbowed him sharply, opening my mouth to explain, but Zeth's stunned reply had the words caught in my throat. "We?"

When I still didn't say anything, Zeth's fury-filled eyes cut to me. Pain peppered his gaze like I was the one betraying him, and I shook my head. I had to explain before this got out of hand.

"He has a lead on a location," I told him quickly. "He's going to take us to it."

"Us?" Conrad's voice pitched higher, incredulous, eyes snapping to me.

I bit the inside of my lip. This... was getting annoying. Ignoring both of them, I scanned the room behind Zeth. The ring was empty, and the crowd was at the cash-out station. A few women were lazily gossiping in their seats. The fights were over.

Walking around Zeth, I bolted for the stairs before the crowd surged for the exit, tossing back, "Come on, boys. We've got a guy to find."

Two sets of footsteps followed close behind, but I didn't dare look back. Nope, I just kept facing forward until we got outside.

Conrad snapped his fingers at the valet, saying, "Get my car," then turned that sharp smile on me. "It's a two-seater, so *Zeth* will have to take his car. I'll text him the address."

Zeth growled, the sound odd coming from a demon, but he'd practically been raised by wolves, so it made sense. He took a step forward, eyes burning at Conrad's words. "You lead. *We'll* follow."

Before the situation could turn into another pissing match, I cut them off. "Zeth's going with you, Conrad. I'll follow."

Zeth's lips parted like he was going to argue, so I crossed my arms and lifted my brow. "It's my car."

His jaw moved from side to side before he glared at Conrad, who sent him an equally annoyed look. They were making it clear that they'd rather have their toenails ripped out and spoon fed to them than ride together, but that wasn't my problem. *I* was in charge. End of story.

A deep green Chevrolet Corvette 3LZ purred beside my jeep, the color almost a match for Conrad's eyes. Sleek and polished, it looked like the perfect counterpoint to my rugged, terrain-built ride, like they'd been bought as a set. One for the city, the other for the mountains. I didn't know why that irked me, but it did.

Snatching the keys from the valet, I called over my shoulder, "Don't lose me, or Zeth will kill you."

Zeth bared his teeth in a grim smile. "I hope you drive fast, vamp, or it's your funeral."

Conrad sneered right back. "I'd never give you the satis-faction."

Well, this was going to be fun.

I COULDN'T HELP but think that Conrad was either really worried that he would lose me… or he had a death wish.

He kept a sluggish pace the entire time, which drove me insane, so I could only imagine how Zeth was handling it in the passenger seat. The image was clear in my mind. Arms crossed, scowl carved deep, throwing Conrad hate at every single mile marker. The mental image had me laughing most of the ride.

Still, I hoped this little excursion hammered my message into their skulls. If they wanted to fight like dogs, I'd treat them like dogs. Let them swipe at each other until it was too much then yank on their leashes, making them heel at my feet. Wouldn't that be a pretty sight to behold?

Conrad turned off the highway early, winding us through back roads and skirting the edge of the city until we hit a dirt road that led into a hidden trailer park pressed against the forest. It was a sharp contrast to the expensive homes and polished city center we'd left behind.

I rolled the windows down, letting the night air sharpen my senses. Gravel crunched under my tires, and the acrid scent of marijuana hung heavy.

The deeper we went, the clearer it became. This was the side of Whitefish that people rarely saw. People lounged on makeshift porches, smoking or drinking, their conversations quiet but their eyes tracking everything that moved. Rows and rows of small box-like, broken-down trailers were propped up on stilts.

A fairy woman with a ratty neon blue ponytail, miniskirt, and a jacket that was pinched too tight caught my attention. Her clothes weren't magicked to conceal her wings, and they were lying flat through the self-cut slits of her jacket. The faint shimmer of her wings sputtered like a dying bulb, so I knew she was running on fumes, too low on life essence.

Life essence wasn't cheap when it came in a bottle, and even if it was concentrated, which meant a little went a long way, most average fairies couldn't afford it. That was why they usually signed up for sex work and sipped on it that way.

A human man whistled at her.

"Cherry! How 'bout a blowjob for a couple months?!"

She didn't even look back.

"Six months!" he yelled desperately when she kept walking. "A-a year!"

That made her pause.

"A year if you swallow, and I'm in control," he bargained.

From my rearview mirror, I watched her lips curl into a private smile. She turned on her heels, walked straight into his trailer, and shut the door. Her wings would glow bright again tonight.

Conrad pulled up in front of a crooked trailer, and I rolled in next to him, killing the engine at the same time Zeth flung open the door.

"How do you stand this guy, Boss Rossey?" Leaning against the hood of his car, Conrad jerked his thumb toward Zeth, his nose wrinkled and his eyes rolling up into his head.

"Don't worry about my second," I shot back. "Worry about finding Donnie or, better yet, Jeremy."

When we rolled in, the neighborhood buzzed with life, the hiss of cats, dogs snarling, a baby wailing, gossip spilling in hushed tones. The moment we climbed out of our cars, silence fell. Curtains twitched, shadows shifted, and eyes gleamed at us from behind the glass. No one moved. No one spoke. They left us to do whatever it was we came here to do but kept an eye so they knew what would be coming next.

Ignoring the stares, we mounted the steps of the trailer and knocked. Nothing. I tried again. Still nothing.

"Well, I gave you a chance."

I drew back my fist, muscle and bone snapping as I shifted just my arm and swung. The door groaned then splintered in half beneath the blow. I stepped through without hesitation.

"Don't make this harder than it has to be," I called into the stale dark. No answer.

Walking through the threshold, I waited for a beat, trying to detect a hidden heartbeat, but there was nothing. "I'll head back to the bedroom. You guys search the living room and kitchen for any clues as to where he's gone."

I didn't wait for their reply before I drifted down the narrow hall and went into the back bedroom. My first thought was that this place was a shit hole.

Sheets stiff with grime, cigarette burns dotting the carpet, a fist-sized hole punched through the closet door. A shotgun leaned against the window like a half-baked threat. The stench of repressed rage and bitter failure clung to the walls. Everything about the space reeked of a man who thought his new wolf power would be his ticket out yet had no idea what to do with it.

I understood now why someone like this would risk life and limb, willing to do anything to claw his way out of a cycle of poverty and shame.

Looking around, I grabbed a few things and threw them on the bed. When I didn't find anything useful, I tore apart the other stuff with no luck either. No calendar, no notebook, not a scrap of intel. Just a faint trace of failure and wasted opportunity.

Yanking open his dresser drawers, I tore through his clothes, searching for even a single clue as to where they could've gone. *Something. Please, fucking anything.*

Just as I threw the last shirt over my head, a sharp *tink* sounded. I glanced inside the drawer and found a glass syringe that had rolled into the front corner. Glass? What the hell was he doing with something like this? It wasn't like he could get sick or die from any human illnesses. And who the hell still used glass syringes? Every human medical facility I knew of worked with some form of plastic.

I carefully picked it up, noticing it was already used. A greenish sheen clung to the inside of the vial, which made me pause. Tilting it toward the light, I watched the tint shift and slide.

What was this tiny bit of substance in the body of the syringe? Poison, maybe? Or was this something Donnie was shooting up? Why the hell would he keep it hidden in his own home? Was this all he had left? Was that why he always seemed to need cash like Conrad said?

The questions stacked themselves higher and higher as I found myself deeper in this goose chase. Maybe Conrad would know.

Kicking my way through the mess, I headed back into the main room where everything had been turned over and ripped apart.

"I don't really know what we're looking for," Conrad said, tearing into a cushion while Zeth rifled through papers on the table. "But I have to admit, I'm finding the destruction part enjoyable. I see why rage rooms are a thing."

His voice edged with disdain and disbelief, Zeth didn't look up as he replied. "You're saying you've never raged out? I highly doubt a *turned* has never lost control, not even once."

Conrad laughed, the sound pompous, mocking. "No, my dear Zeth—" the glare that earned him was sharp—"I've never broken something out of anger. Even the lowliest of things has value to someone. I prefer to capitalize on that value, not sully it."

The conversation was steering into fight territory, so I stepped in, syringe in hand. "Do you know anything about this?" I asked, holding it up toward Conrad.

His eyes lit up when they landed on *me*, not the syringe. He stepped closer, that penetrating emerald gaze searching my eyes, and my heart thumped louder. When my wolf's attention turned to him, her interest skyrocketed, and, for the first time in years, she took over my eyes for a blip of a second. This excitement was something she hadn't felt in a while.

Needing this moment to end, I quickly forced her back down and shoved the syringe closer to his face. "This. The substance inside. Do you know anything about it?"

At lightning speed, he plucked it from my hand and held it up to the light, studying the residue like it might whisper its secrets back.

Zeth slid in close, the simmering darkness of his voice just waiting to bring down his wrath. "Where did you find that?"

"In his dresser, under some clothes." I shrugged, stepping backward to give Conrad some space as I talked with Zeth. "Everything else was junk."

Zeth's hand slid against the small of my back, deliberate and slow. His head tipped closer, and that sweet almond and cherry scent wafted around me as his lips brushed just above my ear. Low enough that only I could hear, he whispered, "Are you sure it's wise to let him handle this? What if he knows more than he's letting on?"

The question made sense, and it was something that any good second would ask discreetly, but my focus was on the heat of his breath ghosting over my skin and coiling down my neck. A shiver ran straight to my stomach, making it clench with want as my body betrayed me. My pulse kicked harder.

I can't do this. He doesn't feel that way. Put distance between us, now.

Stepping away from him before I lost myself to these lingering emotions, emotions I shouldn't be having, I found myself in front of Conrad. Wrenching a breath past the fire in my chest, I gruffly demanded, "Well? Yes or no?"

Conrad shook his head. "Not off the top of my head. Though the color is... interesting. The use of glass tells me it's either veterinary-grade or lab-made." He shrugged and handed the syringe back like it was nothing.

This was getting into an area beyond my depth. Rubbing my chin, I thought about who would have an idea, and one person came to mind right away.

Snapping a picture of the syringe, I found his name and sent off the picture before pressing the call button and bringing it to my ear.

As it rang, both men moved to stand in front of me, one with a set of eager, tempting eyes, and the other with his arms crossed and a frown carved into his face like it was set in stone. All I knew was I didn't have time for any of that nonsense.

"Hello, Miss Rossey," came a voice over the phone, jolting me from my troublesome thoughts.

"Rack?" I blinked, confused for only a second before my brother's frustrated voice bled through in the background.

"Whatever she wants, tell her I'm busy." He paused. "I'm making a masterpiece, the best invention yet, and I can't be bothered. Tell her that. She'll understand. She's the semi-normal sister. The one who'll at least kill me *after* I'm finished."

Closing my eyes, I drew in a slow breath, reminding myself that he *was,* in fact, a genius who had built hundreds of inventions for the family. Plus, driving to Texas to stab him would be a colossal waste of time.

"It seems he's busy at the moment, Miss Rossey," Rack said smoothly.

My nose wrinkled at the sound of a man I considered an adopted brother calling me "Miss Rossey." It sounded wrong. Made me feel old. Decrepit.

"Rack, quit it. I've known you since I was four. It's weird as fuck for you to call me that."

"Ma'am—"

My stomach lurched, and I held back my gag reflex. "Oh, fuck no. Dear god. That's worse! So much worse!" Shaking my head, I tried to erase it from my memory.

In the background, Calix cackled. "Did you just call her *ma'am?* Who the fuck are you, some butler?" His laughter faded into giddy inspiration. "Oh, wait. A butler. I like that. You can be Alfred to my Bruce Wayne!"

There was a long pause before Calix shouted, "Ow! What the hell was that for? It's a good idea!" Clipped steps echoed, then a door slammed in the background, and I wished I could see the disgust on Rack's face at the thought of being my brother's Alfred. That would be hilarious.

Rack spoke again, his dry voice coming out with a bit of heat. "I don't think your brother is in the *right state of mind* for this conversation."

I tried and failed to hold in my chuckle. "What the hell would he do without you?"

A long silence stretched before Rack delivered a truth bomb that shook me to my core. "One of you would be tasked with keeping him on track and focused."

Cold dread curled through me, my body instinctually recoiling from the receiver. We knew better than to *ever* wish that job on anyone else. None of us could handle him the way Rack did. I silently thanked the stars for the role he played in this family.

Sensing my shift in thought, Rack steered the conversation back on course. Always the professional. "You're calling about the item you sent a picture of?"

I looked down at the syringe still in my hand. "Yeah. Do you have any idea what it's from? Is it something we produce?" It was nearly impossible that I wouldn't already know, but I still had to ask.

"It's definitely not ours. We don't make injectables. Too close to drug production for the human government. We won't know anything until we test the substance and break down its makeup."

"Do you need me to ship this to you?"

"No. The last time your brother visited, he bought the vacant building in Whitefish and built a mini lab. Have your IT man Gil swab it and run some preliminary tests. By the time I get the results… he should be out of his… *creative mode*."

Thinking back, I remembered Calix being the one to hire Gil. Damn double agent.

"Come on, Rack," I called out playfully, "you know we call it his asshole hour."

Rack's parents had been good friends with ours, so when they died when he was thirteen, my parents took him in and raised him alongside us. You would think some of our rowdiness would've rubbed off on him, but that never happened. He was always a stickler for the rules and the "proper" way to do things.

When we all took over as bosses, he distanced himself, drawing lines of propriety we all hated, except for Ezra, who shrugged it off, saying if that was how he wanted it, she wouldn't stop him. Ezra, Calix, and Rack had been thick as thieves in high school, the three of them setting the tone of what to expect from the Syndicate children before Aniyah, Riot, and I got to those grades. So, maybe she understood him better than the rest of us.

This time, Rack gave a low chuckle, and I smiled. Buried under all the formality, he was still the boy I had grown up with.

"Yes. He'll be in a much better state to examine the results." His voice shifted back to business. "I'll send you the coordinates for the lab."

"Don't think I won't have words with him about building a lab here without my knowledge or putting in one of his men and masking them as mine. But since it's helping me now, I'll keep it short."

"That's wise, Miss Rossey." I rolled my eyes. "If it makes you feel any better, he's done this in all of his sisters' base locations."

I took a deep sigh before firing back, "Thanks, *Mr. Rack Marlo*," and hanging up. There was no getting through to that man! Maybe that was why he was with Calix. Birds of a feather and all that jazz.

"That dude's weird," Zeth muttered, shaking his head. I almost agreed, but I knew Rack had to have his reasons for being like that, and I wasn't in a position to pry.

With answers on the way, I slid back into boss mode, turning to Zeth and handing him the syringe. "I'm sure you heard. Cal built a lab in town and apparently has someone in place who can run the tests. Get this to Gil and have him run the test. Tell him to send me and Rack the results ASAP."

Zeth's hand circled around the syringe, nodding at me before his eyes flicked to Conrad then back to me. "Why don't we go together?"

I shook my head, pinning him with a look that said I needed him to follow along with what I'd ordered, not what he thought was best. Plus, the test had to be run immediately, and it would be faster if we split up. "Conrad and I will check the rest of the place, see if Donnie stashed any more."

Turning to Conrad, I asked, "Can Zeth borrow your car? I promise he'll return it." Taking Zeth's concern about the turned vampire to heart, I still wanted to grill Conrad, and letting him have access to his own car would make that harder. It only made sense to have Zeth borrow his.

Conrad studied us, his hand slowly going into his pocket. His controlled features and sharp eyes gave nothing away. My hands fisted as I started to wonder if I was going to need to demand his compliance—because I would if I needed to. Being a boss, you always needed to be ready to flex your strength. I just liked giving people the illusion that I could be nice about it.

He pulled out his keys, a large grin splitting across his face as he handed them over to Zeth. "Of course." His deep green gaze settled on me. "Whatever I can do to help the Syndicate."

Even as he said it, I felt it; he knew something was off, yet he still walked right into it, facing me with his head held high. There was something incredibly… admirable about that.

I really hoped I wouldn't have to kill him. It would be a shame to get rid of those good looks, great body, and savvy business mind.

NOVA

"You know, when you asked me to stay behind, I thought you were either going to kill me or I'd finally convinced you to have sex with me. I did not expect to tear apart a dingy trailer from top to bottom, laminate board to laminate board, using me for manual labor."

Ripping out the last drawer from the second bedroom dresser, I dumped its contents on the bed. "You never know," I called out absently. "The night's still young. Killing someone doesn't take that long." And it all depended on what he said.

As for the latter... it was tempting. My body ran hot just thinking about it.

He puffed out a laugh, but I could see the hesitation in his body, the way his back was never turned toward me. It was cute that he thought that would help him.

Through the corner of my eyes, I watched him roll up his sleeves before he smashed his fist into the wall, making sure he hadn't hidden anything. I couldn't help but study the way those strong forearms tensed up before he swung. When he tugged his arm out, his white shirt getting all dirty and his hair skewed, it made my stomach clench. Maybe this place was too confined. His sophisticated citrus-and-spice scent was too strong for me to escape its pull on me.

Turning away to keep myself focused, I called over my shoulder, "We need to make sure there's nothing else. I don't want anyone stumbling upon something they shouldn't. That's how issues with the human government start."

"You're the fucking Syndicate," he said as I made my way over to the kitchen where he was. "Tell the human government to pound sand." He made the motion of wiping his brow, though we both knew he wasn't sweating. It was just an automatic response from his human days when his body overheated.

Leaning against the wall, I crossed my arms as he tore down the last of the cupboards. "Oh, yeah, sure. Start a war with the human government, one I'm sure they've been waiting for, with both sides dropping bodies left and right." Kicking at some of the mess we'd made, I sighed. "That just sounds like... a whole lot of hassle."

He flung his head up to look at me, genuine curiosity sparking in his eyes. "So, what, are you saying the Syndicate can't handle it?"

Rage burned hot in my veins, and I was on him in a flash, knocking him onto the floor with a loud thud. Claws around his throat, I choked him out as I transformed my teeth into fangs, snapping them in his face. His face contorted, real fear finally making an appearance as he kicked and shoved at me, pulling at my arms to break free, but I only pressed in harder. As his face started turning blue, I let my fangs retreat, but I kept him pinned to the floor, claws digging into his throat.

"We may not want a war," I leaned in close, making sure he understood every syllable, "but that doesn't mean we've grown weak. We just see the world through a different lens."

Retracting my claws, I rose and stared down at him as he turned on his side, gasping for air. "We understand the nature of things. We'll always need ants, lieutenants, and kings. That's what makes the world go round. It puts money in our pockets and fuels our pleasures. Killing all the ants doesn't mean the lieutenants will pick up the slack, and there's no way the kings will go backward without trying to destroy everything just to keep their spot. It's a delicate balance of keeping the status quo while building insurances and counterpoints to ensure success."

He glared up at me, clutching his crimson-covered throat, and I backed up a few steps to let him rise. His gaze landed on my hands, and I lifted one to my mouth, licking my bloody fingertips.

That acidic taste filled my mouth, and a jolt struck me like a lightning bolt. My tongue went slack as my muscles locked up. Heat surged through my veins, curling around my core and pulsing with need. Staggering back from the shock, my spine hit the wall, reminding me to breathe.

Taking a few quick breaths, I focused on the pounding of my heart, the sound echoing in my ears. To make matters worse, my wolf raced in circles in my head, growling something inaudible over and over.

A pulse of heat bloomed at my wrist, but I ignored it, trying to stop the spinning in my head and push away the fuzzy, consuming sensation.

"Hey," he rasped, his voice still raw from my claws tearing at it from the inside. "Hey... are you okay? Nova?" He stood up and moved closer to me, one hand outstretched, but I jerked away.

"B-boss. Rossey," I croaked, desperately clinging to the line I'd drawn in that parlor. I could not afford to look weak in front of him. Attracted? Fine. Horny? If I couldn't hide it. But weak? *Never.*

Pressing my palm to my chest as if that would keep my heart from busting out of it, I glared at him. A rumble of a growl came from my lips, letting him know I was seconds away from tearing him limb from limb, and he sighed heavily, dropping his arm and his head. That signal of submission helped my fear of looking weak begin to dissipate.

I didn't know what was happening, but everything was somehow heightened and blurred all at once. Whatever this was, I had to shake it off. I needed control again, but there were still burning questions that only he could answer.

"Follow me," I barked, kicking off the wall so I could dart out of the trailer and into the forest.

His footsteps trailed after me, though the deeper we went, the more hesitant they became.

"Nov—I mean, Boss Rossey, where are we going?"

I drew in a deep breath, filling my lungs with the forest. The damp musk of soil rose first, rich with decaying leaves. The air was cool and crisp, sharp enough to clear even the densest mind. Aromatics like pine and juniper wrapped around us, grounding me. Slowly, the fog in my head thinned.

The trickle of a babbling brook sounded only a dozen steps away, and I bolted toward it. I just needed a splash of that water in my face, and I'd be fine—better than fine. I'd be back in control and ready to face Conrad.

"Okay," he huffed behind me. "If this is some tactic to confuse and disorient your prey, then, yes, you've succeeded. What the hell is going on, Nov—I mean, Boss Rossey?"

He kept calling me by my name. Why did he keep doing that? Did he not fear me? Did he not respect me as a leader, as a Syndicate boss? Had I been too lenient with him?

My shoes stopped right at the edge of the brook, and I bent down to scoop up some of that ice-cold spring water and splash it across my face. Thankfully, the burning heat inside of me subsided. The fog in my mind cleared, and I could finally focus. That feverish want that had taken over my body lingered in the background, almost like it was simply biding its time, but it no longer consumed me.

Standing on shaky legs, I lifted my chin high, ready for the next round. A glance at the moon told me it was the early hours of the morning, so I had to make this quick.

When I began to stalk toward him, he backed up a step, eyeing me, until I crouched and swung my leg around, hooking it behind his. He dropped like a felled tree.

He slammed onto the ground with a groan. "Ahh! What the fuck, Nova!"

This time, I fully shifted into a wolf, pouncing on top of him. My body hovered over his, paws pinning his arms to the ground. Instead of squirming or screaming like I expected, he simply stared up at me, waiting.

"If you're going to kill me, just do it." He stuck up his chin, and his muscles underneath me relaxed as he accepted his fate. My wolf whined in my head.

That wasn't the reaction I was going for, so I shifted back. Now naked on top of him, I asked in the most menacing tone I could muster, "What do you know about that substance? Tell me *now*."

In a calm, cool voice, he answered as if we were sitting across from each other in his office. "I don't know anything about it. It's not something I'd want to know if I came across it, anyway. It would put me into trouble with the Syndicate, right?"

"That never stopped anyone from doing what they do," I barked back, but his lips pressed into a thin line.

"Why should I trust you?" I growled viciously, pressing into him harder, my fingers digging into his arms for emphasis. His body quivered beneath mine, but not from fear. If anything, it felt like he was restraining himself, fighting against his natural instinct to meet the bigger, badder predator.

"I don't know why," he admitted, his voice raw. His deep emerald eyes searched mine, desperate for an answer to some question he hadn't spoken. "I don't understand any of this myself, like why I'm reacting in ways I normally don't, but I *do* know that I want to help you." He blinked, and that desperation turned into steel. "I can use my connections to other turned supes to find out if anyone else knows about this."

I still didn't understand it, but I knew in my soul he spoke the truth, so I eased up on my grip. My chest quickly rose and fell as I whispered, "And why would you do that?"

His lips split into a bright smile, which blinded me for a heartbeat, wiping my thoughts clean. Then, in one swift motion, my back hit the forest floor. Now, Conrad was above *me*, still smiling like he'd finally gotten his way.

"Because, for some crazy, strange reason, I want you to like me. I want it so badly I'd burn favors I've collected and use all my connections to make it happen."

He surged forward, capturing my lips with his, but this time, I didn't fight it, didn't push him away. I let the heat consume me. Wrapping my arms around his neck, I pulled him closer and kissed him harder.

Though this was hardly my first kiss, it was only one of two in my life that consumed me completely. Fire erupted in my veins as he moaned against my mouth, and that lava spilled over. Tugging him to me so tightly all I could think about was having him close, having all of him. I could feel him growing against my thigh through his pants, and it excited me.

The kiss broke, and Conrad's eyes roamed over my face. "Is this for real?"

I tilted my head, brows furrowed in confusion. He looked off to the side.

"I don't want you to call this a mistake later. To regret it."

Cupping his chin, I forced his gaze back to mine. "And why would I regret it?"

A crack broke his armored confidence, and his voice bled honesty. "I'm a turned."

My face pinched in confusion, I shook my head. "And? What

does that have to do with us fucking in the middle of the forest?"

When he didn't answer, I took a page from my little sister Aniyah and made the first move. Unzipping his pants, I wrapped my hand around his cock and gave it a squeeze. The gasp he gave was sweet, full of shock and awe, and I wanted to hear it again.

"Tell me," I murmured, moving my hand up and down as his eyes fluttered at my touch. "What does that have to do with us fucking? What does that have to do with having your dick inside me?" Lifting my head, I pressed a soft kiss to his neck while keeping my hand movements steady. "I can barely fit my hand around you, and you keep growing harder. I'd say you'll do just fine performing the act. What else are you concerned about?"

His mouth opened, but only clipped, heady breaths came out.

Enjoying the heat coursing through me, I rolled us, reclaiming the top position. "Now..." My fingers worked expertly, undoing his pants and sliding them down to his thighs. His cock sprang to attention instantly, the glistening, silky head pointing straight at me, practically weeping for me. "I think you have far too many clothes on," I murmured, my voice teasing. "It's not fair for me to be all naked and you to be all covered."

I lifted a finger, morphed it into a sharp claw, and hooked it into the collar of his shirt, ripping the fabric down the middle. As the white fabric fell to the sides, my eyes feasted on what laid before me, and I flicked my tongue against my fang.

Lean, taut muscle was spread out in front of me like a damn snack. Each groove and line looked good enough to eat. His body wasn't bulky or his skin stretched out like all the fighters I knew, no, this man's body was honed for life's *other* pleasures. My hands roamed his chest, tracing each line. I enjoyed the quiver of every muscle I touched, eliciting low, desperate groans from him that vibrated against my skin. His gaze devoured me like I was everything and nothing he'd ever imagined. I liked that. I needed that.

"Fuck, Nova, I need to touch you." His hands latched onto my ass, tugging me closer as he rubbed his cock along the slit of my heat. Every stroke, every press of his hardness sent shivers coursing down my spine.

"When we're like this, you can touch me however you like." I was surprised when the words came out of my mouth, spoken to a man I'd known less than twenty-four hours, yet they felt right. My body knew some kind of truth before my mind did.

His hand gripped my waist as he shifted up to a seated position, claiming my mouth with teeth and tongue, exploring as if memorizing every single insatiable moment. The kiss was both languid and frenzied, his internal war reflected in the desperate rhythm of his mouth. My core clenched in response, aching, empty. I wanted him inside me.

Screw whatever war he was fighting. I would win mine.

Breaking the kiss, I rested my temple against his shoulder, both of us panting, craving more. My hand slithered between us, wrapping around his cock. A hiss escaped his lips, the sound setting fire to every nerve ending in me. His hands roamed my body, desperate to claim every inch of skin he could reach—my neck, my shoulder, my collarbone— needing that skin-to-skin feel.

Quickly, I got on my knees and positioned myself over him before I thrust, impaling myself on his cock, driving that desire deep into my core. A guttural moan tore from his throat.

"Oh, fuck!" His hands gripped my back like cool iron, fingers digging into my flesh. I imagined claws raking my skin, and a pang of dark pleasure shot through me. His forehead pressed against my chest, his heady breath skating along my nipples, making them tighten as he clung to me.

I rode him relentlessly, savoring the shuddering heat, the way he broke beneath me with each thrust.

"So fucking warm." He groaned, lips and tongue tracing across my skin as he murmured, "so fucking wet."

I tangled my fingers in his burnt-blond hair, tilting his head back. His eyes glowed with unchained hunger, dark need spreading to every corner of his expression.

"You're a fucking witch," he growled, part anger, part awe. "You trapped me, and now I can't feel anything but this… ever again."

I threw my head back, laughing into the night sky, keeping up those slow, tantalizing thrusts, driving us both higher and higher. His hands devoured every line of muscle, every taut inch of skin, gripping greedily. I loved hearing his curses mix with his need. In this moment, I was seen and utterly desired.

The raw, carnal rush of being the sole object of someone's attention and adoration was intoxicating. No pretense, no power games, no strategy. Just primal, unfiltered want. Every moment with Conrad was instinctual, a give-and-take of pure, unbridled need.

I wanted to drown in it, to lose myself completely.

A rustle to my left snapped me from the haze, and I paused. My gaze sharpened, instincts flaring. Was someone watching? I'd gut them before they saw even a second more.

"Please, Nova."

Conrad's fractured voice drew me back, and the noise faded into nothing. I looked down, struck by the sheer, devastating beauty of him. Fangs out, lips glistening, eyes darting from my neck to my eyes, raw desperation was written across every feature.

He wanted not only my body but my blood. Most born vampires used blood for control or mating, but turned ones had no such luxury of choice. They needed connection, physical and visceral, to draw what they craved.

I lifted my hair, offering my neck, letting anticipation coil tight around my senses.

His soft, plush lips traced a trail from my shoulder to my neck, each brush creating electric sparks that pooled in my core. My breath hitched, and my hips rolled, riding every wave, every pulse of heat. One hand cupped my neck, gentle, grounding. The other claimed my breast, his thumb circling my areola in slow, maddening strokes that made me arch into him.

Then, his fingers pinched, hard, and I screamed. At the same moment, his fangs sank deep into my skin. My mind went blank, drowning in fire and desire, and my body trembled uncontrollably, completely consumed by the pleasure of each pull at my neck.

It had never been like this.

After Zeth's rejection, I really wanted to split sex from the desire for partners, for a mate. It drove me to turn to strangers, casting blur spells over my face so no one would recognize me. It was just body parts meshing together. Mechanical, impersonal. Heat, yes, but only from the act itself, not this slow, devouring fire that rose higher with every touch.

Then Aniyah's Twenty-first birthday happened. Liam happened.

I knew I wasn't soft or delicate. I wore muscle and control like armor because I had to. When Liam and I clicked, I thought I had found someone who saw outside of that. Someone who could see the locked-away part of me. The woman that wanted to flirt, and joke, and swoon at soft, sultry words. But it had all been a farce.

That night, I nailed that door shut, chained it, and threw away the key. I would never be that vulnerable again.

I wasn't made to be wanted. I was made to be strong. To lead. To control.

The sharp pull at my neck dragged me back to now. My legs wrapped around Conrad's back, and I held on tight. All of those feelings bled into the background as I moaned his name.

His hands gripped my waist, and, with inhuman speed, he drove me up and down, hard and fast, until the forest blurred into flashes of green. The only sounds left were his carnal grunts and my broken moans as he sucked at my neck and fucked me raw.

"Ooh, oh, fuck! Conrad. Haah... aaah!" My voice fractured, repeating those words like a broken record as my body bounced helplessly in his grasp while I clung to him with everything I had.

Heat burned at my wrist, searing through me, and I almost told him to stop, to figure out what that burning was, when he yanked his mouth from my neck and growled into the forest like the apex predator he was. He pushed me back onto the ground, and all thoughts of pain left as every thrust of his hips pounded me into the earth, skin smacking, friction igniting every nerve.

"Grab my neck."

My eyes snapped open, looking up into the green fire of his gaze. I tilted my head, silently asking if I'd heard him right.

He seized my hand mid-thrust and curled it around his neck, teeth bared, muscles taut. "Claws out. Grab me tight. I want to fuck the woman who could snuff me out without thinking twice."

His words ignited the fire in my veins. My hips lifted instinctively, grinding against him all while keeping a tight grip on his throat. My breath caught, and my whole body clenched as I cried out. Waves of pleasure pooled in my core, mingling with the wet, sloppy rhythm of our bodies, and I came so hard my eyes crossed.

His head tipped back in ecstasy. Hot, guttural moans vibrated against my grip, fighting their way through. Then, like a light had switched on, his gaze snapped back to mine, unflinching, demanding. He was determined to consume me, to break me entirely.

He hooked his arms under my thighs, lifting them up just to push them as far to the ground as they would go, stretching me so wide I thought I would split apart. Every inch of me was pulled taut, muscles straining, and the delicious ache drove stars behind my eyelids. My breath came in ragged pants, muscle pounding against muscle, and my own desire was dripping out, making a mess between us.

"We're not done, Boss Rossey." His mouth was stained with my blood, fangs bared, gaze searing. "I'm going to fuck this tight little pussy so hard you'll need to be carried out."

A shuddered whimper escaped me, a sound I'd never heard myself make. His eyes softened for the smallest moment, and my heart skipped a beat, a slice of vulnerability beneath that feral exterior. "But only for my good girl.... Will you be my good girl?"

My body already craving a second orgasm, I bit my lip and nodded. His grin widened, and his arms eased their grip, giving my bruised body a brief reprieve.

He brought my hand to his lips, tongue brushing over my fingertips, tasting me, and I shivered, molten heat pooling deeper with every lick.

"Now," he murmured, moving my other hand to his neck while still sucking and licking at the first. "Claws out, piercing skin, and I want you to squeeze hard. Choke me while I fuck you. Don't let go until I've made you come again. Understand?"

I nodded, shaping one finger into a sharp claw. He chuckled darkly, dragging it into his mouth, sucking and licking at it as his tongue sliced open and blood oozed from his lips. He moved to kiss my palm and down my arm, leaving a blood red trail as he went. It was primal and dirty, like we were making an offering to the moon goddess.

Moving that hand to meet the other, I enclosed both hands along the column of his throat. Heat radiated from the taut muscles beneath my claws, and his skin was slick with blood.

He thrust harder, faster, and I opened my mouth to scream, but his lips crushed mine. The coppery taste of my blood mingled between our tongues, his raw need pushing the kiss harder, faster.

I tightened my grip, pulling him just close enough to whisper, "Fuck me, Conrad. Fuck me so hard I'm forced to let go."

His arms pushed my thighs higher, spreading me wide as he relentlessly drove into me. Every inch of him thrust inside, filling me, stretching me, dragging ragged gasps from my throat.

Thwop.

Thwop.

Thwop.

My claws dug in, ripping shallow lines into his skin, almost like I was marking him. My wolf purred in my head at the thought, and I shoved that away as soon as friction sparked fire across my nerves. His eyes darkened, pupils wide and glowing, watching me gasp, pant, and shudder. He licked his lips as my muscles clenched around him, grasping him tight.

His thrusts became frenzied, neck veins pulsing, face flushed, but his gaze never left mine, commanding, claiming, tethering me to him.

Held in a savage lock, neither of us yielded until the heat in my core exploded. The tingling between my thighs busted into a storm that left me breathless and silent.

My claws retracted, hands slipping from his neck.

Like a tether snapping free, he roared into the night. "Oh, god, fuck! Nova! Fucking. Take. It!"

Liquid heat spilled into me as he pumped until he was spent. I was trembling and utterly wrecked, but the satisfaction and contentment I felt was worth it. Every thick, velvety thrust, every moan, every pulse of muscle was raw, carnal, *ours*.

Conrad collapsed atop me, chest heaving, gulping air like he couldn't get enough. I threaded fingers through his burnt-blond hair, massaging his scalp, feeling every beat of his racing heart that matched my own.

"I don't know about you, but that was my first time fucking in the forest." His head tilted, grin tugging at his lips despite his exhaustion. "Who knew I liked it wild?"

Licking my lips, I teased, "And who knew Mr. Businessman could fuck like that? You surprised me."

He closed his eyes, leaning into my touch, soaking in the contact. We savored the aftermath until the buzzing of my phone shattered the heat bubble around us. Reality had come knocking sooner than I thought.

I gave myself one more second to close my eyes and take a breath, enjoying the afterglow of great sex, before I tapped his shoulder. "Time's up."

With a groan, he reluctantly rolled off me. "Can't you just tell Zeth you're busy?"

I glanced at my shredded clothes and sighed. Luckily, I always kept a spare set in the car. Unlocking my phone, I saw missed texts from my siblings and a voicemail from Zeth asking if I needed help questioning Conrad.

Nope. That part of the presentation was done. Completely.

"Let's go take a nap and have a lazy afternoon." His hopeful voice was cute. "We could crash at my place and—"

I lifted my hand and saw he'd already got up, pants buttoned, his shredded shirt in hand, eyes bright like he was excited by the idea of spending more time with me. I wished it were that simple. I wished *I* were that simple.

"I can't." I closed my eyes. It was time to go back to the real world. "I need to get back. Check on the sample, then follow the lead where it takes me."

"Then how about I go with you?"

Looking up at him, I shook my head as if he'd lost his mind. "No. Now that I know you're not involved, you're no longer tied to it." My words sounded cold, so I quickly added, "Thank you for all your help. I truly appreciate it, but we'll take it from here."

See, Nova? Nice. Easy. Clean. No strings. Then why does my chest ache?

"Wait. Wait. Wait." He stomped up to me, and I folded my arms across my chest, standing my ground. Naked or not, I was still a boss. "Are you saying you're done with me?"

His eyes bounced between mine, silently begging me not to say yes, so I didn't answer. I didn't want it to be true either, but this was how it had to go. He didn't need to be tangled in something he wasn't part of. This was Syndicate business.

Deliberately not looking back, I stepped around him, walking down the path we'd used. "I'll take you home. You don't have to worry. And if you suffered any losses from missing the fight tonight, I'll compensate you."

Did I just fuck him and tell him I'd pay him? Yikes, Nova. Probably not the right phrasing.

161

I had made it about halfway when a blur of motion stopped me. Conrad was positioned right in front of me, eyes ablaze.

"No." His green eyes locked on mine, his mouth tight, arms crossed like a steel barrier. "Donnie and Jeremy are my friends." Even he winced at his wording, but he quickly doubled down. "I want to help."

I cocked an eyebrow. "Didn't you say they were just acquaintances?"

"No. Friends. Fellow turned supes I've helped. You don't go helping every random acquaintance, do you?"

I shrugged. True, I didn't, but I also didn't have time for dead weight. I brushed past him, only to have him yank my arm back. I growled, surprised by his resolve.

"I know someone Donnie might've told," he blurted, running a hand through his hair before standing his ground. "A promoter he keeps in touch with. If anyone knows what Donnie was up to, it's him."

Was this just a ploy to stay involved or if he was really trying to find a way to be around me? Maybe he was being honest. Maybe not. If he lied, I could kill him.

That voice deep inside cooed, *"But could you really?"*

I bit out, "Where's this promoter?"

His lips twitched, but he stayed firm. "He'll be in town for a major fight in a couple days. The Grosky versus Banner fight that you're putting on."

It wasn't just a fight; it was *the* fight. The one that was going to be televised across the nation. The one for which I had celebrities and rich people, both supes and humans, begging me for seats. Money, fame, the works. I'd even built a new dome facility, making the in-person fights exclusive to the elite and the few celebrities who could afford a seat.

The only exception was I had a lot of media coming for this first fight, both big and small, wanting everyone to have this playing in everyone's faces.

Looking him in the eyes, I knew I couldn't ignore the lead. The syringe. The sample. What if it was inconclusive? What if it led nowhere? I had to follow all the leads, wherever they went. It was my job.

"Fine," I relented.

I stepped up, chest-to-chest. "And if this guy turns out to be a dead lead or hasn't talked to Donnie in a while, I'll make it my personal goal to ruin every business venture of yours. You waste my time, and I'll make sure your time doesn't even matter. Understand?"

A sinful smile stretched across his face, sending shivers down my spine. "You got it, Boss Rossey."

I took a breath, leaning forward just slightly, still drawn to him. His eyes turned molten as they looked down, and I was suddenly very aware of how naked I was.

Snapping out of it and spinning toward the car, I said, "Let's go. I need to get you home so I can shower."

His voice whispered near my ear, "You could always shower at my place?"

I closed my eyes, realizing that getting him home would be a battle of wills all its own. What the fuck had I gotten myself into?

11

NICK

Thud. Thud. Whack.

What is she looking for in that dingy trailer?

Thud. Thud. Whack.

Who is that man with her?

Thud. Thud. Whack.

What's going on? What am I missing?

Whack. Whack. Whack.

Why does he smell different than other vampires? Who is he to her?

Whack.

A growl crawled up the back of my head, the beast in my chest clawing at the thought of her on top of him, her voice screaming into the night sky, face etched in pleasure.

WHY?!

"Shit, Nick!" My thoughts broke. Kevin was standing behind the punching bag, holding it as sand spilled from the broken seam. His mouth hung open as his eyes kept darting around then back to me. "You broke the fucking bag!"

Squeezing my fists at my side, I reminded myself I was supposed to lie low, not call attention to myself. Shit.

"Dude!" Kevin punched my arm, and I looked down at the spot, missing the ache that used to be there when I was human. "You're the strongest turned wolf I know!"

He whispered that last part, glancing around like he was making sure no one else heard.

"Aren't all beas—I mean... werewolves this strong?" I still didn't understand why he was so surprised.

He puffed out a chuckle like I was an idiot, then threw the broken bag to the side and waved his hand over the sand on the floor. The air shifted like it was being sucked into his palm, then his fingers twitched in one direction, dragging all the particles with them. Air mage.

"I'll get another bag. Hold on." He jogged off, leaving me with my thoughts.

After the tournament, the large Latin werewolf had split us into two groups. My group was told to train at a facility closer to town the next day, while the others stayed behind. I hadn't known until I showed up that morning that the fighters here were either destined for the professional circuit or leadership positions in the Syndicate. Some of them had even been handpicked by Nova, which irked me... I mean, it irked the beast in my chest.

Looking around at all the top-of-the-line products, pristine work-out gear, and magic items for training, I had this sinking feeling like I didn't belong. Was I here because of that fight? I wasn't the best fighter, but it had been my favorite activity at the police academy, and I'd gotten best in class. I knew I'd do okay, especially with heightened speed, agility, and strength now on my side. I guessed I'd impressed her?

A surge of pride rose in me. I was *pleased* that she saw value in me but quickly realized how ridiculous that was. Proud that a supe mob boss liked my fighting? Pitiful. I was here for a job. That was all I needed to focus on.

It wasn't long before another trainer stepped forward and split us into pairs, telling us this person would be our training partner. I was paired with Kevin, an easygoing mage who liked to talk—a lot.

I reminded myself that this was good, an easy way to remain in the background while staying in the know, but his incessant chatter was already grating on my nerves. It had only been the first day, and I was already tired of him.

Or is it because you stayed up all night, watching her?

Shaking off that nagging voice, my mind drifted back to the scene I'd been trying to erase. Her hand locked around his neck, claws digging in, claiming him. His hips slammed into her like she was his salvation, like there was no air left in the world except what came out of her mouth. They moved together as if the forest itself had been built as their private suite.

My gut should be curdling at the thought. Repulsed or, better yet, indifferent about the whole situation. It should have been nothing more than a passing breeze, a detail to note and dismiss. All I needed was her location, her patterns, the kind of intel I was supposed to be gathering, but that wasn't what happened. My gaze had glued itself to her, fists clenched, body trembling with an ache that had nothing to do with restraint.

I wouldn't have been out there at all if the other fighters hadn't wanted to shift and run off their injuries because we healed faster in wolf form. I'd taken it as an excuse to unleash the beast inside of me because he was already clawing underneath my skin, begging to be let loose.

I hadn't known it would catch her scent. Hadn't known how far it would go, but the second it inhaled her, a tether snapped taut, pulling me toward her with the force of magical magnets.

After my turning, I'd read about the thing called mates. How the beast chose the one it believed to be your perfect match. It had always sounded too much like soulmates, too romantic, too binding. How could this thing possibly know who was perfect for me?

Still, the fact remained that it was in control, and it bothered me.

I just remembered being laser focused and running. I had followed a small trail into a clearing, looking around with these beastly eyes. Even with it being cold, a small brook burbled against the stillness of the forest. Underneath the moonlight, the water looked like threads of silver weaving its way down between the frosted edges. It should have been serene.

Instead, it became a stage, and when my eyes found her on the ground, naked, along with that vampire, I nearly howled into the crisp sky. Her hair caught the moonlight, a white halo over taut muscle and supple curves. Her body was bent and arched, a weapon ready to go off. Forged in beauty and brutality, she was living proof that such opposites could live in the same flesh.

Then he rolled her to the ground, green eyes flashing, and claimed the spot that... that I felt was mine.

As soon as I realized that feeling came from the beast inside, I expected it to lose it, to lash out and rip him apart. I liked the thought of that, so I didn't fight it.

My pulse pounded like war drums, every instinct braced for the fight, but, to my surprise, the beast didn't move. It just stared. Watched.

I wanted to scream at him. To yank out this thing inside of me and tell it to do its job. I just didn't understand. Wasn't this supposed to be sacred? Wasn't a mate worth fighting to the death for?

Instead, he fed me something worse. *Jealousy.*

Pure, gnawing, white-hot jealousy. It slid under my skin and lit me up from the inside. With every touch that vampire laid on her skin, another spark lit.

The second his teeth sank into her flesh, the beast jerked, paw lifting as if he might finally spring into action. My heart thundered with relief, ready for the bloodbath, but then he stilled again, leaving me wrecked with wanting.

The jealousy twisted—not just in anger that someone else was touching her but in hunger. A deep craving to touch her that way myself. To feel her nails carve into my skin. To hear her gasp my name instead of his. The beast concocted mental visions and shoved them in my face. Me driving into her, tasting every inch of her body, marking her so thoroughly she wouldn't remember the green-eyed bastard existed… and my stomach churned, becoming sour, after I realized I liked it.

Fuck, I liked it too much. Even in this beastly, fur-covered body, I could feel my cock ache. It was hard and insistent, as though my body had already made the decision my mind refused to admit. I couldn't take it anymore.

I told him to charge, to tear them apart, to take what was ours. If I was going to have this thing inside of me, he had to be useful for something!

Instead, it answered back in broken words. *Mate. Not accept us. Not yet.*

I didn't know what the fuck that meant, but the human side of me hated how they moved together, hated that I couldn't look away, hated that I burned for her when I should've been recoiling instead. She screamed her pleasure into the wind, and the sound ricocheted through me, wild, unchained.

Absently, my paws moved. Leaves rustled underneath me, and her head snapped in my direction. I stayed as still as possible, hoping her trained wolfish eyes didn't find mine. I was grateful when the vampire's pleas caught her attention, giving me the chance to slowly back away. This was getting dangerous.

I dragged us back to the facility, even though the beast whined in my head that he wanted to stay, but I couldn't. I was raw. My soul felt like it was put through the ringer, and I just needed a second to breathe. To come back to myself.

Almost mechanically, I shifted back, put some clothes on, and made my way back home in a daze. Plopping down on my bed, I promised myself that I'd be able to let it go once I got a good night's rest. This fixation was just because everything was so shocking and new. I could push through this after I got some sleep... but sleep kept mocking me.

Every time my eyes closed, my mind was filled with imaginings of her body writhing under mine instead of his, the way she would tremble in my arms, her cries sharpened by the marks *I* left on her skin.

It was why I went to the training facility so early. Why I'd already broken a sweat by the time the rest of the group got here. I couldn't get her out of my head. Rubbing both hands over my face now, I bitterly muttered to myself, "Why the hell did it have to be her?"

"Okay." Kevin smiled, breaking the spell she had over me. A new bag floated behind him. "I got this one. Instead of the laces being magicked, the whole bag's under protection. I think they gave us that old version because... well, you know."

Kevin tried to shrug it off, but I had no idea what he meant. "What do you mean?"

He eyed me up and down, raising a brow at me like I was an idiot. Instinctively, I went into cop mode, scrambling for an excuse or a distraction to divert him. Then he asked, "Wait... how long ago were you turned?"

I shrugged, not wanting to give away too much. "Not long. A few months."

His eyes nearly popped out of his skull, and his voice shot high. "Holy shit! And you're already that strong?!"

I looked down at my fists, not knowing what to say. It wasn't like I'd been trying all that hard. In fact, I'd been lost in the

171

memory of last night, getting angrier with every punch instead of controlling my strength. A rookie mistake.

Kevin glanced around before leaning closer. "I'm guessing you haven't spent much time around other supes yet, huh?"

I shook my head, relieved it wasn't too obvious.

"Well," he said, lowering his voice, "I hate to be the bearer of bad news, but there's an unspoken hierarchy in the supe world. Whoever's strongest is the top dog, no matter the species." His pity-laced eyes met mine. "Turned vampires and werewolves are naturally weaker than born ones. And since the demons, fae, and mages are all born with their magic, that makes the turned ones... well..." he looked around before mumbling, "looked down on."

Great. Just fucking great. Fire churned in my belly. Since I'd been turned, I'd been ostracized by my friends, dumped by my girlfriend, and cut off from my job. Now, I was hearing that the very community I was now supposed to belong to saw me as the lowest of the low. A bottom feeder.

It hadn't even been my fucking choice! My mind raced as my body shook. I hadn't begged some werewolf to turn me. It was an accident. I'd been trying to help someone. Protect someone. Be the fucking good guy!

Why did my life have to turn out like this? Why did I have to be cursed with this thing inside me? What did I do to deserve it?

The beast growled in the back of my mind, and I snapped, "Shut up, you! You're the problem here!"

"Woah, hey," Kevin exclaimed, hands flying up. "I don't think that way! Don't bite my head off!"

I realized too late that people were staring. A few heads had turned, eyes glaring. Shit. "Sorry," I muttered, turning my back to them. "I wasn't talking to you."

Kevin eyed me like he didn't believe it but went back to holding the punching bag. "Look, this is just a gentle warning. Outcast to outcast. The whole reason they paired us up is because they think we're the weakest."

I shifted my feet, needing something to do other than just stand there and take his words. "What do you mean? You can move air with your hands. You could fling an opponent around. How is that weak?"

Tilting his head, he gave me a look that said he pitied the size of my brain. "That's exactly why. Mages are capped as to how much magic we can use during a fight."

He nodded toward the punching bag, so I went back to my jab-hook-kick combo while he kept talking in that hushed tone of his.

"Having a mage throw someone around with their power isn't entertaining. If you want the big bucks, want to be a professional supe fighter, you need to make it a show. Something people want to watch, to root for." He gestured to my shoulder. "Drop your left shoulder when you punch. Now, vampires can use their teeth, but they're not allowed to suck you dry. Demons and fairies have to apply and show their magical style before they're even admitted to try out."

My brows pulled tight, and he sighed, his gaze flicking toward the ceiling like he was already exhausted with me. "It wouldn't be fun to watch a demon smoke his way out of being punched for five rounds, and no one wants to see a fairy sing someone to sleep in order to win. It's all about finding that balance of low power and ingenuity versus strength to make it exciting."

I paused mid-combo, sweat dripping into my eyes. "What about werewolves?"

He shrugged. "They don't have any rules. Fighting has always been a werewolf sport, run by the Rossey clan of the Syndicate." His voice dipped lower, and I leaned in, throwing light jabs just to keep busy.

"If you don't know your history," he said, "the Rossey clan started as just werewolves, ruled by Manic Rossey. When his son, Ax, took over, he opened the clan to other species, but they had to prove themselves, and everyone was hesitant to change. It wasn't until this new generation of Syndicate bosses came in that those rules got scrapped. Now, the Rosseys find a use for anyone, no matter their skill. They're taking these fights out of the supe underground and commercializing them. Making them available to the masses." He shrugged again. "But like all new things, they needed rules so humans could handle the bloodshed and would dump their money into betting on us."

I stopped, wiping sweat from my face, and lifted a brow at him. "Doesn't that piss you off? They still run those illegal underground fights, but the pay's trash. So, the only way for someone like us to get to the professional level is to be a weaker supe and get beat up? That doesn't sound fair."

His smirk curved slowly, almost lazily, like my words amused him. "Fair, but that's a human way of thinking." Even though his face stayed smiling, his eyes flashed bright, his magic flaring up. "Nothing's fair in life, my man. You fight for what you want. You take what you can. And you live with no regrets."

Lifting his arm, he flexed for me. "That's why I still keep my body sharp and train my air magic to help me in small ways, like making me faster or my hits land harder. I use just enough to throw them off balance and maybe, just maybe, get in a good shot that will go my way. Plus—" he bared his teeth in a grin—"I'm not afraid to get beat up when there's that much money on the line. Supe money and human money are all green. More risk, more reward."

I wanted to roll my eyes, but his words lodged under my skin. It made sense in a twisted way. They couldn't die from a few rounds of beating, not really. Still, the justice-devoted part of me flinched, feeling restless.

"Kevin! Come here a sec."

We both turned our heads. The trainer waved him over.

"Ugh, duty calls. Be right back." Kevin jogged off, leaving me alone with my thoughts.

I grabbed my water bottle and tipped it back, letting the cool liquid wash away the heat in my throat. That was when the air stirred beside me. Earthy soil laced with a sharp, metallic copper smell stung my nose, a scent that screamed *vampire*. My first instinct was to walk away. I had no interest in making small talk with bloodsuckers. The only thing that stopped me was the faint undertone of human in the mix. A trace that reminded me of the one she'd been with last night.

"Hey," a voice drawled, "you've got good form. Decent strength."

I glanced sideways. Leaning against the wall was a tall, lanky vampire, skin stretched over sharp bones, his slicked-back corn-yellow hair doing nothing to distract from the sunken hollows of his cheeks. His clothes hung off him like they belonged to someone else. My cop instincts flared. This guy was bad news, but this was a gym full of supes. Bad news was everywhere. So I stayed put, muttering, "Thanks," before taking another drink.

"But you know it's not enough, right? They're still gonna set you up to fail."

I shrugged, though irritation prickled under my skin. Why the hell was this his business?

He edged closer. A growl slipped from my throat before I could stop it.

"Easy, easy." He held up a hand, speaking out of the corner of his mouth. "I'm trying to help you out as a fellow turned."

That froze me. Kevin's words echoed in my head. *Turned.* That explained the faint human scent. Maybe that was why Nova's vampire had smelled similar.

Taking my silence as permission, he pressed on, his voice quickening with feverish energy. "Haven't you ever wanted to prove it? Show them who the fuck they're toying with? We've got the same urges, the same pull to dominate, but they get an advantage just because they were born that way? Don't you want a level playing field?"

I almost told this fucker to buzz off. I didn't want anything to do with him and whatever he was offering. Nothing good could come from him.

Before I could do that, the last words from my lieutenant came to mind. After receiving my report about that first fight night, he'd called me into his office. He leaned on his desk with greedy eyes, ordering me to stay deep undercover for the long haul. He didn't want me just sniffing around juveniles who walked on the wrong side of the road. He wanted the big fish—something that could make headlines, something he could bring to the mayor to shove the Syndicate out. Maybe this guy would lead me to the thing I needed to put the nail in the coffin.

I didn't know where this vampire was going, but my gut told me to follow the thread.

Taking another swig of water, I muttered around the bottle, "Go on."

He turned to face me fully this time, a grin spreading from ear to ear. Just as he opened his mouth, the gym erupted, buzzing with movement as bodies surged toward the entrance in a tidal wave.

The vampire beside me froze, eyes widening, fear swallowing his smugness whole. He dug into his pocket, pulled out a folded scrap, and shoved it into my hand. "Here," he rasped urgently, darting eyes flicking toward the crowd. "Call me after. I'll help you. Like I said, us turned need to watch each other's backs."

The last word had barely left his lips when the air shifted. The scent of honeysuckle hit me, sweet and intoxicating. My gut twisted. It was *her*.

Nova Rossey.

The beast inside surged, vibrating against my skin, tail-wagging in my head. Pitiful. Fucking pitiful.

I turned to ask the vampire what he thought of her, but he was gone. Air. Nothing but the ghost of his scent.

"All right, fighters!"

Her voice boomed from the ring, commanding, bright, as she gave us a salacious grin. She spun slowly, arms stretched wide. "I'm in a good mood, boys. Who wants to take me on, huh?"

My jaw tightened until it ached. Images of her tangled with that vampire in the forest flared behind my eyes. Rage seared my veins, bitter and sharp.

I wanted to take her on. No... I wanted to work out every ounce of this aggression and make her see me.

12

NOVA

"I told you, he's clean." Setting my toothbrush down, I spit into the sink and bit back the urge to snap at him. If I were in his position, I'd probably be questioning me, too, but not this damn much. And I'd sure as hell not do it the second I rolled out of bed.

"Fine. Okay," Zeth huffed, leaning against the doorframe, arms crossed. "You've told me that a couple of times." His eyes slid over me, sharp, accusatory. "But I still don't understand why we're meeting up with him in a couple days at the fight."

"He knows someone going to the fight who might have answers about where Donnic is." I pushed past him into the kitchen, grabbed a bottle of water, cracked the top, and took a long swig. Anything to cool the heat crawling up my neck.

Keep it clean, Nova. Keep it business. He didn't need to know we'd fucked each other senseless. Or that a part of me wanted to see him again.

Zeth's gaze cut through me, searching. I turned away before he could read my face. With how he was acting, I knew one thing for sure. When he met Conrad again, there were going to be fireworks, and not the fun kind.

"Why can't he just tell us who it is, and we make him talk?"

Fuck. That was actually a good question.

I scanned the room for an escape route. Keys. On the table. Perfect. Snatching them up, I shrugged into my jacket while he called after me.

"We can talk about this later," I said, flashing the keys over my shoulder. "I need to check on the new fighters, see if any are ready for the prelims next week. I'd like to have back-ups lined up."

As soon as the last word passed my lips, I turned and made quick steps to get away from the conversation.

"Wait for me!" Zeth shouted, his footsteps closing in. "I'll go with you."

Great. A long car ride with his questions buzzing in my ear. Exactly what I didn't need.

I SLAMMED the gearshift into park. "For the last time, he's going to introduce us to someone who might know where Donnie is, which could help us find Jeremy, the kid, and Reece. We don't have any other leads." My voice sharpened. "And he's plugged into a fighter base we've never tapped into." Shoving the door open, I slid out, done with the conversation.

Why the hell couldn't he drop it?

Zeth slammed his door hard enough to rattle the frame, then laughed without any humor.

"Really, Nova? Now you want to tap into turned supes?" He scoffed as if that would never be a possibility. Wasn't that short sighted of him?

Pointing toward the gym doors, I shot back, "We have a turned supe in here. Case in point."

He stomped up close, getting in my face. "That was a fluke!"

That familiar smoky, tobacco-laced cherries and almond scent rolled off him. It usually calmed me, made me anxious, or gave me heartache. Sometimes, all three at once, but now, it was just pissing me off.

Turning my head, I took a shallow breath to clear everything away and pulled open the gym door. "And maybe it's not. We won't know unless we try." I quickly stepped inside, shutting down the argument before it could drag on anymore.

A ball of shadow surged toward me. "B-boss Rossey, what a pleasant surprise!" Her high pitch almost had me shaking out my ears, but I suppressed it.

"Hey, Lucy. How're they all doing? Gideon in yet?"

The ball stretched, forming into the shape of a person before the smoke dissipated, leaving a cute blonde woman with green eyes and muscles that rivaled my own in its place.

"H-he's here somewhere. L-let me go check." The way she scurried off told me she was probably calling him and telling him to get his ass down here.

Gideon, a werewolf, had been part of my dad Ax's old guard. I'd grown up climbing all over him, hanging on his arms and kicking his shins, which was probably why he liked to sleep in on weekends and only gave me reports once a week. He was the best of the best, an elite fighter with the talent to judge what kind of supe would thrive in the organization, and, like me, he was a potential seeker. He and I usually agreed on a fighter, whereas Hime and I rarely did. There was a good balance between the three of us, even if he was on the lazy side now that he had a mate and daughter.

Lucy was Gideon's daughter with his mate, Shera, a demon he'd met once, then chased all over Hell until he convinced her to cross over and build a life with him. A cute love story, one he'd retell to anyone who would listen.

It didn't take long for the fighters to notice I was there and start circling around me like a pack of hyenas.

"Boss Rossey, thank you so much for this opportunity. I won't let you down!"

"Boss Rossey, I've been working on my form just like you told me last time. Want to see?"

"Boss Rossey, what are you looking for in your next fighter? I want to fight Domino next! We'll make you lots of money."

Zeth quickly moved in front of me, barking at them to back off, but I placed a hand on his shoulder and gave it a firm squeeze. When he looked back, I nodded, and he eased off.

"So, you all think you're ready, huh?" Looking around, they nodded, their eyes hungry for the opportunity I could give them. Little did they know, I had come here for just that reason. They needed to prove themselves before I gave them their shot... and I needed to work off a little aggression from my earlier conversation with Zeth.

Shucking off my jacket, I held out my arms. "All right, fighters!" I hopped up on a bench and let my voice carry throughout the gym so all could hear. "Who wants to take me on, huh?"

Some of the more seasoned fighters' brows pinched as they weighed whether it was worth getting their asses beat, but the young guns, the ones with something to prove, yelled out, "Me! Me! I will! Pick me!"

I could feel Zeth's glare searing my back, probably still pissed at me for not consulting him about bringing Conrad in on this job, but I couldn't take it back now. He just needed to get used to the idea. It wasn't like he had to like the guy to work with him. We just needed as much help as we could get. I could hear the clock ticking in my head and just knew Ezra was waiting by the phone for an update.

Well, probably not her. It would most likely be Arion, but he would stop whatever she was in the middle of to answer me. He was the best of the best when it came to right-hand men. A secretary, bodyguard, accountant, and lawyer all rolled into one. It was hard to catch Ezra without him by her side. I admired their relationship, but at the same time, I craved more of an equal partner, and I didn't know if Ezra was... built that way.

Shaking all that off, I hauled myself up and jumped over the cage before pointing to a vampire with blond hair and bright blue eyes that sparkled with confidence and the thirst to prove himself. It was the look you had when you'd never tasted a loss, and, for some reason, I really enjoyed breaking those young ones' spirits.

"You," I said. "Come on up."

His eyes went wide with hunger as he sliced his way through the crowd, using his speed to get into the cage. The rest circled around, trying to get the best seat in the house.

*"What's your name?" I cracked my knuckles as I circled the ring, studying him for any weaknesses.

Mimicking my movements, he made sure to stay across from me, eyeing me up and down like he couldn't wait to show the rest of them how good he was.

"Benson." He took a second to bow. "And I would just like to say this first. Taking you out will do me no pleasure, Miss Rossey."

I stopped and gave a full-belly laugh that rang throughout the whole gym, pretending to wipe my eyes at the thought. "Oh, Benson, I'll remember you, but not how you're hoping."

His brows furrowed, his mouth stuttering as he searched for words, which only made the moment all the sweeter.

"Don't beat the poor kid too much. He still has drills to do today!"

Glancing over my shoulder, I saw Gideon next to Zeth and Lucy, yawning. "Glad you could get up and grace us with your presence, princess."

Lucy looked up at him then back at me, wringing her hands. She was always nervous whenever Gideon and I were in the same room. While Gideon and I viewed fighters the same way, we always ended up arguing about something or another and unintentionally broke something... usually something expensive. Last time we fought, we accidentally started a fire in a restaurant a couple streets over. The fight had been over the proper way to kick for maximum damage.

That night, I had been scolded by his mate Shera. I'd never been so afraid in my life. Gideon had a fierce mate, and I

---

* Manbitch by Haiku Hands

could see why he always just did what she said. It was safer that way.

"What can I tell you?" His smug voice carried over all the bodies around me as he adjusted his pants. "Shera's insatiable on the weekends."

The crowd of mostly men chuckled, murmurs of how they "gave it" to their girls at home echoing down the line. The few women in the room rolled their eyes in unison, used to the idiot talk. Men's egos were so damn fragile.

Thinking he could get the drop on me with my back turned, Benson sped forward, going for a right hook. My wolf's senses skyrocketed as I felt the air around me move.

I leaned back, grabbed his extended arm right in front of me, and threw him to the other side of the cage. He bounced off the titanium chains and landed on the mat with a thud.

Turning back to Gideon, I pointed at him, warning, "I'm gonna tell Shera you said that… in front of all these people."

His face turned white as a sheet, and he mouthed, 'You wouldn't.'

Lucy covered her mouth as she giggled, and I winked at her. I was *absolutely* going to call Shera after this. He was one hundred percent dead by the time he got home.

I was too busy gloating to notice young Benny boy had gotten up and was now coming at me by faking a left hook while switching to a right kick. As soon as my back bent to dodge the kick, he was on me, using his body weight to take me down. It was inevitable.

So, instead of fighting it, I went with it, going down but throwing my left arm behind his neck, looping it back beneath his chin with a firm grip, and throwing my body weight to that side so I landed on my knees with him secured in the headlock.

Circling my right arm around to my left wrist, I pulled with my right to choke him out harder. As a vampire, he couldn't die from asphyxiation, but it was still unpleasant and frightening to feel like you were choking to death.

He gave it his best shot, wiggling around, trying to throw his body left and right, but all he did was put more strain on his neck, which equaled more pain. I hunkered down, keeping my center of gravity planted, and watched his face turn blue.

Clawing at my arms, trying to kick me or punch me didn't work, and he ended up tiring himself out. When he finally tapped out, I let go and stood up with my hands high. The crowd went wild.

Roars of cheers filled the space. It's not that I took a lot of pleasure in taking down a young buck like this, but there was always going to be one like this in the new recruits, and I liked to establish dominance early. They needed to know I was confident I could beat them all. If they didn't, they would smell blood in the water and think they could come for me. There was always someone who thought they could steal the top-dog spot with just brawn on their side.

I looked down at the mat to see Benson gasping for air like a fish out of water, crawling, his fingers gripping the mat. Defeat and disappointment clouded his eyes, so I crouched down.

"Hey. Know that when you come at me fast, I can feel the wind shift, so save those quick punches for up-close shots— stuff the others can't get away from. When you want to be sneaky, go slow. Catch them off guard by doing the opposite of what they think you'll do. Kay?"

I watched the depression in his eyes melt, a renewed sense of vigor taking over. Biting his lip, he nodded his head. Giving him my hand, I hoisted him back up and shook it before turning to the rest.

"Anyone else?"

Most of the ones chomping at the bit sealed their lips and looked away, suddenly hoping I didn't remember how eager they'd been to take me on earlier.

"I will."

My smile froze as I looked into a set of sharp golden eyes glinting beneath the lights. His lips were pressed into a frown.

Nick. The turned wolf I'd bet on.

Heat flared across my wrist, a dangerous pulse I ignored as I straightened, watching that large frame stalk toward me. My eyes devoured him before I could stop myself, tracing the shift of his shirt over the grooves of his stomach. I didn't need to touch him to know those abs would be hard enough to dig my fingers into.

Nova, girl, keep your shit together. Be strong. He means nothing.

My wolf stirred restlessly in my chest, bringing with it unease, confusion, and hunger. She wrestled with the emotions as I shoved them down, locking them up tight. At least until I was done wiping the mat with him.

Schooling my features, I let a cocky grin curl across my face as I cocked my hip. "Come on up, then. I've always got time to show you all who's the boss and why."

He prowled forward, golden eyes locked on mine, and warmth spread from my left arm through the rest of my body. My breathing turned shallow, betraying me, as he opened the cage door and stepped inside.

"Do we just start whenever?" His voice was a low growl, threaded with anger.

I arched a brow. *What the hell did I do to piss him off?* I'd helped him get here, fought for him, even. Hime never would've given a turned wolf a chance like this without me pushing for it. He fucking owed me.

The more that thought circled, the hotter my blood ran, rage burning away those flickers of attraction. This wasn't flirtation. This was war.

"Go whenever you feel like it, pumpkin. It's no swe—"

His fist flew, a solid right hook, but I slid aside with ease, my counter kick snapping into his side.

He absorbed the blow and shook it off without dropping his guard. I bounced on my toes, circling, while his golden eyes scanned every twitch of my muscles, calculating. I wasn't about to let it be that easy.

I baited him with a few backward steps, letting him think he had me retreating, then I dropped, palms catching the floor as I kicked out at his legs with both of mine for maximum damage. He barely saved himself, managing to jump in just the nick of time, but my heel still clipped the top of his foot, rocking his balance. He stumbled on the mat, and that was all I needed.

I launched myself toward him at full force. Midair, my bones cracked, fur tearing through my skin, letting my wolf explode into the space between us. His eyes widened as he raised his forearm, saving his throat from my fangs at the last second.

Wrestling me on a good day was bad enough. Wrestling me in wolf form was a nightmare.

My jaws clamped tight, tasting the hot bite of his skin. Blood. My wolf screamed at me to release, to spare him, but I shoved her weakness away. He took advantage of the hesitation, hooking my paw with his foot and throwing his weight to the side so we rolled.

Pinned, I shifted back in a blur, escaping his grip on me with my bare fists flying. My knuckles cracked against his jaw. My knee drove into his stomach, his growl vibrating against my skin like a promise.

I caught Zeth's glare from the corner of my eye, concern tangled with fury. *Finish this now, Nova,* I told myself. Prove him wrong. Prove them all wrong.

I slammed my head into Nick's. His pained cry filled the cage as blood gushed from his nose, splattering onto me and the mat. The scent was sharp, coppery, mesmerizing. I slid in it, using the new slickness of my skin to twist free from his grip.

In seconds, I was on his back, arm locked beneath his chin, legs cinched around his waist like I was a psycho spider monkey, hanging on with all my might. I squeezed hard, every muscle straining, to make him break.

Tap out. Tap, damn you. I don't want to destroy you.

The crowd banged against the cage, savage voices calling for blood. My chest clenched. I hated them for wanting me to rip him apart. I hated myself more for not wanting to.

Having a weakness was death. Rossey bosses didn't go soft.

Tightening my hold around his neck, I made sure not a puff of air could escape. His legs kicked out, so I wrapped mine around them, too, making it so he was stuck with no outs, no hope, and still, he lasted longer than I thought he would.

It took a good minute or two of strapping him down in this position for that thick head of his to finally realize he wasn't going to win, for that hope to be snuffed out. Those light taps on my thigh came, and my whole body tightened right before I blew out a breath and let my arms drop away.

He didn't gasp for air like the vampire did, no, this man took short, quick, angry breaths, actively trying to calm himself down as I sat up. Blood was streaked everywhere—along the mat, my body. I must've looked like a mess.

The crowd erupted, voices crashing against the steel.

"That's it! That's our boss right there!"

"You're no match for her! No one is!"

I got up with raised hands, and the noises grew louder. Respect shined bright in their eyes, and their admiration reminded me. *This is why, Nova. You can never lose. Never bleed in front of them. Number one, or nothing. Number one, or you could lose everything.*

But after the stick, they needed a little carrot.

Raising my hands to shush the crowd, I let my voice boom through the cage. "Since these two fighters were brave enough to step into the ring with *me*," a ripple of chuckles rolled through the arena, "I'm giving both of them tickets to the Grosky versus Banner fight!"

A rumble of shock and disappointment surged. Voices overlapped with some complaining about the insane ticket prices, while others grumbled that they'd have happily taken a beating if they'd known the prize.

Exactly the reaction I wanted. The reward was never about handing out freebies; it was about honoring the ones with the guts to take the risk. The ones who stared down someone who could kill them yet still chose to step into the cage. Rewards like this were a way to champion the type of fighters I wanted.

When the cheers dulled, I crouched down. Nick's bloodied face tilted toward me, eyes still blazing even through the mess. Patting his shoulder, I leaned in so no one heard me. "Not a bad prize, right? You did good. Remember, you deserve this spot."

His fingers caught mine before I could pull away. My breath caught.

Up close, his eyes swirled, liquid gold, molten, alive. Magic hummed there, something otherworldly, but it wasn't the power that unstrung me. It was the grin. That crooked, dark, hungry slice against his tan skin and plush lips. A grin that whispered of dark corners and stolen kisses.

His gaze dipped to my lips. Heat scorched my veins. My heart thundered like I'd sprinted across the globe, every instinct urging me to close the distance even though I couldn't dare.

His hushed voice slid over my skin like a caress. "Not bad. But I'm more looking forward to seeing you in a dress."

I rose slowly, locking eyes with him, but the tension was thick as smoke, clinging, choking. Heat coiled low in my belly, raw and insistent. Part of me wanted to tackle him right there, tear the shirt from his body, and claim him in front of every gawking face.

How dare he. How dare he leer at me like that, reducing me to a trembling pulse and shaky breath.

And gods help me, how dare it excite me? How dare the first thought in my mind be to buy a new dress just to see lust twist his features when I wore it.

I closed my eyes, forcing a breath as I clawed for composure. *No. You're Nova Rossey. You don't pant after a man for a smile. You don't crumble for heat and pretty words.*

When I opened them again, I gave him a glare sharp enough to cut, but inside, my wolf trembled with restless desire.

"We'll see," was all I could bite out before turning to leave, only to be smacked in the face with the sight of Lucy rubbing herself against Zeth. Her hand slid up his jaw, cupping his face like she already owned him, like they were lovers. Maybe they were.

A growl clawed its way up my throat, my wolf flashing me a vision of tearing Lucy off him with our teeth and hurling her across the room. My fists clenched so hard my knuckles burned, and I snapped my gaze away. *He's not ours. Never will be.*

My wolf whined, low and wounded, telling me I was wrong, but I shut her up with the only truth that mattered, the memory of him not being in the training room the next day, my grandfather telling me he needed to train Zeth separately. His rejection was loud and clear.

That silenced her, forcing her into the corner of my mind where she couldn't argue with the facts that gutted us both.

The cage door clanged as I shoved it open and stormed out. My watch buzzed, and I saw a text from Calix.

Cal: *Come to the lab. Now.*

My pulse jumped. Was he here? When? Why hadn't he told me?

Looking back to tell Zeth, I was met with the scene of a smiling Zeth holding Lucy's hand on his chest. My lungs squeezed, and a ragged breath came out before I turned on my heel and stormed to my office.

I had stuff to do, a territory to protect. I didn't need anything else.

Grabbing the extra set of clothes I always had available, I yanked them on with hands still shaking from the adrenaline of the fight. I grabbed a jacket and the keys to my bike.

I usually didn't ride my bike in the winter, but this was an emergency. Either I left now or I risked killing a lieutenant's daughter... and maybe ripping out Zeth's throat for good measure.

Gideon caught me on my way out, worry creasing his face. "Are you really going to tell Shera what I said?"

The wobble in his voice cracked through my rage. A laugh ripped free, jagged, desperate. "Who knows?" I shrugged, watching despair creep into his eyes. "Maybe you just need to learn to keep your mouth shut about your wife and her urges when she isn't around to defend herself."

His head bobbed frantically. "Yes. I totally agree."

Ignoring him, I called over my shoulder, "Taking the bike." Whirling around, I walked backward with a grin I didn't feel.

"I wonder how mad she'll get when I tell her you said that in front of the whole gym full of fighters?"

His voice broke, sharp and panicked. "Nova, please! I'm too young to die!"

I waved him off without turning around. I wouldn't call her, but he needed to sweat over it. Served him right.

My steps carried me back toward Zeth and Lucy. They were now just talking, but although they were standing at an appropriate distance, the sight still twisted something unnameable inside me. As soon as he turned to look at me, I shoved the keys into his hand. His vivid aqua eyes locked on mine, scrambling like he'd been caught.

"Nova, what—"

I cut him off, voice tight as wire. "When you're done, just park the jeep in my garage. I got to go, and I'm taking the bike." Then I spun on my heel, not trusting myself to stay.

I heard him stammering apologies to Lucy at my back, causing me to speed up. I refused to let him catch up to me, to let guilt sink its claws in. I wasn't his keeper. I wasn't his anything. He could do whatever he wanted with whoever he wanted. That was what friends did. Kept their distance, stayed in their lane.

My wolf stayed silent, hollow, and that silence cut deeper than any scream.

The sight of my matte black Ducati Panigale V4 nearly made me cry with relief. A fast ride, that was all I needed. Speed, cold wind, and distance. Anything to shred the ache in my chest.

I rolled my baby out, swung a leg over, jammed the key into the ignition, and turned. With the engine's purr between my legs, a small measure of relief hit me before a pair of inked hands closed around the handlebars.

"Where are you going?" Zeth's breathless growl was right there, too close.

I didn't look at him. *Couldn't.* "Calix is in town. I'm meeting him." I yanked the bar free from his grip, eyes locked on the horizon. "I've got this. You don't have to leave. Looked like you were... getting somewhere, and I don't want to get in your way."

"What are you talking about?" he spat out before he paused. "Are you talking about *Lucy*? That was—"

I threw up a hand, choking on words that felt like glass in my throat. "I don't need to know. Just don't fuck in my jeep." Twisting the throttle, I tore off, not brave enough to hear whatever excuse he wanted to give me.

The wind whipped against me, feeling like small slices across my face, and I let it. Better to focus on the sting of cold air than the breaking in my chest.

When my eyes blurred, threatening to spill over, I told myself I wasn't crying. Something had gotten caught in my eye since I didn't have much gear on, leaving too quickly for any of that.

That's what I get for not wearing a helmet.

1 3

NOVA

Arriving at the address Rack had given me, I parked my bike in front of the old, decrepit warehouse, then I sat there for a second, taking several slow, deep breaths that came from my battered soul. The exhales that followed expelled all the tension I'd been holding, all the confusion and pain. Letting all of it go before I went in to see my brother, who would know instantly if something was off, was a necessity.

That warm, hot tingle on my wrist, the one that had burned relentlessly since I'd left, finally began to subside, transforming from fierce intensity into nothing more than a dull, persistent ache that echoed through my bones. I looked down at my wrist then, studying it with desperate hope that something, anything, would give me answers, but it looked exactly the same as always. No marks or lines marred my skin, no visible evidence of the torment I'd been experiencing. The sight left me utterly confused as to what any of it could possibly mean.

When Aniyah had described how her tattoo burned, she'd said it was like taking a shot of pure lust, craving the mates the tattoo was meant to hide, but mine hadn't felt that way at all. Instead, it had been more of a slow, agonizing burn, like something foreign and confusing was forcing its way into my very body, trying to take root where it didn't belong.

The burning sensation had flared when I was with Conrad, fired up like a live wire when my eyes met Nick's, and ached with a deep, throbbing pain when I felt highly emotional around Zeth.

I could accept that I was attracted to these three men, as that much was undeniable. I could even accept that I wanted to explore the physical side of things with them. But to be mates? The very idea seemed impossible, like trying to convince myself that the sky was green or water flowed upward.

I'd felt something inside of me break after I realized that Zeth really wasn't coming back. That my kiss and confession were rejected in the nicest way he could think of—disappearance. That stupid, stubborn hope that I'd found my perfect partner sunk to the bottom of the deep, dark ocean in my soul, never to rise again. My wolf had been so certain, and it was even harder for her to face his nice rejection, so I took up the slack, knowing I had to be the strong one for the both of us.

It was one of the reasons I got the mate-blocking tattoo. You couldn't have what was already taken. At least that was what I thought until Conrad and Nick showed up, making my wolf react like they possessed the rope to where that hope had sunk and were slowly, carefully pulling it back to the surface.

The question that haunted me now was whether someone who had been rejected could eventually find another mate, or even less likely, *multiple* mates. I'd never heard of such a thing before, had never even dared to dream it might be possible.

A flash of Lucy touching Zeth's arm came to mind, making my skin crawl. Why did my heart still bleed for Zeth with such relentless persistence? I'd agonized over him for what felt like an eternity, torturing myself with thoughts of what could've been, what should've been. I just couldn't carve him out of my heart, no matter how much I wanted to, no matter how much pain he continued to cause me.

As I stared at my wrist, I could still feel the phantom vibrations of the tattoo gun as she had layered magic into the mate-blocking spell. The memory was so vivid I could almost hear the buzzing sound and feel the needle piercing my skin over and over again.

The more I stared, the bigger that small spark inside me grew, flickering like a candle flame in a gentle breeze. Could I find a mate again? Was my body responding to Conrad and Nick as potential mates? Were they replacements for what I'd lost or something new entirely?

"What the fuck, Nova?! It's cold as fuck!" Calix's familiar voice cut through my spiraling thoughts, and I puffed out a laugh despite everything. "Not all of us have a built-in heater in our DNA."

Swinging my leg over my bike, I waved at my brother, heading in his direction before his complaining got any worse.

His shoulders were hunched, his arms folded tightly across his chest, looking at me like everything was my fault. "You know how I feel about the damn fucking cold."

I shook my head, unable to suppress a small smile. "It's April! What did you expect?"

"Not to freeze my balls off, Nova! That should never be an option! Come on!" He waved me in urgently, tucking his hands against his sides and mumbling under his breath about "damn wolves" and "should bury them in the ice to teach them a lesson." His complaints were so typical, so perfectly him, that I felt some tension leave my shoulders.

I pressed my lips together, keeping my chuckle to myself. It was genuinely nice to see him, even with all his complaining and dramatic flair. His presence helped me let everything else go, let me focus on what *really* mattered—my territory, the Syndicate, our legacy. These were the things that would outlast whatever romantic confusion I was experiencing.

He threw open the door with gusto, and, luckily, I caught it before it smacked me in the face. *What a whiny little prince he is.*

Magic rippled over the space around me as soon as I stepped through the threshold. It washed over me in waves, the sensation like walking through an invisible waterfall. The space before me was night and day from the junky exterior, a complete transformation that spoke to my brother's incredible ingenuity.

Magic pulsed along the walls and ceiling, creating an invisible barrier that separated the pristine white and stainless steel room inside from the harsh elements outside. White walls stretched in every direction, broken up by several glass half-walls covered with complex equations and formulas. Several stainless steel tables held microscopes and magical tools that hummed with barely contained power. A large refrigerator dominated the back wall next to a massive metal machine filled with trays of vials, its mechanical arm moving with precise, hypnotic movements as it picked up vials and scanned them with methodical efficiency.

This was a full-fledged mini version of the lab he maintained at home in Texas, and, somehow, he'd managed to bring all this equipment here without my knowledge. For a second, I was in awe of what a sneaky, brilliant, evil genius he was. *Glad he uses that brain of his for us.*

The machine in the far back corner beeped insistently, and he was over there in a flash, his vampire speed making him appear to have teleported. He studied the readout on the computer next to it, his expression growing more serious by the second.

"Well, shit." He raked his hand through the icy locks that perfectly matched mine, and when his golden, pink-hued eyes sliced over to me, I could feel the gravity of whatever he'd discovered. "You really need to see this."

Straightening my shoulders despite the weight of impending bad news settling over me, my heavy steps carried me over to where he stood, ready for some long, drawn-out explanation. Calix always tried to teach me something or show off his skills. It was frustrating when I just wanted him to get to the point, but that wasn't how he worked.

Usually, Rack or Ezra had to endure these detailed explanations, saving the rest of us, but today, it looked like I was the unlucky tribute.

He pointed to the screen. "As you can see by the numbers, it looks like N-14A and the metabolic compound OF-67 are slowly introduced to the variant, making it a stable isotope. Then here…" He tapped on another screen. "You can see the numbers over time, showing the growth of the different compounds that end up becoming radioactive, and you know what *that* means."

With his hands on his hips, glaring as he talked, I glanced at the screen and tried to make sense of all the numbers and acronyms displayed, but it was complete gibberish to me. The incomprehensible mess of scientific jargon might as well have been written in ancient hieroglyphics. In fact, maybe I could figure it out if it was in picture form. I wasn't a damn scientist!

Throwing my hand toward the screen in exasperation, I exclaimed, "No. No, I don't! What the hell am I looking at?"

Calix's eyes rose toward the ceiling with a heavy sigh, and my fingers curled into a ball, ready to punch him just to make myself feel better. Leaning over, his fingers punched in a few keys then pointed to the screen with renewed patience. "Look. Watch."

The display transformed into what appeared to be a video, showing several blob-like shapes floating around in what I assumed was some kind of cellular environment. At first, they seemed harmless enough, just drifting aimlessly, until something green appeared and attacked the blobs with shocking violence. The assault was swift and brutal, and I found myself leaning forward despite my confusion.

With my attention fully captured, I watched in horrified fascination as the blobs were taken over by the green and began to grow larger, like they were bulking up, becoming more substantial. The transformation held for what felt like an eternity, the enhanced cells maintaining their new, powerful state, but after some time, they gradually turned black and began to disintegrate. Their edges became fuzzy and indistinct before they started to disappear entirely, dissolving into nothingness as if they'd never existed at all.

"Whatever's in that vial," Calix explained, his voice taking on the clinical tone he used when discussing his work, "attacks a supe's DNA and inflates it. Almost makes the cells stronger, more powerful than they should be. Over some time, the cells eventually run out of power, and the enhancement slowly disintegrates them from the inside out."

He pressed another key, and the screen switched to a grid showing multiple videos of the same horrifying process I'd just witnessed. Each one followed the same pattern—initial attack, enhancement, then destruction.

"I tried this with different supe races' DNA and got the same result every time," he continued, his finger moving across the screen to point at various examples. "Except," and, here, his voice took on an even more ominous tone, "with human DNA." He pointed to the only video where the cells hadn't turned green. "Instead of destroying it, the substance clings on and adapts with it, almost like a parasite finding the perfect host."

As I watched the human cell video, I could see he was absolutely right. The green cells didn't attack and destroy like they had with the supernatural DNA. Instead, they simply clung to the sides of the human cells like some kind of symbiotic organism, but the effect was still disturbing in its own way. The human cells moved in a faster, more agitated motion, as if they were being pushed beyond their normal limits.

"What the hell is it doing to them?" I asked, though I wasn't sure I wanted to know the answer.

Looking up at my brother, I saw him shrug with the kind of casual gesture that belied the seriousness of what we were discussing, then he sighed like this was far more work than he'd wanted to do on a weekend, which was typical Calix. Brilliant but perpetually lazy.

"I don't know, and I won't know unless I test it on actual humans, and we're absolutely not doing that," he spat out, disgusted with the idea.

Even though my brother could be lazy and was, admittedly, emotionally unstable, he still held certain principles that he refused to compromise on. One of his strongest beliefs was that you didn't mess around with genetics and cellular makeup. He always said that experiments like that almost never went the way you wanted them to and that combining magic with DNA manipulation was just asking for absolute disaster.

I knew that Ezra didn't share his moral concerns about such things. Early on, she wanted to see if Calix could create something that would boost supernatural powers, pushing the boundaries of what our kind could achieve. He had refused her request outright, and it ended up becoming an issue at the Syndicate boss table.

We voted on it. The final tally was two to three, with Calix winning the argument. Ezra had to drop that particular idea and move on to something new. I thought it would be an issue, something that would divide us, but in typical Ezra fashion, she pivoted to the next opportunity without holding onto any emotions, putting her laser focus on legitimizing our portfolio instead.

That was when I knew without a shadow of a doubt that Ezra would do anything for us. She could tear another person into shreds, but when it came to the family, to keep the Syndicate whole, she would sacrifice anything. Even her own goals.

As I sat there staring at the computer screen, watching those horrifying videos play on repeat, a spike of pure rage hit me like a physical blow. The emotion was so intense it nearly knocked me backward.

I should have been notified that something like this was out there! What the hell were my lieutenants doing? Were they just sitting around twiddling their thumbs while this nightmare unfolded in my territory?

This was my damn city, my territory, my responsibility! The thought burned through me like acid, but just as quickly as the rage had come, it was replaced by something even worse... shame.

Pictures of Ezra's furious scowl and my parents' disappointed faces floated through my mind like accusatory ghosts. How the hell had I not known what was going on in my own backyard? The question haunted me, and with my recent failures piling up, I was forced to face a devastating realization: this was on me.

All of it.

I was the boss, the one in charge, the person everyone looked to for leadership and protection. I should have had a tighter grip on everything and everyone under my command. There should've been no cracks in my organization, no weaknesses wide enough for this kind of threat to slip through undetected.

My thoughts flashed to the last couple of days, and I felt sick with self-recrimination. I'd been focused on all the wrong things. Who cared about mates or this temperature-changing tattoo when something potentially catastrophic was loose on my streets? What kind of Rossey boss let this shit slide under their watch?!

"Fuck!" The word exploded from me as I slammed my fist down next to the computer, the sound echoing through the sterile lab like a gunshot.

"Hey! Hey! Easy!" Calix zoomed around me, his movements a blur as he frantically clicked on the keyboard, caught several things that had fallen off the table from my outburst, and finally began petting the machine like it was a beloved pet. "Don't take it out on Maria! She's just the messenger!"

The fact that he'd named his machine Maria would have been amusing under different circumstances, but I was too wound up to appreciate the humor. I jumped off the seat and began pacing, my body filled with spiky jitters that made me feel like I might explode if I didn't keep moving.

I forced myself to pause, think rationally. Why would someone create something so volatile and dangerous?

From a business standpoint, it made no sense at all. Even if someone wanted to rig fights and make their supernatural fighter extra strong, the enhancement would just kill them later, destroying their cash cow. So, it couldn't be for business purposes, which meant it probably wasn't a rival coming for us either, since they would be affected by this, too.

Maybe it was a human? Someone trying to systematically wipe out supernaturals? But then, why had it been found with Donnie, a turned werewolf? If genocide was the goal, Donnie definitely wouldn't be where I'd start. He was hardly a significant target.

"You okay, Nov?" The concern in Calix's voice was genuine and unmistakable, cutting through my spiraling thoughts.

I raised my head, folding my arms to make myself stop moving. To look calm. "Yeah, why?"

He had settled onto the stool I'd vacated, crossing his legs at the ankles and folding his arms in a gesture that reminded me of our father, Falcon. The resemblance was striking and somehow comforting. "Because you were sitting on your bike in a complete daze when I first saw you, then you freaked out over this whole mad scientist situation."

I gestured toward the machine that had analyzed the samples, exasperated by his casual attitude. "What do you mean? This is *huge*, Calix! There's about to be complete chaos in my city, and I should have known about it. I should have been on top of this from the beginning."

Calix's eyes narrowed, and his head cocked to the side in that particularly annoying way he had—telling me I was stupid without saying the words. It was infuriating.

"Nova," he said, rising from the stool with deliberate slowness, "this," he flicked his fingers dismissively at the computer, "this can be handled. You *will* handle it. It's what we do. It's what we've always done for generations."

He took a few cautious steps toward me like he was approaching a wild animal that might bolt or attack at a moment's notice. "You know we have your back, and you have the full power of the Syndicate at your disposal. All you need to do is make one phone call, and you'll have an entire army at your command."

He moved closer, his expression softening into something that looked almost sad. "But whatever's going on in here," he gently tapped my forehead, "and here," he tapped my sternum, right over my heart, "is messing with you, Nov. I can see it written all over your face. What's really going on?"

Fuck. He was absolutely right, and I hated that he could read me so easily. I rubbed my face with both hands, trying to get a grip on myself and my scattered emotions. "I'm just..." I started, then stopped. How could I possibly explain everything that was tearing me apart inside?

I was heartbroken over someone I should let go of but couldn't seem to release. I was perplexed by some turned wolf I shouldn't see again but knew I would. I was trusting a turned vampire I had just met based on nothing more than this inexplicable feeling in my gut. I shouldn't be focused on any of that romantic drama when I had real, serious problems to deal with.

But I couldn't say any of that to him. If I did, that would mean I needed help figuring it out, and the one thing I was not going to do was ask my brother for relationship advice. Other than Aniyah, my other siblings weren't the best source of info in that department.

I also didn't want to admit how completely my personal life was interfering with my professional responsibilities, so instead, I avoided his perceptive gaze and settled on a half-truth. "Tired," I puffed out. "I'm just tired."

His frown deepened, and I could see he wasn't buying my explanation for a second. "I know when something's bothering you, Nova. I've known you your entire life."

I blinked, and a set of strong arms pulled me into a hug. It felt like being embraced by steel. Despite the hardness of his vampire physique, the coolness of his skin was oddly comforting, a balm to my overheated emotions.

He whispered against my hair, "If you don't want to tell me what's really going on, that's fine. I get it. I understand the need for privacy. Just know," he gripped my shoulders and pulled away slightly so those eyes that perfectly matched mine could stare down at me with a glimpse of genuine brotherly love, "we're here for you. All of us. Whatever you need, whenever you need it. That's what makes us stronger than anyone else who might come against us. That's what makes us Syndicate. Makes us unstoppable."

Knowing with absolute certainty that he was right, I nodded. I'd always had my siblings' backs without question, never thought less of them when they called on me for help or support. In fact, I had enjoyed those moments when I could help them, when they needed me. Those times confirmed my place in this family, in this world, proving that I mattered and belonged.

Drawing on that strength, that unshakeable foundation of family loyalty, I took a deep breath and squeezed his arm before I let go.

His eyes settled back into their normal expression, and a lazy smirk formed on his lips as he crossed his arms. "You know that doesn't give you license to boss me around, so don't even try it. Also, I'll just hand off most of the work you send me to Rack anyway because I'm a busy fucking man with better things to do."

I lifted a brow at him, knowing he only half-meant what he was saying. Typical Calix. Always trying to maintain his image as someone who didn't care too much about anything.

Throwing my hand around to indicate the elaborate lab surrounding us, I said, "Sure. Right. That's why you came running to this little replica."

He laughed loud and hard, his face turned up toward the ceiling in genuine amusement before he said, "Well, I want to do the fun stuff. The boring administrative crap can go to someone else."

Shaking my head, I mumbled, "Gods, I feel bad for Rack. He has the worst job of them all, dealing with your lazy ass."

"Don't worry about him." Calix waved off my concern as he glanced down at his watch. "He's perfectly fine where he is." He smiled in a way that immediately made me suspicious. "Speaking of seconds, yours just rolled up outside."

My heart began to pound, and without warning, thoughts of him and Lucy came flooding back. The memory of him smiling down at her as she clung to him was so vivid and painful that my claws popped out involuntarily, my wolf responding to the uncontrollable surge of jealousy and possessiveness.

"Oooohhhh." Calix rubbed his hands together with obvious glee, a savage glint sparkling in his eyes. Of course, my personal drama would be the most entertaining thing he'd seen all day. "Trouble in paradise? Need me to knock him into tomorrow? Bleed him until he collapses from blood loss?"

When I sliced a deadly glare at him, his voice went up a hopeful octave. "Maybe just punch him in his stupid demon face? Just once? For funsies?"

"What's your deal with him?" I asked, genuinely curious about his obvious animosity. "You've never liked Zeth, not even when we were younger and he was just another Syndicate kid hanging around."

Calix glared down at his watch as if the timepiece had personally wronged him, and I barely caught his angry muttered words, "I hate a weak will."

What the hell does that mean? The comment was so cryptic and loaded with implication that I knew I was missing some crucial piece of information.

Before I could ask him to elaborate, Zeth's loud voice rang out from somewhere outside the building. "Nova! Are you in there?" A complex mix of emotions ran through me—anger, longing, frustration, and something that might have been relief.

Did he leave Lucy to catch up to me? How had he found me here? Had he asked Rack for the location? And if so, why? I'd given him full license to stay behind and hang out with her, practically encouraging him to pursue whatever was happening between them.

Maybe he felt guilty about the whole situation? I knew he'd had women at his place a time or two, but this was the first time it had happened so blatantly in my face, the first time I'd been forced to witness it so directly.

As I thought about everything going on, the serious trouble I was facing with this mysterious substance, the threats to my territory and my people, I still somehow had enough emotional energy left over to focus on Zeth and his romantic entanglements. A disturbing thought occurred to me.

Are we just holding each other back? Were both of us unable to move on and find happiness because we were constantly in each other's daily lives, always being reminded of what we couldn't have? Did I need to change that?

"Before you go," Calix called to my back, completely ignoring Zeth's increasingly urgent calls from outside, "I want you to know that this place is coded to let you in anytime. The magical locks will recognize you and grant you access whenever you need it."

He grabbed a few sheets of paper from one of his workstations and darted in front of me. "It's not complete yet, but here's a list of all the chemical compounds I identified in that sample. If you can't find a source or a dealer through normal channels, try following the ingredients instead. I'll also check the coasts to see if this stuff is being brought in from outside the country."

I carefully folded the papers and tucked them into my back pocket, their weight a physical reminder of the responsibility I carried. "Thanks, Cal. I really appreciate this. First, Aniyah had to deal with all that bullshit, and now *this*."

He nodded, but his expression fell by the second, growing more and more serious. "Aniyah. That lady she was fighting. How she described her turning…" He looked back at his lab, his body vibrating like it was itching to do something.

"You think this has something to do with that?" I lifted up the papers and watched his eyes narrow.

"Maybe." He turned around in a circle, answering me absently. "I'll have to see if I can scrounge up some samples to test against, but I'll let you know." His eyes lost focus as he stared at the wall, muttering to himself.

I had turned away from him, not wanting to disturb the mad scientist, when he called out, "Also, I'm going to send the details to Father."

I opened my mouth to object.

Our parents were on a well-deserved trip overseas, so I didn't want to bother them unless absolutely necessary, but Calix shook his head before I could voice my concerns.

"I don't want to disturb them either, trust me, but I have to do this. I need to see if he's ever encountered anything like this before, or if we're dealing with something completely new. His experience might help us figure out who's behind this and what they're really after."

Biting my lip, I was torn between wanting to handle this on my own and knowing he was right. Having experienced eyes on the problem was smart. More ideas, more information, more resources... even if it meant admitting I needed help.

"Fine," I finally agreed, "but tell me what he says the moment he responds. The second he gives you anything, I want to know. Got it?" I jabbed my finger at him to make sure he understood I was dead serious. Calix had this frustrating habit of finding out important information then getting distracted by other projects before sharing it.

He put his hand on top of my head and ruffled my hair, turning it into a knotty mess. I yanked away and growled in annoyance, pushing my claws out and swiping at him. He dodged my attack, using his supernatural speed to appear across the room in a blink. Smart fucking vampire knew exactly how far he could push me.

"You got it, little sis." Raising his fist in the air, he grinned like a complete psycho. "Talk to you soon!"

I had opened my mouth to respond when a loud banging echoed from one of the walls. Calix's expression immediately became murderous.

"If you don't quit fucking with my lab, you damn demon, I'll rip your horns out and shove them up your ass!" he yelled at the door. "Don't think I won't do it, because you know I absolutely will!"

The pounding stopped immediately, and I smirked at Calix. Being a violent psycho was definitely a family trait, so sometimes you just had to laugh it off and appreciate the effectiveness of a good threat.

"I'll be expecting that call soon," I warned him. "If I don't hear from you within a reasonable timeframe, I'll hunt you down myself."

With my hand on the door handle, he laughed. "You'll have to catch me first, and we both know how that usually goes."

Shaking my head at his arrogance, I opened the door and immediately ran into my panicked second.

Zeth's hair was sticking up in several directions, and there was a jittery energy about him that hadn't been there when I'd left him with Lucy. His whole demeanor screamed anxiety and distress.

"What the fuck is going on, Nova?" he demanded, his voice tight with worry and confusion.

Looking at him with a much calmer head than I'd had earlier, I sighed deeply, exhausted by our complicated situation. I needed to face this head-on. We needed a significant change, needed to finally address what had been festering between us for far too long.

"Let's go to my house," I said, my voice steady despite the turmoil in my heart.

"We need to talk."

14

ZETH

We need to talk.

Those four syllables hit me like a hammer to my chest. I froze mid-stride, boots stuck in the gravel parking lot as she climbed back onto her bike. My heart slammed against my ribs so hard I thought it was going to bust out of my chest.

She wanted to talk? My mind spun. Had Calix uncovered something? Was she worried about the substance? Or was this about whatever had been bugging her when she left?

Yeah. No. Of course, it was Syndicate shit. It had to be. Then why did my gut sink at those words?

I opened my mouth to ask why we couldn't hash it out right here, but then I caught her reflection in her bike's side mirror. Her shoulders sagged beneath the leather jacket, her cheeks hollowed. She wasn't really looking at me, just staring past my shoulder, jaw tight, fingers drumming along her thigh, and alarm bells clanged through my skull.

*She'd never looked at me like that before. Not when we were training together as kids, not when I came back and demanded my role by her side, not over the past five years that I'd been back in my rightful place. Never.

The pull to use my magic came hot and fast. If I could just read her emotions, get a taste of what she was concerned about, I could figure it out on the way to her house and have a solution to her problem, but that damn voice in the back of my head spoke up. *Don't do it. You know she doesn't like it when you do that to her.*

My mind flashed to earlier when I wanted to use my power. When she was fighting that turned wolf and jealousy rose up in my chest when their eyes met. If it wasn't for Lucy distracting me with all of her annoying, stupid questions, I might've tried to leap into the ring myself.

No. I needed to take a more direct approach.

Swallowing hard, I pressed my palm to my chest where the pulse pounded like a war drum. If only I could spin her around, look into her eyes, and coax it out of her. I'd find out whatever had fractured the light in those beautiful, sunset soul catchers so I could apologize and fix it. I was here to solve her problems. My whole reason to be here and stay by her side.

Stepping forward, I reached for her elbow. The instant my fingertips hovered near her shoulder, her whole upper body flinched away. My arm froze in midair. Did she not want me to touch her? My arm fell limp at my side, my breath caught in my throat painfully.

---

* Heartless by Diplo ft. Morgan Wallen

What had I done to make her this upset? Why was she acting like this? Why wouldn't she look at me?!

My chest trembled. I didn't understand. I'd done everything I could. I kept quiet as I watched her fight with that turned wolf, kept my fury buttoned shut, even while my blood screamed to explode. When she left, I called Rack and begged for the coordinates, then raced over here as fast as I could and banged around until she could hear me. Why was she pushing me away?

I ached for a cigarette right now. Anything to burn away this electric tension buzzing under my skin. Something was wrong, catastrophically wrong, and I couldn't unfeel it.

Without glancing back, she kicked the stand up and turned the key. Her bike roared to life, the engine's growl rattling my skull.

"I'll meet you at my house," she called, her flat voice devoid of her normal, easy tone. Then she tore off down the sunbaked street, whipping up a cloud of dust that stung my throat. In a second, she was gone, a distant silhouette swallowed by the haze of dust.

A volcano of panic erupted deep inside my chest as I stood there, watching her leave me like a doomsday omen. My pulse drummed in my temples painfully. The world felt taut, my soul on the brink of exploding.

"You know what? You're a fucking idiot."

Calix's mocking voice sliced through the haze like a blade. I spun to find him leaning against my car, arms crossed, with an infuriating half-smirk curling along his lips as if he'd been waiting the whole time.

A sharp ache split through my jaw. If I'd been human, my teeth would have splintered. *He's a boss. Her brother. Don't let him get to you. Ignore him. Get to the car. Focus on Nova.*

I tried, gods, I fucking tried, to pivot away and leave him standing there like the self-satisfied bastard he was. I should've known better. He was a Desmond after all.

"That's why I don't like you." His voice followed me, lazy, cruel, his words tumbling out and picking up shards of my anger. "Pure idiotism. We don't need that kind of trait in the family gene pool. So, keep this up." He flicked his chin at the empty street where Nova had vanished. "You're doing me a favor."

Heat crawled under my skin. My muscles coiled tight as bowstrings. Beneath the surface, my demon magic hummed, a low, hungry vibration that wanted out. Wanted to hurt.

Only two people knew the truth, that I was powerful enough not just to read emotions but to *manipulate* them. My fingers twitched with the urge to make Calix cower, ripping that smug grin from his face and stripping away the oppressive superiority he draped over me like a noose.

It would feel *so* good.

But I shoved it down. Hard. *Remember the consequences.*

One small moment of letting go, of letting myself feel, and my manipulation magic slipped out. I was devastated when her eyes changed and she said the words I'd always wanted to hear. All under the influence of my magic.

I didn't sleep that night. The only thing rolling around my head after all was said and done was that I needed to learn how to control it. I needed to be useful to her... so I called Manic.

A full year away from her was painful, but mastering restraint and control was more important. My mess up, my desperation for her to love me, cost me time apart from her. Every day felt hollow and vacant.

I was so excited after I mastered my power, knowing that I could now return to where I belonged. She was a little mad at me, but nothing could ruin us, right? No amount of her anger could keep us from being where we belonged. I could work on softening her anger, proving that she should never regret picking me.

My spine went rigid, every breath shallow enough to cut. My throat burned with unshed fury as I forced a stiff nod and turned on tight hinges, palms sliced from how hard I'd clenched them. Every step toward the car rattled with the promise that something inside me was about to snap, and I wasn't sure if it would be him or me who broke first.

Starting a fight with Nova's brother, Syndicate boss or not, was a bad idea on its own. Doing it after he'd just helped her? Even worse. *Breathe. Don't fight him. Not worth it.*

The crunch of gravel behind me made the hairs on my arm stick up, ready.

"I know what you want, Zeth Carter." Calix's voice dropped lower, closer, like a devil whispering in my ear. "I can see it even if she doesn't, and I'm telling you here and now—you're not worthy."

The words sunk into my skin, searing me from the inside out. *I know that,* I wanted to tell him. *Why do you think I haven't pushed harder? Why do you think I keep my distance? Why do you think I've been holding back?*

Heading for my car, I knew he'd never understand how much it cost me to keep myself in check when every nerve melted only for her. How many times I'd swallowed the urge to kneel, to beg for another chance. I'd never let my power ruin it again. I'd wait for years, decades, *centuries* for her to feel the same way for me if she would let me. If she would only open her heart just a crack.

"And she knows it, too."

My hand froze on the door handle, heart clenching so hard I heard it crack.

A rush of air brushed my neck, then his voice was suddenly right there, hot and poisonous. "I've even heard she's hanging out with a turned vampire. I mean, I don't want her to stoop *that* low, but anything's better than you, right?"

The last thread of sanity snapped. Rage and pain surged molten in my veins, and I couldn't keep it contained anymore. My power burst out, hungry, fast, and overwhelming. A smoky web crawled along the ground like a dangerous fog, meant to cripple him, to drag him down into the feeling of agony and make him beg. I wanted to see him *break*.

When I stepped forward and the haze cleared, a blur of motion landed right in front of me. Calix was standing there, arms crossed, smirk intact.

"You think us bosses don't know everything about our seconds?" His gaze dragged over me with disdain. "Whenever we announced our seconds, we had to give reasons, and everyone had to agree. I was outvoted on you. But all of that is to say—" he spread his arms in a mocking invitation—"I know about your little emotional manipulation trick, and now I know I can outrun it."

He turned his head, looking off into the distance. "Looks like you've got about a fifty-yard radius. You're welcome for the test."

I didn't think. Didn't feel. Just *moved.* My fist cracked against his face, the crunch of bone loud as a gunshot. His grin shattered, his head snapping sideways.

For a moment, everything stilled. Calix's head slowly turned back toward me, eyes lit up in untapped rage. Those rosy eyes turned sharp, a predator considering prey.

His fingers brushed the spot I'd hit. Whatever I'd broken was already healing, but my body still vibrated, craving another hit, another rush of violence after years of swallowing it down.

"That was a good shot." His voice was eerily calm, still water hiding a riptide. He rubbed his face and twisted his neck to peer at me with a cruel smile that promised retribution.

My stomach dropped as I gulped. *I just punched Boss Winstale in the face. Fuck!*

Calix grinned wider, blood on his teeth glinting as his vampire fangs caught the fading sunlight. "You won't get another, Carter."

Pain detonated in my stomach before the words even finished. My body went airborne, back slamming into a tree with a sharp *crack*, my ass slamming into the ground as splinters rained down all around me.

Fire erupted in my chest, sudden and merciless. My teeth ground together as the pressure gave way—hard, splintering pops that crushed the breath out of me.

I folded inward, lungs stuttering, each inhale carving me open from the inside. Deep beneath the pain, broken pieces shifted and scraped, clawing toward one another, knitting back together far too slowly, every second a fresh kind of torture.

"Now that we've gotten our frustrations out of the way..." He crouched in front of me, lazy smirk back in place. "I'll give you some advice. Do your job. Leave my sister alone. She has no room in her heart for a man like you. Stay in your lane."

He got up, giving me a pitiful look before turning away from me.

Something inside me went cold and absolute. The fury didn't burn anymore; it locked into place. Dense and unyielding, the hard, cutting stillness edged every thought.

I knew I wasn't good enough for her. I knew I messed up, but I'm hers whether she wants me or not. His opinion of me doesn't change that fact.

I wanted to be the man she needed. I wanted to give her my all and let her choose. If she rejected me, it would gut me, but I deserved no less. Still, if there was a sliver of hope, I would take it. I would make her see me and prove to her over and over that I was the right one for her whether her wolf wanted to mate with me or not.

With my mind made up, I focused on his back and unleashed my power again. This time, it hit. I felt it sink into his psyche, and my veins lit up with that addictive high.

"I'm not weak," I whispered, knowing he heard me as I shoved raw pain down the connection. Calix groaned.

I got up on shaky legs, puffing out a laugh as I stalked closer, power thrumming in my veins. Years of being underestimated boiled up—

His hand shot out, snatching my throat and lifting me like I weighed nothing.

What the fuck? His body should've been locked in torment.

His eyes were bloodshot and blown wide. Blood dripped from his lip, and his fangs were bared. He looked monstrous, nothing like the smooth, controlled Calix I knew.

He snarled. "You think we haven't been trained to resist mind manipulation? Fairy, mage, demon—it's all the same."

Even before his fingers squeezed, I'd lost my breath. *They've been trained for this? They know how to resist it?* Hope blossomed in my chest. My mind was focused on only one thing, and it wasn't the pain Calix was inflicting.

I wheezed, clawing at his arm, desperate to hear the truth. "Did... Nova get... this... training... too?"

He glared at me, bows pinched, before dropping me like dead weight. My power snapped away from him.

"Fuck." He shook his head. "I don't like that feeling," he muttered, rolling his shoulders.

Coughing a few times, I croaked again, "Did Nova... get that training?"

For a heartbeat, behind all his fury, I caught a flicker of something unexpected: respect.

"Yes, dipshit! We all did." He looked around, exasperated. "Did you really think Nova would have a second who could control her? Do you think we would let her?"

The words hit me harder than his punch. *I can't control her.*

For years, I'd been repeating it in my head like a curse. It had been the reason I told her no. My whole body suddenly light, the years of guilt lifting away like smoke. I bolted for the car. I had to see Nova. Had to talk to her. Explain. Maybe, just maybe, we could start over.

My stomach coiled tight, breath coming in erratic bursts, but my heart was light for the first time in months. I didn't even register the pain from Calix's punch anymore.

"Where the fuck do you think you're going?" Calix shouted after me.

I raised my hand without looking back. "I don't have time to deal with you anymore. I need to talk to Nova."

Slamming the car door shut, my engine roared to life, mimicking the way my own soul had come back online. Gravel spit under my tires as I tore out of there, Calix shrinking in the rearview, arms crossed, glare sharp, but the corner of his mouth had lifted.

He played me. Again.

Fucking Calix.

It didn't matter because, tonight, I'd prove I wasn't the weak link he thought I was. The time for caution and patience was up. I was going to show her that she was mine.

15

NOVA

*The cool rim of the glass pressed against my lips, bringing with it a steadiness that held me back from the cliff's edge. I'd been filled with pain and frustration all afternoon, but now the chilled Hellfire liquor slid down my throat and smoothed the edges of the storm, a clean burn that cut through and settled into my belly.

I told myself I wasn't punishing him. I was *freeing* him. I kept saying the words to myself over and over until they sounded like the truth.

It was cruel and selfish to keep him chained up next to me and perpetuate this toxic loop we were in.

My fingers closed around the crystal glass until the engraved initials bit into my palm. The thoughts scraped on the insides of my skull like claws, striking sharp and deep. I shook my head and guzzled down the mind-numbing liquid. The burn made the feelings dull. Manageable.

---

* Fade Out by Kami Kehoe

Somewhere behind my thoughts, my wolf whined, a small, protesting sound that coiled under my sternum. If she truly thought I was making a mistake, she would have slammed forward, been insistent. Instead, she stayed back, sending me a reluctant, soul-deep ache, one that made my throat tighten and breathing difficult.

My wolf was always ready for a fight. Even when she was silent or at her lowest, she would rise to the occasion if doling out pain and blood was called for. She never gave up on Zeth either, pushing me, always pushing me to make him ours. When he smiled at me, I could almost feel it, the connection inside of me reaching out for him.

I'd felt that way even when he was a gawky kid, his limbs too long, at his dad's side. His eyes were downcast when we met, and the second he lifted that mop of sun-kissed brown hair and those aqua-green eyes found mine, I was gone. Instantly, my thoughts changed. I knew I wanted him, now and forever.

Even now, the memory made my stomach twist.

Banishing the past, the red numbers on the stove clock glared at me. Where was he? I thought he had followed me, he always did, or at least kept pace. I'd left him in the dust on purpose, but still, my chest threatened to cave in with every second he didn't show.

And that's the type of thinking you need to let go of, Nova. Closing my eyes, I took a deep breath. *Maybe he went to see Lucy?* As the dull pain in my chest strengthened, my mind kept going. *What's going to happen to them once he leaves? Maybe he'll take her with him?* My jaw clenched. *Wouldn't that be perfect. The two of them moving away together, making a new life.*

I slammed my hand on the table, and the glass toppled against the wood, the sound a sharp reminder. "Let it go, Nova," I murmured to myself. "You have bigger things to worry about. You're the fucking Rossey boss. One man is *nothing*." The words felt brittle and weak, even to me.

Pulling my shoulders back, I forced my spine to steady, becoming a pillar. I needed to be strong. I needed to take this love and shove it so far down that it had nowhere to go. Eventually, over time, it would disappear and fade into a memory. *At least I hope so.*

My wolf whined again, and I couldn't take it.

Shut up! This is best for everyone. She sank back into the dark corners of my mind, and I breathed a little easier. I couldn't be weak about this. Plus, she seemed interested in Nick and Conrad. She would get over it.

They're not a substitute for Zeth.

Boots on the porch echoed, and my pulse jumped. Needing something to do, I got up and pulled another glass from the cabinet, pouring three fingers into each like an offering. If he already knew I was agitated, I could pin it on Calix. Half-lies were easier to swallow with liquor.

"Nova." His voice, low, ragged, made the room tilt. I rose before I could rehearse the goodbye I had planned. Corking the bottle, I watched him as he came in—how his shoulders carried him, how his throat bobbed when he swallowed. Pain and something hotter lanced through me. I bit the inside of my cheek until I tasted copper.

Lifting my glass to hide the way my fingers trembled, I took a drink. The burn steadied me once again, settling in my stomach as my muscles tingled with the numbing effect. "Sit,"

I said, kicking at the chair across from me. The single word came out flat, businesslike. "We have a lot to talk about."

Silence pooled between us like oil, thick and uncomfortable, but I welcomed it. It gave me time to shape the sentences I wanted to say, to pick the knife with which I would cut him loose, but how to broach the subject?

My mind scrambled through options: reassignment, Calix's warnings, the training he'd mentioned. All of them sounded like evasions. None of them sounded like the mercy I wanted it to seem like. I watched the glass in my hand catch the light and tried to feel nothing.

The sound of glass dragging along the table caught my attention. He yanked out the seat right next to me with a screech as he turned the chair to face me. Heat crawled up my neck; my wolf shifted inside of my chest, my muscles tensing as his scent filled the space around us. Sweet, smoky, and dangerous. I took another drink to steady myself.

This was ridiculous. I had much bigger problems to occupy my mind with—the men I needed to find, the human boy in need of a rescue, and the bastard who was dealing drugs in my territory. *Get a fucking grip, Nova.*

"Yeah, we do." Zeth tipped his head and finished his drink like it was nothing. I couldn't stop watching his throat work, the way the glass blurred the planes of his face. An old, irrational desire rose in the back of my mind—*grab, bite, claim.* The feral pull made my teeth ache for a taste. I caught myself and reached for the bottle again, pouring us another three fingers because movement steadied me. The sound of liquid hitting glass filled the room with something honest, giving me courage.

His eyes flicked to the bottle, then to me. My mind and urges were still waging their own battle, but now was not the time. I set the bottle down between us, fingers hovering over the crystal as I tried to make the next sentence clean and concise.

"First…" My voice cracked, but I took a beat, steadied it, then tried again. "First, I need you to know Calix tested the substance. Long story short, someone's made an injection for supes, something that makes us stronger, faster, and sharper, but only for a time. Once the cells burn out, it kills us from the inside, down to the cellular level."

Zeth's jaw flexed, his lips parting in a low hiss. "Shit." His fingers raked through those brown locks streaked with rebellious blond, tugging the ends as if the pain anchored him. He stared down at the table for a heartbeat before looking back up at me, his eyes swirling like a sea storm, lost in thought.

I nodded and tipped the glass against my lips. The liquor burned, cold and clean, fuzzing the edges of my mind even though my tongue sharpened. "We need to get a handle on this now. My brother's going to tell Ezra soon so she knows it's top priority, but since we found it at Donnie's, I'm guessing those men she needed me to find are involved somehow."

My sigh came out with an all-too-obvious tremor. Long nights ahead meant no time for softness.

Zeth nodded, his phone already in hand. His thumbs hovered, waiting. "Got it. Should I have the men scour the city?"

"Yes." My voice steadied as he began to type. "Focus on turned hangouts and underground fights. It would make sense for them to use those that fly under the radar as test subjects.

Make the smart men the leads on this. We don't want to tip our hand and let them know we're on to them. If they get tipped off, they'll go underground, and we'll lose this chance."

He typed faster, and I watched the light from his screen flicker across his face. On the drive here, I'd been telling myself that letting him go was the right thing, that it would've happened eventually, but my mouth dried up like ash. I couldn't say the words out loud.

"We're not just after dealers," I added. "We need the distributors, the lab, and the maker. At this point, following the drug to its root is our game plan." I fished a folded sheet from my back pocket and slid it to him. "Also have Kalen look into chemical purchases. These are the basics. Cal will send me the full list later. See if anyone's ordering this crap in bulk."

Zeth didn't even glance at the list before snapping a picture and firing off a message. "Got it. I'll keep him on task and get it over to you ASAP."

Tucking his phone back in his pocket, he leaned forward, elbows braced on his knees, and, for a moment, I saw not the soldier or my second-in-command but the boy who had once grinned at me with his whole heart. Determination glinted in his eyes now, like steel catching sunlight.

"We'll get them, Nova. We'll show them the Syndicate isn't to be fucked with. We'll make them pay for ever thinking they could slip this past us. I'd say it's about time we had a good hunt."

A wolfish smile curled along his lips, warm and sharp all at once, and my lips betrayed me by mirroring it. "I know, Zeth. Even if we have to call in the cavalry, we'll get these bastards. We'll make them pay in blood."

Moments like this were intoxicating. The steadiness in him, the fire. They were a lifeline I'd leaned on more than I'd cared to admit, but lifelines could strangle, too.

Taking a deep breath, I locked my resolve into place. I was Nova goddamn Rossey. I could do this. I could let him go.

"After all this business is done…" I made my smile wide, almost congratulatory, despite everything inside me screaming not to say it. "It's about time you got a promotion, don't you think?"

His head jerked back like I'd struck him. "P-promotion?" His mouth shaped the word as if it didn't make sense.

I pushed forward, pretending not to hear his heart skipping a beat. "I want to honor your dedication and good work. You've done a hell of a job helping me build this into the fighters' mecca I dreamed of, and I'm so close to solidifying that."

Leaning forward, I punched his arm lightly, playing at cama-raderie, even though my words tasted like acid. "Now, it's time for your dreams. I'd love for you to be somewhere strategic, like the South, to cover the East Coast, but it's your gift and your choice. Whatever works best for you."

He sat frozen, eyes wide, shoulders stiff enough to crack. The silence stretched, and my stomach clenched. I rushed to fill the space with more words. "If you need to talk this over with… someone, that's fine. We have time until all this mess is sorted. I just wanted you to start thinking about it. Make plans."

"Someone?" The bite in that word cut straight through my act. I tilted my head, unsure what he wanted from me.

Why was he looking at me like *I'd* gutted *him*? Did he want me to bless him and Lucy? To hand him off to her with a neat little bow? *I'm trying, aren't I?*

I grabbed my drink and downed it in one shot, trying to drown the hurt raking up my throat. I was opening my mouth to tell him I hoped he'd be happy, with Lucy or whoever, when he dropped to his knees in front of me, catching my hands in his.

"Why are you doing this?" The deep, pain-filled desperation in his voice caught me off guard. "Why are you pushing me away? What did I do? I can fix it. Whatever it is, whatever you want. Just… please don't leave me behind."

Those last words struck like stones thrown into water, their ripples smashing through my composure. I shot up so fast my chair toppled, yanking my hands free. "Leave you behind?! Is that what you think I'm doing?" My voice shook with each word, fury and pain grinding against one another.

"*I'm* not leaving anyone." My body vibrated, a taut wire ready to snap. "*You're* the one leaving *me*. You're going to find your mate, start a family, and be so fucking happy. And I—" my voice broke into a growl—"I'm going to stay here, rejected, focusing on my business and my family."

I glared at his beautiful, panicked face. "I'm going to let you go. I'm going to release you from this toxic mess that's been eating us alive. We're going to move the fuck—"

I didn't get to finish. He surged up, hands framing my face, before his lips crashed onto mine, swallowing the rest of my words like they were never meant to exist.

*The rich taste of cherry-laced tobacco slid across my tongue as his mouth claimed mine, taking, testing, tasting, coaxing me to respond in kind. The flavor was hypnotic, the smoke laced with a tart sweetness, and, before I could think better of it, I threw my arms around his neck, pulling him down to me as I surrendered to the craving I'd been starved of for years.

Gods, it felt good. *Too* good.

We took a few stumbled steps together until my back hit the kitchen counter with a dull thud, the impact sending a tremor up my spine. His tall, muscular frame caged me in, heat radiating off his body as his hands came up to cradle my face with a gentleness that made my throat tighten. My eyes burned, unbidden tears threatening to spill.

"Don't let me go," he pleaded against my lips. "Keep your claws in me." His mouth claimed mine again, and I just couldn't stop him.

Why is he doing this to me now? Why tear me open just when I'd built walls thick enough to survive him?

The questions clawed at the back of my mind, but I held them back. Terrified that if I spoke them aloud, if I demanded the answers, he'd stop, and the desperate, selfish part of me couldn't bear for him to do so. Not yet.

I knew this was dangerous, that this could end in a mess for us both, but the cold, rational voice inside me had been outshouted. If this was all we'd ever get, then I would take it, take *him*, for one night. The least he could do was let me have this before I let him go.

---

* Wave by Meghan Trainor ft. Mike Sabath

My body moved on instinct. My legs wrapped tight around his waist, my hips tilting to rub shamelessly against the hard, thick length between his legs. His low moan vibrated into my mouth, breaking apart the fragile control I had left, and my legs squeezed him tighter into me.

"Fuck, Nova," he groaned against my lips, his breath hot, voice raspy like it'd been years since its use. "You taste so good."

His hands slid under my jacket, dragging my shirt up as his palms cupped my breasts. The flick of his finger across my nipple sent a violent shudder through me, and my wolf howled her answer. *Mate. Mate. Fuck mate.* The word pounded in my skull like a spell, and, for once, I didn't silence her. I did what she wanted, what we *both* wanted.

A burn sparked at my wrist, but not hot enough to truly register through the fog of liquor and years of repressed hunger. I was done holding back. I wanted to feel. I *needed* to feel. At least once.

I tore off my jacket, top, and bra, scattering fabric around the floor like a flag of surrender. His tongue dragged a molten path down my chest until his mouth closed around my nipple, sucking, circling, teasing, while his other hand toyed with its twin. My head dropped back against the cabinet as he trailed kisses down further, an involuntary purr slipping out of me at the sensation.

"I love that sound," Zeth murmured against my belly, his fingers playing at the waistband of my pants. I hissed at his touch, biting my lip to keep from begging.

"Another sound I like," he taunted, and the sharp pops of my zipper unfastening ricocheted off the kitchen walls. My pulse spiked.

"I wonder what kind of sound you'll make when I touch you *here*." One hand worked my pants off as his other brushed along my slit in a feather-light stroke that made my hips jerk forward, craving more, needing everything.

"Quit wasting my time and—" The words broke off as he discarded my pants, lifted one of my legs over his shoulder, and dove into my pussy like a starved man.

His tongue licked and sucked greedily, and the messy sounds made my entire body tighten, the pleasure almost too much.

"Oh—oh, shit," I gasped, tangling my fingers in his hair, tugging hard to keep myself from going over the edge. He moaned against me, and the vibrations shot up into my core, making me clench around his tongue. I needed more, all of him, right now.

As if he'd read my thoughts, his hands gripped my ass, fingers digging into my skin hard enough to make me cry out. He chuckled darkly, lifting my other leg over his shoulder until I was trembling in his hold. "You better hold on tight, Nov," he cooed. "I'm not going to fuck you in the kitchen."

That was all the warning I got before he hoisted me up like I weighed nothing, his mouth still buried in me, and shivers of fear skittered along my skin.

"Oh, shit!" My legs clamped around his neck, and I gripped down on his hair for dear life. His tongue flicked at my clit, my whole body seizing with the jolt. How the hell was he going to get me upstairs? At this point, my thighs were around his head, and my pussy was covering his view.

Not giving me time to think, his tongue moved faster, flicking back and forth, making my eyes roll back as my claws slid free. Leaning over his head, I lightly raked them down his back while he carried me out of the kitchen, his stride steady despite my nails scoring his skin.

He paused at the wall by the stairs and lifted his head with a smug grin. When he spoke, his words were breathless but still teasing. "I know this house like the back of my hand," he said, "but I *will* stumble if you keep distracting me."

My world narrowed to him, the way his desire-consumed eyes caught mine, the scent of us hanging heavy in the air, the soft burn of alcohol blurring the edges of my vision. It was like stepping out of time. How could this all feel this good when he'd broken my heart so completely? But right now, none of that mattered. This moment was ours, for better or worse.

"Then I guess you'd better concentrate," I whispered.

His tongue dragged against his glistening lips, and I bit my lip in response. His fingers on my ass creeped closer and closer until he slipped two fingers inside of me at a slow, tantalizing pace that was driving me insane.

My eyes slammed shut, fingers twisting in his hair because they needed something to hold onto in order to keep me grounded.

*"Look at me, Nova." The command in his voice had the boss in me wanting to bark at him, but the mate who loved him wanted to follow the command, and tonight, the mate won.

My gaze locked onto his, those Caribbean green eyes swirling with unbridled passion. He cooed as he stepped up the stairs, "Even if you never say the words, I can see them in

---

* Never Ever by Omido

those gorgeous rose gold eyes. I can see your need, your desire for me. I can hear them begging me for more." The fingers in my pussy pumped in and out, working me up notch by notch as the wet noises grew louder. The moans that tumbled out of my mouth were raw and husky.

His eyes watched everything, memorizing every twitch, every reaction to him and his words. Even when he reached the top of the stairs, he didn't look away, just turned left and went down the hallway, telling me to duck my head when we made it all the way there. The booze went straight to my head, and I got dizzy, my fingers gripping him harder, trying to steady myself.

In my confusion, I went to climb down, to see where we were going, but Zeth's grip on me became tighter, and he bit the inside of my thigh.

"Zeth!" I cried out, glaring down at him, but he gave me a toothy smile in response.

"Close your eyes, Nov. Trust me to make you feel good. To take care of you." His words came out like a plea, begging me to give him everything in this moment.

A piece of me hesitated, reminding me that I was a Syndicate boss. I needed to be strong and in control. All those thoughts I lived with day in and day out circled in my head, but when I looked down at him, I realized I *wanted* to let go. I wanted to trust someone with a side of me that wasn't strong. The piece of me that wasn't all fists and fury but was softer, lighter… feminine. The piece that was always meant for my mate.

The heat from my wrist crawled further up my arm, filling my body with a warm, safe glow, and I made my decision. Closing my eyes, I whispered, "I trust you."

Like it was timed, his fingers in my pussy pumped harder, faster, and my breath hitched. His lips closed around my clit, and my mouth dropped open soundlessly as he flicked his tongue in time with his fingers.

My hips were unable to keep still, thrusting against his face, making sure he was surrounded by me and my scent. Nothing had permission to take up any space in his mind—except me.

Just when we worked up a tantalizing rhythm that pushed me higher and higher, heat coiling low in my belly, his teeth ran along my clit before he sucked on it like he was taking my soul with his mouth.

The orgasm that had been building exploded from within me. My pussy clenched down hard on his fingers, and I threw my body backward as I screamed his name.

For a second, it felt like I was floating in the air, encased in the pleasure of fully letting go, letting the euphoria take over my body to do with it what it willed. That was until my back landed on something fluffy, and my eyes snapped open.

Zeth's eyes searched mine, his cum-soaked hands lowering my legs from his shoulders to sit around his hips. "Gods, you're beautiful. I can't wait anymore," was all he said as his hands fumbled with his pants. His cock sprung out, slapping against my thigh before he grabbed it and shoved it into my wet and waiting pussy.

At this angle, head and back on the bed, ass in the air, legs wrapped around his hips, he sheathed himself deep inside of me. My thighs trembled as he fucked me through the after-shocks of my orgasm.

"Fuck. Fuck, Nova." His grip on my hips became bruising as he rutted into me like a mad man. All that commanding patience was stripped away from him, leaving only the starved man who needed to take and take from me.

His face twisted up in a painful kind of pleasure, sweat dripping from his forehead as his body shook. I liked seeing the effect I had on him. I liked it far too much.

I smirked up at him, enjoying the view until he glared down and growled. His hand snapped out and slapped my clit, which sent a shattering rush down my spine. His fingers rubbed at my clit as he pounded into me, his long, fat cock banging against that spot inside that made me choke on my own moans.

"You thought you were done?" A cruel laugh spilled from him. "I have time to catch up on."

It seemed my body agreed with him since heat burned up from my belly like he was reaching inside of me and tearing it out of me.

"That's right. Clench down on me hard. Never let me go. Fucking take it all."

My eyes rolled back into my head as bliss was yanked out of me, and my moans turned into desperate pants. His thrusts grew erratic, and with clenched teeth, he cried out, "Fucking take it. All of it. *All of me.*"

His thrusts slammed into me, reaching so deep I felt the warmth of his cum fill me. "Nova. My Nova."

His Nova. Yes. That's what I want.

He released me with a groan, my body sagging into the

mattress as my bliss made me twitch with the fading pulses of our fuck session.

I patted the spot next to me, wanting him to know he could be at ease and catch his breath. I knew I did.

I wasn't expecting him to yank at both my legs and roll me over. I yelped in surprise, looking over my shoulder to yell at him, then froze.

Zeth was heaving big, long breaths like he wasn't a demon but a beast, his eyes narrowed into slits, muscles taut and bulging. Everything screamed that he was dangerous and I should get away, but that thought only made me even more breathless with want.

"I promised myself," he huffed, "that I would have *all* of you."

When my brows crinkled in confusion, his hand cupped my pussy, collecting his dripping cum before rubbing it between my cheeks. My eyes went wide, and his mouth split into a grin. "I'm going to have all of you, Nova." He worked a cum-covered finger into my ass, and I couldn't help the whimper that fell from my lips.

He rolled his head at the sound, his neck corded as his hard length grew along the back of my thigh. Silky, thick, and hard. "Tell me I can have you, Nova." The words were more of a command than a question.

The rational side of me buried under booze and lust poked its head out, telling me not to do it, to stop here. That he wasn't ours.

His other hand rubbed at my clit, and that lustful wave swallowed that voice back under. I wasn't thinking about tomorrow or the next day or the next, just living in the now with him.

"Yes, Zeth," I moaned. "Take all of me."

NOVA

Shifting against the cool, magicked sheets, I hissed out a breath. The temper-charmed spell woven into the fabric of my comforter was always perfectly chilled against my naturally warm body, but right now, nothing was cooling me down. That Hellfire booze had been a mistake. Sure, it was great because of the lack of hangover, but tingling pinpricks crawled up my spine like a hundred restless fire ants.

It would ease after a couple hours, but although it wasn't painful, it was annoying to wake up to.

I stretched, hoping to shake it off, and my foot nudged something solid behind me... warm, alive. A sleepy groan rolled across the mattress.

"Mmm... warm. Cozy," Zeth mumbled, his voice dragging with a husky edge.

I froze. My chest went tight. Last night flashed behind my eyes in fractured, heated fragments: his mouth, his hands, his voice growling my name. My teeth caught the inside of my cheek hard enough to sting, anything to keep the sound rising in my throat from escaping.

What the hell did I do? I'd sworn I'd let him go. Let him be free of me and our fucked-up situation. And instead... instead I'd taken him, again and again, until neither of us could move anymore.

A full quiver of sharpened thoughts pierced my soul. *What if this wrecked everything we'd built? The friendship and camaraderie? What if he thought he could... treat me the way he did last night in front of the Syndicate?* Oh, no! That would not fly.

And what about Lucy? Hell, I didn't even know where they stood! Had I just let myself become the other woman? Every muscle in my body clenched at the thought. What did he want from me now? What could he possibly have been thinking?!

Even if this was just a fuck, this wasn't my usual pattern. No clean break. No names forgotten as I left. No spending the night next to him. No neat compartment to shove it in. With him, there were threads, questions, and a thrum in my chest that wouldn't go quiet.

I dragged my hands over my face and bit back a groan. *That's it! No more Hellfire booze. Ever.* I was forever off the sauce because, apparently, it turned me into someone reckless enough to chuck every boundary I'd built straight out the damn window.

He stirred again, and I went still, every muscle tense, every sound putting me on edge. Peeking over my shoulder, my focus softened as I watched him sleep. Hair a tousled mess, breath even and slow, lips curved faintly, something peaceful and content. It was the picture of a man who'd fed every appetite to complete satisfaction. Against my better judgment, a smile tugged my lips.

Even through the chaos in my head, one truth pulsed beneath it... Zeth knew how to fuck. Not just well, devastatingly well. Addictingly well. Dangerously well. I hadn't felt this wrung-out, this satisfied, in longer than I wanted to admit, if ever.

Who knew he had it in him?

His face scrunched, nose twitching as loose strands of hair brushed his face. The urge to sweep it back rose before I could stop it. What harm could it do? Just a touch. Just to keep him asleep. I needed him to stay asleep while I processed everything. Plus, he'd worked so hard last night; he deserved the rest.

I slid my fingers into his hair, combing it back in gentle strokes. Silken strands slipped over my skin until something sharp kissed my fingertip. I hissed and drew my hand back, but his soft, sleepy moan caught me. "Nova. Oh... Nova."

I froze. Heat flushed up my throat as I realized he was still asleep. Was he... dreaming about me? Even after last night's extensive activities? What a little sex beast he was. Maybe it was the demon genes?

Something poked out through his hair. My heart gave a heavy kick, and I leaned closer, pulse hammering in my ears. He moved again, burrowing his face into my pillow and taking a nice big sniff before settling down. The thing rose another half-inch, smooth and wickedly pointed.

No. It can't be.

I blinked, but the vision didn't fade. Two deep metallic black stubs, one on each side of his head, poked through his locks.

Smooth, tapered to a needlepoint sharp enough to break skin.

Horns. Demon horns.

My whole brain went offline. There were no thoughts—only the desperate need to go.

Trying to be as careful and slow as possible, I slipped from the bed like it was rigged with explosives, heart pounding, every nerve ending screaming for distance. Those were fucking horns... horns that grew when he said my name and smelled my scent!

Snagging a sports bra and leggings from the floor, I practically ran from my room and down the stairs. I quickly scrawled a note for form's sake and left it on the fridge before I bolted for the back patio.

Dropping the clothes onto the table for when I came back, I took off into the forest naked, knowing that I wasn't going to spend a lot of time in human form. I needed to run. I didn't know where or why, but the act itself would make me calmer.

The moment my bare feet hit the earth, I took off, going zero to sixty in mere seconds. The mountain air cut at my skin, each lungful sharp enough to hurt. *Fucking horns.*

Demon horns only emerged for their mates.

Did he know? How long had he hidden this from me? Did he know when I confessed to him six years ago? Did he know when he came back? Was it me, my power, my position, that made him hold back? Did he want me and my body, but not the bond?

The questions tangled tighter and tighter until they became a noose. I couldn't breathe. Couldn't think.

Tears prickled at the corners of my eyes, threatening to spill over. My whole world had been thrown into chaos, but a Rossey didn't cry. No. We pushed through with our strength, got mad, and made the world bend to our will... but I had no idea what that will was.

That familiar heat flared up at my wrist, confusing me even more, but I refused to look at it. To acknowledge it. No. I was going to let all of this fade into the back of my mind. I was going to let her take over and save me from embarrassing myself any further.

My bones cracked and reshaped mid-stride, fur bursting over my skin as my wolf took me, slamming the human voice into silence. Four paws hit the ground, claws digging into soil, and the world became pure and clean. Pine and damp earth filled my lungs, the rush of wind in my ears, the pulse of the forest around me.

No Zeth. No horns. No questions. Just the wild, the run, and the single primal beat in my veins.

I didn't know how long I'd been running, how far I'd gone. I just let my wolf take the reins and do with us what she wanted, letting the peace of not being in control settle my troubled soul.

———

THE FUR along my spine prickled.

A presence pressed in at my back, not close enough to hear, not careless enough to snap a twig. Just weight. Attention. It moved when I moved, slipping through brush and hollows with stealth.

I let my stride settle, then veered off the trail without warning. Leaves crunched under my paws as I cut downhill, angling toward the creek. There was nowhere to hide in open water, nowhere to watch without being seen.

If they wanted to keep me in their sights, they'd have to step into the light.

THE CREEK BROKE through the trees in a flash of blue silver. I tore down the bank and skidded to a stop at the water's edge, breath burning, heart slamming hard enough to rattle my ribs.

I lowered my muzzle to the stream, letting the cold bite my tongue, letting the surface ripple as if I were nothing more than a thirsty animal.

Beneath the chill of the water, the air thrummed tight and alert. A breeze brushed my ears and lingered.

Then I caught it.

A heartbeat. Steady. Close.

Maybe it was a lost human. Too blind or too arrogant to heed the warnings nailed to the tree line. Maybe it was someone foolish enough to believe four legs and fangs were something they could handle.

My wolf rolled beneath my skin, a pleased rumble vibrating through my chest. *Let them try.*

I let my shoulders loosen and my stance soften, all the tension bleeding out of me on purpose. Beneath the calm, I reached inward and brushed a thought against my other half. *Circle wide. Let's catch our little shadow.*

She moved without hesitation, slipping into the brush behind a jagged boulder that resembled a broken cliff face. We went still.

A muted crunch. A ripple through the air. The fur along my spine lifted, one slow prickle at a time.

Before I could move, the wind turned, and the scent found me.

White musk, warm and living, threaded with heat and wildness. It didn't just fill my lungs; it sank past bone and blood, straight into the place where my wolf resided. My instincts surged, sharp and aching, tugged forward by an undeniable call.

It pulled at my core, a low summons that bypassed thought and reason alike. Not temptation... more like recognition. As if some part of my soul had lifted its head and gone still, listening.

My breath hitched. My pulse stuttered then roared beneath my skin.

A shadow stepped forward. Black fur caught the sunlight, each ripple of muscle beneath it sleek and fluid. Then I saw the wolf's eyes. Deep, molten brown locked on mine, whispers of forever and secrets traveling between us.

The forest fell away like magic.

The world dissolved into stillness and heartbeats, mine tripping over his. Time didn't matter, only the distance between us, charged and fragile. My wolf spoke one word in the back of my mind, her tone reverent.

Mate.

The word loosed a shiver that ran down my spine, curling low in my gut. I felt it in my bones, in my breath, in the space between each heartbeat.

Without thinking, I moved toward him. The second my paw pressed into the dirt, he jolted, then ran off in the opposite direction.

That was all the invitation my wolf needed.

She launched forward, joy and hunger colliding as we gave chase. His scent streamed through the trees, heady and addictive. It clung to the back of my throat, making every inhale feel too full.

He glanced back, tongue lolling out in a teasing grin that sparked heat in my belly before he darted faster. The sound of his paws drummed against the forest floor in a rhythm I couldn't ignore. The chase changed, becoming something else, something that got the blood pumping and my mind running wild. Something... intimate.

Heat surged beneath my fur, and heartbeat synced to the pace of his. Even knowing it was play, my wolf wanted more. Not just to catch him, to *claim* him.

The land shifted, familiar terrain rising in my mind. I angled off, herding him toward the glen, a hidden hollow wrapped in waterfall mist. Perfect place to corner him.

I darted close enough to nip his flank, my teeth grazing fur. He twisted, dodging, breath puffing white in the cool air. Each dodge drew a spark, each brush of movement a promise.

He broke through the clearing, skidding to a stop just before launching himself into the air, heading for the pool of water to escape me. I leapt after him without hesitating.

Bones cracked and twisted midair, fur giving way to skin. I collided with him, tugging him to the side, rolling in the air until our bodies slammed into the damp grass of the water's edge. His fur was so soft and lush, I wanted to sink my face into it. The strength of that sudden desire nearly made me forget what I was doing.

His weight pressed into mine, solid and burning hot even through the cool night and dense fur. My knees braced on either side of his ribs, my breath tangling with his. For a heartbeat, all I could feel was heat and pulse and skin. *Got you.*

A tremor rippled through him. Black fur receded like smoke, leaving sun-warmed tan skin beneath my palms. Sweat glistened along the lines of muscle carved by motion and moonlight. My gaze lifted and locked onto familiar brown eyes, wide with shock.

Nick.

His name fractured something within me.

Heat surged from my wrist, shooting through my veins with the heat and strength of a wildfire. The mark blazed, its burn delicious and somehow alive. My body ached with it, every nerve attuned to him. His scent deepened, wrapping tighter around us until I could taste it on my tongue.

Don't you dare, I warned myself, but the thought came and went with the wind.

My fingers dug into his wrist, grounding me in the moment's

fragile edge. My voice came out rough. "Why were you following me?"

His eyes flickered, voice a low rasp. "I—I don't know." Shame and confusion threaded through his words. "Something inside me just... took over. Then I was there. Watching you." His chest rose and fell, then he whispered, "He was... called to you."

The space between us pulled taut, humming with instinct.

That warmth I'd been fighting at my wrist coiled low, molten and alive. My gaze betrayed me, caught on the stubble on his jaw, the damp hair sticking to his forehead, the curve of his throat as it bobbed. The urge to lean down, to *taste*, burned through me. His pupils dilated, lips parting, breath mixing with mine.

"Is this... normal?" His voice was soft, unsteady. "Does this happen to all of you?"

That one word, *you*, snapped something inside me. Did he really think he wasn't part of us now?

His cock pressed against my thigh, the heat of it searing my skin, and my breath caught. My wolf took that moment to flood my mind with visions of tangled limbs, grass beneath bare skin, and the scrape of bark against my back. My thighs trembled, my exhale shaky as I tried to get a grip on myself. Every muscle in my body coiled tight, ready to spring.

"Sometimes." I gulped. "It's normal for us wolves to let our instincts help make our decisions, to lead us to the right outcome." The words came out steady even though my nails were digging crescents into the earth. I bit back the truth. I didn't want to tell him that I'd never lost control before, not when it felt like I was about to lose it now.

My arms trembled. Sweat beaded at my temples. In the back of my mind, my wolf's voice rose to a howl. *Take him. Now. Here.*

"It's just instinct?" The desperation in his question had me tilting my head before he added, "Something that doesn't mean anything else?"

His gaze dropped to my bare chest, lingering there. His tongue darted across his bottom lip, there and gone in a heartbeat. Between us, his cock twitched, and I realized what he meant. *Ahhhh. So, he has a hard time sifting through his wants versus his wolf's.*

"No," I said, wanting to see what he would do if I gave him an out. "It doesn't need to mean anything beyond what it is."

*The lie tasted bitter on my tongue. I could practically feel my wolf rolling her eyes at me.

My chest tightened, ribs constricting around lungs that suddenly couldn't get enough air. Everything in me knew whatever happened next would change things, but the blood thundering in my ears drowned out the warning.

His jaw worked. His fingers flexed at his sides, curling and uncurling. The tendons in his neck stood out like cords.

I had started to pull back, not into being with someone who didn't want it, when I heard him growl, "Fuck it."

His hand shot behind my neck, fingers threading through my hair, then he yanked me down hard and fast. Our lips crashed together, opposing waves in the ocean, violent and unyielding.

---

* Bad Choices by Kode

He tasted like desperation, longing, and something darker I couldn't quite put my finger on. Whatever it was, I devoured it. Pressing closer, I tried to swallow what haunted him and replace it with the heat building between us. My wolf surged forward, clawing its way through my control.

I ground my hips against him, already slick and aching for more. A growl rumbled up from his chest, vibrating through my mouth and straight down my spine. My eyes fluttered as I swallowed it, keeping it for myself.

My wrist pulsed, sharp, insistent, demanding my attention. Just as I was going to look, he slipped his hand between us, gripping himself before dragging the head of his cock across my clit. Slow. Deliberate.

More. The thought exploded through me. *All of him. I want it. I need it.*

Nick's hands clamped onto my ass, lifted me up before I had a second thought, and slammed me down onto his cock.

Stars burst behind my eyelids. My spine arched, head thrown back. The stretch burned, pleasure and pain twisting together until I couldn't tell where one ended and the other began.

A phantom ache from last night flared. Zeth's name flickered through my mind, and I could sense the pesky feelings of pain and hurt flaring up. Before any feelings could settle, Nick thrust up, rough fingers finding my clit, slamming all those feelings back into the box that held them.

His hoarse voice barked out, "Don't think of anything else but me. It's my dick you're on."

The words scraped out of him, raw and possessive. Zeth's

image sank back into my memory, and I focused on the warmth blooming in my chest, unfamiliar and... terrifying.

He grunted, and I looked down, falling into those eyes full of dark fire. A rich, smoldering brown that caught the light like burnished mahogany. All I could think about at that moment was how badly I wanted those eyes. I wanted them to see me as more than the Rossey boss, more than just the women on top of him. I wanted more from him. I wanted him to be—

"Fucking mine."

Nick moaned, "Yes," and my eyes flared. *Did I say that out loud?* His fingers dug into my hips hard enough to bruise as he grunted, "Yours. Fucking yours."

My body froze, heat rising from my cheeks as my heart kicked against my ribs.

His smile was all teeth, sharp and joyless. "At least for right now, right?"

That thump in my chest crumpled. I forced my lips to curve, forced my hips to move. *I am not about to look like the weak one in this situation.* Instead of speaking, I ground down on him until his eyes rolled back and his breath stuttered.

"Yeah. You're mine... for right now. As long as this," I eyed his chest, running my hand down it, digging my nails into the grooves, "lasts."

His whole body clenched underneath my touch, and before I could say another word, he flipped me. My back hit the ground, knocking the air from my lungs. His cock drove into me, hard, fast, relentless.

"You're fucking mine, too." Each word was punctuated by a thrust. "Don't. Forget. That."

255

His fingers clawed at the ground. The earth crumbled beneath his palms, turning to powder. He froze mid-thrust, staring at his hands like they belonged to someone else.

Hooking one leg around him, I dug my heel into his ass, pulling him deeper inside of me to wake him the fuck up or distract him from freaking out about the fact that he was now a monster. "Harder. Fuck me harder."

Lost, uncertain eyes met mine, and, for a second, I felt for his predicament. It wasn't easy for your life to get turned upside down, but now wasn't the time to wallow. Now was the time to enjoy the perks of being a supe.

Rocking myself up, I cupped his face and bit his lip hard. Tangy copper took over my tastebuds before I swiped my tongue along his lips. Just like when you fought, sometimes you needed to draw some blood to get you to focus.

His fingers swiped at his mouth, dragging crimson across his chin. "What did—"

I caught his lips with mine, tongue digging into the spot where I'd bitten him. Caught up in the mix of his blood in my mouth and his scent in my lungs, my pulse stuttered.

"You're a werewolf now." I ran my thumb along his lip and showed him the lack of blood. "Your skin heals fast." Staring at his mouth, my core clenched, and I licked my lips. "Losing a couple drops of blood is nothing, but it can satisfy the animal inside you."

His gaze locked on mine, searching, but I didn't look away. Didn't hide the predator that laid beneath these eyes. He needed to see the truth.

While I didn't want him to see me as his boss, I also didn't want him to see me like some of the weak human women he had likely bedded in the past. I could handle the animal he kept locked up.

His head bent down, hips rolling slow and deep while his mouth made a thick, wet trail up between my breasts. Once he got to my collarbone, my weak spot, I let out a small whimper. His lips curled along my skin, then he bit down. Hard.

The sharp sting dissolved into heat in a flash. A raw moan tore from my throat. His tongue swept across the wound, tentative at first, then he lapped at it, drenching my pussy.

The sound of his heartbeat thundered in my ears. Between my legs, his cock swelled harder, and my lips curved. There it was.

"Let him out," I whispered into his ear. "Fuck me like you've wanted to. Like you've dreamed about." His rhythm stuttered. "You know I can take it. *All* of it."

He slid out of me fast, and I cried out at the emptiness. I was about to tell him I was disappointed when he lifted and turned my body like I was weightless, slamming my top half to the ground, leaving my ass in the air.

His hand pressed between my shoulder blades, pinning me down, and my instincts came up, demanding I kick at him and shove him onto the ground. Seconds away from doing just that, his fingers slid inside me, and my mouth dropped open. His thumb circled my clit, spreading the wetness around until my hips bucked and writhed beneath him. All thoughts of getting back at him dissolved into the pleasure that overrode it.

"I'll give you what you want, Nova." The head of his cock pressed at my entrance. My breath caught. Blood rushed in my ears. "I'm going to fuck my ma—" He paused, and his hand clamped down on my hip harder. The punishing pressure of his grip sent fresh wetness pooling between my thighs.

His chest was on my back, lips brushing the shell of my ear as he cooed, "Even if this is only for tonight, you won't forget it. Won't forget *me*. I'll make sure of it."

Those were his last words before he drove into me like a madman. No build-up, no hesitation. A few hard thrusts, then he found his rhythm, brutal and relentless. Lightning shot down my legs. My muscles turned liquid. My eyes rolled back, my jaw slack as he pounded into me again and again and again.

Skin slapping against skin echoed off the rocks. The sound bounced back to us, amplified.

"Fuck, Nova. Your cunt's so fucking tight. Goddamn." His palm cracked across my ass. The sting rippled through me, stealing the breath from my lungs.

Everything sharpened. The mineral scent of soil. The distant roar of falling water. The bruising grip of his hands that marked deeper than any cut. The coil in my belly wound tighter and tighter, making it hard to think about anything else but him fucking me until I couldn't take it anymore.

Claws raked down my back. Skin split open. A howl tore through the air, and I almost laughed. *Yes. I want it all. Give it to me.*

The pain and pleasure crashed together. My body convulsed, spine arching as I screamed, "Oh, fuck. Nick. Fuck. Fuck. Fuck!"

He hissed as I clenched around him. His hips jerked, rhythm breaking as he pumped his cum deep inside me like it never belonged anywhere else.

"Nova," he cried out. The husky, ragged sound was filled with something that made my chest ache for more, but of what, I didn't know.

As my orgasm came to its crescendo, I collapsed against damp earth. When the chilled soil kissed my overheated skin, the burn at my wrist cooled, and I sighed. Nick kept fucking me at a slow and steady pace as I spasmed around his cock. His lips pressed a soft kiss to the center of my back before he crashed down beside me, chest heaving.

With other wolves, I'd always stayed on top and kept control. Even when my appearance was masked with magic, I never let anyone have the opportunity to wield that kind of power over me.

But Nick was different.

Maybe he didn't trigger my territorial instincts because he was a turned? Maybe it was the tattoo pulsing at my wrist, reminding me that not only he but Zeth and Conrad seemed to be able to pull this side out of me.

All I knew was having him pin me down, rutting me into the dirt, using my body until we shattered... it ignited something inside me.

Something I wanted to believe in again.

First Conrad, then Zeth, and now Nick. I covered my eyes with my palms and sighed.

. . .

I'D NEVER HAD boy problems. That was Aniyah's territory. Maybe I should call her and get some advice because, right now, I couldn't walk away from any of them, and if this tattoo could talk, I bet it would tell me I shouldn't let them slip through my fingers.

I DIDN'T HAVE time for this.

Fuck me.

NOVA

The air hung heavy with sweat and heat, with the echo of what we'd just done as our breaths slowly found the same rhythm. The earth beneath us still held our warmth, and my heart beat hard, insistent, urging me to linger. To lift a hand. To follow the sharp line of his collarbone. To press closer until there was no edge left between us, only shared heat and forgetting.

But that wasn't what he was here for.

Just sex.

The thought landed sour, brittle. The way my wolf had stirred for him, the flare of heat at my wrist when we were in contact, all of it pointed to him being my mate, but the question cut deeper than the pull. Was I his?

I couldn't survive that answer again. The hope. The rejection. The hollow aftermath.

Eyes flicking to the side, I saw him on his back staring up through the canopy, jaw tight, brow drawn down like he was wrestling something far heavier than me. I huffed a quiet breath and looked away.

He hadn't even made peace with his wolf yet. The idea of a mate was miles beyond his reach, and I didn't have time for this. That was all second compared to my position and territory. My reputation.

So, I buried it. All of it. I locked the wanting away and settled into what was safe. What was simple.

A buzz came from my watch on my wrist, pulling me back to reality. There was no rest for the wicked. Pushing up from the ground, I brushed off the dirt that clung to my thighs as if even the ground didn't want to let go.

"This was great…" My heart tugged, and I put on a fake smile. "But I gotta go."

The words stumbled out awkwardly, too light for what we'd just done. My chest tightened. Fuck, I sounded pathetic.

His gaze flicked to mine, then down. A muscle jumped in his jaw before he forced a stiff nod. "Yeah. This was… interesting." His voice carried that rough post-shift rasp that made my stomach twist. "Is it always this… intense for you werewolves?"

"You werewolves?" I shot back before I could stop myself. "You know you're one of us now, right?"

His eyes flared, his mouth opening before he took a second then closed it. Reluctant acceptance locked down his face, but I noticed the way his throat worked and the faint tremor in his fingers like he was holding something inside.

"It's going to… take me time to get used to."

There it is. That edge of pain he was trying to hide. And I, god help me, wanted to smooth it away. To tell him everything was going to be all right, that I could help him see the benefits to being a wolf. The urge to lay my head on his chest, feel his heartbeat against my cheek and tell him I was here now, rode me hard. But I didn't. Couldn't. Not right now.

"Right," I said instead, voice too tight. I tried to step back, the universal signal that this was done, but my body refused to move the way I wanted.

"Well, see you around." I forced myself to turn before my voice could betray me further, cheeks flaming, pulse still stumbling over itself.

"Or at the fight, remember?" he called after me, getting up off the ground.

The words stopped me cold. Right. The fight tomorrow. With Nick, Conrad, *and* Zeth. My stomach dropped. Perfect.

I'd never been in a situation like this before. Did I just play it cool? Ignore their stares? Ignore their questions? *What would Aniyah do?* She had much more experience in that department than me.

Her teasing voice ghosted through my mind. *I'd make this one blush. Maybe mention how good he felt, then tell him I'm already looking forward to round two. Maybe ask if the other two could join?*

Nope. Absolutely not.

Instead, I pivoted, smirking just enough to hide the chaos bubbling inside me. "Right. Now that I think about it, do you need a suit?"

263

His brow furrowed, hands finding his hips. "You need a suit for a fight?"

"It's a legendary fight," I teased, taking slow backward steps. Each one made the air between us hum. His eyes darted down, then snapped back up, guilt and desire warring in them. He was trying so hard *not* to look at my naked body. "It's going to be televised. Famous people are coming and everything. You gotta look sharp."

When he still didn't say anything, I added, "I'll send you something." A grin curled my lips. "Can't have one of my boys looking like a slob when he's representing me."

"You don't have my address," he said, his voice rough yet almost amused.

That made me laugh. "I got it, Nick. There's nothing in my territory I don't know about or can't get when I want it. Remember that." I pointed at him, making sure he knew what I meant.

When his smile wobbled, I winked at him then shifted and ran away before I could change my mind.

The forest blurred around me, but the rush of wind on my fur was barely enough to cool the heat he'd left under my skin. No matter how far I ran, that scent, *his scent*, lingered, clinging to my skin.

Getting closer and closer to my house, I realized I'd have to face Zeth even though I didn't think I was ready. Just thinking about it gave me an uneasy feeling. Did I yell at him? Berate him with questions? Ask him why he lied to me? Did he lie to me?

All of it was just too much, especially with the big fight being tomorrow. I just didn't have the luxury to be freaking out right now. I had shit to do.

Watching the windows, I waited until his back was turned to brew his coffee, then I carefully slipped onto the deck and snatched the clothes I'd set on the chair before I left. For a split second, I felt bad, knowing that I should talk to him, but then I played it out.

Morning, Z! Had a nice fuck with Nick. Wanna talk about us? Yeah, nope. That sounds like a disaster in the making.

Standing on the side of the house, I slipped on my jeans and shirt before tugging on my boots as quickly as possible. Heading to the garage, I fumbled a text to Zeth about a last-minute video meeting with a lieutenant. *A lie to buy time,* I told myself. *Just need to buy myself a little space to sort it all out.*

My wrist burned when I glanced down, that now-familiar ache prickling under my skin. The heat Nick left was different—steady and slow-building—reminiscent of a piece of coal that kept glowing no matter how much air you gave it. Zeth had been all wildfire and flames. His heat licked at everything until reason burned away. Conrad's pull felt like a tease, a simmer that could flare into a bonfire with the right spark. Names and flavors of longing crowded my head until I felt like I was going to explode.

There was no time for this. Looking down at my watch, I saw I had an abundance of emails to get through. People needed to figure out last-minute details about tomorrow's event. A text from Glen came through, saying he couldn't find anyone ordering the chemicals on Calix's list in large quantities, which reminded me what had to be priority.

The poison on the street, leads that need to be followed, a televised fight that could put me on the map. This territory was mine to sharpen and make great. Mates could wait. They had to.

I grabbed the jacket off the hook in the garage and slipped it on, covering that warm wrist as if the leather could seal it away. Then I silently rolled my bike out, pushing it through the trees until the service road opened. Only then did I kick it to life, heading toward the gym.

A buzz came from my wrist, a reply from Zeth, but I ignored it. Out of sight, out of mind… at least that was the plan.

Gideon was waiting in the back lot, arms crossed and foot tapping. His scowl was loosened into that particular brand of worried fury that meant actual problems. Seeing him made my pulse steady. Pile on the work. I needed the distraction from my life.

"Nova," he barked the second my boots hit the asphalt. "I told Lucy, and now I'm telling you. She's not allowed to date anyone in the Syndicate."

Images from yesterday popped back into my mind. Lucy's hands on Zeth, the way she'd laughed for him. I cracked my neck and moved past him, teeth bared in a smile that didn't reach my eyes. "Sure. Yeah. Whatever. It's up to you."

Gideon followed, hot and loud. "I'm serious. She's my only daughter." He planted himself in front of my office door and threw his hands up. "I don't want her with some thug." With a nod, I maneuvered around him to open the door and head to my desk, but he just followed me in. "She deserves some idiot in a high-rise who can give her pretty things and have a nice, easy office job. Something that won't put her in danger."

I sat down, folded my hands on the desk, and kept my voice level. "What do you want me to do, G? Set her up with someone? It sounds like those are the types Ezra knows. They'll still be tied to the Syndicate one way or another. I can steer her toward the legit side of the business if that's what you want."

The fight in his shoulders softened for a second, then hardened again. "I just want your second to keep his dick away from my daughter."

I almost blurted out—*his dick was inside of me last night*—but a growl from my wolf rumbled in my chest, staying the words. Instead, I let my silence be the answer. I didn't even know what I or Zeth meant to each other yet, and I had no right to police anyone's heart, even if it made me want to break something.

Before I could say more, a Zeth-sized shadow filled the doorway. "No disrespect, G, but I don't want Lucy. Never have, never will." His voice was calm, though that last part sounded like it was meant just for me to hear. Gideon grabbed his collar and slammed him into the wall, raw fury in his face.

"What the fuck is wrong with my Lucy, you prick?!" he spat.

Zeth didn't fight back, raising his hands like a man who had learned how to be careful. "She's not my type," he said, eyes flicking to me with something unnameable that made my chest bruise and swell at once. "I've always seen her like a little sister, not a woman."

I could hear Gideon's teeth rattle, and I moved between them without thinking, my palm landing on Gideon's arm. "You can't have it both ways," I said. "You can't crucify him for not wanting her, especially when you didn't want him to begin with."

Gideon shoved him against the wall again, a warning, before he slowly let go, his face collapsing into a tired kind of defeat.

"You're right, Nova," he whispered. "I know you are, but..." He swallowed hard before facing me. "I don't want to be the one to see her eyes go dim when her little crush on this asshole," he threw his thumb at Zeth, "goes fucking south."

Gideon rubbed his hands over his face again and took a long, deep breath before asking me, "Can you tell her? She respects you."

My jaw ticked as I went back to my desk. Several emotions flooded me at the thought of telling her to back off Zeth, including my wolf itching to tell her to back off her mate, and that worried me. In the state I was in, I could do more damage than good, and Lucy was still Syndicate. Still family.

Zeth answered for me. "I'll tell her. I'll be firm but gentle." His voice was low and calm, trying to put Gideon at ease. Gideon's glare softened into a warning, the kind parents felt before storms. "You better not hurt her," he snapped, then he stomped out, leaving us with the echo of his anger.

For a second, the room hung between us, words unsaid, the clench of something dangerous and tender. I watched Zeth's hands, the slow tug of his sleeves, the way his jaw tightened as if chewing on regret. My fingers found each other under the desk because they needed something to do.

"Thanks," I said, but the word felt thin. We stood there, two people with more between them than either wanted to name, the air tasting of restraint and longing.

*"Where did you go this morning?"

His voice was smooth, *too* smooth. It held the kind of calm that was as peaceful as a blade pressed against the skin. I didn't need to look up to feel the heat of his gaze drilling into the side of my face.

"For a run," I said, keeping my tone flat. "Letting my wolf out."

The sound of my voice felt foreign, too controlled, too casual. My fingers twitched as I clicked through my emails, forcing my eyes to stay on the screen instead of him. The soft hum of the computer was safer than the silence between us.

He didn't answer. I could feel the shift of air as he walked away. Zeth was too quiet when he wanted to be, too deliberate.

The door clicked shut.

I froze.

When I finally looked up, he was leaning against the door like he owned the room. His eyes were darker than I remembered, the kind of dark that swallowed everything in its reach.

"Finally," he murmured, "you're looking at me."

I forced a tight smile, folding my hands on the desk to keep them from fidgeting. "Is there something you need, Zeth?"

For a second, he just stood there, lips pressed into a thin, angry line, then he took a step closer. "Yeah. I want to talk about last night."

---

* You Broke Me First by Tate McRae

My throat tightened, and I looked away. The cursor blinked on my screen, mocking, steady, waiting.

"We fucked," I said, pretending to type. "Got it out of our system. Let's move on."

The lie tasted like acid.

A soft set of steps creeped closer to me, making my whole body tense up. "What if I don't want to move on?" I swallowed hard. "What if I want to do it again? What if I want to kneel down in front of you right now, part your sweet thighs, and—"

"Zeth." His name broke from my lips, coming out sharper than I meant, but it was the only thing keeping me from drowning in the sound of his voice and the memory of his hands on my skin. The way his mouth felt on me as we fell into bed.

Then Gideon's face flashed in my mind, his fury, his heartbreak for Lucy, and all I could remember were all the women who'd claimed pieces of him before I ever could. That hurt and anger from this morning began to run through my veins once again.

My tongue lashed out before I could stop it. "What the fuck, Zeth? Do you need it so badly that you take it from any woman you can get your hands on?"

His head snapped back like I'd slapped him. "W–what?" His voice cracked, confusion carving lines across his face. He looked to the door then back at me. "Are you talking about what Gideon was thinking? I told you, I've never thought of her like that!"

"You could've fooled everyone with the way you two were pawing at each other yesterday." My arms and legs crossed automatically, a weak shield against the anger clawing inside me, calling me to demand he pay for his betrayal with his blood. "While I was fighting, by the way." I gripped my arms so hard I thought they would break off.

His eyes widened like the realization just hit him. "Is *that* why you were mad at me yesterday?" His hand raked through his hair, tugging at the strands as he huffed and took a step closer.

"Didn't you see me push her hand off me? She's like that with everyone! I didn't want to humiliate her in front of a crowd," he threw his hand out, motioning to where all the fighters were training, "but if that's what it takes, I'll do it."

His hand fisted at his side, eyes narrowed on me. "I'll walk out right now and tell her there will never be anything between us. I don't even find her attractive!"

I rubbed the bridge of my nose, torn between feeling bad for the girl and being excited by the prospect. It was very un-bossly of me. "No," I sighed, hating how much I actually cared about the people under me. "Don't do that, Zeth. That's just mean, and I don't want Gideon to kill you. Plus, she's not the only one."

That got him. His jaw tightened, eyes narrowing as he stepped in closer. "What else?" His voice dropped, low and deadly calm. "What other misconceptions do I need to clear up so we can be together?"

The last word cracked me open, and my hand slammed against the desk. "I know about them!"

He blinked, brows pulling together. "Them?"

"The women that go to your place at night once a week!" I snapped, the words tumbling out faster than my breath.

"You didn't think I'd find out? You didn't think I'd smell them?"

"Women?" His voice broke with his disbelief. "There are no women, damn it! I haven't had anyone in my bed for six years." His hands hit my desk hard enough to make my laptop wobble. "You think I could stomach touching anyone else after you?"

The emotion in his voice wasn't anger; it was armored heartbreak.

"If you're talking about the girls that I've posted around town to gather intel, then, yes, I've had females come to my house to tell me what they've learned and who was doing what, but that's my damn job! It was better for them to meet me at my place so they didn't blow their covers."

His words trailed off with a pained sound. "You thought I…. You always thought…."

Everything about him—the way his words cut off, his head hanging down, and his hunched back—hit me like a punch to the gut.

He circled the desk, moving slowly, deliberately, until he was standing over me. His hands gripped the armrests of my chair, trapping me—not with force, but with the weight of everything we'd never said. His breath brushed my cheek, and I could smell the truth on him, raw, desperate, real.

"I don't see anyone but you," he said, his voice breaking. "You're my everything at work, but I want you to be my everything all the time."

His words wrecked me in the best of ways, and I couldn't help but lean toward him. Hope peppered my mind until I remembered this morning. The horns. Did he know we were mates? Was that the first occurrence? If those words came from a place of awareness instead of ignorance, the sharp pain in my chest would've become unbearable because that would mean he'd chosen to hurt me.

"Why now?" The words came out edged and hot even though I tried to keep them from turning venomous. Everything I'd buried, every ounce of confusion, longing, and humiliation rose in a flood that burned my throat.

I shoved back my chair and shot to my feet, fists tightening until my knuckles cracked. "Why would you care what makes me upset? You rejected me!" I jabbed a finger into his chest, every syllable reopening a wound. "You. Rejected. Me."

He didn't flinch, but his eyes, those summery turquoise eyes, had gone storm-dark, pain streaking through them. His lips parted, breath hitching on words too heavy to swallow. "I didn't want to," he said, swallowing hard. "I've only ever wanted you, wanted *us,* since we were kids."

That still didn't answer my question. I scoffed in his face, turning away from him. I was done feeling like shit. I was done not having an explanation.

His hand shot out, gripping my arm and yanking me back to face him. "I mean it, Nova." His words rushed out, desperate. "I—I..."

The hesitation raised my hackles. "Don't put yourself out on my account," I snapped, tearing my arm free. The metal desk screeched across the wooden floor as I shoved it aside, heart pounding as I made my way around him.

I made it two steps before he caught me again. His inky arms wrapped around me from behind, locking me in place. My back hit his chest with a force that knocked the air from my lungs. His breath became ragged, shaking against my ear.

"I couldn't control it," he said, the words slicing me open. "That day, when we sparred, I got so worked up, and it-it just burst out of me. My manipulation magic. I couldn't stop it." His voice quivered as he rushed on, sounding almost panicked. "I thought... I thought you confessed to me because I *made* you feel that way."

I tried to turn, but his arms only tightened. His face pressed into my hair, the heat of his breath shuddering against my neck. "I didn't want you to hate me for something I couldn't control," he whispered. "Didn't want to lose my spot next to you. I didn't want to see you regret me. I couldn't handle knowing the thing I wanted most was never real to begin with."

His body trembled behind me, but his arms never gave up. "I wanted to stay by your side forever," he went on, his voice stripped bare. "But to do that, I had to learn control. It was the only way I could be by your side again. I never wanted to hurt..." He faltered, breath stuttering against my skin. "My *mate* like that again."

The word *mate* hit me like a surprise fist in the face.

He admitted it. *He fucking knew.*

I tore myself from his grip, and this time, he didn't stop me. When I turned, the sight of him gutted me. His face was a battlefield, agony shadowing every line, regret bleeding through each trembling breath he tried to steady.

"You knew?" The words escaped in a whisper sharp enough to wound.

He flinched but managed a single nod.

SYNDICATE FISTS

"Since when?" The words were half-accusation, half-plea, wishing for his admittance not to be real.

His throat bobbed as he swallowed. "I didn't know for sure until after you made me your second. That night, my horns grew when I was… thinking about you as I pleasured myself." A shaky smile ghosted across his mouth, gone as quickly as it came. "But if I'm honest, I think I've always known. Felt it in here," he said, pressing his hand to his chest, "since the moment I laid eyes on you."

His eyes softened, those turquoise orbs reaching out for me. "I know you know it, too," he said quietly. "Last night… I saw your mate-blocking tattoo light up. Just for a second. I saw it, and I knew you felt it, too." He took a step closer. "Just like your sister, we can break it."

My gaze fell to my wrist, to the dull ache that pulsed there. Once it had burned like wildfire—now it just throbbed, muted and sad.

I shook my head, trying to reason with myself, to breathe past the storm clawing inside me, but years of hurt and rejection fortified the door to that part of me I'd kept locked up for so long.

"So… what, then?" I shrugged, tired of feeling like this with him. "You didn't confess after I got the tattoo, so what was the plan, Zeth? What were you going to do once you realized your *mate* had chosen to block you?"

He straightened, shoulders squared and strong. "You're my boss," he said simply. "I had no right to challenge your decision, so I decided I would settle our working relationship first. Make things steady here before I tried to win you back, slowly. Turn our friendship into something more until it felt natural. And when it did…" His voice softened, a sad smile

275

flickering over his lips. "I was going to ask you to marry me."

My breath caught.

He must've seen the shock on my face because his mouth curved slightly, though it didn't reach his eyes. "I don't need a bond to know we belong together," he said quietly, glancing at my wrist. "That tattoo? It wasn't going to stop me. Not from you. Not from *us*."

For a moment, my wolf howled with joy inside me, wild, euphoric, but the darker part of me, the part that still remembered the day he'd walked away, split open instead. Every piece of pain I'd buried came roaring back, and this time, it didn't just ache.

It burned.

"Do you have any idea how much I've agonized over this? How painful your rejection was? How hard it's been to cage those feelings?" The words ripped out of me, leaving me shaky, exposed, and before I could stop myself, a growl rolled through the room.

I closed the distance between us, my heart pounding so hard it hurt, then I shoved him back. The chair caught his legs, and he crashed into it, eyes wide as he rolled back.

"Can you even imagine what it felt like when my best friend, the person I knew was my mate, vanished for a year?" My voice cracked, but I didn't stop. "Do you know what it's like when your wolf cries in your head over and over for someone who's gone, and you have no choice but to live with that sound?"

Zeth didn't answer. The muscles under his shirt twitched as I said each word, but he kept his eyes on me, chest heaving like he couldn't breathe. Regret, love, guilt, and pain swirled in his eyes, everything tangled up, just like me.

I leaned in until I could see the gold flecks trembling in his eyes, then my voice lashed out in a violent whisper. "You're the reason I got this fucking tattoo. I thought if I've already been rejected by my mate, why the hell would I ever hope for another?"

The hit landed. I saw it when his eyes flinched, his mouth opening and shutting before he bowed his head to me. My chest burned, air coming too fast, yet I still couldn't stop. It wasn't enough. I wanted him to hurt, to feel a small amount of the pain I'd felt for years.

Crossing my arms over the ache in my chest, the words slipped through my teeth before I could stop them. "Turns out, you're not my only possible mate. I've found others."

His head snapped up. The tension in his face shifted from shock to agony. The chair creaked as his hands gripped the arm rests, his lips pressed shut. The pain in his eyes was deep, bruised, the kind that crawled beneath your skin and stayed there.

I'd wanted to hurt him, and I'd succeeded... but it felt like I was bleeding out.

Mom's voice drifted through my head, sharp as ever. *Don't fight angry. But if you do, win it.* This didn't feel like winning.

Something cracked, and Zeth surged up from the chair. My mouth dropped as his horns tore through his scalp, black and gleaming, and for the first time, I saw the true demon instead of the man. "Who?" The word came out rough, animalistic. His aura darkened, shadows curling along his shoulders.

I didn't move, didn't speak. Just closed my mouth and caught myself as my body swayed toward him. This side of him was… alluring. I wanted to touch his horns, see if it really was an erogenous zone.

"Who is it, Nova!?" His hands clamped on my shoulders, trembling, not from fury but from how hard he was holding himself back.

I tore myself away, tilting my chin up in defiance that barely masked my shaking voice. "Conrad," I bit out. His eyes flared. "And Nick."

The roar that followed wasn't just anger, it was heartbreak turned monstrous. He spun, driving his fist through the wall with a sound that made my heart jump. Dust rained down as he shook his hand free.

I forced a bitter laugh. "Great. Add that to my to-do list." My voice wavered despite my attempt at sarcasm. The broken furniture, the scuffed-up wood flooring, the shaking in my hands, it all felt too fitting. Two people who'd finally come apart after pretending they never would.

"Look," I said, my voice rough, "we need time. Space. To think." I gestured between us, the word *us* having all the sharpness of glass in my mouth. "Separately."

His jaw clenched so tight I could hear it. "How do you know?" The question came out half-yell, half-plea.

I lifted my brow at him, eyes flicking between the fist-sized hole and him. He closed his eyes and took a breath. After a few seconds, his horns retracted. His chest heaved like he'd just run a marathon, and when he finally lifted his gaze to me, I saw the sheen of tears he refused to let fall.

"When I was with you last night," I said, touching the spot on my wrist, "the mark flared up." Hope flickered in his eyes, small, fragile. I needed to be honest with him. It was the only way we could get through this, whatever this was.

"But it did with them, too."

He froze, breath stuttering before escaping in a jagged exhale. His hope shattered so visibly I felt it in my bones.

"I haven't told them yet," I went on quietly, "but I will. My wolf... she responds to them, and she's never responded to anyone but you."

That undid him. His shoulders slumped, his body folding in on itself. Every trace of power bled out of him until he was a ruin of the man I knew. He pressed a hand over his heart, and, for one dizzy second, I almost reached out. Almost took back the words that had hurt him so.

Instead, I turned away, building that boss mask up brick by brick until I felt safe again, letting all the hurt and pain slide down my back as I straightened it.

"I'm working from home today," I said, the words steady but quiet. "Someone's out there tampering with supe DNA in my land. That's what matters right now. The rest—" I waved at the wreckage "—can wait."

I turned to the door, looking back toward him as I asked, "Can you focus on this? Or do I need to call on someone else?"

Footsteps shifted behind me. He stopped just short of touching me, his breath brushing my shoulder before he stepped back. "I got it, Boss." The words came out hoarse, threaded with grief.

I nodded once, then left before my mask could crack. Through the gym, I kept my stride even, chin up, face unreadable. I could feel the heat of his gaze on my back, heavy with everything we didn't say.

Outside, the cool air hit me like a slap. My throat burned, my chest tight. But no tears fell. I refused to let them.

I was a Rossey, and Rosseys didn't shed tears, didn't show disappointment or sadness.

That was when the wolves descended and ate the weak, and I wasn't weak. I was fucking Syndicate.

NOVA

"It seems like some of the local turned supes have been going missing. There are three that have been confirmed by their families as missing and another two that have recently disappeared, reported as not coming home or showing up for work."

Glaring down at the receiver, I pushed my breakfast of cooked steak aside and growled in frustration. "Good work, Devin," I replied, "but I need you to see if you can find any leads as to where they could've disappeared to." I needed something, just fucking *something* to give me a direction to dedicate myself to. Fucking anything.

He told me he was going to dig around some more, and before I hung up, I reminded him to check all the dump spots we used to get rid of bodies. Whoever it was might be trying to hide what they were doing by blaming it on us.

"Got it, Boss. I'll let you know." *Click.*

As soon as he got off, I shoveled the protein into my mouth, trying to eat my feelings and fill my stomach to drown out my wolf's incessant whining. She was hurting, and I knew that. I'd separated her from her mate, one that said they wanted to be with her, too, but I was having a hard time getting over the pain, the hurt. I needed time to think and work through this.

It was years' worth, so it was going to take me longer than a fucking day.

A whole day and night of not seeing him, not saying more than a few words via text, was torture in of itself. I'd watched those little texting dots run and run and run until a one-word reply came through, and disappointment seeped in.

I didn't realize how big of a space Zeth filled in my daily life. With how much it hurt to be away from him, it was almost as bad as being with him while not being able to have him.

So, it seemed I was fucked either way.

What made it worse was that Geof Groskey was supposed to fight tonight, but he'd missed his flight in Germany and wouldn't be stateside until tomorrow. I had to scramble to see who was available and could get here on time. I finally got some fighter from Brazil, Deslen Tacnon, that was already stateside and ready to go as the underdog against Copland Banner. His manager promised me that he would make this fight worth it, claiming this would put Deslen on the map. I was in no position to argue, so I gave him the slot. One massive problem fixed.

Shoving another mouthful of that perfectly seared meat in my mouth, I chewed lazily. The flavors slid across my tongue without meaning, just texture and warmth filling a body that felt too cold inside.

There was no shortage of work for either Zeth or me since the fight was tonight. Everything needed to go perfectly. The venue was getting set up for the media, and the celebrities were piling in. My most trusted men were already holding down security, so all I needed to do was show up and smile.

Ezra had called me first thing this morning, asking if I needed anything or wanted her to fly out, even if it was just for support. I told her I was fine and not to waste the jet fuel. I wanted to show her that I could handle this all on my own. I could pull my weight, helping the Syndicate become more, just like she wanted.

Calix texted me in the sibling chat.

Cal: *Sending you a surprise.*

Cal: *You're welcome.*

Cal: *I'm the best brother ever.*

My brows pinched, but before I could respond, Aniyah's texts flew in.

Niyah: *You're our only brother*

Niyah: *It's not hard*

Niyah: *It's much harder to be the best sister*

Niyah: *Which you know...*

Niyah: 😈

Riot chimed in, sending well wishes. Short, clean, and to the point.

Riot: *Don't worry. You got this.*

Sometimes she made me laugh by just how little she said.

Nova: *Thanks, guys.*

Nova: *Make sure to watch!*

As soon as I hit send, a message from Ezra followed.

Ezra: *All the casinos nationwide will be showing it, utilizing all the prime TV spots. We also have a few promo videos running, advertising the new fighter as a dark horse pick. I'll tell you what the take is by the end of the night.*

I puffed out a chuckle after reading that. Good old Ezra, already thinking about how much money the fight was going to make and how to maximize its visibility. It was her way of supporting me as best she could... and I appreciated it.

Feeling a little more myself, I went up to take a long, hot shower—the kind where it was so hot your skin almost burned off—which felt good. Somehow, all my problems melted away beneath that water.

After the shower, I got a text from Conrad.

Conrad: *Excited to see you tonight.*

Rolling my lips into my mouth, I tried to keep myself from smiling too wide.

With Conrad, it was easy. I could feel his eyes on me, wanting me, not assessing me, and I liked it. Furthering his own business ventures felt like it was second to enjoying me, and I liked that. I knew where I stood with him. I wasn't trapped in this will-they,-won't-they situation like with Zeth.

Despite initially thinking of Conrad, my mind drifted to Nick. Had he gotten the present I sent him? I couldn't have him representing the Rossey clan in anything less than a suit, so I'd made sure he had one. I sent off a quick text, asking if he got it and if it fit all right.

It took him a while to text me back. Those damn little dots kept popping up then disappearing until a picture came through. It was him holding the suit up against his dripping wet body, like he'd just taken a shower. I bit my lip, and when the warmth at my wrist intensified, I almost texted him to come over. Almost.

Throwing my phone on the bed, I went to my closet and opened it, looking at the black silk pants and sheer top I'd picked out for tonight. It was one of my only outfits that was fancy enough for this event. I was more of a jeans and top kind of girl.

Thinking about all three men being there tonight, looking stunning in their attire, I lamented my decision. *I should've bought a dress.*

Shrugging my shoulders, I slid the pants on, accepting my lot in life, like always. It was then that a text came through from Zeth, and my heart stopped.

Z: *Incoming*

What? My face scrunched as I typed out my reply, but before I could send it, the sound of heels clacking against my hardwood floors echoed from below.

"The party of the family is here!"

My eyes went to my door. *Aniyah?* Closing my closet, I made my way to the stairs and looked down to see my younger sister directing people with racks of clothes to come into my house and set up.

"Yep, right there. Oh! And that one over here. I want the maybes to be on this side."

Tightening the band on my robe, I went down and watched my five-foot-nothing sister, decked out in black thigh-high stilettos and matching stocking, toe my boots near the door with a scowl. "Get those out of here," she mumbled before throwing her designer leather jacket and purse onto the couch. She twirled toward me in her pleated black mini dress and threw her hands up.

"Surprise!"

Crossing my arms, I looked her up and down. "You going to a funeral?" It was odd to see her in all black. Her long, wavy white-blonde hair, which reached the center of her back, was the only contrast.

Putting her hands on her hips, she announced, "I'm downplaying my looks and style to heighten yours." When I lifted a brow, her lips wiggled in amusement. "Or maybe I lost a bet with my mates, and this was the outcome." She shrugged before mumbling, "They know I love my sparkles. I'm beginning to think they have a goth girl fetish, which, I mean, I'm in, but just fucking ask me. Is that so hard?"

I needed to stop the rambling before it got any worse. "Don't get me wrong, I love seeing you... but what are you doing here?"

Her heels clicked as she came closer, an evil twinkle in her eye. "Because, dear sister, tonight's a big night, and I knew what you would be wearing..." She flicked her hands at my robe, opening it enough to show the pants I hadn't even buttoned yet. "This," she finished in disgust.

"Hey!" I closed the robe, feeling more self-conscious about my outfit choices than showing my full bare chest. "Ezra wears stuff just like this!" I thought the defense made sense, but Aniyah wasn't buying it.

"I mean, sure, but she makes it a sexy blend of feminine and masculine, like pairing a set of trouser pants with a lacy bra and long chain necklace. Or when she wore that suit top and long jacket with nothing underneath or those pants that had a half-skirt on top."

She eyed me like she knew me better than myself. "And let me guess, you planned to pair this with a sleeveless white tunic that went up to your neck, showing off nothing but your muscular arms." You'd think I was planning to commit a crime based on the level of offense in her voice.

"I like my muscular arms..." I weakly mumbled the protest, not feeling as passionate about my defense as I usually would.

She moved behind me, circling her arms around me. "Yes. Yes, of course. Your arms are gorgeous, but you have a taut and tempting stomach, some gorgeous, shapely legs, and a rack that is just *screaming* for some attention." I jumped at the sting she gave my ass when she smacked it. "Not to mention these gorgeous big booty cheeks will have all the boys chasing after you if we accentuate it a little."

Shrugging her off me, I growled, frustrated about the whole situation. She knew that I was self-conscious about my figure or lack thereof. She just laughed, patting me on my arm. "This is why you need me here today. I'm going to help dress you and do your makeup and hair. Just like the old days!"

Clapping her hands in excitement, her iridescent wings came out as she flew backward and started to pull the covers from the racks. My eyes doubled in size when I took in the rows and rows of dresses. Had she robbed a whole boutique and brought it to my house?

"What is…" Daring to move closer, I lifted a diamond-studded pink fabric with two fingers. There was only a scrap of fabric up top that would barely cover my nipples, then a thin stretchy bit of fabric that connected to the bottom. These scraps were a dress? Half of the bottom seemed to be missing!

"Oh, I love that one, but looking at your face, it seems like that's not the one for this occasion. Maybe when you take someone on a date… to my club?" Her lips tipped up wickedly. "It would be the perfect dress to fuck in. You wouldn't even have to worry about it." She pulled it out and put it up against her body, miming what she was describing. "Just peel down this part for them to play with your breast, and they can easily push the fabric in the back aside. Two seconds, and bam! You're ready for entry!"

Grabbing the hanger, I put it back into its spot, tucking it behind another one. "Yeah, *so* not for this event."

She rolled her eyes. "Fiiiiiiine. But the next one I pick for you, you put on. Okay?"

After my small, regretful nod, she flew to another rack, sifting through all of the dresses.

"I'm surprised one of your mates isn't here with you," I said as I fingered a simple black dress with a deep back.

"Oh, Rasmus is always close, whether it's by camera or in person, but since I told him he couldn't hack into your system, he demanded to come with me. Maso came to keep him in check, and they're both outside. I told them to make themselves busy while we had girl time." She lifted an emerald green dress just as I pulled out a black one.

"No! You're not wearing black, navy, tan, or grey tonight. Nothing in your normal color palette!" Like she was showing me what she meant, she plucked a canary yellow monstrosity and put it to the side.

"I'm not—"

She lifted her finger, her teeth clenched. Her normal carefree and sexy aura showed a crack of her frustration. "You *will* try what I pick for you."

Seeing that deranged look in her eyes, I nodded, not wanting her to have a meltdown in the middle of my house. I'd just finished this construction six months ago, and I really didn't want to have another bill for this property for at least a couple months.

Throwing my hands up, I moved to sit on the couch, letting her do her thing. You wanted to see if someone was a good fighter, tell you if they could last five rounds, or had the temperament for security work, I was your girl. This was Aniyah's territory. I just had to trust the process.

Glaring at that yellow dress, I knew it wasn't going to be the one. The process didn't need to tell me that, which meant it was in there out of spite. Great.

It didn't take her long to pick out what she wanted and move us upstairs to my bedroom since it was the only room that had floor length mirrors.

She handed me the stack of dresses with the ugly yellow one on top and told me to dress in the bathroom area to give her the full reveal effect of me entering the room. Keeping my grimace inside, I took the dresses and went around the corner.

"So," she called out as my bed creaked, "who are you fucking tonight?"

I stuck my head around the corner. She was lying on the bed, head hanging off the end as she checked out her nails. "How am I supposed to know that in advance? Also, who said I'm fucking anyone tonight? It's a work event."

This time, she rolled her eyes. "Uuuhhhhhh! Nova! Why can't it be both?!"

Smirking at her, I tugged on that stupid yellow dress then moved to stand before her.

She rolled onto her stomach, her lips rolled into her mouth as she tried to keep in a laugh, then she flicked her fingers at me to go back. "Okay. Okay. You're right. That one's not for you."

Rolling my eyes, I went back and picked up the next one, which was an off-the-shoulder emerald green dress with a sweetheart neckline. It was full-length with a little flare at the bottom where it touched the floor. It was so silky and girly that I couldn't help but handle it with care.

"Don't bother telling me who you're going with. We both know it's Zeth," she droned, annoyance sharpening her tone.

In the middle of zipping up the back, I paused at his name. The person that was once such a standard part of my life felt so distant. Honestly, for a split-second, I doubted that he was going to be there, and that hurt more than I wanted to admit.

"And we all know you're not fucking him tonight." Her laugh echoed as I bit my lip and kept quiet. I wasn't going to lie, but I also didn't need to confirm anything, right?

Silence followed. I wanted to move on, so I stepped out, looking down at the dress. "This isn't bad…"

Air rushed around my face, stray strands moving in the wind, and when I looked up, bright pink eyes swirling with a golden hue were an inch from my face, her wings fluttering in the background as she narrowed her eyes on me.

She looked around, eyeing me like she could see through to my soul, and I almost told her to quit it before she blurted out, "Are you telling me that you finally made Mr. Long-ingly-Waiting-Forever the happiest boy in the whole world?!"

I glared at her, unsure how I wanted to handle this. I didn't like the disrespect toward Zeth, but at the same time, I was chastising myself for wanting to defend him. It was complicated, so I blew it off. "It's not a big deal. Nothing's changed."

She grabbed my face and pushed my cheeks together as she said with certainty, "Everything's changed."

I smacked her hands and waved her off, needing to divert her attention from the topic. I tugged down the zipper in the back, nodding my head as I went back. "Okay, so green in the maybe pile."

Picking up the next dress, I was trying to figure out how I was going to get all the straps around my body when Aniyah rushed in. "Oh, my god. Where? When? How? How long?"

"How long?" I stepped into the dress, but that was as far as I got. The straps fit tightly around my thigh when I tried to yank it up. Nope. Not the right spot, and now my legs were tangled in this thing.

With a huff, Aniyah helped me out of it, yanking the dress from my fingers. "How long? How long was his dick? How long did he last? How long was your orgasm? You know, the normal things."

"I don't know..." I shrugged, looking around for an escape route. "Let's just say long on all accounts."

She moved the dress around, stretching her arms through it before motioning for my head. I bowed down as she shucked it over. "Ooohhh, that's what I like to hear! Now you just need a few more!" She tugged the fabric down, brushing the smooth, silky fabric down my body, adjusting a lot of the straps across my boobs.

"Yeah, about that..." I admitted, trying to figure out how to ask her about my current guy problem without telling her too much.

Her jaw dropped, crying out in praise as she did a little dance on her toes until she almost fell flat on her face, me barely catching her in time.

She popped up like nothing happened, whirling around to face me. "Oh, hell, it's finally happened. There's so much we need to do! I have to catch you up on *all* the new sex positions." She spread her legs far apart before doing a deep squat. "I'll give you some tips on how to stretch out that pussy for more than one cock."

"Whoa, whoa, whoa!" I threw out my hand. "Calm your ass down. No one said I was going to fuck them all together!"

Her eyes narrowed on me before she threw her hands up in the air. "Why the fuck not? It's amazing. Fucking wonderful. Ten out of ten. Everyone should do it. And this might be the only shot I have to pick out your orgy dress!"

I took a step back, not knowing how to process all the things she just said. "Excuse fucking me?"

She shook her head. "What?! It's not a bad thing! It's just..." She half-heartedly shrugged. "You're more of a we-need-to-connect-before-we-have-an-orgy type person."

"Oh, yeah," I puffed out, a little miffed. "And what are *you*? A let's-fuck-as-long-as-I'm-wearing-a-skirt type person?"

Her head bobbed up and down as she counted off her fingers. "I need a hand up my skirt, on my ass, one covering each breast, and a hand around my neck for good measure."

Slumping my shoulders, I rolled my head around in frustration. "Look, just because I don't fuck twenty-four-seven doesn't mean I don't fuck." I stopped myself from telling her about Conrad and Nick, both in the forest, in public, where anyone could see us! Not that I wasn't monitoring that as well.

Aniyah's sweet face scrunched up. "I know that! If you want to have a one-night stand, you will. If you want some hot, dirty sex in a bathroom, you will. What I mean isn't about being sexual, it's about what you want in the end. Sis, you're the type that wants that sweet kind of affection and loyalty after the sex. The kind that makes your heart melt onto the floor when they give you those bedroom eyes."

I folded my arms and scoffed. She added, "I want that fervor kind of love, the kind where their hands and eyes can't be off me for too long or they go crazy." She stepped back and smiled, leaving me in my thoughts as she grabbed something and came back. Hand in my hair, she twisted strands at one side into a braid, using golden rings as decoration, while she left the other side down and loose.

She was done quicker than I thought possible, then she shoved me into a chair with the order to close my eyes. Soft bristles covered my lids.

"Look," I huffed, "is it so bad to want someone to love me for me? Inside and out. The woman *and* the boss?" When she paused, I looked up to see her brows pinched, mascara wand in hand.

"They will. The ones that matter, the ones meant for you… they will. Inside *and* out."

Looking at the conviction on her face, something inside me melted. How could she be one hundred percent sure that I was going to get that kind of love? My heart was too full, so I tilted my head and smirked. "When did you get so smart? Is it because you're an old lady now?"

Her eyes swirled before she pinched me underneath my arm. I cried out, rubbing at the spot she knew I hated. "That's what you get for calling me old!" Her lips tipped up as she finished my makeup.

"Come on. Look." She stepped back and pointed to the mirror. "You're fucking gorgeous, Nova. Now, tell me thank you. Go on. I need to hear it."

Looking at my reflection, I almost gasped. Without a thought, I stood up, running my hands over the dress that somehow made my athletic shape look womanly.

While the dress was a bit risqué for me, I couldn't deny I looked good. The color was already eye-catching, a burnt orange that highlighted my tan skin. The cross-shaped halter had two lines of silk in front of my chest, accentuating my boobs as they spilled out on both sides. A little peekaboo showed triangles of skin where the top connected to the hip, leaving my taut stomach on display. The rest was tight around my hips, flowing into a mermaid shape with a slit up the side that left some room for movement.

She had made my eyes into these dark, smokey pools that held a pink jewel in the center, drawing you into them. My lips were nude with a bit of gloss. Kissable. It was something I never would've picked for myself, but even I had to admit that I looked strong and beautiful.

"I'm waiting." She tapped her foot.

I turned and gave her a hug. "Thank you, Niyah. I couldn't have done this without you."

She grabbed me tightly, reminding me of when we were little... at least until she called out, "Go get 'em, killer. Get all those dicks!" Then she smacked my ass, again.

Just as I was about to tell her to turn the fuck around so I could smack her ass, the doorbell rang. We looked toward the door.

She gave me a look. "Who the fuck rings the doorbell?"

Moving around her, I responded with a sigh. "Normal people, Niyah. Normal people."

She grunted and rolled her eyes.

We made our way down the stairs, and I padded over to the door on bare feet, calling back a request for Niyah to grab me some shoes as I yanked it open. "Hell—" I paused as Zeth turned around. Cigarette in hand and his hair slicked back, he looked entirely too good in his suit. I swallowed the rest of my words.

He looked so good, like forget-about-everything-we'd-talked-about, throw-him-on-the-porch, and-lick-up-every-inch-of-him good.

When I yanked myself out of my little fantasy, I noticed his eyes were about to pop out of his head. His cigarette was on the floor even though his hand was still up, his eyes slowly devouring every inch of me. *"Fuck,"* slipped from his lips, then his shoulders stiffened, and his eyes grew tight. "Fuck." The second fuck didn't sound as good as the first one.

"That's right, big boy." Aniyah slid up next to me. "Your job's going to be ten times harder tonight." She leaned down to put a set of strappy golden heels at my feet, then stood up and stared Zeth in the eyes. After a second of silence, her lips thinned. She narrowed her eyes on him then lowered her gaze to the heels.

He immediately fell to his knees. "I-I'll help you into them. Just put your hands on my shoulder."

I did as he asked, glaring at Aniyah's smiling face as his hands carefully lifted my foot, sliding it into the shoe and buckling it. Once he was done, his hand ran up the back of my calf, making my fingers dig into his shoulder blades. His muscles tightened as he took the second foot and shoe and did the same slow, tantalizing thing. Once he was finished, he paused, staring up at me from below like I was his day and night, his sole reason for living. I could fall into a gaze like that.

"Now, I told you once, but I'll tell you again..." Aniyah's devilish voice came from beside us, bursting the bubble. "Make sure you get some dicks wet in that dress. If it doesn't have some kind of cum stain on it when you take it to the cleaners, you didn't use my gift right."

Zeth's head dropped as the hand on the ground balled into a fist, shaking from how hard he was squeezing. *Fucking Aniyah!*

"Since my work is done, I'll clean up here then take the jet home. Let you have your place to yourself for the marathon tonight." I almost snapped at her to stop it, but her dark-haired demon suddenly appeared next to her, kissing her arm and shoulder, those red eyes looking at her like a puppy longing for his master.

She glanced down at her phone, moving her neck so he could kiss her there as she lamented. "Lucus is already asking when I'll get back, and I can see Alic is checking my location every ten minutes. Those are the mate signals to get home before they come to drag my ass back."

A car zipped around the corner and parked out front by my door. My sister's wolfy mate—and a somewhat reluctant friend of mine—came out and up the stairs.

"Nova." He nodded at me, his eyes filled with nothing but irritation and respect. If he wasn't my sister's mate, I might say some shit right now, but as soon as his eyes connected with hers, they lit up, turning into these sky blue orbs of happiness.

"Maso." I nodded as he passed me and went to my sister, who giggled at something Rasmus said in her ear.

Maso grabbed her chin, all intense and purposeful energy, and kissed her like it was the first time. Rasmus watched with those red eyes, the tips of his lips lifting as his hands trailed all over her. I knew what the three of them were going to do in my house before they left—I wasn't stupid—so I mumbled, "Clean up and don't ruin the furniture," and left it at that.

Motioning to Zeth that we had to go now, he took my elbow. His featherweight touch, so different from before, had me biting the inside of my lip. We only made it a few steps down before Aniyah called at my back, "Remember what I said, Nova! Stains! I want to see some stains! Send me pictures or else I'm going to send a glitter bomb to the gym and make all those boys shine bright like diamonds!"

Closing my eyes, I could picture all of the fighters throwing a fit as glitter stuck to them, making a damn mess of my gym. My hand shot up, waving at her like a white flag as I went down the stairs as fast as I could.

Looking out the side of my eye, Zeth's jaw had tightened. This car ride was going to be *very* uncomfortable.

Fucking thanks, Aniyah.

19

NICK

Nova Rossey was the third child born to Rayla Desmond of the Syndicate. Her biological father is Ax Rossey, but she was raised by all of the Syndicate leaders—Lex Devil, Falcon Winstale, Avery Glovefox, and Cosmo Desmond. All five men were Rayla Desmond's mates, and, through their union, they officially made the Syndicate one family.

One big happy, bloody family, huh?

I shut the file I was re-reading in hopes that I could find something that would help me tonight. I pored over every piece of data and documentation I had on Nova Rossey. When I started this job, I'd planned to lean on what I already knew about the Syndicate, hoping to get more firsthand info the deeper in I got, but now, I wanted to know everything.

For as long as anyone knew, the Syndicate had always been a crime family. Even in the earliest days, under Ternin Desmond, Syris Glovefox, Manic Rossey, Easton Winstale, and Rathe Devil—Nova's grandfathers—they'd savagely killed people, earning their riches by being the baddest supes around. There were claims that they were all descendants of either royalty or the firsts of their kind, which was why they were so strong, so unstoppable.

Then the Awakening happened.

In the years that followed, humans warred with supes until the American government brokered a simple treaty with those five men. They ruled their people, keeping them in line how they saw fit, while we ruled ours. We would live separate lives while sharing the same space.

As I scrolled through the redacted accounts of what they did to their own people, I grimaced at some of the photographic details. From what I could tell, any punishments in those first five years after the treaty were brutal, swift, and public. Their tactics were merciless and violent, but they produced results.

Supe blood had soaked the streets of most major cities; satellite pictures told a grisly story. By the end of the fifth year, human deaths at the hands of supes had dropped to almost nothing, which was proof of their grasp on their people.

The Syndicate was a band of thugs who had carved their empire out of death and destruction. The only difference between them and others was they were a solid, impenetrable unit, one that even other powerful supes couldn't break through... until the magical bombing that took out the bosses' mates as well as Rathe Devil.

That attack had scattered them, forcing them to carve out territory and plant bases all over the United States. Hunkered down in their separate spaces, they reestablished their rule and maintained their iron fist as law.

Their nefarious activities included money laundering, corruption, assassination, prostitution, racketeering, arms dealing... the list went on. Since their crimes mostly involved other supes, the government and law enforcement agencies had chosen to look the other way, just glad they didn't have to deal with the supes themselves.

Then the next generation met up. Nova's parents.

From the documents, it seemed they hadn't gotten along at first, but they'd come together to take out Vincent Devil, Rathe's brother. Again, most of the information was redacted, so the motive had been hard to figure out, and it didn't say what happened to him after the fight.

Soon after that, Rayla had claimed her adopted brother and four other Syndicate heirs as her mates and promised the government she would bear five children, one for each faction of the Syndicate, to keep the treaty intact.

If you thought the next generation, raised in the post-Awakening era, would be calmer or more level-headed than their predecessors, you would've been wrong.

Instead of maintaining the status quo, they had made Vegas their home base while setting up lieutenants and interconnected groups to handle day-to-day operations across the United States. That expansion had extended the Syndicate's reach, pushing into suburbs and outskirts that had previously gone unmanaged.

For their generation, most of the pictures and videos, evidence as to how they ran the Syndicate, had been scrubbed from the internet. A small few had been left out there, feeling more like a purposeful warning than something forgotten about.

One video showed Avery Glovefox leaning against a wall, twirling a wedding ring on his finger as he sang a haunting song. The werewolf in front of him held a knife to his own chest, carving out letters to the song Avery was singing. He screamed as the blade sliced up his skin and bones until, finally, he'd torn out his own heart and collapsed. Avery then walked up to the body on the ground and crushed the heart beneath his shoe, all while complaining about getting blood on his wife's new gift.

It wasn't until they had Calix, Ezra, Nova, Riot, and Aniyah that those kinds of videos and photos stopped appearing publicly. My guess was that even criminal parents wanted to limit what their kids saw of them. Still, there were stacks of eyewitness accounts and he-said/she-said tales suggesting everything remained vicious and bloody—just not for public consumption.

It wasn't until five years ago that the kids had officially taken over, seizing their parents' seats and spreading out from their central base in Vegas, reclaiming the locations their grandparents had previously vacated. Each of them had taken over the faction that best suited their skills rather than simply inheriting the seat that "belonged" to their species, which rocked the Syndicate status quo.

Even with the distance, the Syndicate bosses operated as one organization, but it did appear Ezra Desmond had assumed the head leadership role.

She ran the money side of the Syndicate, though she was handling it differently from her predecessors, rubbing elbows with human politicians and big-business CEOs. She'd launched a string of Syndicate-funded orphanages for supe children, as well as other charities, while also setting up legitimate business ventures. It seemed her goal was to change the Syndicate's reputation from a bunch of thugs to affluent business owners and entrepreneurs.

When I asked around, although it was clear the Syndicate still struck fear into most supes' hearts, public opinion had started to shift. Some praised the newer generation for creating clean jobs and supporting the supe community; others condemned them for trying to infiltrate human businesses and blurring the clear species lines.

I figured that was why my captain had it out for Nova, wanting me to focus on her operation and report if any humans were involved and/or harmed. He didn't care if she mercilessly beat and killed other supes. He wanted me to find any dirt that could be considered a breach of the treaty so he could kick her out of the state.

He was not alone in his feelings against supes.

Hell, I'd always felt an ache of resentment that crawled beneath my skin whenever I saw supes swagger through town like they owned it. Their superiority wasn't subtle. The glances, the smirks, the way they moved as if the ground bent for them. Just because they were faster and stronger didn't mean they were better. Didn't mean they could look down on us humans.

This had been my family's home long before their kind arrived with their shiny cars and modern mansions, building over land we'd bled for. They prowled the streets in packs, confident, untouchable. The human kids around here had started mimicking them—picking fights, posturing like wolves. I'd seen what that imitation turned into. Infected everything. Beatings ended up going too far. Aggression rose with no purpose. Poor humans turning to them, willing to work underneath them for just a scrap of that power and money. It was manipulation and chaos.

Becoming a cop had felt like a way to take back some of that power, to reinstate order when the world had gone wild.

But that illusion hadn't lasted long.

Flashes of the night I was turned still tore through me. Claws raking my back, the girl under the brush crying for help as the forest filled with unnatural growls that no normal animal could make. I'd carried her out of there, bleeding and shaking. I'd saved her but condemned myself. That first night, the pain that had ripped through me was unbearable. The tearing of skin, the unrelenting fire that burned in my veins until I was covered in fur and standing on four legs. Everything had changed.

In just one night, a single claw mark to my back, and I was no longer on the outside looking in. I was the monster I'd spent my life hating.

I could still feel the ache in my knuckles from that first shift, how the bones broke and reshaped, how my lungs burned. The next morning, I'd woken up naked, caked in dirt and blood, a mangled deer sprawled beside me. I'd stared at it for hours, waiting for the nausea to come, but what I'd really felt instead was fear because, deep down, some part of me *liked it.*

The strength. The clarity. The wild pulse in my veins that whispered, *"You belong to this now."*

Clenching my fists, I reminded myself that I was human. Took a few slow, deep breaths to ground myself. To focus.

The mission. Infiltrate the Syndicate. Gather proof. It should be easy, especially now that I'd caught her attention.

Mate.

The word pulsed inside my skull, the beast's low growl curling through my head. I shoved him down hard, burying him under the same walls I'd built to hold back everything else.

Mate? I almost laughed. I didn't know anything about that. Didn't *want* to. But the image of her body against the forest floor lingered. The memory of her heat against mine, her scent that took over my senses, the way her gaze dared me to try to resist.

I wasn't a beast. I was a man. A cop. I didn't stalk women, didn't take what wasn't offered, didn't *want* to throw her to the ground and fuck her until she forgot her own name and only called out mine.

Except I did.

The thought had acid crawling up my throat.

My gaze landed on the Armani suit she'd sent, still in the box, smooth and immaculate. Earlier, I'd run my hand over the fabric, afraid to touch it too long, afraid I'd ruin it. Was this her idea of control? To show off what she could do? What she could buy me?

I should be disgusted, should throw the suit into the dumpster, but my legs and arms wouldn't move. A single thought had completely captured my mind. *Why do I crave her attention?*

Lifting my arm without thinking, I inhaled my skin, filling my lungs with her even as I hated it. Her scent, wildflowers and sweet honey, still clung to me from our fuck in the woods, and I couldn't stop gulping it down. I wouldn't have pegged that scent for her, not with the way she carried herself, but somehow, it fit. Somehow, it felt like it *should* be hers.

And worse, it felt like it should be *mine.*

I shoved my arm away, disgusted by the heat rolling through me and the whisper of want curling under my ribs.

Dragging my open laptop onto my lap, I forced myself to focus. To remember *who* she was. A criminal. A killer. A damn supe.

The files didn't soften the image. Photos of bodies. Reports of fights she'd won with brutal efficiency. A demon flayed open for disrespecting her sister. A werewolf left broken after crossing her. Every word painted her as untouchable, terrifying.

When I thought back to the fight we'd had, I could still see it. The dangerous spark behind her eyes, the precision in every strike that allowed her to take down her opponent swiftly and without mercy. The beast inside me stirred, *admiring* her, recognizing something that mirrored itself.

Mate strong. Perfect.

My jaw tightened, but I couldn't disagree. She *was* strong.

That thought, that memory, it bled into another. Her body pressed to mine. Those sculpted thighs parting for me, that toned back bending against my chest. Just picturing that powerful body beneath me, writhing in pleasure from what I was doing to her, made blood rush to my dick.

But that wasn't what I wanted. No. That was what the beast inside me wanted.

What I wanted was someone like my ex, Faith. Soft. Sweet. Someone who needed protection, who needed me to feel safe and secure. That was the kind of woman I wanted by my side... right?

Why couldn't I remember her face anymore? Why couldn't I recall the sound of her voice or the scent of her hair? My memory of Faith was disappearing like she'd never existed, replaced with a set of jewel-toned pink eyes and a wicked smile.

I closed my eyes, trying to think about and feel what my life had been like before I'd been turned, but it was slowly slipping away from me like sand through my fingers.

Maybe it wasn't memory loss. Maybe it was instinct.

Maybe the man I'd been wasn't disappearing but being replaced by him, the beast. This thing that called Nova *mate.*

A buzz sliced through the silence of the apartment, and I glanced around, looking for my phone. As soon as I saw the screen and who the message was from, my body went still.

For a heartbeat, I didn't breathe—*Nova.*

It was short, simply asking about the suit she sent. Just a simple text, nothing special, but it was her. Her words. Her attention. My pulse kicked hard against my chest.

My eyes drifted to the bed where the suit laid stretched out like a promise, sharp, tailored, and expensive as hell. A piece of her world sent straight into mine.

I told myself I should ignore it. Hell, a part of me wanted to rip it in half, to tear the damn thing apart and send it back. I needed to prove that she didn't have any kind of pull over me. She was a criminal, the enemy, and my mission. She was everything I was supposed to destroy.

But the thought of her eyes sliding over me while I wore *her* gift made something inside me purr. I could almost see it, those cool, assessing eyes flicking down my chest, the corner of her mouth curving in that quiet, dangerous satisfaction. The idea of her gaze lingering on me, of *wanting* me, hit harder than I wanted to admit.

Why the fuck did I want that? Why did I care what she thought?

Yet, I found myself moving before I could stop. Standing. Picking up the hanger. Holding the suit against me like a fool. I snapped a picture and sent it off, fingers hovering over the screen even though my brain screamed *don't*.

Too late.

Her reply came fast. A smiling emoji, then a flushed, hot-faced one. My lips twitched before I could stop them.

A gangster, a goddamn crime boss, was texting me smiley faces.

It should've been ridiculous. Instead, it made my chest feel tight, and the room got hot.

By the time I'd forced myself into the suit, I felt like someone else, someone sleeker, more dangerous—her world's version of me. The fabric clung perfectly, moving over my body like magic. I caught my reflection in the mirror and hesitated.

I looked like *her type*. The realization shot spikes of thrill through me even as I told myself it shouldn't.

When I stepped outside, a black car was idling at the curb. Of course, she'd send one. Of course, she'd orchestrate every detail.

The door swung open, and my pulse jumped. Did she come to pick me up? Was that why she wanted to see me in my suit?

When a head of blond hair popped out instead of a mane of white, my stomach dropped, and I scowled.

"Hey, man!" Benson, the vampire who fought Nova before me, beamed, waving his arms like I couldn't fucking see him. "Isn't the boss great? She sent us this sick ride!"

My lip curled before I could hide it, a low growl catching in my throat. A stupid sting of disappointment twisted in my gut. What the hell was wrong with me? Why did I care that it wasn't her?

Because a part of me had pictured it. Her smirk. The way her natural perfume flooded the space around me. Her thigh brushing mine as she told me what to do with that voice that could cut and caress in the same breath.

Forcing that image away, I climbed in, sliding to the far edge of the seat to put as much distance as possible between me and the idiot with me.

It only took seconds for me to realize he talked way too much for my liking, so I tried to tune him out. He kept yapping about the fight, about how he learned a lot by being "smacked around" by the boss, how it was "worth it" since he got tickets to the fight. I nodded occasionally, just to make sure he didn't try to talk to me even more.

Under the chatter, my thoughts spiraled. The wolf inside me prowled restlessly, low and hungry. It wanted to see her. To *smell* her. To remind her who he was.

I clenched my jaw, running the Miranda rights in my head just to remind me that I had a human side, one that didn't believe in mates. He growled at me in my head, and I recited the words louder.

This mental game went on and on as we went deeper and deeper into the woods until the trees broke. As though it had appeared with magic, a mega mansion was suddenly there, like it had grown from the woods themselves. Massive, secluded, it settled into the side of the mountain like it had always been there. It was the kind of place power liked to hide.

It should've set off alarms. It should've made my stomach twist with dread.

Instead, the first question that popped into my head was what did she look like tonight? Fucking pitiful.

We rolled up a long, guarded drive, tailing a convoy of glossy foreign cars until the red carpet unfurled at the foot of the stairs. She stood at the top like a carved promise. Golden caramel skin, hair shining like she was a star plucked from the sky, eyes the color of a slow-burn sunset. The smoky orange dress clung to her in all the right places, the fabric sliding over hips and chest, making every man jealous he wasn't that scrap of fabric.

Something inside me snapped the moment I saw her. I didn't remember stepping from the car or climbing the steps; my world narrowed to the way light pooled in the hollows of her throat, making my bones shake. When those eyes latched onto mine, the rest of the world blurred and fell away until all that remained was the heat of her gaze.

A shadow folded into my periphery—Zeth—coiled and dangerous, his face full of sharpened patience. He didn't blink; he watched me the way hunters watch prey: with purpose. Like he knew everything and was waiting for his moment to strike.

He was close enough to press his hand around her waist, fingers digging into her side like he owned that spot. The motion made the beast in my chest let out a low, ragged sound in my head that vibrated across my sternum. My muscles so tense they were about to snap.

Zeth whispered in her ear, pointing at someone below. Nova smiled at me, a small, casual curl of her lips, before she turned away, but Zeth's fingers stayed as he stared me down.

The beast wanted blood. My hands itched to close around his throat. Not to kill, no, that would be tidy, almost merciful, but to make him understand with bone-aching pain that I belonged at her side.

"Hey, Nick." She twisted out of his grip and took a few steps forward then stopped short. Her eyes scanned our surroundings as she held herself in place, then looked me up and down. "Looks like the suit was the right size."

Why did she stop? Why did it irritate me that she looked around first? My neck grew tight as I gave her a strained smile.

"Yeah. You have good taste."

She stared at me for a beat longer until Benson slid up beside me, a ball of excitement. "Thank you so much, Boss! I'm so excited for the fight. Thanks for beating me up!"

A slow, small grin crept up her face, more calculating than an actual smile, and she nodded. "Your seats are behind us. Make sure to train hard, and maybe next time you'll be in the front row or, hell, maybe up on that stage."

Benson's eyes went wide, like his head was about to explode, and, for the first time since I'd seen him, he was speechless. The grin on his face said she was his goddess and he would follow whatever she told him.

Rage flared, hot and ridiculous. My gums pricked as my fangs begged to break free. To tear his head clean off for smiling, for breathing in her space, for looking in her direction. It was then that I realized the brutal violence that swirled inside me, aiming at Benson, was wholly different from the feelings I felt around Zeth. *Why?*

I'd been around her and other men before, hell, she worked mainly with other men. Yet, here, the simple tilt of Benson's mouth, flashing his fangs at her, made me imagine his blood slicking the carpet. I didn't like him even looking at what was *mine*.

It felt wrong, animalistic, and utterly inevitable.

Mate. That damn word threaded through me again with the pulsing certainty of a heartbeat. The wolf snarled his approval at the idea of claiming, of marking. The human part of me flinched at the possessiveness, at how easily those thoughts and feelings came to me.

A gush of air swirled around me as a presence zipped next to her, and, in a flash, I was looking at that turned vampire from the woods. Conrad, I thought his name was?

He bowed before her, her hand in his, as his lips caressed her right hand.

My jaw tightened so hard the tendon in my neck jumped. Images of me shoving him down the stairs while listening to him scramble almost had me laughing out loud, but then the beast inside me called out, *He mate, too.*

My body stilled. *What the fuck does that mean?*

I could feel something inside of me unraveling, but I knew this was not the moment to let that happen. Tapping into my training, I focused on things that I knew for sure.

My badge number. The oath I took when I started on the force.

When I was finally out of that freak-out mode, I took a breath and reminded myself that this was only a job and not to get caught up. My heart thumped loudly, but it was in two simultaneous rhythms. One was slow and legal, by the book, while the other wanted to break out into war.

How many goddamn mates does this woman have? A small fact from the files I had at home popped up in my head, and I recalled her mother having five mates. I cracked my neck at the thought.

"You're a vision, Miss Rossey. Absolutely good enough to eat." Conrad's words made that urge to punch him in his smug mouth even harder to resist.

A soft giggle leaked out from her. Her eyes fluttered and breath hitched before she calmly said, "Thank you. You don't look so bad yourself." The sound tore something inside me. That was what she was supposed to say to me!

A copper taste filled the back of my throat as my brain and soul fought for who was in charge of my body.

You're a cop, the human part scolded. *You're undercover. Keep the job clean.*

The wolf in my head snorted, a mocking sound that set me off even more. *She laughed... not for you.*

Shut the fuck up, you fucking dick!

313

When I looked up, I could see I was not the only one having a problem with this damn vampire.

Zeth's face mirrored mine, and it made me feel marginally better. Tension in his shoulders, jaw tight behind manners he didn't want to have, a rage that was barely kept in check. The solace I found in that was shameful. Being a criminal's ally in fury felt like betrayal and relief all at once.

Suddenly, Nova's expression slid into business mode, cool and lethal. "We have things to talk about, don't we? Let's head inside."

Conrad smiled and offered his arm. She took it, her boss mask fully in place like armor. Benson and I fell in step behind, while Zeth claimed her other side, scowling like he would gut the next person who dared breathe too close to her.

As we moved, my mind kept circling back to the strangeness of it. How quickly my protectiveness had become possessiveness, how easily the thought of hurting some nobody had calmed the thunder in my ribs. Jealousy, I realized with ugly clarity, wasn't just a human ache. It was even more heightened, more dangerous, more powerful in this supe body I now possessed, and that frightened me.

What if I lost control?

I puffed out an annoyed breath. All of these people were dangerous, each of them hiding their own beast beneath their skin.

Tonight, the air tasted like power, perfume, and danger, and I was going to be right at the center of it, just like I needed to be.

20

CONRAD

I'd been losing my damn mind these past few days. Work was supposed to drown out the noise, keeping my head clear, but every time I paused, she was there. The phantom heat of her pressed against me. The rasp of her breath when it caught. The memory of her claws tightening around my throat, making me feel more alive than I ever had.

All it took was a moment of pause, then a memory would invade my senses, and, suddenly, it was all I could think of. Her in my secret room, on my desk. Between her thighs in the woods. Without fail, my pants would tighten uncomfortably. It was getting to be tiresome to handle. Always having to relieve myself just to focus again. It was so mechanical, pathetic, yet still never enough.

Afterwards, when I'd taken the edge off, I'd catch myself staring at my phone. Should I text her? Call her? Ask her to come over just so I could see her... hear her... taste her again?

It was hard not to relive the moment my fangs sank into her skin, the immediate jolt of ecstasy when her full, rich blood hit my tongue. Right then, I'd known I was done for.

One sip, and I was lost. She tasted exactly like she smelled, honey-soaked wildflowers and summer heat. Sweet and floral with a sharp undertone that hit the back of my throat and went down smoothly. It wasn't just the blood that distracted me; it was the unshakeable high of just being around her.

More than once, my thumb hovered over the call button, but every damn time, I stopped myself.

What if she didn't feel the same pull? What if I was just another name she forgot once the thrill was gone? A woman like her didn't waste time on men who couldn't keep their composure or were unable to separate business from pleasure, and I truly thought I was one of those men. But, for some reason, this woman had me all tied up in knots, and I couldn't figure out the right move, the closing deal, so I put away my phone, counting down the hours until the fight event where we'd agreed to meet.

In the meantime, I'd been busy digging through reports, listening to back-alley gossip from the turned supes I knew. While I didn't get a lead on a mysterious substance, I did find out a few turned supes had gone missing. There was no connection between the missing supes other than being the kind no one paid much attention to. They had nothing to lose, and that meant they were easy prey.

It stank of intention, like someone was cherry-picking them for something they didn't want anyone to know about. Partner that with the vial we'd found at Donnie's place? It stank of nefarious deeds.

To prep for the meet-up, I reached out to Frank, the connection I had who might know a thing or two. He was a middle-tier turned fighter who'd grown up in the slums and knew nothing else. He did a few things under the table that could get him in trouble with the Syndicate, but he was the only one who might have an ear in the same groups.

When I finally got a hold of him, he dodged my questions, rushing me off the phone as he said he'd talk after the fight at the after-party. I pressed for more, but he hung up. *After the fight,* he'd repeated, and I'd gotten the message.

If Frank didn't want to talk over the phone, then whatever he stumbled into was serious and dangerous enough to make even him extra cautious. That meant I needed to be smarter than usual, not that I ever listened to my better judgment. I wasn't built for rules or restraint. If I'd followed them, I'd still be another blood-starved drifter scraping through the dregs.

Suiting up for the event, I chose a steel-grey color, tailored to me within an inch of perfection. Hair slicked back, smile sharp enough to cut, the mirror said I looked ready. Since most of the attendees would be in black suits, the thought was that I would stand out, making sure she could see me from across the room.

I was wrong.

*The moment I stepped into the venue, my eyes found her at the top of the stairs. That dress... bright, silky, dripping over her body like sin incarnate. She didn't just walk; she *commanded* attention. This was her in full bloom, every curve a declaration that power and strength could be seductive.

My mouth went dry as my chest tightened. I wanted to burn

---

* Haunt Me by Bryce Savage

the image into my mind, to devour it completely, then two shadows stepped into view.

Zeth. Standing beside her like a loyal hound ready to tear out throats the second she breathed. And another—a wolf shifter with the restless look of a man trapped between staying and bolting. She was the sun, and they were locked in her orbit.

My body moved before my brain caught up. I crossed the distance between us in a flash, took her hand from her side, and brought it to my lips, hoping the two shadows burned red.

"You're breathtaking," I murmured. My voice was steady, but my pulse beat like a war drum.

Their glares burned into me, and I couldn't help the smirk that fell across my face. Let them look. Let them know. I wasn't losing to them.

Her cheeks flushed, lips tipping into a smile that hit me square in the chest. For a heartbeat, everything inside me quieted, then I caught her scent again. That mouthwatering perfume of metallic heat made my fangs ache to sink in, to make her mine all over again.

Then her smile changed. The air shifted, cooling. In an instant, she wasn't *my* dangerous temptation anymore; she was the Syndicate's leader. Untouchable. Commanding. Deadly.

Her voice sliced through the haze. "We have things to discuss. Let's head inside."

I swallowed the hunger clawing up my throat and nodded, offering my arm. Even like this, she was stunning.

Now businesslike, she slid her hand into my elbow, and we moved toward the doors. My pulse screamed at me to focus, to remember why I was here.

Still, disappointment sat heavy in my gut. She could switch it off, all emotion, all heat, just like that? I admired that control almost as much as I hated it.

Zeth's glare burned into my peripheral vision. His eyes kept flicking to where her hand rested on my arm, his nostrils flaring. *Not a clueless guard anymore, are you?* Now he looked like a possessive beast ready to tear me apart for daring to touch what he wanted.

Something had happened between them. I could feel it in the way her energy pulsed, becoming colder, sharper. Her eyes shifted to him every once in a while when he wasn't looking, then they'd go back to that carefully crafted Rossey boss mask I was learning more about.

Hearing the turned wolf's huff behind me, his steps clipped and close, I knew I wasn't the only one on edge. A smirk tugged at my lips despite myself.

Welcome to the club, you jealous bastard.

Leading us into the house, there was a massive foyer of silver-accented white marble. Following the path into the house, we went down a long, wide corridor with a red carpet. The lights were dimmed so that it looked like the only thing you could see was the light at the end of the tunnel. As we neared the edge, where the space around us became more and more visible, my eyes flew open.

Staring around, you realized that you were in a concrete dome. Magic shimmered against the curved walls, and about

319

ten rows of seats circled the center where a state-of-the-art ring was right in the middle. The entrance looked like a millionaire's mansion, but the real purpose was this hidden arena in the middle of a mountain.

She tugged my arm to the VIP section, the security guards immediately moving out of our way when they saw her coming up.

A few rows from the front, she said in a hushed tone, "Have you confirmed your contact will be here?"

I nodded, leaning close enough for only her to hear. "Yeah. He's the first fighter in the prelims. Frank Vivio."

Before I could say more, a well-dressed stranger swooped in, congratulating her on the venue. Soon, the vultures flocked, and the rhythm became predictable. Praise her, handshake, ask to talk to her later, then another one would show up. She moved through them like a queen holding court, introducing Zeth, the fighters Nick and Benson, and then me.

The closer we got to our seats, the more the air turned into a cloying cloud of expensive perfume and ambition. I usually loved the smell, knowing it meant money, but, for some reason, with her next to me, it set me on edge.

When we finally sat, I could see the strain hiding behind her practiced smile. The tight pull at the corner of her lips, the faint roll of her shoulders as she exhaled like she'd been holding her breath for hours.

Putting his hand on her shoulder, Zeth threw me a look that could've curdled blood before he excused himself to check on security and stalked off.

That was when a redheaded fairy appeared, wrapped in a golden miniskirt and clear wings. She gave me a set of come-fuck-me eyes as she bent over, pulling her hair away from her neck as she asked me if I wanted something to drink.

I glanced at her neck, the vein pumping right beneath her skin, and normally, I would've, appreciated a taste, a distraction, but tonight, the idea soured my stomach. It felt empty. Wrong.

Just as I was opening my mouth to tell her no, Nova slowly leaned over my lap. Her voice was smooth and controlled when she said, "You're switching sections with James, Lisa. Go. Now."

The vibrations of her authority made the fairy woman freeze, eyes wide with dread, before she scurried off as she professed her apologies.

I almost laughed as a sense of giddiness took me over for a second. Possessive, territorial… Gods, it looked good on her. I turned to tease her for it, excited that she was jealous, and then I saw it.

A mark.

Small, diamond-shaped, and slightly darker than the skin behind her neck, it was half-hidden beneath the fall of her white hair.

The second my gaze locked on it, everything in me detonated. The world blurred out, sound and movement collapsing into silence until only she remained. My pulse thundered. My body heated from the inside out, every instinct clawing toward her.

My mark.

She was wearing my mark.

It pulsed, faint but alive, and she must've felt it too because she sat up and lifted a hand to rub the spot, her brow furrowing in confusion. Then someone called her name, and the spell broke. She turned, smiling at whoever it was, while I sat there like a man struck by lightning.

Even as the crowd rose to applaud the first fighters, I couldn't move. Couldn't breathe. My mind was a blur of disbelief, hunger, and something dangerously close to joy.

My mate.

Nova Rossey was my fucking mate.

For a second, the thought filled me up, making me feel reckless. My chest felt too tight for my ribs. Ideas started tripping over themselves—merging businesses, houses, lives. I imagined her in my home, her things scattered among mine, her scent in every room. Or maybe I'd move in with her, both of us running operations under the same roof.

Butterflies, actual goddamn butterflies, churned in my gut, and I almost laughed at the absurdity of it.

I'd stopped believing this could happen a long time ago. Turned supes weren't supposed to find their mates. Our bloodlines were fractured, our threads of fate frayed with watered-down magic. The chances were slim, and I'd accepted that. I'd learned to live without the ache of wanting something that wasn't meant for me.

Then here she was. A woman carved from steel and fire, strong enough to hold her own in a world built to break us. My perfect match. My anchor. My undoing.

Beneath the joy, fear slid in like a crack through glass. The memory of her face in the woods, cool and detached, as she pulled away before the sweat had dried. The way she'd made it clear that whatever had happened between us was an indulgence, nothing more.

That memory gutted me now.

She didn't know. Or she didn't feel it. Either way, if I lunged too soon, I'd lose her before I even had her.

So, I forced myself to breathe. To steady my pulse. To mask the chaos boiling beneath my skin.

If she wasn't feeling the bond yet, pushing it would only drive her off, and the last thing I wanted was for her to walk away. I'd been abandoned before. Lost in a world that didn't have time or mercy for a turned vampire whose sire had left him on the side of the road. The thought of her disappearing the same way scraped at something raw inside.

No, I'd be smarter. Slower. Patient. I'd make her fall without realizing she was falling.

When she finally looked at me and *felt* it, when she realized what we were, she wouldn't just accept the bond.

She'd *want* it. Her wolf would want it.

"Nova Rossey!"

A fire mage with a thick Latin accent swept up to her before I could blink, dragging her into a bear hug and kissing both her cheeks like they were old lovers. My eye twitched. "Thank you, thank you! I promise you won't be disappointed in Deslen. He's top tier, top notch. I swear on my grandmother."

My jaw flexed. The sound that left my throat was almost a growl. My vampire fangs poked out on instinct, sharp and aching for a throat, *his* throat. Every inch of me screamed to rip him away from her, to make him remember whose air he was daring to share.

The words he just said registered in my head, and I took a step back. Deslen. That was the fighter she had put in last minute. This was business.

Nova smiled at him, but it was all teeth and polish, the kind of smile that said, *you're useful, not special.* My chest loosened a fraction, then the frustration came back, sharp and bitter. I looked around. Where the hell was Zeth? Wasn't it his damn job to keep idiots like this away from her?

"It's nice to see you, Antonio." Her voice dipped in warning as she tugged on his hand. "I'm sure he'll work out just fine, but if he doesn't, I know where to find you."

Sweat beaded along the mage's brow, and the rising stench of panic came before she released his hand with a small, amused laugh. She turned to me like this was always a part of her plan.

"Let me introduce you to Conrad Mecariee." She glanced at me, smiling as the golden rings in her hair shined. "He runs some fights you might be interested in."

She turned and motioned toward him. "Antonio Ramirez, he's got some talent in South America that might interest you. He's looking to expand into turned fighters, so I think you two will have plenty to discuss."

Her tone said it wasn't a suggestion, so I obliged, turning on my business mask.

Shaking his hand, I forced civility into my grip when all I wanted was to break his hand off. Small talk flowed out of me like muscle memory, polite, effortless, the kind of charm that made men laugh even when they knew I'd gut them in business later. She was handing me an opportunity on a silver platter, and I played the part she expected until Antonio finally took the hint and disappeared back into his seat.

Then she leaned in close.

Her scent surrounded me in wildflowers with a fresh sweetness that made me salivate. My pulse stuttered as the air around her became hotter.

Her hand slid up my thigh, deliberate and slow. Her voice brushed against my ear. "I expect a twenty percent finder's fee on whatever comes of that."

Her fingers tightened just enough to make my breath hitch and my heart pound.

A sharp laugh tore out of me, too loud, too unguarded. A few heads turned our way, but I didn't care. This—*this*—was why she fit so perfectly in the jagged edges of my world. She was power wrapped in silk, ambition that smiled while it bit.

When she looked at me again, her eyes gleamed that golden blush color, swirling with a kind of predatory calm that made weaker men step back and walk away. Her plush lips flattened into a thin, unreadable line. Her hair, that ashy blonde mane, fell across half her face, half-light, half-shadow.

It should've been intimidating. Instead, I wanted more of it.

I couldn't hold back anymore. The tension that had been winding tight since the moment we sat down snapped. My hand found her jaw, fingers sliding into her hair as I made sure my thumb skated over the mark.

She gasped but didn't stop me.

I tilted her face toward mine and captured her lips.

It wasn't gentle. It wasn't patient. It was full of desperation, months of denial and hunger packed into one reckless moment. Her lips softened beneath mine, and, for one fleeting heartbeat, she kissed me back.

Her hand, the same one that had just threatened me, slid higher. Her fingers brushed my crotch. Her tongue grazed mine. Heat flared between us, and the world narrowed down to just the sound of her breath and the thud of my heart.

Then a crash broke the spell. Glass shattered somewhere behind us, followed by a muttered "Shit!"

Nova pulled away, breath unsteady, eyes darting to the floor. The guy behind us, Nick, was already crouched, trying to scoop up shards with a bleeding hand.

A tall male fairy in a pressed vest appeared like magic, conjuring a vacuum that swept away the mess in seconds. Nick muttered something, his jaw tight, as he sat back down when the male fairy said he would bring him another.

The air changed. The tension was back, thicker, heavier. Nick's stare drilled into the back of Nova's head.

What the hell was that about?

Before I could ask, Zeth returned, settling beside her with that infuriating calm. "Looks like I missed a part of the show," he said, voice dry as ash.

Nova froze when their eyes met. An entire conversation was exchanged without a single word, then she turned away sharply, murmuring something about watching the fight. I didn't miss the color creeping up her neck or the way her knuckles cracked as she clasped her hands together.

Something had happened between them. Recently.

The realization hit hard, followed by another. The jealousy I'd felt toward Antonio wasn't the same as what I felt toward Zeth... or even the wolf behind us, Nick. They were different kinds of threats.

When I thought about it, her mother had been famous for having multiple mates, so why wouldn't Nova be the same?

The thought should've angered me, but instead, it twisted into something sharper, more strategic. Wanting her all to myself hadn't changed, that fire still burned as fierce, but I could play the long game. I always did.

Business had taught me this much: every obstacle was just an opportunity in disguise. Every challenge was a chance to plan smarter.

So, I'd adapt. Watch. Wait. Learn her rhythm. Learn theirs.

Because no matter who else thought they had a claim, in the end, she'd be mine. My mate.

One way or another.

With Nova's attention locked on the fight, I didn't fully register the heat of someone's glare until I turned away. I found a set of turquoise eyes staring at me. Zeth. His cutting stare sent a message, clear and simple. *Go away. Leave her alone. She's mine.*

I met his look with a slow, knowing smile, my eyes flicking to Nova's before finding his again. Then I let my tongue drag across a fang, giving my unspoken response. *I'm not going anywhere.*

His nostrils flared, lip curling just enough to flash teeth. The expression was pure animal, almost feral. He might be a demon, but that man had been raised by wolves. Unfortunately for him, if that was supposed to scare me, he needed to take more lessons from Nova. Now, *her* glare could skin a man alive.

The crowd roared as the fight officially began, but it was just distant thunder beneath the silent war between Zeth and me. No words. Just tension thick enough to choke on. Every breath, every subtle twitch of muscle, was another round in our private brawl.

Now and then, I caught movement from behind. Nick's eyes flicked toward Nova, then back to the ring, a quiet shake of his head following. He wasn't a threat, not yet. Just another moth circling her flame.

A wave of gasps rippled through the crowd, breaking our stare-off. My gaze snapped back to the ring just as a massive sepia-skinned fighter with long braids twisted midair, bones cracking and reshaping until a black jaguar the size of a horse landed on padded feet. The lines of shimmering magic stayed on his fur, marking him as a fae shifter.

The shifter lunged, sinking his fangs into a vampire's forearm before the strike could land. With a brutal twist, he flung the bloodsucker across the mat like a discarded toy.

So, that was Deslen Tacnon. I'd heard the name whispered among the underground circuits. Fast, brutal, untouchable. Seeing him now? I could tell why the whispers seemed to chant his name. He was a cloud of shadow wrapped in muscle and fury. A rare species, too.

Too proud and too protective of their shrinking lands, most jaguar shifters didn't cross over from Faerie. Their kind loved fiercely, fought harder, and birthed rarely. To see one here was a sight worth the price of admission alone.

Across from him, Copland Banner, the reigning vampire heavyweight, looked almost mortal by comparison. His jabs were quick, his footwork sharper than most, but Deslen danced through his blows like smoke, turning defense into art, his counters precise and devastating.

Beside me, Nova leaned forward, eyes lit with feral excitement as blood splattered across the mat when one of Deslen's uppercuts connected. Her lips curved, the gold in her gaze burning bright. With every blow that landed, I could hear her pulse thump faster, could *see* it against her skin. Watching her thrive in the chaos was addictive, so much so that I didn't even realize he'd delivered the final strike until the crowd erupted, bodies surging to their feet in a collective roar.

Deslen stood victorious, the vampire sprawled at his feet, unconscious. The announcer's voice boomed, declaring him the winner by knockout. I barely heard it, too busy watching the reflection of the fight still flickering in Nova's eyes.

Then Deslen took the mic.

"I dedicate this fight to you!" he roared, his accent thick and rich as his finger pointed straight at Nova. A hush fell over the crowd. "I've finally found you! My mate. The woman I'll marry! This win, and every win to come, belongs to you!"

Every head turned toward her, and my gut sank. Oh, *hell*.

Nova froze, her eyes narrowed into slits before she rose up out of her chair. Her body trembled as her right fist clenched. Power coiled around her skin, and you could almost see the bones starting to bend as the atmosphere bent away from her heat.

Her voice became lethal. "Who the *fuck* do you think you are to say that to me?"

Oh, shit. This was about to get messy.

21

NOVA

The second my eyes locked on Deslen Tacnon, strutting around the ring to his hype song before the fight, something in me bristled. It wasn't awe or curiosity; it was a warning. Pressure, low in my gut, coiled tighter with every step he took. I didn't know why, but I could feel it building like static before lightning hit. Something was off. Something was about to break.

When he climbed through the ropes and came closer, my wrist burned, a familiar flare, but I told myself it was nothing, just my proximity to Conrad, Nick, Zeth. They'd all triggered it before, but this burn came on sharp and fast, becoming vicious in seconds.

Heat spread under my skin like wildfire, crawling up my arm until I had to clench my jaw to keep from wincing. I rubbed it, pretending to fix my watch, pretending I wasn't one second away from tearing at my skin just to make it stop.

The itch deepened as the heat climbed higher. For one wild heartbeat, I thought I might actually lose control, but I refused to let anyone see that. Not the cameras, not the fighters, not the world, so my face stayed calm and my hands steady while every nerve inside me screamed. Tonight had to go perfectly. I wouldn't let some stranger's presence throw me off balance.

Watching him fight made some of the tension ease as I got lost in his movements. The way his body bent and moved was so fluid, so graceful. I knew right then and there I had to have him for my ring.

I could see it all now—the contracts, the promotions, the endorsements. We could call him *The Midnight Jaguar.* Even his damn nickname sounded like profit. That was all I needed him to be—marketable. Useful. Not... whatever my wrist was trying to tell me.

The ref lifted his hand for the win, and the crowd went wild. Just as I was about to get up and clap, someone gave him the mic.

"I dedicate this fight to you! I've finally found you! My mate. The woman I'll marry! This win, and every win to come, belongs to you!"

My mate.

The words hit like a slap. For a second, I thought I'd misheard him, but the crowd's reaction told me I hadn't.

Heat surged up my throat, burning away every shred of composure I'd fought so hard to hold. My pulse pounded in my ears, and the bond mark on my wrist blazed like it was laughing at me.

He didn't just say what I thought he did, did he? Not *here.* Not in front of *everyone*. On national television.

I wanted to laugh, to tear the mic out of his hand and tell the world he was delusional, but all I could do was stand there, fists tight, nails biting into my palms, fury trembling just under my skin.

How fucking dare he.

How dare he look at me like that, like he owned something he hadn't earned. I hadn't even said two words to the man!

And the worst part? That stupid, traitorous burn under my skin didn't fade. It pulsed harder, mocking me with every beat.

"Who the fuck do you think you are to say that to me?"

The words tore out of me before I could stop them, sharp and clean like the crack of a gunshot. Deslen Tacnon had barely finished his little speech before I was on my feet, fury flooding my veins. What the hell was he trying to do? Impress me? Humiliate me? Make me a spectacle?

Every eye in the room burned against my skin, and the heat of embarrassment licked up my throat, threatening to show on my face. I smothered it under the familiar weight of authority and rage. Anger was easier. Anger was safe.

My pulse raced, each beat syncing with the grind of my teeth as my hands curled into fists. The part of me that I'd locked away for tonight, the ruthless, unshakable Syndicate boss, was clawing to get out. It wanted to make an example of him. To show the world that I was *not* to be fucked with. It wanted blood, or at the very least, obedience.

National television be damned.

I should've walked away. Should've told Zeth to drag him to me later so I could handle it in private like Ezra would've done—cool, composed, and untouched by emotion—but I wasn't Ezra. She was the ice queen who could slit your throat without raising her voice. I was fire. Wild and uncontained. I burned too bright, felt too much. When I loved, I loved hard. When I raged, the world felt it.

And right now, I was shaking the whole damn room.

My jaw tightened as my heels clicked across the floor, my body moving before my brain caught up. Even in a dress and stilettos, I reached the cage and gripped the top bar, hauling myself over in one fluid motion. Chiffon billowed behind me, a wave of silky fabric cutting through the light. When my heels hit the mat, the sound echoed. The crowd was so quiet, the air itself was holding its breath.

Good. Let them watch.

Deslen stood there in the center, grinning. As I took him in, I realized that this man was gorgeous, and that only made me madder.

His skin was carved bronze, gleaming under the lights, jaw sharp enough to cut deep. Dark hair spilled past his shoulders in a mess of braids and loose strands that screamed wild freedom. Every inch of him radiated strength. And that scent —fuck.

It hit me the moment I got close. Sweet strawberries tangled with peppercorn spice and a hint of vanilla. It wrapped around me, warm and dizzying, flooding my lungs before I could brace for it. My wolf stirred, low and hungry, inhaling like she'd been starving her whole life for that scent alone.

I forced her back with a snarl. I didn't care how good he smelled. He'd made a mistake. A public, unforgivable mistake.

"My mate," he cooed, lips curling into a smile that dripped with something dangerously close to adoration.

I didn't think. My hand shifted, claws bursting through skin as I grabbed him by the throat and yanked him down. His knees slammed into the mat with a heavy thud, the sound rippling through the crowd. Gasps followed, sharp and delicious. I half-expected him to fight back, to make me work for it, but he didn't. He just looked at me with those soft yellow eyes, calm, unyielding, like submission was his choice and he reveled in it.

That only pissed me off more.

Tightening my grip, my claws biting into his skin, I cut off his air until his pulse fluttered weakly against my palm. I leaned in close enough for the cameras to lose the sound. "You made a mistake," I whispered, my voice clipped. "You're going to take it back, right now, or I'll pop this pretty head clean off and end your career before it even starts."

Pulling back just enough to look him dead in the eyes, I continued my threat. "Then I'll reattach it and hang you in my gym by the wrists as my personal punching bag."

The cameras couldn't see the small tremor in my hand. Couldn't hear the roar inside my chest. My wolf was clawing up my ribs, furious that I was threatening him, furious that I wasn't *listening*. Her growl tangled with my heartbeat, a soundless echo of need and protest.

And still, he didn't flinch.

"If it's… what my mate… wants," he rasped, the words broken and raw, "then please… get rid of… what… displeases you," then motioned to his body.

His words hit harder than they should've. Those pale-yellow eyes stayed open, steady, trusting. *Too trusting.* He could've broken my grip. He could've ended this. Instead, he knelt there and offered me his throat on a platter. Who the fuck was this guy?

My wolf howled inside me, furious, desperate. *He's ours.*

I clenched my teeth until I tasted blood, fighting her with everything I had. I was the boss. I was in control. I was the power.

But the way he looked at me...

The heat, the surrender, the sheer madness of it... it was enough to make even a Syndicate boss hesitate.

When I looked down at my wrist, the world dulled into static. The noise, the crowd, the flashes, everything vanished beneath the sight of that thin, fine-lined wolfsbane plant wrapped around my arm like inky vines. The tattoo that was supposed to stay invisible.

Someone called my name, but it was distant, muffled. I couldn't look away. Each delicate flowerbud throbbed with a faint pulse, having a heartbeat of its own, until something cracked open beneath my skin. Heat surged through me, curling up from my belly and clawing through my chest in trembling waves. My breaths became shallow, each one threatening to splinter me apart.

What the hell is happening to me?

My fingers loosened, and Deslen collapsed to the mat, coughing and gasping for air. The crowd roared back into focus just in time for someone to shove a mic in my face. Questions hit me like bullets.

"Was he right?"

"Are you his mate?"

"Tell us what that means for the human audience. Are you now married?"

I closed my eyes and dragged in a breath until Zeth's voice cut through the chaos. I clung to it, needing something to ground me as I told myself, *Hold it together, Nova. At least until you get to the damn car.*

Ignoring the wildfire tearing through my veins, I lifted my head and smiled seductively at the crowd, hoping they didn't see the sweat rolling down my neck.

"He's not bad-looking, huh, ladies?" My laugh came out sharp and hollow. The crowd hesitated, eyes darting between me and the cameras, so I pushed the act harder, channeling Ezra's easy charm.

"No, no, I joke," I said, waving my hands in the air, still smiling, though my jaw ached from holding it. "I was a little upset, don't get me wrong." I casually shrugged as if I wasn't one wrong word away from breaking apart. Humans already thought we were a violent bunch, so it shouldn't be hard to sell it as a regular fight between supes. Maybe a misunderstanding?

"Due to the language barrier, he mistook mate for partner." I eyed him on the floor with a smile, "This will make my legal team throw a fit, but what the hell!" I threw my hands up and chuckled before holding one out to help him up. "Right before this fight, Rossey Fighting Enterprise signed Deslen, so you'll be seeing a lot more of his fights to come."

Deslen rose slowly, that unshakable grin plastered across his

337

face. With a smile, I threw my chin to the crowd, and he nodded, turning to wave at the crowd like my lie was gospel.

The humans ate it up, laughing, clapping, completely oblivious. The supes, though... their eyes told another story. No one mistook *mate* for *business partner*. They knew, but I could deal with them later, ripping their hearts out one by one if I had to. The humans were the ones I needed to convince.

Letting go of his hand, I clapped for Deslen as they buckled the championship belt around his waist, then I began to retreat, heading toward the cage door. When Deslen tried to follow, I cut him a warning glance. *You. Stay.*

He froze, his expression flickering before he fixed on that charming grin and turned back to his adoring audience.

Zeth, Conrad, and Nick were waiting just outside the cage. Zeth started to speak, but I shook my head. He shut his mouth and moved in beside me, solid and silent. His presence steadied me just enough.

"How about a drink? I know I need one," Conrad said, looping an arm through mine. I leaned into him for a heartbeat, just long enough to feel the weight shift off my shoulders.

Then my phone buzzed against my thigh.

Of course, it would.

Reaching into the hidden pocket of the dress, I pulled it out and caught the name flashing across the screen.

Ezra. Video chat.

Oh, fuck.

I pushed my way out as fast as I could, the roar of the crowd snapping at my heels. "Zeth, get the car," I called back, but he already had his phone out and was ordering someone to bring it around the front fast.

Voices called after me—people trying to either rub elbows or talk to me about that epic ending to my first televised fight—but I couldn't deal with them now.

I felt someone covering me, and Conrad's voice followed, tossing out clever excuses with ease. Something about an after-party and having a tight schedule tonight. Lies, every one of them, but I appreciated his help in saving face.

I glanced down at my wrist, where the faint outline of the wolfsbane plant twining around my forearm pulsed again. Warmth rippled through me like liquid gold, and my knees buckled from the force. A pair of rough hands steadied me.

"I gotcha."

I looked over my shoulder and met a set of metallic-gold eyes clouded with concern. Nick. I drew strength from them and got my feet back under me.

The limo was already waiting at the curb, its door open. I barely hit the last step before diving inside and sliding all the way to the back where the partition was up. My fingers fumbled as I swiped the screen, answering the incoming video call.

All four of my siblings filled the display.

Aniyah's squeal nearly blew out my eardrum. "Oh, my god, girl! You bagged a *behemoth*! Lucus kept covering my eyes because I wouldn't stop pointing out the bulge in his shorts! You're gonna be *blessed* tonight! Stains on top of stains!"

Two fingers went to my temple, massaging it before I responded to my sister. "Aniyah—"

Ezra's calm voice cut in. "You handled the press well. Most humans bought your explanation, and now that Deslen's repeating your story on camera, it should hold—at least publicly."

"But not with the supes," I muttered because we all knew the truth.

Her expression iced over. "Riot, keep your men on the chatter. First hundred supes who mention it—break their legs and make sure to use the slow-healing poison on them. Next hundred? Make them disappear. That should send a message."

Riot nodded once, dark and sharp, her fingers moving across her phone. "On it." Without missing a beat, she asked, "Should I kill him tonight?"

The air in the limo thinned, and my chest tightened. I knew she was doing her job, helping me, even, but the thought of Deslen lying dead somewhere, that open smile gone cold, tore at something raw inside me. My wolf howled deep in my soul.

"No. Don't." The words slipped out before I could stop them. My hand fisted on my thigh.

I didn't really know this asshole, and I was already defending him. Fuck! I didn't need this right now!

Silence stretched. All four pairs of eyes on my phone were fixed on me. Calix ran a hand over his face and sighed like the weight of the world had already crushed him once today. "Nova," he said softly, "don't tell me that—"

"I don't know." My voice came out tight. The wolf inside me was pacing, snarling, "*yes*," but my mind refused to listen. The tattoo burned faintly, giving me all the proof I didn't want. All I knew for sure was that I didn't want Deslen to be hurt physically.

"We don't have time to cover up or explain a high-profile death, which, after this fight, he would be. Plus, I need to focus on this substance problem. I have a lead I'll talk to tonight." Staring at Ezra, I hoped she understood that I didn't want to talk about what she was worried about. Not yet.

I sighed. "For now, leave him."

Ezra watched me for a long ten seconds, eyes unreadable, before nodding slowly. "Agreed. The green goo takes priority."

Of course, she'd call it that. Ezra could topple big corporate conglomerates and convince an educated man to purchase air, but when it came to naming things, she had the imagination of a brick.

I cleared my throat. "Any updates?" I needed to talk about anything to move on from this conversation.

Calix nodded. "I'll send what I have soon. I'm comparing the compound to the tissue Ezra preserved from the creature that attacked Aniyah. If they match, the incidents are connected."

"And someone's targeting us," Ezra finished, her tone matter-of-fact. The call went quiet as that reality sank in. Having an enemy that we knew nothing about was a big issue, one that would affect us all.

Right at the most inopportune moment, my wrist pulsed and heat rolled through me again. My thighs trembled. My body felt like it was perched on the edge of something vast and uncontrollable.

"Nova?" someone said, but I couldn't answer. Not until I forced my breathing to steady. When I opened my eyes, my siblings were watching me, each of them waiting for an explanation I didn't have.

Riot broke the tension. "It was... enjoyable. The fight. You did a good job." I sent her a silent thank you.

Then Aniyah jumped in, laughing and teasing, describing how her mates were currently trying to outdo one another with ridiculous feats of strength since she'd made a comment about liking the muscles on the fighters. She winked and whispered about how she was about to let them use her as a sexy barbell. Make gym time finally work in her favor.

Calix groaned. "Aniyah, if you mention your sex life one more time, I'm cutting one of your mate's balls off."

She gasped, immediately retaliating by telling him she would cut off one of his in return. The two of them started bickering, and their noise filled the space, chasing away the echo of the mark pulsing under my skin.

"Enough," Ezra said sharply, shaking her head before focusing on me. "Nova, you did good. I'll have numbers in the morning. Celebrate tonight for a job well done. All of us are proud of you."

I nodded, told them all thank you, and ended the call. Setting my phone on the seat beside me, I let my eyes close for a moment, knowing my night wasn't over yet. I still needed to talk to Conrad's contact.

The silence in the limo didn't bother me; it felt... safe. Three sets of eyes still lingered, but instead of pressure, they brought a strange sense of calm.

Wait. Three?

I blinked and looked up. Conrad, Zeth, *and* Nick were watching me.

"Where are you going?" I asked Nick.

"With you guys," he said simply. "Benson met a girl and took the car."

I exhaled hard through my nose. The last thing I needed was another body tangled up in this mess, but at least he was already in the Syndicate ranks, which meant I owned him. I'd just count him as free labor.

"Fine," I said. "You can help, but you follow my lead with no questions asked."

He nodded, and I sat up, taking a breath before reminding everyone, "Nothing that is said leaves this car. Is that understood?"

A round of nods went all around, and I turned to Conrad. Those forest-green eyes had a way of cutting through my chaos, so I took a breath. "We need to make a plan for how we're going to find your lead and get him somewhere to talk."

Despite the layers of tension between us, the three of them easily fell into their roles as they started to talk strategy. I tried to focus, but my mind kept drifting back to him.

Deslen.

I didn't dare look down at my wrist again, didn't want to feel that warmth spreading, that pull tightening in my chest. I shoved the thought away, choosing to cling to the question that popped into my brain. How was he dealing with the sudden fame?

Under all the noise, one word whispered through my mind again and again—steady, insistent, undeniable.

Mate. Mate. Mate. Mate.

2 2

DESLEN

"Deslen, is what Miss Rossey said true?"

Looking at the human woman in front of me with a mic, the man next to her holding up a camera, I nodded, keeping my voice steady even though my pulse was racing. Lying wasn't an option, not when my mate's scent still clung to my skin, reminding me of what kind of a mate I wanted to be for her.

Also, I didn't want to give her another reason to be mad at me, still feeling the pinpricks of her claws on my throat, the warmth of her palm pressed against my airway. I didn't hate that exchange, but I didn't like the anger in her eyes, not when it was pointed at me. Not when I'd only just found her.

Another person shoved a mic in my face. "Are you excited to be signing on with Miss Rossey?"

"Yes," I said quickly, nodding so hard it probably looked rehearsed. "It's... something of a lifelong dream."

That much was true. Since I started this journey, I'd wanted to find my place, a tribe beyond blood, a home beyond the one I left behind. In one of her prophetic dazes, my grand-mother, the old seer of the Tacnon jaguar clan, had told me, *"You will find your heart beyond the veil."* I didn't believe it at first, not wanting to leave my home, but now, I carried those words with me like a promise carved into bone.

Years had passed since I crossed over, and I'd spent too many lonely nights dreaming about what my life could be. Each season spent searching had stripped away more and more hope until even my reflection had started to look like a stranger.

Then I met Antonio.

He was loud, fast-talking, full of wild ideas. He'd seen me fight for some cash, he said, and promised the world if I made him my manager—fame, fights, fortune. None of it had mattered to me, not really, but when he promised to take me around the world, I took the chance, hoping I could find her along our travels. My mate.

He'd spent his last coin to fly us here on a whim. No fights lined up, no guarantee of anything. We were running on faith and desperation, just as I'd spent every day on the human plane. Then, by some divine twist of fate, I'd found her.

A deep rumble built in my chest before I could stop it, a pleased purr that came from somewhere ancient. The human reporters flinched and stepped back, while the supes leaned closer, eyes wide with curiosity.

"Since this is your debut, do you have anyone you'd like to fight in the ring?"

I clenched my jaw, forcing my smile to stay in place. *When will these questions end?* My gaze swept the crowd, searching for a way out. My chest ached where that invisible golden string connected me to her, already tugging me in the direction she'd gone.

Before I could move, Antonio appeared at my side, his hand clamping down on my arm. "People, people, one at a time!" he said with a grin that didn't quite reach his eyes. "We'll be sitting down with Miss Rossey soon to discuss Deslen's potential future."

We were? That was news to me, but if it meant seeing her again, I was all for it.

Leaning toward him, I muttered under my breath, "Vamos lá. Não quero deixar meu amigo esperando." *Let's go. I don't want to keep my friend waiting.*

He waved me off without looking. "Não seja ridículo e estrague esta oportunidade incrível." *Don't be ridiculous and ruin this incredible opportunity.* Then he turned me back toward the flashing lights, a storm of cameras erupting right in my face.

The sudden burst of light made my instincts flare. I lifted my arm to shield my eyes, muscles tensing, the predator in me uneasy with the feeling of being trapped in this bright, noisy cage of light. I didn't want to embarrass my mate by freaking out and swiping a claw at them to get them to stop.

I could still feel the look she'd given me before she left, that icy calm masking her fierceness underneath. The silent warning, *Don't fuck this up*, was heard loud and clear.

I'd already done enough to anger my mate. I didn't want to give her any more reason to stay that way.

Another reporter pushed her way through, shoving up her glasses as she sneered. "And you're aware that Miss Rossey is a gangster for the Syndicate? Does that bother you? Having someone like that in charge of your future? Aren't you scared?"

The word *gangster* made my ears twitch. I blinked, confused. Antonio had told me she was influential, powerful, even, but not much more than that. Certainly not that she was some big crime boss who ruled from the shadows.

I thought back to the starlight locks that wildly framed her face, eyes like molten rose gold, sharp enough to cut. The way the air bent around her when she moved. Dangerous? Absolutely. But danger was beauty in its purest form, and if that was what she was, then I didn't mind bleeding a little.

"She's given me the opportunity of a lifetime," I said, keeping my tone measured. "One I'll dedicate myself to day and night to prove my worth."

The golden thread between us pulsed weakly, a fragile thing since it hadn't been solidified. Each second she drifted further away made it fade a little more until it felt like sand slipping through my fingers.

Panic bloomed in my chest. The ache was primal. My grand-mother's words echoed again. *Find your mate and keep the line alive.* I couldn't lose her. Not after all these years.

"N-no more questions," I stammered, pushing through the reporters before they could throw another one at me.

Antonio's voice rose behind me, barking my name, demanding that I come back, but I just lifted a hand in farewell and kept going.

He'd understand someday.

I didn't just want a mate. I *needed* her. She wasn't simply my destiny; she was my reason for breathing.

Black jaguars had always been a proud people. The strongest of the shifter species in Faerie, we were born to be soldiers, guards, protectors of the fae courts. Serving the royals had once been an honor, a calling worth bleeding for, dying for. Our lives had meaning when our claws defended something greater than ourselves.

Then Faerie began to rot from the inside. The land warped, its magic growing sour, and the fae royalty twisted along with it. Generation after generation, they grew crueler, turning their fangs and fury on not only their enemies but on their kin. When the realm finally fractured, Faerie started to shrink, royal factions tearing into each other for what scraps of power remained.

Entire bloodlines vanished in that war, and by the time the dust settled, only a handful of jaguars had survived. My grandmother, uncle, and I were the last from our tribe.

When the fae started escaping to the human realm in droves, I begged them to come with me, to start over. My grandmother only smiled, her gnarled fingers stroking a flower that bent toward her touch like it loved her. She said she couldn't leave, not while Faerie still needed her. It was her home—and her grave if need be. What she gained from Faerie she needed to give back in blood and bones.

My uncle, just as stubborn as his mother, stayed with her, so I did, too. For years, we lived off whatever the dying land could still offer. In Faerie, time was stretched thin; days lasted months, and years blurred. By the time I was grown, I'd accepted that this was my life. I would stay to protect them and fade beside them when the time had come.

But my grandmother had other plans.

349

One night, I woke under a strange star-filled sky, the taste of sleep-magic still thick on my tongue. Later, lucid snippets of that night came to me. My uncle had carried me across the border into the human realm. He left me there with only a folded note in my pocket and a burning talisman carved into my shoulder, the kind that only Grandmother knew. The kind that barred me from ever crossing back.

I didn't read the note. Instead, I screamed and wanted to rebel at my grandmother's decision.

Night after night, I cursed the glowing border until my voice broke, clawing at the magic until my hands bled, demanding it open and take me home. For months, I raged, fought, starved, and wept at its edge. Only when I had nothing left, when the world had gone quiet and I laid on the cold ground in despair, did I pull out the note.

Her handwriting was shaky but clear. She'd written that Faerie had spoken to her, showing her a vision she could not ignore, a future for me beyond the veil. One filled with laughter, love, and a family that was stronger than any other, one that could weather any storm that came its way. This future meant our line's survival. She wrote I would find my mate, someone strong and fierce, someone who I would have children with, children that would thrive for a millennia and beyond.

If I stayed in Faerie, she warned, I would wither away, dying long before my time, and she couldn't bear that thought.

So, she ensured that I couldn't come back, that I could live out my destiny. She hoped that I would realize this was the better choice one day.

After days of reading it over and over, I realized that finding my mate was my only option. The only way to make living in this realm worth it.

I got up off the earth and went to the nearest city, doing odd jobs as I drifted from city to city on foot. My grandmother's note stayed in my pocket, giving me the strength to keep going, and for ten long years, I searched. Each moon, each city, I kept going, but the hope that I started with kept withering, layer by layer, as time went on. Until tonight.

Because tonight, I found her.

It was her scent that caught my attention first, wrapping me in an intoxicating trance of sweet honeydew. It crawled under my skin, curled in my chest, and made my knees weaken with want. I nearly stopped fighting, lost in the pull of it, as heat rolled through me in waves. I'd never touched a woman before, never wanted to until now. I'd waited for this, for *her.*

I'd watched enough of our jaguar shadow as a cub to know what to do, how to please your mate as both a man and the beast within, and I wanted to please her. To make her mine in every way that mattered. My mate. My salvation.

My feet picked up their pace, passing all the people that were gawking or pointing at me. I needed to talk to her, to explain everything. Just as I saw the massive doors to the outside world, someone yanked me into a dark hallway, breaking my line of sight.

Pissed at my focus being interrupted, a growl ripped from my chest before I even saw who it was.

"Whoa. Whoa. Save that kind of fierceness for the ring, boy."

I straightened and took in the human man before me. His body was soft and bloated, golden rings flashing on every chubby finger as he gestured with them while he talked. His breath was a rancid cloud that made my face twist in disgust. My first impulse was to swipe at him, to get him away from me and clear a path with claws and teeth, but my mate's face flashed in my mind. Reminding myself of how she behaved around humans, I forced my hands to stay where they were.

If she wanted civility, I would give it. If she wanted a representative, then I would be one. I would show her how valuable I could be.

Breathe. Be the man she can parade in front of cameras. I smiled and nodded for him to continue, willing to give him a minute or two before I went back to hunting down my mate.

"Now, my boy," the man crooned, looping an oily arm through mine and steering me down the dim corridor. He wasn't afraid of me. His confidence made my hackles rise, but all I thought about was how pleased my mate would be that I was able to handle this filth with a cool, calm demeanor.

"What you did out there was stupendous! The fight of a lifetime! Seeing you shift and take the champ... man!" His praise spilled over me, and I nodded. The truth was simpler: I'd trained for this. My uncle had taught me the art of war—how to move, how to survive against the strange and the powerful. Fighting beast to beast, I knew exactly how to win and survive.

He pushed harder, his breath slick against my ear. "You deserve the lights. The cameras. Worldwide. Figurines, movies—name it." As he spoke, his saliva pooled at the corners of his mouth, and his jowls jiggled. Cold humor curled through me. *This human's greed and hunger for spectacle is grotesque.*

"You were built for this life," he said, squeezing my arm as if to claim me. "You were made for this purpose."

"My purpose is to find my mate and have cubs," I answered, and the words left no room for anything else.

His grin soured into something oily. "Girls? I can get girls—hundreds. Have your fun. If one gets pregnant, we can—" he gestured as if bargaining a livestock sale"—sign the child over. The public loves a family man. Single dads sell."

The image he painted sat heavy and foul inside me. Girls. Other women. Children who weren't hers. My body recoiled as if the idea had a poisonous taste. Sweat pricked my skin. Heat pooled low and ugly. The thought of having a cub with anyone but my mate felt like a slap to the throat.

He kept yapping away. An agency solely dedicated to me, being the first supe he'd championed. All while a volcano of pure rage built up inside me, erupting when I couldn't take it anymore.

When I shoved him against the corridor wall, his rings clanged, and his heart rate picked up. The rancid stench of fear rolled off him as he gasped. My fingers dug into his windpipe as I leaned in, voice animal-like. "Get this through your thick, fat skull: there's nothing in this world you could offer me that would make me sign with you. Next time you cross me, I'll snap your neck between my teeth… human or not."

He hit the floor like a sack of rotten fruit, scrambling away on hands and knees before bolting down the hall. The urge to take him down and shred him to pieces tugged at my bones. I wanted to let him run, let him think he was safe, then show him the meaning of real fear. I imagined ripping out his esophagus and presenting it to my mate as an offering. In Faerie, trophies were proof of devotion. *Would she understand that here?*

The temptation to tear after him, run him down to the ground, and hear his high screams fade into the night rode me hard, but I took a few breaths and let the instinct go. She wanted the humans placated, not murdered in the spotlight.

Patience, I told myself. There were other gifts I could give her —better ones, chosen with care. I would not cheapen the start of what we might be with something grotesque.

Turning my attention back to the hallway, my nose picked up the faint sweet melon thread that tugged at my heart, so I followed it. Voices ahead drifted into focus. A man in a suit and red tie, a woman wobbling in sequins. "Did Nova leave already?" the man asked, scanning the hall. "I wanted to talk to her about an opportunity."

The woman cackled uncontrollably behind him. "She's not investing in your business, *Kyle*." A smirk on her face, she began hiccuping. "She's a hardened mob boss who changes into a wolf and tears hearts out. She's not interested in your dinky security business."

I sank back into the shadows, about to ignore these two in favor of following my mate's trail, when the wobbly-footed woman spoke again. "I did hear she was going to the after-party... but you have to be invited. I don't think you're invited, *Kyle*."

My mate. A party?

Stepping out from the shadows, I emerged right in front of the woman slurring her words. She shrieked and flailed her arms, about to fall backward, but I caught her, setting her upright with a gentle hand on her elbow.

I gave her my second-best smile—sweet, practiced, the one that opened doors more easily than violence. "Where's this after-party?" I asked. "And how do you get an invitation?"

I was going to see my mate and talk to her even if it was the last thing I did.

23

NOVA

Something was wrong. Terribly wrong.

The vent blasted cool air across my skin, but it didn't have the intended effect. Instead, the chill only sharpened the heat rippling through me. My pulse thudded in my wrists, in my throat, in my whole body, making every move uncomfortable.

We had been talking about the plan when my body sent a chill up and down my spine. Like it was a warning before a scorching heat bloomed underneath my skin.

I tried to cover it up, turning the nearest air vents toward me when they weren't looking, but it didn't help. Then it hit me, like a scent bomb detonating in my chest, and I gasped, dragging in mouthfuls of air. Each inhale burst with flavor, the vivid taste alive on my tongue as it filled my lungs.

Zeth's smoked cherries—dark and sticky—merged with Nick's clean white musk until the air thickened into something sweeter, heavier. A sharp streak of citrus cut through the sweetness, chased by sandalwood and spice that burned its way down my lungs. Every note tangled together until my mind was dizzy, drowning in an ocean of scents and desire that drove my body crazy.

My wolf rolled over inside me, shameless and eager, tail wagging, belly bare. Not in the least bit helpful!

I told myself to get out of the car, to breathe fresh air, to think about anything but them, but my hands wouldn't move. My chest rose and fell in rapid succession. My thighs pressed together of their own accord, and I hated how much I liked being suffocated by their scents.

A cool, smooth hand landed on my thigh, and the breath I'd been holding came out in a shuddering plea.

"Are you okay, Nova?"

Conrad's voice dragged me under, and I lolled my head in the direction of his voice. Concern softened those moss-green eyes until they blurred behind the memory of his mouth on my skin in the woods, making my body burn hotter. My teeth sliced into my lower lip, blood spilling across my tongue as I held back a plea.

A small, sane voice in my head told me to stay seated, to pretend it was nothing, but every nerve in my body leaned toward him, begging for more.

His thumb stroked my thigh once, innocent, maybe, but it sent shots of lightning up my spine. My eyes slammed shut as my fingers clenched the leather seat, nails biting in, trying to ground myself as my pulse throbbed down below.

He tilted my head up, my lids cracked open to see his curious lifted brow and questioning gaze locked onto me. Guilt twisted through me like a blade.

The marks on my arm ignited, each bud pulsing in a different rhythm, and none of them mine.

He shrugged out of his jacket and leaned in close, a crooked half-smile tugging at his mouth. "I've got you, Boss," he murmured.

The laugh that left me cracked through my dry throat, sounding small and strangled.

*He knelt, his eyes on me like they would never let go, and my heartbeat tripped. Fangs slid into sight, slow and alluring, from behind his smile. My breath hitched; my body tightened. His fingers brushed the fabric of my dress up, and my breath stuttered. Even the soft sound of sliding silk sent tremors up my thighs.

"What the fuck?" a surprised voice muttered, breaking the spell. A low growl vibrated through my chest, my wolf angry at the interruption.

"Shhh," Conrad soothed, coaxing me. "Don't worry about anything else. Anybody else. Just focus on me."

His hands mapped the length of my thighs, and his lips followed, the heat of his breath causing goosebumps to follow. My body arched toward him before I could stop it.

My lips parted in a gasp as his teeth grazed the inside of my thigh. My body opened up for him, begging in a primal response.

"More," I heard myself whisper. "I need... more."

Conrad lifted one of my legs, draping it over his shoulder before he gave me one last devilish smile. "Oh, you're going

---

* Worship by Ari Abdul

359

to get more, Boss. I want you to feel how I devour you from the inside out. I want all my tastebuds to scream your name."

A whimper tore from my throat at his words. Desperation clouded my mind. My thoughts fragmented as my vision blurred at the edges. My hips rolled forward in small, involuntary movements, my body pleading for what wouldn't come out of my mouth.

"Mmmmm," he hummed along my inner thigh. The vibrations teased my sensitive skin, and I gasped, a wordless plea for him to keep going. "Your cunt smells *divine*, Nova. I'm going to feast tonight."

Before I could process his words, his cool palms cupped my ass with lightning speed, fingers digging into my flesh. He'd lifted me effortlessly, so high that his elbows pressed into the leather while my bottom was suspended in the air.

He gave my pussy one long, languid lick, flicking his tongue along my clit at the end. My head slammed back against the headrest. My spine arched so severely the bones felt like a bow drawn taut, and my hips thrust forward shamelessly, chasing his mouth for more.

"Fuck, your pussy's gorgeous," he whispered against my inner thigh, then those teeth slid into my flesh. With one long, deliberate pull, he sucked from my vein.

"Aaahhhh." The sound slipped from my mouth unbidden as he drank from me. When I looked down, his eyes were still fixed on my pussy, watching it clench in rhythm with each pull at my thigh.

His fingers dug deeper into my ass, the tips creeping dangerously close to entering both holes. My body shook, not from fear, but from a need so visceral it had stolen my breath.

"Conrad. Please." My voice cracked, hoarse and raw. He released my thigh with a wet *pop*, his tongue soothing the wound before his gaze returned to mine. Devotion, praise, loyalty, want—all of it swirled together in those eyes—eyes that I should've been wary of, but, in that moment, hesitation had no place here. Both my body and I needed him to deliver on his promise, to take the edge off and help me regain my focus.

I slid my hand into his caramel-blond locks, my voice breathless as I commanded, "Fucking lick me clean, then, and don't stop until I've come all over that gorgeous face."

He didn't need to be told twice. He dove in, making sounds that filled the car with carnal pleasure, wet and hungry. My hands gripped the leather so hard the fabric split beneath my fingernails. His touch, those sounds, our combined scent flooded my senses. My eyes rolled back as his tongue circled my clit and lapped at my center with single-minded devotion.

"Fuck this," came from the other end of the car, but I didn't acknowledge it. All I wanted was for Conrad to continue, for me to come so my body would finally calm down. There was still so much to do that night, and I needed to be focused.

Leather creaked, and Conrad took that moment to spear my core with his tongue. My eyes popped open as a moan tore from me. Molten sea-colored eyes flashed before my face. A mouth covered mine, warm, wet. His tongue collided with mine, swallowing that moan as if he'd always meant to claim it as his own.

Cherries filled my nose, and I knew who'd kissed the daylights out of me. *Zeth.*

His hands cupped my breasts, pinching my hardened nipples through the silky fabric, turning my body into a trembling mess.

When his mouth broke from my lips, Zeth stared down at me. Although his eyes were lit with anger, his lust was written on his face, both sides battling for dominance. Hoping to help him decide, I breathed out his name. That desire took over as his grip turned rough.

"You think I'm going to just let this asshole do this in front of me without making my claim? You're *mine*, Nova Rossey."

I swallowed hard, scrambling for what to say about all that, but Conrad didn't let me think. He paused, causing me to look down at him. He put his fingers in his mouth, licking around them liberally before looking up at me, shoving those two saliva-soaked fingers past the tight ring of muscle at my backside.

"Oh, fuck, Con," burst from my lips as the vampire staked his claim.

Zeth's eyes surged with fire. His hands gripped the fabric at my breasts and tore it apart. The loud snap of threads breaking bounced around the car as his mouth circled my nipple and bit down hard.

"Aaahhhh! Fuck! Yes!" My breathing became labored, ragged. My body wound tighter and tighter as Zeth tortured me with his rough treatment from above while Conrad licked and sucked at my clit, working two fingers in and out of my ass with maddening precision.

"Fucking animals." The groan came from the other side of the car where Nick was sitting, his hands gripping his thighs so hard

I thought his fingers would snap. His back rigid and hunched, his eyes drank in the scene, caught between sin and salvation. He wanted it but couldn't come to terms with that desire.

Too fucking bad. He wasn't human anymore, and he needed to accept that. And supes… we liked to fuck.

I cried out Zeth and Conrad's names while staring at Nick, and they moaned mine in return as they continued with renewed vigor.

For a second, Nick looked like he was about to lunge forward, to say *fuck it*, but then he snarled at himself and turned his head away.

Normally, I wasn't the type to beg for sex, didn't enjoy convincing someone or pulling them in, but my body needed more despite how hard the two men were working me over. So I changed tactics.

"Nick," I whispered desperately. Lifting a hand from my side, I reached for him with a plea that normally would have caused me shame, but right now, all of that went out the window. I needed him, and I was willing to do whatever it took to get him.

His whole body flinched. He didn't want to watch, but curiosity won. His gaze slowly turned my way.

"I need you," I choked out.

He puffed out a humorless laugh, his eyes flicking to Zeth and Conrad before returning to me, his silent *'yeah, right'* coming out loud and clear.

The deep ache inside only intensified. The need to have all of them pulsed at my wrist like a second heartbeat. I almost slammed my fist down beside me and demanded he come over, but I had a feeling that would have made him angrier.

My brain scrambled for a way to reach him. To get him to give in to his animal side. His pants were tented, his eyes keeping me in his peripherals. He wanted this just as much as I did, but he was thinking with his human head, clinging to human norms.

"You're right, Nick," I called out, moaning as Zeth rolled one nipple between his fingers and tongued the other. "It's animalistic." Conrad hummed in agreement against my core, and I desperately clenched around him. "More of a need to fulfill, so don't think too much. Just go with your instincts."

His whole body turned my way, though his eyes still held doubt.

"What does your wolf want?" I asked as his eyes widened before dropping to his hands.

That was when Conrad took one hand away from my ass and shoved three fingers into my pussy. My eyes flew wide as I cried out.

"Leave him." Conrad's voice was darker than I'd ever heard it. "If he wants to deny himself, let him. We don't need a weak link."

Zeth chimed in, his mouth still on my breast as he chuckled. "We'll make sure you don't miss him. Don't worry about it. We got you." His teeth sank in, sharp and deliberate, a warning wrapped in desire.

They were right. I closed my eyes. If he didn't want to, then I wasn't about to try to convince him any further. I'd just enjoy—

A hand grabbed my chin from my other side. Liquid gold eyes swirled a vibrant haze, blazing with lust that almost glowed. "Just with you. Only with you." Nick's breath brushed my lips, his words hovering between a vow and a threat. From the tone, I didn't know if his joining was a good thing or a bad thing, but my lips parted for him just the same.

His words slid through me like cool water, easing the tension from my shoulders until my breath finally came free. Everything narrowed to the tight coil of sensation winding higher inside me.

Nick's hand closed around my throat, holding me in place before he descended on my mouth, capturing it like every last bit of me had been his all along. Even after the others had left their mark on me, his touch hit harder. All it took was a kiss from him, and I came undone, opening like flower petals who had long been denied the sun. It was jarring how much this man affected me. How all of them affected me together.

For a few glorious, life-altering seconds, I had all three mouths on me, pleasing me. One would make me ache and burn for more, while another would cool the sensation, then the next would build it back up again.

It was dizzying and disorienting, but I was finally able to let instinct take over. My arm gave one last pulse, a thundering beat that echoed through all of us, and my muscles locked, every inch of me wound tight until the tension snapped. Heat tore through me in violent waves, scorching me from the inside out, and I clung to them like they were the only things keeping me from going under.

Hearing Conrad slurp and suck up all of my cum had sent me over the edge again. My hips thrust up against his face desperately, and a second shockwave hit me. This time, I tried to scream, but the sound never made it out of my throat, my hands gripping Zeth and Nick so hard I knew they had marks on their flesh.

All three of them kept up their kisses, touches, and licks through the aftershocks of my orgasm. As I sagged into a puddle in my seat, completely spent, their hands became surprisingly gentle. Soothing me, they cooed my name while my brain tried to reboot.

Nick grumbled under his breath before pressing a lingering kiss to my neck. His teeth grazed my skin, pressing just hard enough to make a sound slip out of me, then, just as fast, he pulled away. Slouched into his seat, he stared out the window with accusing eyes.

Zeth lifted his head, lips flushed and swollen, his gaze still fastened on me as though the sight of me calmed him. He bent forward until our foreheads met, both of us slick with heat and breathless. He inhaled deeply and deliberately, drawing in my scent.

Conrad set my leg down with careful hands, folding his arms across my thighs and resting his head on my lap. He looked up at me through his lashes, lips and chin glistening, a lazy smile curving the corner of his mouth. "Did that help, Boss? Feel any better now?"

The question hit somewhere low in my stomach. My body was still humming with the echo of what had just happened, but when I mentally checked, the chaos in my body had quieted, the fever fading to a steady, satisfied warmth. "Y-yeah. Much better."

My hand lifted before I thought to stop it, my thumb brushing against his bottom lip. He gently caught my wrist, eyes darkening as he nibbled along my pulse, and I had to bite back another sound.

Turning my head, I brushed a soft kiss to Zeth's nose, the closest I could manage without moving too much, and whispered, "Thank you."

"Fuck," Zeth muttered, his fingers tightening around mine, his chest rising and falling too fast. The hand at my waist found its way around me like he needed the contact to stay anchored. "Anything for you, Nov."

Down the car, Nick still hadn't moved. His reflection in the window was all sharp lines and tension. I smiled faintly. "Thank you, Nick."

His eyes slid toward me, a sidelong flicker, before he gave a single, stiff nod and looked away again.

Part of me hoped he'd figure out how to stop fighting himself, how to blend that human restraint with what burned underneath before it tore him in half.

I glanced down. The shredded remains of my dress hung in scraps around my waist. "Shit," I muttered. We were supposed to be headed to the after-party, and I was *not* walking in like this.

My watch buzzed.

Niyah: *Forgot to tell you! I left a backup dress in the trunk.*

Niyah: *You can't wear a cum-stained dress out, Nov! That's tacky.*

Resting my head back on the seat, I thanked the heavens for having a pushy little sister. Tacky or not, I was just relieved I wouldn't have to walk in half-naked. If it was all supes, I could make some wolfish excuse, but there was bound to be some of those rich humans there, and I didn't want to freak them out. I typed out a *thank you* and rapped on the partition, telling the driver to pop the trunk.

"What are you doing?" Zeth's harsh, commanding tone had me lifting a brow.

"Aniyah packed me a backup dress," I said with a tired laugh. "Unless you think I should show up like this?"

I dragged my fingertips down the center of my bare torso, and three sets of eyes tracked the motion like starved hyenas.

"No."

"I'd advise against it, Boss."

"Are you crazy?!"

The last came with enough bite that I leaned over to look at its source. Nick avoided my gaze entirely, acting like he didn't just have an outburst.

I smirked. "Guess *that's* unanimous."

"I'll get it," Zeth said, already reaching for the handle before I could protest. The door slammed shut behind him.

Conrad watched him through the tinted glass. "He's going to be the protective one."

"And you're not?" I teased, my voice still hoarse.

With a grin, he leaned closer as if sharing a secret. "I'm more of the let-you-do-what-you-do-and-catch-you-if-you-fall' type."

I crossed my arms, mostly to hide how much I liked that answer, but his eyes dropped to my chest anyway. The heat I thought we'd satiated sparked back up in his eyes. I wasn't normally the type men ogled, so the attention made butter-flies flutter in my stomach. I kinda liked it.

He tilted his head toward Nick. "That one's the stubborn one."

Nick's low growl vibrated from the far seat, and I couldn't help the quiet laugh that escaped. "Nick is not amused." Before he could reply, the door opened, and Nick shut his mouth, but I was still curious as to what he was going to say.

That was until Zeth climbed back in, holding a sleek, green satin crop top with spaghetti straps and a high-waisted pencil skirt that looked like it was made for me.

He handed it over, and I grinned, already picturing Aniyah's smug face. She knew I liked the sleek, athletic style, so she'd saved it on purpose. The fabric caught the low light, vivid and rich in color, shining like a jewel. I quickly changed while the boys failed miserably at not watching with hungry eyes, telling me they were ready for more. Now.

I gave them a knowing smile and smoothed the skirt over my hips as I couldn't wear panties with the skirt being so tight. *Maybe later,* I thought. *Right now, we have work to do.*

Before stepping out, I snapped a photo of the torn remains of my orange dress on the seat and sent it to Aniyah.

Nov: *Does a ripped dress count as a stained one?*

Her reply came so fast she had to have been waiting for my text.

Niyah: 👑

Niyah: *I'll fucking take it*

Niyah: *Though I'm a little disappointed.*

I shook my head, smiling despite myself.

Nov: *That's all you're getting. Sorry.*

Her response popped up almost instantly.

Niyah: *Fine.*

Niyah: *On a side note, I think Ras is right.*

Niyah: *I might have a cum fetish. WHO KNEW!???*

I groaned under my breath. This must be what Calix felt all the time. Shaking my head, I typed out my response.

Nov: *Another line on the list of things I don't need to know about my sister.*

By the time the car rolled up to the after-party, another ping lit up my wrist.

Niyah: *At least I'm dedicated to my craft. #JoinTheCumSide*

I snorted. "Fucking Aniyah." She was a menace but a loveable one.

24

NOVA

"I don't like splitting up. We should just stick together. Less risky that way." Zeth's voice was edged with concern.

I took a deep breath, reminding myself he wasn't trying to be an overprotective idiot just because we'd fucked. He was just being a good second—cautious and loyal to a fault. *Right?*

"No." I let the finality hit before continuing. "I want to cover more ground. It's not like this is our regular turf, and we don't know the layout of this mansion. Conrad showed us Frank's picture, so if we all look for him, we'll find him faster, and it'll be easier to drag him away from the crowd."

Maybe I'd rough him up a bit, make him regret not coming to me with anything he knew first, but that part didn't need to be said. Turned or born, a supe was a supe, and the Syndicate reigned supreme. He needed to be reminded of that, and I was damn good at reminding these motherfuckers.

The three of them continued to look like they were silently weighing my judgment, and I snapped. My index finger lengthened into a claw. I pointed it straight at Zeth's throat since he was the closest, but I was talking to everyone.

"Do you need me to beat your ass right here and now to remind you who the fucking boss is?"

Zeth's gaze flicked down to the claw, then back up to me. He knew better than to test my patience tonight. After the messy end to the fight, I really needed a win, and getting a lead on this was my only hope.

When I turned the claw toward the others, Nick jerked back like I'd burned him, but Conrad lifted his hands in playful surrender. That earned the smallest curl of a smile from me, and I got a wider grin from Conrad.

Behind closed doors, I might bend to their will, might moan their names into the dark, but when it came to Syndicate business, I was judge, jury, and executioner. No debate. No exceptions.

"So, we're just gonna take him out back and beat the shit out of him until he tells us the answers to our questions?"

Nick's tone wavered between disgust and curiosity. I closed my eyes for a beat, letting the air slide through my lungs. He still didn't get it. I reminded myself that he was still fresh to the supe world and thinking about this through a human lens.

"I run this town," I said, my voice flat, final. "Everything goes through me. People know that. That's why they respect me... or fear me." My voice dropped lower, the words becoming sharp and certain. "I'm the police here. Just not the kind you're used to. Not the kind that wastes time sitting across the table while they question you with a coffee in hand."

His Adam's apple bobbed, and although he glared at me and huffed like I'd personally insulted him, he didn't argue. Damn fragile human.

"Most of the people at this party either work for the Syndicate or are desperate to. For example, the homeowner's a broker trying to get in our good graces, so I saw an opportunity." I shrugged, leaning back into the cool leather seat. "I hate planning parties. Told him if he handled the after-party for this event, I'd put in a good word with Ezra. Now, he's my bitch, which means his house is fair game."

Nick looked to Zeth and Conrad in question, like I was just talking out of my ass, which infuriated me. The former ignored him completely in favor of looking down at his phone, while Conrad gave a small shrug that said everything. *That's just how it is.*

The car rolled to a halt. Zeth reached for his belt as he spoke, already shifting forward. "Let's go. Most of the guests should be inside by now. Frank included."

Agreeing with his assessment even though he was being a little bossy about it, I reached for the door. His hand caught mine mid-motion, firm and possessive.

"I go first."

When I lifted a brow at him, he gave me a sheepish grin. Softening his voice, he reasoned, "It's safer that way."

Before I could say a word, he slipped out, his eyes slicing through the darkness before turning back to me. His gaze softened as he extended his hand and nodded to say it was all clear.

I took it, letting him pull me up since I was in a skirt and not my regular pants. His other hand caught my waist and lifted me. For a second, his eyes dragged down my body and back up, two live flames that burned through me as his thumb ran against the silky fabric at my waist.

He stepped in close, lips hovering next to my ear. "Even though this one isn't ripped up, I don't like it," he murmured. His thumb moved up, brushing the strip of bare skin between my top and the skirt. "Don't like others seeing you like this. It's too tempting." His breath brushed my neck, his voice rough as he muttered, "Makes me want to commit mass murder just to keep the image all to myself."

A shiver slipped down my spine, my knees threatening to give. This wasn't the careful, restrained Zeth who kept his distance and hid behind childhood friendship. This was raw hunger. Possession. This version of him that had been stripped bare and was unafraid to want... I liked it. Too much. Too fucking much.

No one had ever told me they wanted to kill just to protect a memory of me. Twisted as it was, it felt... sweet. *Real*. Proof that this wasn't born from a momentary lapse of judgment or fear of losing me. This side of him had been simmering beneath the surface all along, just waiting for its moment.

Still, he didn't get to have it easy—not after rejecting me.

Brushing my hand up his chest, I leaned in. "Some of these people owe us money," I whispered. "Let's wait to commit mass murder until after they pay up, okay, my second?"

I patted him lightly on the cheek, teasing. His body swayed closer, eyes zeroed in on my lips, his breath growing unsteady.

When his mouth inched toward mine, I slid my hand down his chest—slow, sensual—tilting my head up like I was going to accept whatever he was going to give, before turning my head and strutting away from him. I left him standing there, flushed and frustrated. *Karma's a bitch.*

I felt his gaze burning into my ass as I walked ahead, biting back a grin when he muttered under his breath about smacking that ass later. I liked the way he wanted me, hot, angry, hungry.

Is this how Aniyah always feels? No wonder she strutted around cocky and glowing. No wonder her men could barely keep their hands off her. Was this what it meant to have a mate?

I mentally smacked myself over that single word. The word that I thought I would never utter.

Focus, Nova. Don't start calling them your mates. It's just a tattoo that heats up whenever they're near and a wolf whining in your head. Plus, you have a job, a duty to fulfill first. You have obligations and responsibilities that are more important right now. When all of this is over, we'll figure out what they are—or aren't. For right now, just use the help.

Behind me, Zeth was barking at the others. "Fucking move! Don't stick your hand out like I'm supposed to help you!"

A sharp smack followed, then a threat and the shuffle of feet. I almost looked back but decided against it. *Let them sort it out. They're big boys.*

"I'm going to tell Nova we need to reevaluate who she keeps on staff."

Conrad's smooth voice carried a new edge, sharp enough to make me glance over my shoulder. He was a hard one to rattle, so when it happened, I paid attention.

There they were, Conrad and Zeth, nose-to-nose, each vibrating with barely contained fury. Conrad straightened his jacket with a smug smile that screamed provocation. I rolled my eyes. Those two were fire and ice, opposites that refused to mix.

Still, thinking back to what happened in the car earlier, satisfaction curled low in my stomach. Maybe that friction between them had its uses. Heat and cold—two sides of the same delicious coin, and *I* got to reap the benefits.

"Get your fat asses out of the way!"

Nick shoved past them, exasperation written all over his face. The other men growled in unison at the interruption, but I silently thanked him. Those two needed to keep it to themselves or go into the ring and work it all out. My mind couldn't help it, picturing both of them shirtless, bloody, and sweaty. I bit my lip to keep from offering it as a suggestion. *Later. Maybe later.*

Zeth started ranting about how his ass was tight enough to bounce a coin off of, and Nick's disgusted grimace almost broke my composure. I might've laughed if someone hadn't called out my name.

Every sound around us died. The men's attention snapped to me, then to whoever had spoken, their collective glare sharp enough to strip paint. Another talk I needed to have with them: stop death-staring every man who looked my way.

I turned, forcing a polite smile when I saw it was Mr. Shafer, one of the VIPs for the event, walking toward me with open arms. "Nova Rossey! As I live and breathe. You look stunning."

He leaned in, his overwhelming cologne assaulting my nostrils, and I tried to breathe out of my mouth as he delivered two air kisses. The things I endured for paying clients.

"Oh, you flatter me," I said smoothly. "Did you enjoy the event?" Making a move to head into the house, I nodded to the bouncer at the entrance who was one of my men.

"It was one of the best shows I've seen in ages!" he said, taking a slow sip of his drink. Then came the pause, the telltale hesitation of a man about to ask for something. "I was wondering… what might it cost to arrange something like a private fight? Just for a circle of close friends." His eyes gleamed over the rim of his glass with something dark and depraved. "I'd love to see Deslen fight again."

The moment he said Deslen's name, something feral coiled inside me. My wolf surged up, calling out for his blood, his bones, his throat for penance. I smiled instead, tight and brittle.

"We haven't finished signing Deslen yet," I said, keeping my tone pleasant, "so I don't know his schedule." I motioned for the bouncer to come over. "But we'll take your number and get back to you."

His excitement drained faster than spilled liquor. "Oh. Of course. Please do. No amount of money is a problem. Just name your price."

My smile stayed fixed in place as I imagined how easy it would be to tear this human apart and let him see what a *real* predator looked like. Instead, I nodded toward the bouncer. "Kevin will get your information. I'll be in touch."

Inner Ezra. Just channel your inner Ezra and smile while you picture all the horrible things you will do to this person.

"Now, if you'll excuse me..." I moved around him, patting him on the arm. "I need to greet my other guests." Then I turned and walked toward the entrance, heels clacking against the concrete as I left that asshole in the dust.

"Zeth," I called. He was beside me instantly, every inch the shadow I still relied on.

"Make sure you get his info from Kevin, then I want a deep dive into his life." My jaw ached from how tightly I was clenching it. "I want *everything*—who he does business with, where he eats, who he fucks. Everything."

I stopped, turning toward him with a grin that was downright nasty. "Then give it to Ezra. Tell her he needs to be *drained*. ASAP."

"Drained?" Nick's voice came from my right. Conrad drifted closer, listening.

"If you need someone interrogated, protected, beaten, or scared into talking, you call me," I said. "You want someone's life ruined, their social standing tarnished, every asset gone, every cent in their account bled dry? You send it to Ezra."

A dark laugh slipped free. "She'll make sure that when I call that man, he won't be able to afford a private fight, let alone another ticket to my event again."

Conrad's tone became cold. "And that, Nick, is why the Syndicate's feared. They can be your best friend or your worst enemy. People either bow to them or burn themselves trying to bask in their light."

I turned my head toward him, brow raised. *And which one are you?* I asked silently.

He stepped closer, forest-green eyes locked on mine, his confidence rolling off him in waves. "Lucky me," he said quietly, the vibrations of his voice rolling over my skin, "I like the warmth."

Beside me, Zeth scoffed as he rolled his eyes, but my lips twitched. That was the perfect answer, and he damn well knew it. My mind drifted back to that car and what this man could do with his mouth. *Nova! Not now. Work. Then play.*

Twisting away from him before I did something embarrassing, I stepped through the doorway of the massive three-story mansion packed with people. Music blasted, but you could still hear the buzz of people chattering over it. Everywhere I turned, women were in their glittering finest, showing off their goods, while men pounded shots and boasted about their latest exploits. All of it looked like a whole lot of work just to search for one man. Made me glad I brought extra help today.

"It's time to go hunting, boys." I could feel them circling around my back. "Zeth, you take the perimeter. Nick, you take the first floor. Conrad, you take the second, and I'll take the third." We broke away in unison, with Conrad and I heading up the stairs, Zeth out the door, and Nick moving into the thick of the first floor, all of us in search of our little target: Frank.

Going up the stairs turned into its own kind of obstacle course. Every few steps, someone stopped me to introduce themselves, trying to make small talk I had no interest in. Conrad helped until he got to the second floor and peeled off. By the time I reached the third floor, the press of bodies had thinned and the hum of voices below faded into a low, steady murmur.

Enough people had seen me to confirm I'd made an appearance, which meant I needed to blend in. Plus, I wanted to take Frank by surprise if I found him. The catch was always sweeter that way.

I slipped into an empty corner, tapped the finger reader on the side of my watch, and waited. The faint vibration beneath my fingertip told me the spell was activated, so I closed my eyes and pictured the woman I wanted them to see me as. The image formed of a mid-forties fire mage with chestnut hair, unremarkable brown eyes, and a sharp nose, the kind of face you forgot the moment you looked away.

A shiver of magic rolled across my skin, spreading from my wrist to my shoulders, then down my back to my heels. My reflection in the nearby glass blurred before snapping back into focus, the plain stranger I'd imagined staring back. I waited a few more seconds, giving the rune magic time to settle, then stepped back into the hall.

Gods, I loved my brother. He might be a menace half the time, but when it came to creating things that shouldn't exist, he was a genius. These watches were proof of it. The sleek little devices clung to our wrists like shadows until we called them forth. They were communicators, trackers, and, in the right hands, weapons. But my favorite feature? The cloaking spell.

For people like us, with our rose gold eyes and pale, ashy hair, it was impossible to blend in. We were walking beacons, just like our mom and Tata Ternin, but with one press of a button and a clear image in our mind, we could be anyone. The rune magic didn't just change how we looked; it could wrap us in the energy of another species entirely.

Now, invisible in my fake skin, the crowd's attention slipped right past me. No lingering stares. No interruptions. Just silence and space to move. Perfect for searching the floor in peace.

At first glance, the third floor looked to have several hallways, each with their own set of doorways and openings, which was exhausting. Why did someone need this many damn rooms?

Scanning each hallway, I listened for anything odd, and when I got to the last corridor, the air turned frigid and empty, as if the house had exhaled and forgotten to breathe again. Intrigued, I went down the hallway, seeing the difference in the heavy drapes and rugs that shimmered with magic with each step. The magic was swallowing the sound I was making, which created an eerie sense of silence. The shadows all around didn't feel empty so much as expectant. Hollow.

Quickly, I moved from room to room, pressing my ear to each door, listening for voices or heartbeats before I opened it and searched the space. A dark rosewood bedroom with a chest of sex toys. A study that yielded shelves of books on various rune magic and an old whiskey decanter. A guest chamber smelling of lavender gone stale. Room after room, yet no Frank.

Getting to the end of the hallway, my nose tickled when I closed the door. A thick layer of fine grey residue coated the tabletops. I ran a fingertip along the surface, narrowing my eyes on the thin layer of grime that appeared on my finger.

My eyes flicked around, seeing that the film covered everything. Every door knob, table, and door frame held the same untouched dust... except the second-to-last door on the right. Its brass handle shone bright. *Bingo.*

As I made a beeline for the door, something rolled over me, and my instincts began to scream. *Turn back. Nothing here.* My wolf growled at the intrusion, letting me know it was all false, something conjured with rune magic to steer people away from the door, and I smiled.

Smart, but also telling.

With my mind trained for this kind of magic, I pushed through it and pressed my ear against the door. No movement, no sound, so I cautiously eased a hand toward the knob. A powerful sound rune spell could muffle everything, even if you were having a battle on the other side.

The hand not on the knob shifted into claws, and I crouched low, listening again, searching for the subtlest of signs, but silence was all that answered. Time ticked by with my patience wearing thin.

Fine. I shrugged. *I can handle whatever is past this door. No problem.*

Standing up, I took a step back, rocking my weight back to kick. but my peripherals picked up movement at the mouth of the corridor. I turned to face it just as two shadows slid into the light and broke the hush.

If it was some idiot partygoers, then I just needed to get rid of them. Killing the illusion magic with a tap, I readied myself to tell these two to beat it, but a familiar set of turquoise eyes cut through the dim. Alongside my second was Nick, his brows knit with concern. Great. Backup.

Lifting my index finger to my lips, I pointed to the door I

was about to kick. Zeth came in close, his voice low enough that only I heard it. "Conrad's holding the entrance."

Giving him a thumbs up, I pressed the button on my watch again, letting the disguise shimmer back into place. Nick's nostrils flared; he inhaled the room like a hound catching a new trail, eyes narrowing at my illusion. *Oh, don't like that you can't smell me?*

Ignoring his questioning eyes, I turned back to the door. It was time to find out who was inside.

I stepped forward and planted my foot, aiming for my heel to hit near the handle. Wood exploded under impact in a sharp, splintering crack that turned the silence into a jagged thing. The door swung open, and the room answered.

At the center of the bedroom, a tall man with slicked-back hair and neon-green eyes that had a faint glow was huddled together with just the man we were looking for, Frank. Their arms were stretched out like they had passed something between each other.

Frank was the first to react, snarling at the intrusion. "Who the fuck are you? Get the fuck out!"

Smiling like I didn't hear him, I stepped in further. As soon as I did that, Zeth and Nick entered behind me. The green-eyed man's eyes bounced around, his pulse skyrocketing before his gaze went to the window behind him. It took just a second for him to look at us, then he bolted for the window. Glass crashed to the floor before I could get my first word out.

"Get him!"

Zeth and Nick burst forward, both of them jumping out the

window like shadows unhooked from the wall, going after our now second lead. I turned to face the target.

"Hello, Frank," I called out, hands open wide as I stepped toward him. "I have some questions for you." He gulped, gripping something inside of his jacket. "This might sound a little old fashioned, but... we can do this the easy way," I cracked my knuckles, "or the hard way. Your call."

His face twisted, lips curling in rage. "Who the fuck are you, bitch?!"

I stopped for a second, forgetting I still had on the cloaking spell, and Frank lunged. His full weight slammed me to the floor, the impact cracking through my spine and knocking the air from my lungs. My claws burst free on instinct, raking deep into his back until I felt the tug of tearing skin and warm, slippery liquid beneath my nails. His roar rattled the walls, raw and furious.

Dragging one hand away, I shoved my other hand into his side, claws slicing through muscle like butter. I twisted my hand inside of him until I felt something give. "What the fuck are you doing, Frank? Who was he?"

He swung for my face, but I tilted just enough that his fist met hardwood instead. Throwing his weight to the side, he rolled away from me, staggering to get up while clutching his bleeding side. The wound had already started to knit itself closed, red threads drawing together. I pushed to my knees, chest heaving.

"None of your business, bitch," he spat, voice cracking.

"Wrong answer."

I thumbed the cloaking spell off, and his fury stuttered, collapsing into dread the second my real face surfaced. Fuck,

I loved moments like that, when the break between rage and realization settled in, and they finally understood exactly *who* they'd picked a fight with. The scent of fear always followed close behind, sour and sharp.

Licking at my claws as I stared him down, my bloodied mouth curved into a deceptively soft smile. "Now, tell me, Frank... what were you two talking about?"

Faint laughter carried from the hall. Conrad. I could hear his smooth, calm tone. "Oh, don't worry about the noise. Probably a couple having a great time. I wouldn't mind having some of those wall-shaking times myself, am I right?"

Good. He was keeping people away. My grin stretched wider right before Frank bolted for the window.

"Oh, no, you don't."

I leapt, bones shifting midair, fur bursting along my limbs. My wolf hit the floor in front of him, lips curled, growl rumbling from deep in my chest. He froze, then jerked the hand from his jacket. A gleam caught the low light, thin, deadly. A knife.

"I–I'm not g-going to let him use me," he stammered, trembling. "Not l-letting him use m-my body. It's m-me or y-you. So l-let's go, b-bitch."

His words snagged in my mind. *Use his body?* Before I could ask, a faint shimmer rippled across the blade, catching my eye. Magic was carved into that blade. I took a careful step back.

"That's right!" he shouted, his voice breaking. "He told me to... c-convince you to talk, then k-kill you with this!" Sweat poured down his temples, his skin waxy, eyes fluttering every which way. This man wasn't scared of me; he was scared of someone else. This *him* he was talking about.

He lunged for me, almost catching my side before I jumped back. I needed fucking answers, which meant I couldn't kill him. Looking down at his hands again, I sniffed the air. I couldn't smell any elemental magic enhancements, which meant it was spellwork I didn't recognize.

We circled each other, his breath hitching and my claws flexing into the hardwood. Every twitch of his wrist, every flick of his gaze, I watched for my opening. I only needed one. When a faint voice echoed down the hall, his eyes flicked toward the sound. That was when I lunged.

He moved faster than I expected, but instead of trying to slice me up, he threw it at me. Unable to dodge it fully, it sliced up my inner thigh.

White-hot agony tore through me, followed by a pain unlike anything I'd ever known.

The damn knife felt like it *bit* into me.

My wolf screamed inside my skull, a sound that was halfway strangled to silence as she was shoved back then ripped away from me. My wolf body shifted mid-leap. Flesh, not fur, hit the floor.

The world tilted, colors too bright, sound too sharp. My thigh pulsed wet beneath my palm, and I gripped the wound as hard as I could until my hands began to shake, blood slipping between my fingers. The cut was deep, main artery deep, and it wasn't closing.

It wasn't fucking closing. That was not good.

My eyes started to go out of focus as I heard him mutter, "I-I have to kill you." His voice came from the other side of the room. He fumbled with something, and I heard a bullet load into a chamber. "I n-need to kill Nova Rossey. I need to k-kill you. It's the o-only way."

Hearing my name pass his lips sent rage slicing through the haze, and I used all my strength to roll where my instincts told me to. A gunshot split the air right beside my ear.

I rolled until I felt something hard stop me. A wall. Still disoriented, I tried to keep my wits about me. I sat up with my back to the wall, trying to figure out my next move.

A roar sliced through the air in front of me. This one was deep, guttural, feral. It filled the room, shaking dust from the ceiling.

Frank screamed. The crunching sound of bone meeting bone filled the air, something ripping in between the cracks until a wet gurgling sound was all that was left.

I pressed my hand to my thigh, trying to blink away the dizzy state I was in while searching for my wolf in my mind. She was there, but it was like there was a wall between us, thick and humming. The magic was still burning under my skin, eating away at the edges of my power.

Except for my heartbeat and the faint drag of something heavy moving, the room was quiet. I reached out with my senses, tasting blood and magic in the air. *Focus. Anticipate.*

A light tread, four-footed and careful, slowly moved closer, but it wasn't the pattern of a predator hunting. Each step was slow, cautious, hesitant. The air shifted with it, carrying a wave of emotion that wasn't mine: sorrow, regret, fierce protectiveness that wrapped around the edges of my fear.

I should've flinched when something wet pressed against my thigh, but I didn't. Focusing on what this beast was doing, I realized it was using its tongue to lick at my wound. Warm, steady, and deliberate, it coaxed the heat and pain out of my body until my breath evened and the shaking slowed.

Somewhere in that strange rhythm, my body began to relax on its own. The wall between me and my wolf thinned, threads of gold weaving through the dark. The licking became less insistent, more soft, lightly tracing my skin, and heat curled low in my belly. I let go of the fear, the pain, the fight, just *felt*.

The magic's burn faded as my pulse steadied. My wolf stirred beneath my skin again, no longer locked away.

Whoever the creature was, I could feel it. An apology pulsed through every careful touch, each deep breath. This creature was taking care of me like it owed me, like it was mine.

The tongue shifted upward, just shy of my center, and I couldn't help the soft moan that tore from my throat. The licking continued, slow and deliberate this time. I didn't know what was going on with my body, but the more the beast licked at my skin, the more liquid my bones became. My legs moved, falling open, thighs trembling as pleasurable magic raced up and down my back.

The change between emergency healing and sensual tasting came quickly. The air around me shifted, and hands gripped me, fingers digging into my flesh as they spread me even wider. The voice that followed was low, accented, breaking on the words. "My mate. My love."

Then a long, wet stroke lapped at my center, and my spine turned into jelly. My mind was muddled with magic and pleasure, not letting reason make its way through.

"More." The word scraped out of me, barely recognizable. The familiar scent of spicy warm strawberries filled my lungs, and I let it seep into my pores, wanting to drown in it.

The hesitation vanished. His mouth worked me over, nipping, licking, mapping every inch of me. My breath caught. Stopped. Started again in short, desperate bursts. A whine built in my chest.

Each touch came slowly. Deliberately. Heat layered upon heat, building in waves that never crested. My hands fisted against the hardwood beneath me, nails biting into my palms. My hips rolled, seeking more pressure, more friction, more everything.

My vision sharpened, then it blurred again as I squeezed my eyes shut. He held me there, balanced on a cliff's edge, never letting me fall.

"Please." My voice cracked.

Forcing my eyes open, I looked down to see the wound on my thigh was now smooth, sealed skin. Below it, rich brown hands touched with gold were curled around my thighs, the strength of his hold whitening his knuckles.

I looked up. Pale yellow eyes stared back. Dark loose strands fell around his face like a lace curtain. His mouth glistened.

"Please what?" His rumble vibrated through my bones.

I blinked again before recognizing who it was. Deslen. He was on his knees in front of me, resting between my bare legs. His smile curved, slow and knowing. His tongue dragged across his bottom lip like he never wanted to stop tasting it, tasting *me*.

"Please," I called out absently, my gaze completely captured by the movement of his tongue. "Make me come."

Light flooded his expression before something sharper replaced it. One hand slid down my thigh, and he leaned in toward my face, close enough to smell myself on his lips. A shudder rolled through me, and I almost closed my eyes again until his forehead met mine. His hair fell forward, shutting out everything else.

"I would kill hundreds—" Two fingers pushed inside me. I gasped, back arching. "—thousands, for you, my heart."

His fingers moved. In. Out. The rhythm threatened to unravel me. His forehead pressed against mine harder, grounding me, calling me to look deep into his eyes.

"I want to kill that man all over again for daring to hurt what's mine."

My heart slammed against my ribs. Heat flooded my cheeks. Pressure built behind my chest like it was getting ready to break open.

A moment of rational thought hit me at that moment, clearing my mind of whatever was happening between us. He didn't know me. How could he be so sure? How could he give his whole heart so readily? *And to me?*

Unable to keep my desires at bay anymore, I surged forward, crashing my mouth against his. The taste of us together, a slice of sweet magic with a twinge of copper, caused a moan to vibrate between our lips. The mark on my arm flared white-hot, but I couldn't focus on anything except his mouth, his fingers, and this moment.

A third finger entered, stretching me, and stars burst behind my eyelids.

His hand wrapped around my throat, tilting my head back as he swallowed my gasps. His thumb found my clit and circled, firm, relentless. Three fingers pumped hard and fast, pushing me over the edge as my body locked up, clenching so hard I felt like something might break.

The orgasm that ripped through me spread across my body, and I tore away from his mouth, crying out his name.

He groaned against my neck, teeth sinking in hard. Wet heat splashed across my stomach, and for one glorious second, I felt it. That connection. That golden thread of a bond. Fate tying us together.

Footsteps thundered. Voices shouted my name as my mind came back online. Conrad. Zeth. Nick. I looked up to see all three of them stumbling to a halt in the doorway.

A growl tore from Deslen's chest. He shifted into a massive black jaguar, covering me with his body until he paused. When he took a few sniffs toward the three of them, the tension drained from his shoulders.

He shifted back into his human form. Standing before them, smiling brightly, he extended his hand to them. Completely naked.

"Oh! I didn't know I was blessed with mate-brothers." His confident voice was peppered with excitement. "I'm Deslen. So happy to finally join the pack!"

One second passed, then another. None of them moved to shake his hand. Instead, three sets of eyes dropped to me on the floor instead. Three identical expressions silently said, *'This is your fault.'*

Fuck.

25

ZETH

The scent of blood hit me first, sharp and metallic, before we even cleared the hallway. Not just any blood. *Hers.* That faint floral sweetness that always clung to Nova's skin now coated the hallway, too thick to mistake. My pulse roared, breath catching in my throat.

Conrad's eyes snapped to mine, Nick's jaw locked, and without a word, we broke into a run. The scent grew heavier the closer we got, clinging to the walls and crawling under my skin. It wasn't a trace; it was a flood. Something that never should have happened.

We shouted her name, our voices echoing down the corridor, but the silence that answered only made the scent of blood stronger.

Why? The word kept looping in my head, a drumbeat I couldn't shake. Nova didn't bleed, not like this. Her body healed faster than most, a living wall against pain. Whatever happened had to be bad... and I wasn't there to protect her.

With a heavy, guilt-riddled soul, I shot through the door. The sight of her blood splattered across the floor had my heart stopping cold.

Frank was sprawled across the floor, eyes glassy with terror, throat torn wide open. His chest looked like something had ripped through it barehanded. Jagged tears, splintered ribs, and blood painted across the walls in wild, desperate strokes. A heart sat a few feet away, two fang-shaped holes in the center, crushed under what looked like a massive paw print.

I swallowed hard. None of it explained the scent still flooding the air, the sweet, unmistakable trace of Nova.

A ribbon of crimson led away from Frank and ended at Nova. She was slumped against the wall, the floor around her soaked in dark crimson blood. Deslen knelt between her legs, chest heaving like he'd run until his lungs burned. Both of them were naked and looking at each other like the world stopped and started with the other. The sight punched the air out of me.

Deslen's head snapped up the instant he smelled us. His human form twisted, shaping into the massive jaguar we'd seen at the fight, purposely shielding Nova from our view.

That move lit a fuse in my chest; my hands went ice cold and my jaw locked. I tasted violence along my tongue as my power surged at my fingertips. Every part of me wanted blood. I could see the plan in my head. Grab him, make him answer, make him pay. Conrad and Nick were close enough to help; the math checked out.

The jaguar began to sniff around, moving toward us, and I saw its pale yellow eyes flare wide. His wild fae magic unfurled, and he shifted back into his human form with a bright, curious, almost playful attitude. He rose as fluid as a tide, massive and tall, dick swinging as he took a few steps toward us. A wide grin broke across his face like sunlight. It immediately pissed me off.

"Oh! I didn't know I was blessed with mate-brothers." The words were a sucker punch straight to the gut. Deslen's teeth flashed, eyes bright. "I'm Deslen. So happy to finally join the pack!"

Join... the what? My brain stalled.

Peering around his tall, naked form, I looked at Nova for an explanation. She was naked, too, knees snapping together, a sheepish, exhausted smile tugging at her lips. I knew that look. My chest tightened painfully.

Never in all the time I'd known her had I seen her shield herself while naked. It was a natural state for a werewolf. My eyes bounced between her and Deslen. Obviously, something had happened between them.

She cleared her throat before asking firmly, "Did you catch him?"

Wrong question. My teeth ground together against the urge to ask it. To demand to know what just happened between them. Instead, I settled for, "What happened to Frank?"

She shrugged, pushing herself upright to stand. Deslen darted after her, fussing like an overzealous mother hen, murmuring warnings to be careful and let the magic fully heal her leg.

Magic? Heal her? My brow shot up, and my pulse ticked faster. What the hell had happened to her leg?

"Oh, it's fine now," she said, waving off his concern. "We just need to know if they caught the runaway guy since we killed this lead." She tossed the words out carelessly, rolling her eyes as she nodded toward Frank. Her fingers were locked on Deslen's arm, and her right leg stayed bent, trembling slightly.

I caught it. The weakness. The way she was pretending. She was seriously hurt and didn't want us to know. Then it hit me.

I wasn't there. Not when it happened. Not when she needed someone to stop it. That was supposed to be *me.* My job. My goddamn reason for existing. The hole inside me, the one that had been shrinking since we last talked, ripped open again, dragging everything I had into its pool of despair.

Half-mad with guilt, I almost stepped forward and grabbed her, ready to demand answers, but Conrad brushed past all of us, slow and calm, as if he hadn't just walked into a shit storm. He grabbed a towel from the bathroom, returned to her side, and pressed a kiss against her hairline before wiping at her stomach.

She flinched, though it was more out of surprise, before her cheeks burned. What was he cleaning?

"Why don't we start," he said softly, his eyes flicking to Deslen accusingly, "with why you were sitting in a pool of your own blood. I think I need to know that first."

Her brows knitted, eyes cold, lips pressed into a thin line. I knew that look, the one that made people stop talking and fall in line. The one that always made *me* back down, but not this time. Not with this black hole of despair clawing through my ribs, begging for the truth before it swallowed me whole.

My eyes slipped shut, and I drew in a slow breath, letting my power unfurl like smoke under a door. Soft, silent, invisible. Making sure not to go too fast, not to probe, I coaxed it to seep in like it was as natural as air.

Nick was closest, so I brushed against him first.

The first spark was anger, hot and metallic, snapping against my fingertips, but beneath it pulsed something else, something warm and electric—the tug of admiration, the ache of wanting. For Nova. Buried even deeper was a twisted knot of fear. Not fear of *her* but more of what she might see if she looked too close.

Before I could follow that thread, a flash of molten fury burned through my senses. Conrad. Surprising. *I didn't know the bloody bastard could feel something deeper than a spoonful.*

The air around him felt charged, dangerous, yet his face was calm, perfectly controlled. He smiled at Nova even as his eyes darted toward the dark pool of her blood on the floor. The wrath surged again, hidden behind that steady pulse and practiced restraint. Our resident turned vampire had a tighter leash on his emotions than the rest of us right now, and I was almost impressed.

My magic reached for Deslen next, my lip curled up in annoyance. He was exactly what he looked like: sunlight and laughter, radiating joy so bright it almost stung. Anger flickered when his gaze caught the body on the floor, but the moment he looked at Nova, that melted into something blinding, pure unfiltered bliss. Pride and gratefulness settled over him as he looked at her hand on his arm, and I immediately wanted to gut punch him.

As my power reached Nova, I let it hover instead of touch,

just close enough to sense the emotions she didn't keep locked up. If I brushed against her directly, she'd know.

Frustration hit first. No surprise there. She hated losing control, but then, underneath the irritation, something colder peeked out. Something quieter... something kind of like... fear.

Such an emotion was so foreign to her that I almost didn't believe it.

It wasn't the kind that came from enemies, expectations, or the weight of her family name. This was personal. Her eyes darted between us, her body tight with tension like she was waiting for something to happen.

I jerked in realization and snapped my power back inside me, breaking the connection.

The woman who could stare down a horde of enemies with claws and a smile was terrified of losing people, even the people that were meant for her. She was terrified of being rejected again.

And every ounce of that fear was my fault.

"A knife?!" Nick's voice cracked through the air, dragging me out of my thoughts. His eyes were wild, jaw set. "A *fucking knife*? I thought your body regenerated! I thought it was like... basically indestructible?"

She shrugged away his panicked tone, casually blowing it off in a way that ticked me off. "It was magicked... somehow."

The word hung there—*magicked*—like that explained anything.

We all glanced around the floor again, looking for anything

that resembled a knife, but nothing was here. Nothing but the heavy scent of iron and the residue of active magic.

"It was cursed," Deslen murmured, eyes distant. "Ancient fae magic." His brows knitted together, confusion bleeding into his voice. "But that kind of magic was sealed away before I was born. It shouldn't even exist in this realm."

Conrad's tone was all business. "To recap. He stabbed you, and your body didn't heal—fine. So how are you standing here now without an open, bloody wound?"

A flush crept up Nova's neck, staining her skin pink. She shifted her weight, eyes darting to the floor.

Deslen answered, all smiles and softness, as he brushed his nose against her hair. "When it comes to mates, jaguar saliva neutralizes any toxin. I licked the wound clean with my magic, and it closed up."

I bet you fucking did, was on the tip of my tounge, but Nova's voice came out fast, sharp, cutting through the tension.

"It wasn't just the cut. I couldn't reach my wolf. It was like— like something had slammed a wall between us." She shook her head and closed her eyes. "I could feel her, but I couldn't *reach* her."

With all of us in thought, heavy silence dropped over the room until Nick threw his hands up. "So he licked your leg, it healed, your wolf came back, and you fucked a stranger?"

Nova's head snapped to him, and she took an angry step toward him when a low growl vibrated from his chest.

Deslen moved before I could blink. Tall, naked, and furious, he slid right between them. His easy grin was gone, replaced with a frown carved in stone.

"First," he said, his steady voice edged with something primal, "my mate was hurt. I was going to do anything to make her feel better. *Anything.*" His golden eyes flicked toward Nova, softening. "Second, we didn't fuck. She gave me permission to give her pleasure, making her feel grounded in the middle of all that chaos. I won't let you twist that. Not even if you are my mate-brother."

The words landed like a blow you didn't see coming.

Nova's eyes lifted, a flicker of warmth breaking through her guarded expression for just a heartbeat. I caught it, the spark of memory, the quiet relief she'd felt with him. My gaze slipped to her arm, where inky truth bloomed against her skin. I already knew what he said was true... she did, too.

Nick looked like he was splitting apart from the inside out. His face flushed bright before folding into something raw, something filled with shame and confusion. Deslen's calm tone seemed to dismantle him piece by piece. For once, I was glad to keep my mouth shut.

"Mate-brother?" Nick barked, his voice cracking. "You keep calling me that! I don't know what that even means, but I *don't* have a mate!" Nova's jaw clenched, but that fear flickered in her eyes.

Nick's gaze darted between us wildly, desperate for someone to save him from the truth already clawing its way out of him.

Conrad's voice came next, almost gentle. "Well, I know that *I'm* your mate," he said, eyes locked on Nova. "At least one of them, it seems."

He lifted his hand slowly, reaching toward her. She flinched, and a slice of pain crossed that controlled face. Still, he pressed on, fingertips brushing the skin at the back of her throat. "My mark is here."

Nova flinched and gasped, a sound that was half-breath, half-recognition. Her eyes burned as he pulled back, his gaze daring her to deny it.

The words spilled from me before I could stop them. "You know I'm your mate, Nova." My chest tightened as her shoulders bowed like the truth was too heavy. I exhaled, feeling the fight drain out of me. Acceptance tasted bitter, but it was the only way forward. "And as much as I hate to admit it," I jerked a thumb toward Nick, "this confused bastard's your mate, too… whether he can admit it or not."

Nick's jaw worked soundlessly. Nova's breath came in short bursts, eyes darting between us like a trapped animal.

"And him," I said, nodding toward Deslen. "He's the last one. The final mate."

I dragged a hand over my face, fingers catching in my hair, tugging just to feel some pain on the outside.

Conrad's brow furrowed. "How do you know that?"

I pointed to Nova's arm. "Because that's showing."

Everyone looked down.

From her forearm, dark lines spiraled upward, covering her bicep in inked vines that curled into four buds of wolfsbane. Each one was pulsing faintly as if alive.

Nova stared at them, her shoulders slumping. "Oh, fuck."

The resignation in her voice said everything. She didn't have to say it out loud. She and I both knew what that meant.

"What?" Nick's voice cracked, pitching higher as his panic bled through. "What does that tattoo mean?"

Nova's head snapped toward me, seeking, trusting, and, for just a heartbeat, I soaked in it. That look. The silent pull between us. She *still* turned to me first, even when surrounded by the others. That was something no number of mates could ever erase.

I'd been there before all of them as her childhood friend, her second, her anchor when everything else spun out. The tightness that had been coiling in my chest every time I saw her giving them her attention eased just a little.

"Tell them," I said quietly. The words weren't a command, just a nudge. It was her truth to speak, and they should hear it from her.

Her face fell. Chin dipped. The silence stretched until it snapped, then the words flowed out of her. "I had a mate-blocker tattoo put on after I became the Rossey boss."

Conrad's eyes flashed in realization, his lips flattening into a thin, pained line. Nick blinked, confusion twisting his face as he stared at the ground. But Deslen looked like someone had kicked the ground out from under him. He grabbed her shoulders, turning her toward him.

"You tried to block me? *Block us?*" His voice cracked, raw and bleeding. "Why, Nova? *Why?*"

Guilt churned low in my gut at the hurt lacing his words, the truth settling in hard. I was the reason she'd chosen that path.

Her eyes, glassy but unbroken, locked on mine. The unspoken truth passed between us, heavy and choking. We knew the price of what we'd done.

Before she could speak, a voice from the hall shattered the tension.

"Hey! Look! Someone broke the third-floor window!"

"Do you think there was a fight?"

"Where is the body?"

We all froze, glancing at Frank's mangled form. That would be a problem if someone came by this. Especially a human.

Nova inhaled once, and everything about her shifted. The tears vanished, swallowed back. Her posture straightened, her shoulders squared. In the span of a heartbeat, the vulnerable woman before us disappeared, replaced by the boss. By *Nova Rossey*.

"We don't have time for this," she said, her flat tone cleanly cutting through the air. "If my actions hurt you, I'm sorry, but right now, I have something more pressing to handle. A poison has infiltrated my territory, and I need to handle it."

When no one said anything, she sighed. "We can talk later about," she waved her hands around all of us, "all of this, but not before this is resolved." Her last words were exacting and final.

Her gaze swept over us, sharp and commanding, her unsaid words part question, part decree. *Agree or get out of my way.*

And really, what choice did we have? She wasn't just our mate right now; she was our *boss*. Well, technically mine, Nick's, and now Deslen's.

Her voice sliced through the silence. "Nick, Zeth, what happened to the man you were chasing?"

Nick jumped in fast, words tumbling over each other. "His natural scent was faint, almost gone, but his fear—yeah, that reeked. We tracked that all the way to a canyon."

I clasped my hands behind my back, giving her my report. "While following him, we saw him pass through a rock illusion. That's probably why none of our men spotted the place before as it looks like a regular rock face."

Nick rolled his eyes and covered his face with his hands, though that failed to muffle his words. "Told you we should've gone after him."

"I didn't want to follow because I knew Nova would want to handle this situation herself," I said.

"Zeth's right."

Nova's words landed like a pat on the shoulder and a victory horn at once. I couldn't resist the smirk I shot at Nick. He growled under his breath, lip curling. Yep. He was definitely starting to get in tune with his wolf side.

Nova turned back to business. "I want to be there when we catch these bastards, and I want to see if that substance shows up again. If that cave is a base, we need to know. It's smarter, and safer, when more eyes are on the area."

The air in the room shifted, becoming focused. No more emotions clawing through the space, just her clarity, her command. The Nova I knew best. The one who made chaos look like structure. For the first time in days, I felt... useful again, like I was doing what I was meant to do.

"Timing is everything," she continued. "He thinks he got away, so we still have the element of surprise on our side." Her gaze circled the room, locking with each of ours in turn. "Five of us should be able to handle whatever's waiting."

I gave a curt nod, filling my role as her second, her enforcer, the one who always had her back, then threw a look at the others that said, *'fall in line.'*

"Then it's settled." Nova clapped her hands. "You two lead the way."

She glanced at Frank before pulling out her phone and lifting it to her ear, mumbling to herself. "Please have someone nearby, Riot. Plea—Oh, hey, Ri! Is there any chance you have someone free… like, now, near my location?"

While she finished setting up a clean-up crew for Frank, I picked up her clothes and helped her put them on while she talked. Just like normal.

She looked at the skirt and sliced it with her claws, making it into strips of fabric from the thigh down, ensuring she could move.

Once she was done, she turned, then paused, eyes sliding toward Deslen. The corner of her mouth twitched as her gaze dipped lower.

"Des," she said dryly, "pretty sure we've got time for you to find some pants."

WE MOVED through the trees in a tight line, careful and quiet, every step placed with purpose. The solid rock face we'd watched him enter was just ahead. No guards. No movement. Just stillness.

Nick crouched near the entrance, eyes gleaming. "Right here," he whispered. "Marked a few lines of sight so I wouldn't lose it."

Nova nodded, studying the rock face. "Good thinking, Nick."

He straightened up a little too fast, shoulders pulling back, pride flickering across his face. When he caught me watching, he forced a frown, but it didn't quite stick.

"Deslen," Nova murmured, eyes still on the cave. "You feel any of that ancient magic?"

He shook his head. "No. Just regular runes. Mage work, nothing fae."

She inhaled, rolling her shoulders once before stepping closer to the rock. "Stick with me, boys," she said, a crooked grin tugging at her mouth. "I'll go slow."

The chuckle that followed wasn't much, but it broke the tension just enough. Her confidence, her steadiness, was the thread holding us all together. Without her, this team would unravel in seconds. Nick would be dead for sure, trying to go into this place on his own like he was on some cop show.

When she pressed forward, crossing the threshold of the illusion, magic tore away like fabric. We followed close behind, stepping into a hollow that smelled of damp stone and desperation.

The cavern opened wide, stone walls curving overhead in a low-ceiling dome. No sound. No movement. No life. The silence was so complete it felt wrong, like the cave itself had died.

Nova raised her hand and motioned us forward, her steps light but sure. We followed the narrow passage deeper until she froze, one fist lifted.

Instantly, we stilled.

She pressed herself flat against the wall, head tilted, listening.

"Did you see how fast Netch bolted to the boss?" someone muttered. "Wonder what happened."

Nova looked at me and flicked a finger, giving me the signal. Closing my eyes, I eased my power out like a searching hand and let it creep along the floor.

There were four relaxed but annoyed signatures. The two closest to us were vampires, then there were two further inside, but they were surrounded by a massive crowd of fear and pain. It was so thick I could taste it on the tip of my tongue, so I pulled my magic back.

I held up two fingers and made a fist, then two more and pointed forward, signaling where our targets were.

A rough laugh sounded. "Nah. That idiot's on his last leg. Been messing up jobs, not bringing in quality products. Slipping. This was his last chance to prove himself, and if he fails, he's toast."

Another voice, softer and meaner, chimed in. "Nah, his task was the hard one, rounding up the subjects. Our job's simple, keep 'em here until Doc picks one. Poor bastards. Have you seen what the doc does?" His disgust slid through the words, and it made me curious. If idiots like them were queasy about it, then whatever this "doc" did had to be bad.

Nova's hand stabbed toward Conrad and Deslen, and she mouthed an order to take out the guards closest to us when she gave the signal.

Chains clinked down the corridor, a metallic staccato. One of the voices snapped, "Shut the hell up! This fighting crap stops now. Accept it's over for you and sit the fuck down, or I'll go in and break you."

"Dude," the quieter one hissed, "you can't touch the merch."

"He can't hear a thing," the angry one scoffed.

"He's just down the hall." The nervous voice dipped lower, speaking more urgently. "He could call Doc, and then you'll be the one in the cage."

Nova traced a cuffing motion around her wrists then pointed to me and Nick—*free the prisoners*.

I tapped her hand to get her attention, my expression asking what she was going to do. A dangerous grin spread across her face as she ran a finger over her throat. No words needed. She was going to find the head of this mess and give him exactly what he deserved.

Nova motioned to all of us once, then nodded. When the voices down the hall moved away, she gave us the signal, and we silently moved into position and followed her.

Deslen blurred out of formation first. Fur and teeth swallowed his human frame in a blink. Outside of Nova, I'd never seen anyone shift that fast. Launching forward like a bullet, his jaws clamped around his target's face. The sound of cracking bone bounced off the wall, followed by the wet squelching of bodies being torn apart.

Conrad zipped past me, fingers clenched around another vampire guard's throat in an iron grip. He lifted the man until his feet kicked uselessly.

"Pathetic," he growled. "Picking on turned's that are weaker than you." His hand squeezed, and the vampire's cheeks puffed purple. The idiot clawed at his arms, trying to get free, but it was no use. Conrad was stronger than I thought.

As the guard's legs dangled, Conrad's hand dug into his pants, snatching a ring with some keys and a blank key card from his pockets. He hurled them at me without looking, as if he didn't have time to bother with me. "I'm a little frustrated right now, wishing I could be inside my mate, but I'm learning that violence is the next best thing. I'm warning you… this is going to hurt." His fangs popped out, then he savagely tore into the vampire's neck.

I tongued my teeth to keep from smiling. I might not like the guy all that much, but he seemed to be learning. It seemed you *could* make a gangster out of a businessman… with the right motivation.

A SCREAM SOUNDED, and I turned to see a large black wolf tearing a vampire's chest apart, piece by piece, with his claws and fangs in the most savage, unprofessional way, but fuck if it didn't get the job done. It must hurt like a bitch.

SEEING the fourth guard about to jump on Nick's back to save his buddy, I pushed my power across the ground and into him, dialing up his fear until he was too stunned to fight me off. Taking out the magic gun from my waistband, I aimed it just right and shot him in his back. As soon as the bullet hit his heart, he stopped and fell to the ground with a thud.

A flash of white hair streaked past us, Nova running deeper into the cave. In a matter of seconds, she was swallowed up by darkness until she was nothing more than a vague silhouette against the black.

My chest narrowed with every step she took from my sight. The last time we were apart, she'd come back broken and with another mate. I didn't think I could handle any more surprises like that.

She is your boss, your best friend, your mate. Trust her.

Taking a breath, I turned away from where she'd disappeared to see Nick. He'd changed back into his human form and somehow found time to put on his pants. I knew that his human brain was the reason for that, but I had to shake my head anyway. Didn't other turned supes acclimate quicker than this? Why was he being so fucking stubborn?

If he looked in the mirror, he would see his mouth, hands, and chest covered in the blood and guts of the beings he'd just mauled. Yet, here he was, wasting time on pants before he went to the cages. He was either really shy about his dick or struggling with his other half. *Not my problem,* I reminded myself.

I came up to his side as he was frantically trying to pry open the lock to the door, which was obviously magicked to handle supe strength. When I dangled the keys Conrad gave me in his face, he glared at me like he wished he could incinerate me before snagging them out of my hand and making quick work of getting us inside.

"*Shit.*" Nick's whisper broke the quiet as the magical walls around the cages lowered, and I followed his stare to a cage. It was full of bodies, some scrunched into corners, some huddled in groups, others sitting alone, rocking in the center. They all had their wrists, ankles, and necks cuffed to heavy individual chains. All of them were turned supes.

Muzzles were clamped over most of their mouths, even the vampires. Dirt crusted their hair, and all of their eyes were hollowed out with the same raw terror. No need for my power to tell me how they felt.

Nick went into hero mode, kneeling before the first person in front of him, a werewolf woman, as he felt around for a lock, but there was nothing. Examining the collars further, I followed the large chain from their feet, hands, and neck, all the way around to the back of their head where a black panel connected the chain. No padlock, no visible latch.

Fingering the plastic in my hand, I looked down at the card Conrad tossed me and had an idea. I slid it over the black panel and waited for a few seconds, thinking I was wrong, until I heard a beep, and the screen blinked green. All three locks released in one synchronous thud that made everyone around her jump. Chains hit dirt.

The werewolf woman scrambled away from her corner. Grabbing onto the cage to help her get up, she stumbled out of the cage and onto the ground. She pressed her face to the earth, sobs wracking her body, and I couldn't help but see the scars littering her skin. It didn't make any sense unless... this doctor was testing more than just that enhancement substance.

I had glanced at the tunnel Nova had gone down, about to tell Nick to figure the rest out, when I felt a hand land on my leg. She turned around and clutched at Nick and me like we were anchors, her tears washing weeks of grime from her cheeks.

"Thank you," she cried, her voice torn and raspy. "I didn't want to die like the others. One of that cruel man's experiments."

I wanted to ask her more questions and learn what she knew, but the rest of the captured beings suddenly scooted toward us as fast as they could. Looking back at the tunnel then the prisoners, I knew what Nova would want me to do.

"Fucking hell, let's get this over with," I complained.

Nick and I moved with practiced, efficient hands, passing the key card between us, freeing the rest of the prisoners until only one small person was still stuck in a corner. I stopped in my tracks. That small form was human. A boy.

The lock clattered to the ground, yet the boy clung to the cage, telling us he wouldn't go. He promised his dad he would stay here and be a good boy. I watched Nick's eyes close, then his face completely changed. A calm, commanding voice came out.

When the boy heard that we were here to get him out and find his dad, his head turned, those wide eyes looking at both of us before narrowing on Nick. Finally, he let go of the cage and stood up on shaky limbs. "A-are you O-officer Cordova?" he cried, wiping at the tears collecting in his eyes. "M-my dad told me… t-their was an o-officer that turned. A-are you h-here to s-save us?"

The boy collapsed into Nick's frozen arms, sobbing and begging him to save his dad.

Cordova. The name stuck in my brain, twirling it over and over. Nick's jaw went slack, his whole back tensed up, and warning bells went off in my head. He hugged the boy back, telling him that we were going to try our best, but as soon as he glanced back at me, I knew something was wrong. His eyes were shut down, not giving away any emotion, and that was telling in and of itself.

Something in me snapped. I grabbed him by the neck and hauled Nick away from the boy before I slammed him against the nearest cage. Metal screamed underneath him, and he grunted in pain. Conrad and Deslen lunged, arms out, and grabbed me, their voices sharp with warning, but I didn't listen. Something was off, something that held the metallic tang of betrayal.

I shook off Deslen and Conrad, lunged forward, and gripped Nick's throat, squeezing it until I felt his Adam's apple throb. His eyes darted around the space, pleading. I could feel the fear coming off him, but not for his life. No. It was because of all the lies he had told us.

"Who the fuck are you!" He spat out curses, telling me I was crazy, so I squeezed harder. I could sense that he was trying to shift, but he didn't have the training to do it under pressure. "I'm only going to ask one more time. Who the fuck are you, *Officer Cordova?*"

2 6

NOVA

Seeing Zeth and Nick head for the cages, I went for the dark passage ahead, the one that screamed, "The boss hangs out here!" He'd have some of the answers I needed.

A flicker of satisfaction sparked low in my chest as I watched the others move together, efficient and deadly. My crew. My —*fuck.* I'd just wanted to call them *mates.*

Admitting it felt like a punch to the ribs, but the warmth that filled the space was nice and calming. My head dipped, and there it was, the tattoo winding up my arm. The inked vines shimmered, the buds at their tips glowing soft as they pulsed. I could *feel* them, like their roots were reaching inside of me, knocking against the locked door where I'd kept my heart buried. All they needed was permission to come in.

I clenched my fist. *No. Not now.*

There was still a bastard to find, a bastard who knew things. I didn't have time to waste on glowing vines and soul-bonded men. Maybe *that* was the reason Ezra had pushed for the tattoo in the first place—to keep us from being distracted.

My heart thudded harder despite knowing that. My wolf stirred restlessly, prowling just beneath the skin. She wanted this done, fast, so she could get back to *them.*

The same wolf that had slept for years, waking only for blood and battle, now panted at the thought of her mates. Who knew she would be like this? I didn't.

Snarling under my breath, I told her to get her head on straight, squared my shoulders, and pressed on. The faster I tore through this boss and got what we needed, the faster I could figure out what the hell this bond meant... for all of us.

Just as the rockface veered left, a cry split the air, sharp and desperate. It was followed by the wet sound of flesh parting under a blade and a rhythmic chant that made my skin crawl. *What the fuck is that?*

I pressed my back to the wall, inching forward until I could peer around the bend.

The space beyond opened into a crude excuse for an office. A desk cobbled together from crates was off to the side. Atop it, a lantern burned low, and papers were scattered like fallen leaves all over the ground. In the center stood a bulky turned werewolf in human form, his eyes an unnatural green that glowed like chemical fire.

I knew every pack in my territory, every scent that drifted through my streets, and his smell didn't belong to any of them. He was a ghost in my domain... one who'd been hiding right under my fucking nose.

"No looze endz," he said, voice flat and accented. I thought it was Russian since the s's turned into z's. The knife in his hand pulsed faintly as he said that chant again. Threads of magic lifted off the corpse at his feet, drawing into the blade until it flared violet then settled.

Pain tugged at my thigh, sharp and sudden. That knife. The one Frank had sliced me with. How the hell did this bastard have *that* knife?

He lifted his head slightly, nostrils flaring as he stared into the black space around him. "I can smell you, Syndicate," he said, almost amused. "Your kind always holds the stench of power."

So much for stealth.

I straightened and stepped out into the open. "You know," I said back, my voice edged with a grin, "that's the first time anyone's used 'power' and 'stench' in the same sentence. Pretty sure that's not the compliment you think it is."

His head tipped back as laughter boomed through the cave, bouncing off stone until it sounded less human and more monster—low, cold, and far too pleased with himself.

He lazily waved the knife, the blade catching the dim light as his smile curved sharp.

"You know," he said almost playfully, "I told them we should just *take* you. Change you. Watch that confidence in your eyes fade the moment real power sinks its claws into you. The moment you *understand* what it feels like to know you're inferior."

I made a show of kicking at the ground and pouting my lips. "Aw, shucks," I said. "Guess I'll have to stay like this, then. Just plain old, awesome me."

A chuckle escaped him before his body began to tremble. Muscles ballooned beneath his skin, and dark veins began crawling up his neck. Saliva pooled at the corners of his mouth, dripping onto the floor, hissing when it hit the stone.

I shifted on my feet as his ears stretched into points, fur cutting through the flesh around them. He wasn't a wolf— not exactly. He looked like he was something that had gotten *stuck* halfway, a monster built out of bad magic and arrogance. His eyes burned neon green, bright enough to stain the air around him.

"I'll let you *taste* it," he snarled, jamming the knife deep into the rock wall. The blade hummed, alive. "One hit to the chest would kill you, so I'll make sure you get the full demonstration."

I blinked, and he vanished.

Instinct told me to move, so I ducked and jumped to the side. My eyes landed on the space my head was, hearing the loud crack as the rock crumbled underneath his fist. He turned slowly, grinning, those neon eyes looking like a Halloween decoration, before he came at me again.

This time, my wolf snapped to the surface, bones and fur shifting so quickly that as soon as my back paws met the ground, I launched forward. My fangs found his thigh and sank deep, tearing into the engorged muscle, making it into roast beef.

His roar shook the cave, a sound too big for the space. He swung for me, but I was smaller, faster, *hungrier*, so I slipped out from under the blow. In fluid motion, I launched myself at the rock wall, pushed off on all fours, and twisted to land on his back. My claws tore into his massive flesh, slicing it to ribbons and tearing out chunks with my teeth. Flesh gave way in a wet, satisfying tear.

Blood slammed into my fur, boiling and metallic, thick as rot in the air. It spattered against the stone behind me, a brutal cadence that set my pulse dancing in time.

Adrenaline burned through me, flooding every nerve. My hearing sharpened until I could catch every ragged inhale, every crack of muscle beneath his skin.

With my fangs still buried in his shoulder, I shook my head, tearing deeper. Using my back claws, I raked down his spine until his roars became gurgles, until the cave smelled only of blood and victory.

He howled, knees slamming into the dirt before his hand closed around one of my legs and flung me off him. I twisted in the air and landed on all fours, skidding as grit bit into the pads of my paws, eyes locked on the moving threat.

His hand clutched his bleeding throat, and the wound knit together faster than a normal supe's would, given the damage I inflicted.

"I can do this all night," he spat, his voice raw. "I can spill buckets and buckets of blood and still have the strength to take on a silver-spooned thug of the Syndicate!"

I shifted back into my human shape, planted a hand on my hip, and let a grin crawl across my face. "Is that supposed to be an insult? Cute." I threw my hands up like a showman. "The *Silver-Spooned Thug* has a nice ring. You've picked the wrong racket, bub. You should be in marketing."

His whole frame trembled, teeth grinding so hard that his jaw had to ache. Green fire burned behind his eyes. "We. Will. Ruin. You. All of you."

My fingers morphed into claws at my sides, and my body buzzed, ready for anything. "Plenty have said that before, yet all of them ended the same." Putting my claws over my heart, I pretended to tear it out. "With their heart ripped out and stomped into the dirt. Where you belong."

He bellowed, arms sweeping wide. The cave shuddered at the sound. Dust rattled down, and a thin, hairline crack webbed across the stone above us. Rocks began to tumble.

He didn't seem to care. The moment my attention wasn't on him, he seized the opportunity by slamming me into the wall. Jagged stone bit into my skin as his bulk ground against me.

Air left me, my chest caving in from the weight. I twisted my head and gasped for air, tasting dust and the rank, sour burn of his breath on my cheek. He laughed, the sound filthy. "Under all this muscle is just a woman." With a sneer, he raked his hands up my thigh. "Might be nice to fuck you before I kill you. Last chance to taste you, right?"

Something in me snapped, and a laugh, sharp and bitter, came out. It made his jaw clench. "Please. Your little pecker wouldn't compare to my mates'. You'll just make me miss them more while I laugh at your pathetic dick."

He shook, his anger taking over his mind for a second, and I took advantage. Circling my arms around his, I locked them against me as I thrust my claws into his ribs, slicing along muscle and fat, digging deeper and deeper. He howled as my claws rearranged his insides, the savage in me savoring the pain twisting up his face.

He spat out threats, venomous despite his stammer. "I-I'll ruin you. I-I'll kill you and—" His voice broke, mouth open in a silent scream, unable to finish.

Using that rage, he tried to swing his head down to crush mine, but I let go of him and shifted. My back slid down the rock, tearing it to shreds, and when I looked up, his head smashed into the rock wall with a massive thud. The wall groaned underneath his head, splintering into a web of cracks.

The big bastard staggered back, disoriented, as he pressed his palm to his dented skull with a groan. Dust and small stones rattled from above. The cracks in the wall spread wider, crawling up the wall and overhead, so I knew my time was up. I had minutes, maybe less. I needed to finish this.

I shifted back into my human form and lunged at him, pressing my thumb into his warm, slippery eye socket. There was a wet, fatal pop, and he screamed—a high, animal sound that bounced off the cave. I jumped away from him just as his hands came up to his face, blood slick between his fingers as he tried to catch his dangling right eye, but it was too late for that one. It was already squished like a grape.

In his panicked state, he froze when I leaned closer to his ear. His breathing was ragged and terrified. "If you don't want to lose the other eye," I said, my voice cold as the stone around us shook, "you'll tell me about this doctor. Who is he, and what are you doing here?"

Choppy breaths stuttered out like he was trying to think of what to say, but he hesitated too long. I drove my claws into his chest and felt ribs splinter under my strikes. On the second plunge, I caught a rib between my fingers and slowly twisted it until I heard a sickening snap. His screams finally collapsed into a hoarse, broken croak. "Stop. N-no more."

"Don't make me ask again," I growled.

"H-he's… lake… b-bank," he spat, each syllable a wet, useless thing. My mind ricocheted through possibilities like bullets.

"Lake? What lake?" I pressed. The room began to shake. *Fuck!*

His body trembled. The swollen muscle that had towered over me before slackened, deflating at a rapid pace. His remaining eye flicked down, going wide before he glared up at me.

"They're coming," he rasped. "You won't… survive."

Blood foamed at his mouth. His pupil rolled back, body violently shaking, and I let him go. A wave of red heat shimmered across his chest, settling right above his heart. A sharp crack split through the air. His chest ballooned, then caved in right before my eyes. His body folded to the ground, now lifeless.

What the fuck?

Curiosity took over, so I dug my claws into the warm mess in his chest, tearing through fistfuls of blood-slick tissue until I got to the spot where his heart was.

The inside looked blackened, almost charred, as if something had detonated beneath the sternum. Smoke-scented ash clung to the edges. His heart was nowhere to be found.

The dome above us rumbled, shaking the whole room. A slab of stone separated right above me, and I jumped out of the way. A loud thud sounded right behind me, shaking the ground. Dust choked the air, and stones fell from the ceiling like gravel sprinkles.

Looking up, I saw the knife in the wall, a shining glow rippling across the blade. I wanted that knife, needed to understand what kind of magic it held. Quick on my feet, I bolted for the wall, dodging the speared rocks falling from the ceiling.

Wrapping my fingers around the handle, I heaved with everything in me, but the metal resisted, clinging to the rock for dear life.

"Come on, come on," I hissed. Blood and dirt under my nails, I put both hands around it and yanked. When the blade finally ripped free, a small, high-pitched scream came from it. I stared at it for a second, trying to make sure I heard that correctly.

I had to get this to my family and figure out what the fuck kind of magic this was.

No sooner had I freed the knife from the wall than the ceiling surrendered. Rocks rained down in chunks, and I knew this space would cave in in a matter of seconds. Taking off as fast as I could, I ran for the entrance.

Pushing my legs harder, pumping my arms faster, I kept a firm grip on the knife. Just as I saw the crack split and rock shift right above the entrance, I dove, rolling through grit and heat with a prayer.

Bursting out of the mouth of the mini cave, I rolled right into another rock wall with a thud. Dust and rocks flew at me as the passage collapsed behind me in a final, choking roar.

Slumping against the ground, hoarse, ragged breaths dragged from my lungs, and I spat out grit that coated my face. My whole body ached underneath the skin, and that was when I realized my outfit was buried under tons of stone.

Fucking... whatever. I shrugged to myself. I could steal a shirt from one of the others later. The image that pushed me into motion wasn't clothes... it was them, the men I wanted to check on. Who knew if that cave-in caused something to happen on their side? I needed to make sure everything was okay.

Stabbing the knife into the ground, I quickly pushed myself up. My legs gobbled up the distance between me and the main chamber within seconds.

A thought surprised me as I sprinted toward them. I wanted to see Conrad's steady, calm smile, the way Deslen's face would light up when he saw me, Zeth standing proud with his hands on his hips, and Nick. I wanted to catch that millisecond when Nick's eyes widened, impressed with what I'd done and survived.

I wanted time with them, *real* time. The teasing, the easy laughter, the way their eyes lingered on me until that spark of hunger took over. That thought alone tugged something open inside my chest, the tiny fracture letting in a sliver of warmth I hadn't felt in years. Maybe... just maybe... I could get used to that.

Their voices carried down the tunnel, rough and echoing, and I quickened my pace. When I broke into the clearing, I stopped in my tracks.

Nick was on the ground, one hand rubbing his neck, glaring at Zeth with eyes sharp enough to cut. A human boy hovered over him, wide-eyed, hands shaking as he apologized for something. Across the space, Zeth strained against Conrad and Deslen's hold, teeth bared as he shouted, "Who the *fuck* are you? I'm only going to ask once more before I shove these two aside and beat it out of you. Who *are* you, Officer Cordova?"

Officer?

The word hung in the air like a gunshot. Everything went still.

I turned to look at Nick, every motion being cataloged and assessed. The way his eyes dropped, the hitch in his pulse, the tremor that ran through his fingers. The boy beside him kept glancing between Zeth and Nick, inching his way closer to the latter for safety.

My heart hammered, beating against my ribs so hard they shook. Each thud begged me to reject what my eyes were telling me, to tell me he hadn't been the one to stab a blade into the fragile trust we'd built. He was supposed to be mine.

My feet moved on their own like I was in a trance. Someone called my name, but it didn't get through to me, didn't register. Every inch of my being narrowed on the man in front of me, on Nick, the turned wolf who always had one foot in and one foot out of both worlds.

Nick's head snapped toward me, and his eyes filled with something raw—guilt. That look cut right through my heart, making it bleed, making it hurt even worse than before.

I watched the confession form on his lips before he spoke, but everything felt numb. My mind. My body. The only thing bleeding was my heart, but you couldn't see it.

My steps were steady, but my hands trembled as I kept walking toward him. Up close, the little tic in his jaw, the quick hitch in his breath—all of it confirmed what my gut had already felt.

He lied to me. He was the enemy. Trying to tear me down. Trying to tear the Syndicate down. Trying to take from my family. That spark of rage lit up inside me, and while my heart screamed no, my mind burned with a yes.

"Nova, I—" he started in a small voice, but that didn't stop me.

My fingers flexed on instinct. I pictured grabbing his throat, flinging him across the clearing, and beating that handsome face until it matched the way I felt inside. The boss in me rose to the surface. Punishments were lessons; betrayals were unforgivable.

You don't betray the Syndicate. You don't betray me. The rules tasted metallic on my tongue.

Something howled in my chest, my wolf snapping in protest of my vision of how I wanted to handle the situation. For a single brutal second, my hand obeyed the rage, reaching out for his neck. Chaos descended in my mind, my wolf doing everything possible to fight the urge to make him pay while my mind insisted that this was only going to keep happening if I didn't put a stop to it. I needed to make an example out of him.

But he's your mate... for better or worse.

Pain surged over the rage, and when it was washed away, all I was left with was a hollow hole in my heart. My hand stilled. The damage was already done, and no amount of blood could take that away.

"Don't." The word slipped through my teeth, low and hard. My gaze drilled into those golden eyes that always set something raw and hot under my ribs.

His mouth flattened; disappointment cut across his face, and he straightened, every inch the righteous soldier. The cop. He looked at me like *I* was the traitor.

"Did your captain put you up to this? Are you a spy? An assassin? *A rat?*" Questions rattled out, rapid-fire, but that last one was laced with venom. He flinched and swallowed hard before he spoke.

"Yes." His quiet confirmation set off a bomb in my soul. "They sent me to watch you, to make sure no humans got hurt under you, and to tell them if they did." His eyes went to the boy next to him. The loaded gun.

A hollow laugh escaped me, sharp and humorless. "So, the plan was to cozy up to the mafia queen, win her trust, then plunge a blade into her back later? Mating be damned." I flicked my hand dismissively.

Nick's jaw tightened. "It started out as a job, a mission," he said, the words stumbling out. "But it..." He barked a wry laugh, looking off into the distance. "It switched." He turned to look at me. "I started... I couldn't stop... fuck... I couldn't stop thinking about you."

I shook my head. *Words. Just fucking words, Nova.* Actions were how you learned about someone, how you got to know who they were, and his spoke volumes.

"All the while," I stepped closer, drilling my eyes into his as I spat out, "you were slithering around, gathering intel like some snake." His chin went up, mouth pressing into a hard line. The accusation landed between us, cold and edged.

The boy clung to Nick's shirt, his voice trembling when he spoke. "I-I'm sorry, Miss... d-do you know where m-my dad is?"

Nick's arms tightened around him, shielding him as if I were the threat. Like I would hurt an innocent fucking child becuase I was mad at him! My face betrayed me because I could feel water building behind my eyes.

Something feral unfurled in my chest, and the air seemed to vibrate with it. Claws pressed just beneath my skin, begging to break through. I wanted to tear the walls down, bringing the whole cave down on top of us, but the boy's wide, terrified eyes anchored me. Whatever monster Nick thought I was, I wasn't *that*.

Sucking everything in, I calmed my face and crouched down to face the boy. "What's your father's name?"

"Jeremy, Miss… Jeremy Delton."

So, this was him, the human boy we'd been trying to find. His wrists were rubbed raw from the cuffs, his face streaked with dirt, but he was breathing. Alive. It was the first real piece of good news in hours.That and getting this weird knife in my hands.

"That doctor man took him," the boy said, turning to Nick. "This morning. They took both Reece and my dad. We have to find him!" His panic steadied something inside me, transforming the rage into focus. I wasn't here as a woman scorned. I was the boss, and this boy didn't belong in my world. He needed to be safe and get out.

"Hey."

The kid flinched at my voice, eyeing the knife in my hand before he looked up. His small fingers clutched tighter at Nick's shirt. At least I had his attention. "I'll find him," I said. "I promise you that."

He nodded, and I pushed to my feet. I could feel them before I saw them—Conrad, Deslen, Zeth—closing in behind me, their quiet, solid presence holding me together at the edges.

"Now, listen to *Officer Cordova*," I said, my voice rough when I said the name out loud. Turning to face Nick, I gave him my final order. "Take the boy to the station. Make sure he is taken care of before I send word."

I turned to leave, but his hand caught my arm, squeezing it hard.

"Nova, wait. We need to talk. Figure this out."

The desperation in his voice brushed too close. I let it sink beneath the surface where I didn't have to feel it. "There's nothing to figure out." I yanked my arm out of his grasp before getting into his face, smashing my forehead into his painfully. "If you weren't my *mate*," I shot out, "I'd have gutted you, then tore out your heart and smashed it under my foot."

He glared through the pain in his eyes that shouldn't even be there. What the fuck did he have to be upset about?

"You only do that to people who deserve it—the scum of the earth—doling out punishments that fit the crime."

His tone mocked me, sharp as glass, and maybe he was right. Maybe he did know a piece of me, but I wouldn't give him the satisfaction.

"Sure." I backed up, feeling that rage I was desperately keeping locked up knocking on my door again. "But you're not fucking innocent. You're a liar. A con. A man who does his dirty work for a badge. Don't pretend it's any less criminal than I am."

His expression faltered, and those gold eyes, the same ones that used to make my pulse race, drained of light as the truth laid between our feet. Whatever we'd been before, it had died between us in that silence. A cop and a criminal could never be together.

"Don't come near me again," I said firmly, turning away from him. "I'm hanging on by a thread, *Cordova*. I don't know what I'll do if you test me. So, stay the hell away."

"What about the boy's father?" His desperate tone called forth something inside of me that I smacked down and growled at.

I pushed myself forward, needing to leave. I needed to get out of this place where all I could smell was his creamy, musky scent that I was now desperate for.

"I'll send someone to tell you when we find him."

He called my name as I walked off, the sound echoing in the cave, chasing me. A white button-down slipped over my shoulders, and I looked up to see Conrad's solemn eyes. "Don't send me away tonight," he begged softly.

I nodded, tears in my eyes as I admitted, "I'm not losing anyone else tonight." I slid the shirt off my shoulders and back into his hands. "But I need air. I need to run."

"Zeth," I called over my shoulder, knowing he wouldn't be far away. That was one of the only things I felt like I knew for sure. "Take Conrad and Deslen to my house. Get their prints and signatures set up in the system."

That was all I said before the shift took me.

Bones cracked, skin stretched, and white fur replaced everything human. The forest swallowed me as I ran, each stride pulling the ache further from my chest. Tears fell hot and silent, scattering through the wind, but only the forest saw, and she kept her secrets.

NOVA

"Sooooo, how was your night? Magical? Full of dick?"

Aniyah's voice snapped me out of my thoughts, though not far enough to escape where they always went. I was thinking about that stupid traitor of a human cop turned wolf. *Again*.

One of the flower bulbs inked along my arm thumped faintly, a heartbeat gone weak.

It had been thirty hours since that damn cave. Since Nick and I went our separate ways. To his credit, he stayed gone, just like I'd told him to, yet the emptiness he left behind dug in deep, sour and sharp. I didn't know if I was more angry at him or at myself for missing him like this.

Zeth, Conrad, and Deslen had made an effort to keep me company. Some came armed with half-baked excuses, others with actual work. Either way, I let them. Their presence filled the silence, kept me from staring too long at that hollow space inside my chest.

They were trying to be comforting, I knew that, but every time I looked at them, all I could see was what wasn't there, *who* wasn't there. I was pining like some lovesick fool over a man I barely understood. Pathetic.

It didn't help that I could feel all three of them wanting to talk about the elephant in the room. To their credit, none of them brought it up or put pressure on me to talk about it, but the air between us hummed, tight and electric, charged with their uncertainty and longing.

I could sense their eyes on me, asking me questions without saying a word. Their gazes lingered as I moved around. Sometimes I ignored it, letting them hover while I buried myself in work. Other times, the weight of it pressed too close, and I'd shut the door, locking out their unanswered questions.

I needed an enemy. Something to burn this restless ache out of me. Finding the doctor should've done it, but ever since we released those captives, any potential leads had gone dark. I'd searched all the buildings that used to be banks with no luck.

"Niyah…" I sighed, rubbing a hand over my face. "You got your picture. What more do you want?"

The holographic projection of her perched on my desk leaned closer, eyes gleaming like a cat with a secret. "No, no, that was just the amuse-bouche," she purred, her voice on the edge of laughter. "Now I want the play-by-play." Her grin widened. "A girl's gotta eat, Nov. I need my meat *and* potatoes."

Before I could shut her down, Calix's hologram crackled to life beside hers. His expression was already sour. "What the fuck are you two talking about?"

"Nothing—"

"How much dick Nova got on fight night," Aniyah blurted, cutting me off.

Riot's image blinked into the middle of the chaos. She took one look at Calix's horrified face, Aniyah's feral excitement, and my silent plea for mercy, then sighed, pulled up a book, and hid behind it like she wanted no part of this circus.

"The fuck, Niyah!" Calix barked. "I haven't even had my breakfast yet!" He slammed the mug of blood that had been poised at his mouth onto his desk.

She only smiled, eyes sliding past the camera to someone off-screen. "Then shut your ears, Cal. Even Ras wants to hear what happened. Don't you, my little stalker?"

Rasmus drifted into view, that strange, unblinking devotion on his face. "Oh, yeah," he said easily. "Whatever my star wants is what I want. Very much so."

Glaring at them like they'd personally ruined his morning, Calix groaned. "I think I just threw up in my mouth."

Aniyah's gaze snapped to him, sharp enough to cut. "Just because you don't know how to please—"

"Oh, fucking try me," he shot back. "Ask the woman from last night—"

Ezra's hologram appeared, snapping everyone into focus like a silent command. She sat back in her high-backed chair, fingers steepled, face carved with calm authority. "All here? Ready."

The room froze. Riot put a bookmark in her book and closed it. Even Aniyah stopped smirking. Ezra had that effect. Her voice didn't rise or bite, but the meaning was clear as a brandishing of a blade: *shut the fuck up and focus.*

"Morning, E! You know how much we *love* these early meetings."

Aniyah batted her lashes like she had a scrap of innocence left, her grin stretching so wide it looked painful.

Ezra didn't even blink. "Good morning, Boss Glovefox. Please have your mate leave the room before we start."

Aniyah's smile faltered. Her eyes darted sideways, guilty as a cat caught mid-pounce. A heavy thud sounded under her desk, followed by the unmistakable shuffle of someone trying to make a quiet exit. A head of dark hair appeared just long enough to confirm what we all suspected before the door clicked shut.

Aniyah exhaled, straightening in her chair. "What mate?"

Oh, Aniyah.

Ezra gave her that look, the kind that didn't need words, sharp and annoyed all at once. Within seconds, Aniyah's shoulders slumped, the fight leaking right out of her. Ezra's sigh came soft but final, the verbal equivalent of a closed case, then her gaze shifted to me.

"First off," she said, "between ads, gambles, and the other revenue streams, your fight night brought in over two hundred and sixty-two million. Our total spend came in at fifty-eight. That's over a seventy percent ROI. Excellent work."

On the surface, Ezra's expression didn't move, staying as calm and unreadable as always, but I'd been around her long enough to catch the quiet signals most missed. The faint narrowing of her eyes when she focused on me. The almost invisible lift in the corner of her mouth. The slight tilt of her shoulder, easing into comfort.

Those tiny cracks in her armor were as close as Ezra ever came to a smile, and I felt the warmth of it like sunlight after a long night.

"Thanks," I said, forcing a grin of my own. "I think this'll be good for both sides of the business, above and below board."

"And that Deslen—oh, man." Aniyah fanned herself. "Wasn't he just a snack and a half?"

Heat flared through me, and my fingers curled underneath the desk, gripping my thighs so tight it burned. Her eyes gleamed with that familiar taunting light, making me realize she was fucking with me on purpose... and I just fell for it. I'd given her the ammo she wanted. *Fuck.*

"I've gotta say, Nov," Calix chimed in, voice laced with amusement, "I did *not* see you pulling a publicity stunt like that. That's usually Aniyah's department." He threw his thumb toward her, and she shot him a death glare.

Of course, he just responded with a lazy smirk and a shrug. The two of them were always just one issue away from blowing up at each other.

"Was it?" Riot's voice slid through the noise, soft and steady, cutting the room in half. Everyone turned toward me.

I'd never lied to my siblings before, and I wasn't about to start now. "I didn't know anything about it," I said simply, throwing up my hands in a tired gesture. "Not until it happened. That's why I reacted how I did. It was the only thing I could think of."

Watching that moment later had made my stomach twist. On the feed, I looked like some back-alley thug, spitting in Deslen's face at his grand gesture. It made me look horrible. At the time, it had felt like one more weight I couldn't carry, so I'd exploded.

Calix leaned forward, elbows on his knees, that familiar protective look settling over his features. "You did the right thing. Guys like that see a woman in charge and think they can test her. You showed him who's boss. Hell, you *should've* decked him."

"Oh, my *god*," Aniyah groaned, rolling her eyes hard. "Do you have a single romantic bone in your blood-addled mind? It was a *gesture*, Cal. Devotion! She should've used his body, telling him to prove his words—*all night long.*"

Even Ezra's composure wavered, her eyes flicking aside for half a second. In Ezra-speak, that was practically a nod of agreement. I was annoyed at the heat rising on my neck.

Aniyah grinned, soaking in the chaos. "I thought it was so hot I made Alic recreate it for me," she said proudly. "Before I fucked his face off."

"Aniyah!"

Calix's horrified shout only made her laugh harder. Riot just rolled her eyes, clearly mourning the peace she'd had before joining this meeting.

Ezra's voice sliced through the laughter, calm but sharp. "Enough." She glanced at me, a knowing flicker in her eyes, before steering the conversation back to business.

While the others talked about project updates and business logistics, a soft buzz vibrated against my wrist. I glanced down—Ezra.

E: *Talk to me when you're ready. I'm all ears.*

When I looked up, she had her head turned toward Calix, pretending to listen as he rambled about some new weapons prototype. Her eyes flicked to me for a fraction of a second, a knowing glance, a quick wink, and then she was back to business, asking him a question like nothing had happened.

I didn't know how she always managed to *know* things before anyone else did. Maybe it was intuition, or maybe she'd just learned to read all of us too well. Either way, I was grateful. She was giving me space to sort myself out before the inevitable storm that would come once I told my siblings. Because in our family, once something was spoken aloud, it was carved in stone.

That was why none of us mentioned boyfriends or girl-friends or the people we were seeing or fucking. Saying a name meant it was real, and if you brought someone to the table, that person had better be solid. Once you were intro-duced to the family, you only left in a body bag.

Once we got into the more criminal part of the conversation, I told them all about what happened in the cave, minus the whole Nick thing and who was with me.

"The bastard's eyes glowed the same way as the others,'" I said, resting my forearms on the table. "When he was about to talk, to give me some actual information, his heart exploded."

Ezra's gaze went distant, her hand cradling her chin. "Another silencing spell," she murmured. "Old, complicated."

Riot leaned back, her frown deepening as her arms crossed in front of her chest. "Takes a hell of a lot of magic and knowledge to pull that off. Some of those spells eat at your life force if you're not careful. Most mages won't touch them."

"Not unless you're paid enough," huffed Calix.

"Or," I said, pulling the blade from my jacket and laying it flat on the table, "they're not using the usual kind of magic."

The metal caught the light, the runes along its edge still pulsing faintly. Their eyes widened.

"This is the knife that I texted you all about." I told them where I'd found it, about the man who used it, and about the wound it left on me. I mentioned Deslen and how he healed my leg.

Ezra's brow furrowed. "How exactly did he heal it?"

I shrugged, playing it casual. "His saliva neutralized the curse. Fae jaguar thing." Once Deslen and I figured out what was going on with all of us, I'd tell them it was a mate thing—or whatever the situation was.

Ezra nodded slowly. "Interesting. Good to know, but let's keep that quiet. There aren't many of his kind left."

We all nodded, though Aniyah was already smirking, her eyebrows dancing in the kind of way that made my ears burn. *Why does she think she knows everything?! She knows nothing... I hope.*

"Send the knife my way," Calix said, getting that gleam in his eyes that said he was accepting a challenge. "I'll see what it's made of."

"Will do." If anyone could unravel what was going on with that knife, it was him.

"I'm still digging into this 'doctor' the leads have mentioned," I said, leaning back. "Once I find something worth sharing, you'll all know."

Ezra's gaze met mine, understanding and a clear warning in her eyes. I needed to find this man, and do it quickly.

The conversation drifted on for another ten minutes before wrapping up, all of us saying our goodbyes as their images blinked away.

Grabbing the handle of the knife, I could still feel the pulse of that blade like a heartbeat. I was going to need to double wrap this before I gave it to the courier.

Once everything was done, all emails and phone calls answered, my office turned into a tomb of silence. The last few days had been a blur of chaos and emotion. This was the first moment I'd had to actually breathe.

After what happened with Nick, I'd spent an hour running wild through the forest, trying to quiet my wolf before she tore something apart. She fought with other wolves, went hunting for game, and by the time I came home in the middle of the day, I was covered in dirt and blood. Zeth, Conrad, and Deslen had been waiting at the door, calm and steady, like they'd been there the whole time.

Deslen insisted on a bath, Zeth had movies queued up, and Conrad had Hellfire booze waiting for me in a glass. Even with my heart cracked wide open, they held me together piece by piece.

We'd curled up on the couch, one on each side, another stretched between my legs, watching movies until the sky turned dark. No one mentioned Nick. They just... stayed. Present. Warm.

Conrad left first, groaning about meetings he'd already post-poned before brushing a kiss over my lips and heading out. Deslen followed, saying something about his manager blowing up his phone. Zeth lingered the longest, kissing me deeply enough to steal the air from my lungs before promising to handle the lieutenants and other Syndicate issues so I could rest.

Now, hours later, I sat alone in my chair, the hum of the computer in my office still echoing faintly. My gaze drifted over the wood grain of the desk, the patterns twisting like the thoughts I kept burying in that dark, quiet corner of my mind.

Is it because he doesn't like me?

Nick hadn't seemed to mind fucking me in the forest… but maybe that had been a mistake to him. Maybe he'd been at war with himself the whole time, hating the side that wanted me. Hating the side that saw me as his mate.

That thought gnawed at me as I sat there, staring blankly at the desk. Why would he fight something so natural? Something written into our bones. On our souls. People spent their lives dreaming of this connection, chasing a bond some would never feel, yet he'd spit in fate's face the moment it reached for him.

The second that realization hit, I dropped my forehead onto the desk with a sharp thud.

"God, I'm an idiot." I'd done the same damn thing. Birds of a feather and shit, I guessed.

Yes, Zeth had rejected me, but I'd also been betrayed by men before. Staring down at my fists, I remembered how it felt when I'd heard Liam in that locker room. How it felt to be deceived by someone you thought was truly interested in you.

It was that kind of hurt, the kind that dug bone-deep, the kind that made you want to take the whole damn concept of choice away. But why? Why had I done it?

To keep yourself from ever being hurt again. To hide your weakness.

It was easier that way. I could tell myself it wasn't me, that I wasn't unlucky in love. Men were just too intimidated or too scared, and none of that was *my* fault.

I could blame it all on the mate-blocker tattoo, but that was just an excuse. My shield. The reason I could claim I'd never found "the one" when I knew what the truth was. I thought "the one" had left me.

When Aniyah confessed that her tattoo had stopped working, two things had taken root inside me—hope and fear. Of course, it was the fear that thrived. It grew wild, tangling around everything I wanted until I couldn't tell where it ended and I began.

So, how could I fault him for rejecting something that had been forced on him when I'd willingly done the same thing? I'd beaten him to it, denying myself the opportunity before anyone else could.

And the cruelest part was—I *knew* better. I'd grown up surrounded by fated mates, proof of what that mate bond could be like.

The more I thought about it, the clearer it became. Nick and I weren't opposites; we were *mirrors*. Both lost between what our bodies screamed for and what our minds refused to accept. His mind wanted to stay human, so even if his wolf wanted me, *he* didn't.

If that had been the only source of my pain, maybe I could've let it go. Maybe I could've stopped thinking about him. Then I remembered his true purpose. His betrayal.

He was a cop sent by humans to watch me, to see if I slipped up so they could take advantage. So they could take me and my family down. It wasn't the first time, but the fact that it was him, my mate, sent rage crackling through me, hot and sharp as sparks of steel.

My fingers locked together, knuckles whitening, and something deep inside me trembled. He'd played me. Betrayed me. Betrayed *us*.

But in his mind, he wasn't part of that *us*. He was still human, just one cursed with fur and fangs. A man who hated what he'd become.

The memory of that cave and how he'd looked at me hit like an uppercut. The way he'd pulled that boy behind him, shielding him from *me* like I'd tear into a terrified human child just for breathing the same air as me. That hurt worse than the betrayal. That was how he saw me, as something monstrous, dangerous by nature.

The ache in my chest throbbed. We hadn't even spent that much time together, but somehow, it was enough to make his judgment feel like a blade to the gut.

Yeah, I was rough around the edges. I mean, I'd grown up in a mob family. Violence was in our blood—hell, it was the main way we communicated—but so was control. We hit hard because that was how our world worked. Supes could take it. We healed fast and bounced back, shrugging off things that would kill a human. To us, losing an arm wasn't a tragedy. It was a major inconvenience.

That was why humans feared us. Why they whispered *'monster'* behind closed doors. Why someone like Nick would never want to be tied to someone like me.

I slumped over the desk, exhaustion making my body heavy as stone. My mind was spinning between bad thoughts and worse ones until I stopped trying to rein it in.

If I'd been more his type, maybe he would've looked past my lifestyle, my past. Men did it all the time, falling for women who were bad for them because they couldn't see past a pretty face, but not him. *Story of my damn life.*

The sting in my eyes warned me before the tears came. I buried my face in my arms, trying to choke them back. "Bet his type's some fragile little thing," I muttered into my sleeve, voice rough. "Someone soft he can protect." Men like that, they lived for it, and I was never going to be that. I couldn't.

A single tear slipped free, hot against my skin. I swiped it away, furious.

Don't you fucking cry over him. Don't you dare. You're the fucking Rossey boss. You have to be strong. Show no weakness. Strength is your only defense.

Another one fell, then another, until they came so hard and fast I couldn't wipe them away, carving silent tracks down my cheeks.

My shoulders shook, breath hitching. *This is so stupid,* I told myself. *He's just a man. I have three other mates. Do the math, Nova. You still win.*

But the truth cut through, soft and cruel.

He was supposed to be my mate, too, and he didn't want me.

"Nova? You there?"

Dread knifed through me the moment I heard the voice. An image of my mom popped up in front of me, all warm and excited.

"My rose," I heard Daddy Lex calling in the background, "you're all-powerful and ethereal in my eyes, so you can do no wrong, but... I think you hit the direct button. Those are only for emergencies."

Perfect. Of course, I'd chosen to have a meltdown in the one place where people could still reach me. I should've curled under my covers, in my bed, like a normal person. Hiding from the world.

"This *is* an emergency, Lex," Mom snapped. "I'm their mother, and when I want to talk to them, it's an emergency." Her logic slammed down like a gavel.

A soft tutting came from her other side. "I don't know, Ray. You might see something you're not meant to." Papa Avery? Oh, god.

Mom's scoff was immediate. "Please. It's not like I haven't done worse. What could they possibly be doing that would throw me for a loop? I've fucked five guys at once. I am a fucking goddess." Squeezing my eyes tight, I prayed that this was one of my mom's butt-dial mistakes and she would hang up soon.

"Nova?!" She called my name louder, and I wished for invisibility "Nova! Is that you? Are you sleeping on your desk? That's a little unprofessional."

Nope. No invisibility. Just humiliation.

My dad Ax's voice rumbled out, "Now, Siren, do you want us to bring up all the 'unprofessional' things you've done on your desk?"

She giggled for a second, smiling seductively before she shook it off and scowled. "That was all of your faults. Not mine."

Before this went into a full-on play-by-play of their time together on her desk, I breathed and wiped at my eyes with the back of my hand. Forcing a grin across my face, I answered, "Hey, Mom! How's Europe? Find anything fun?"

Her face tightening, she leaned forward before she inhaled as if the truth had punched her. "Nova! Are you *crying*?"

That was the moment pandemonium erupted. Voices over-lapped, sharp, affectionate, and utterly ridiculous.

"What the fuck?"

"Sweetheart, just tell me who we need to kill."

"Not my Nova. Oh, hell no!"

"All I need is a name, baby girl."

"We should take the next flight home and gut the whole Rossey old guard. She needs a fresh start. It's the most logical solution."

That last one was Father Falcon, and I almost laughed. Ever since I took over as the Rossey boss, he'd been wanting to get rid of the old guard, knowing they would give me a hard time since they were old school. His reasoning was to ensure I was respected correctly, and, in his mind, the only way to ensure that was to put new people in place. He tried to sell it as protecting my reign, but the rest of us called it his way of showing love… and it was out of the question.

I let their noise wash over me, half-embarrassed, fully loved, and absolutely aware that whatever disaster I'd accidentally broadcast, my family would descend like a storm, loud, ridiculous, and fiercely mine.

"All right—out! All of you, out!" my mom screeched, and I took a breath of relief. Talking to the dads about boy problems would be hard since every other word out of their mouths was about how they would make them pay. It was unproductive.

I watched Mom herd my dads like a dog moving cattle, shoulders squared, voice sharp. Men spilled out the doorway, half-grumbling, half-protesting, all wanting information to make this a "quick fix."

Daddy Lex lingered at the threshold, loud and theatrical as always. "I'll make them cry for you, baby girl. I'll even film it! We could have a whole movie night, watching them bawl their weight in tears until they take their final breath! It will be great, and we'll all have a laugh!"

Mom slammed the door in his face, smoothed a stray hair from her forehead, and turned back to me. "All right, Nov. Lay it on me now that the psychos are gone."

I raised an eyebrow. "Mom. You're *also* one of those psychos."

A grin split her face, flashing me some fang. "Oh, but I'm the leader of the psychos, so that means I think about it before I do it." I lifted a brow at her, and she crossed her arms, one corner of her mouth lifting. "Fine. *Most of the time.* Just remember, I'm not the one trying to book international flights right now."

446

That hit a nerve, and I laughed until the sound broke into more tears. I wanted that. I could admit it now. My own pack of lunatics who would flatten the world for me and our kids.

Mom's expression softened. She leaned forward, and the voice we all called her "magic-mom tone" slipped into place: calm, steady, impossible to argue with. "Tell me what's going on. Why are you hurting, Nova?"

I didn't crumble, but I did something worse. I unloaded.

I left out the messy history with Zeth and the mate-blocking tattoo—I wasn't a snitch—but I told her about the four mates who'd shown up, how I'd kept them at arm's length because of my fear. Confessed that one of them had broken my heart and walked away. Explained how confused I was, how stupid I felt for wanting something I wasn't sure was meant for me.

She listened the way she always did, no interruptions, no judgment. When I finished, the weight I'd been carrying didn't vanish, but saying it out loud had made it less absolute.

"Oh, honey." Her smile was kind yet pitying all the same. She chuckled, and the sound was rich and full. "I see so much of your dads in all of you. Calix's focus is so Falcon; Ezra's clean, no-nonsense like Cosmo; Riot feels deeply like Lex; Aniyah, she's pure Avery wildness. And you? You've got Ax's strength—inside and out. But sometimes, I forget you all have a little slice of me in there, too."

I blinked, confused. She reached across the holo and caressed the air like she was tucking back a strand on my hair. "Nov, I was you once. When your dads showed up, I fought them all tooth and nail, swearing it was just some fun and good sex. Then everyone started declaring themselves my mate, and your grandfathers got into trouble.... It was just so much easier to shove those feelings down, telling myself I'd deal with it all later. Sound familiar?"

My head bobbed.

"The hardest part isn't knowing that this is your mate, the one or ones you were destined for. It's the leap, trusting someone with pieces of you, pieces that you don't even understand yet." Her voice was quiet, but the words settled in my chest and started to click back on track like gears.

"That fear of the leap is what's keeping you from going all in. Some people have bigger gaps to leap than others, but the decision is the same for everyone. Is it worth it or not?"

I inhaled, bringing some clarity to my mind as I tried to answer the question honestly. Were these men worth the risk? Could I let myself fall and hope they would catch me? Would I be okay if they said no? Could I be okay if some said yes and others said no? My past screamed 'no,' my heart whispered 'maybe,' and my wolf screamed 'yes.'

"Once you figure that out, you'll know what to do," Mom said, folding her hands and reclining as if the problem was so simple and I'd just misread the map. "And remember—if it fails, if you get hurt, you're never truly alone. You've got your siblings, your dads, your grandfathers, and me, who'd tear the world apart for you. All you need to do is ask, and they'll come running."

She glanced at the door where a muffled voice snapped, "Move! Some of us are trying to listen!"

She rolled her eyes and threw her thumb over her shoulder. "Or just show up crying and you won't have to say a damn thing."

The image of my ridiculous, murderous family circling my mates like vultures made me laugh, a real, breathy kind that pushed out a little more of the darkness in my heart.

Daddy Lex's voice came through the wood. "This is *not* me asking, my rose, but Falcon said that he wants to talk to Nova about the substance, which is more important than your girl talk about stupid boys that we will just kill anyway. *His* words, not *mine*!"

"I'm going to fucking shoot you and melt your face off!" Father Falcon yelled, the sound breaking his usual iron calm as Daddy Lex gasped in shock.

"But that's my best attribute! That and my dic—" His voice cut off with a loud bang against the door, and a scuffle sounded on the other side.

Mom rolled her eyes but stood up. "I guess we have to call your siblings and talk about business. Are you okay with that?"

I nodded. The hollow that had sat under my ribs loosened enough to let me stand tall. "Yeah. I wallowed long enough. Time to sort this shit out."

She gave me a soft smile, winking at me as she opened her mouth. Another loud bang came from the door, followed by sounds that said the scuffle had escalated to a fight.

She snapped her head toward the door, voice whipping out in a queen's command. "All right! You can come in, but no talking about killing or chopping people's balls for her, okay?!"

It was silent until a chorus of muffled 'okay's and a grumbled 'yes' leaked through before the door opened, which had my sides bursting. My mom was a boss. Always had been and always would be.

I let the ridiculous warmth of my parents in, both the armor and the absurdity. For the first time in days, I felt like I was able to breathe. Whichever way it went, I was definitely going to be okay because I had some crazy people who loved me at my back.

28

NOVA

"I didn't really have all the lab equipment that I wanted, but I made do with the stuff here in Ireland, and Calix did some testing and sent me the reports. This, partnered with what we've been finding on our travels, was interesting enough to bring to your attention," Father Falcon shared.

After my conversation with Mom, my dads came in, each of them flickering to life with their own hologram, then we patched in my siblings for a family discussion.

Calix butted in first, of course. "Let's talk about this substance." He shuffled around mountains of paperwork on his desk. "Hold on."

Father Falcon's mouth tightened as the shuffle grew louder and more papers fell off his desk.

He finally exploded. "Calix! How is your desk in such a state? How many times have we had this conversation?!" His normally neutral features were wide and tight.

Calix didn't look up. "I know where everything is." He switched to the other side. "It's fine." He went deeper, still digging around. "Just—ah, found it!" He held the paper up high, triumphant, as though he'd just pulled Excalibur from a heap of forms and documents.

Father Falcon groaned, his body visibly shaking as he tried to keep his normal ninety-degree angle posture. "Where did I go wrong?"

Daddy Lex leaned back, hands behind his head. "Cheer up, old man. Kids will be kids. At least they're out of the house, right?"

Every hologram turned to him. He smiled and shrugged, enjoying the attention. "What?! That's what I hear lots of parents complain about."

Ezra quickly steered the ship back on course. "Calix, we know that this substance attaches to supe DNA and amplifies powers. Right?"

Calix quickly went into intellectual mode, lifting the paper in his hands as his proof, forgetting that we hadn't seen it. "That's what I thought... at first." His words began to come out faster, layered with the thrill of discovery. "But as I started to do a more in-depth study, dissecting the data, I noticed some irregularities."

He moved his chair closer to the video reader. "Human DNA rejected it immediately. Without any magic to use as a food source, the foreign cells quickly became dormant. But when I tested it against supe DNA, it latched on tight like a parasite. After the attachment, its behavior became more like a steroid, artificially pumping up the host's magic, but once it reached max potential, it burned out, consuming the host's magic until there was nothing left."

His eyes scanned our parents' holograms. "I asked our parents to look at it, see if they've run into this before. That was when they said we all needed to talk about what they've been dealing with overseas."

Mom nodded and leaned back, fingers interlaced, the picture of grace sharpened by danger. Her wavy ash-white hair and golden pink eyes matched mine and my siblings, though her gaze was shadowed with the years she'd experienced. While she looked like she wasn't a day past thirty-five, her mannerisms were that of an experienced gangster.

"Nova's territory wasn't the first place this *stuff* surfaced." She looked at Apà Cosmo, who unfolded his arms, his frown deepening.

"Not even the second," he added, his no-nonsense voice sharp and concise. "While traveling, we've been meeting with leaders of supe organizations like ours across the continents, per Ezra's request." Ezra dipped her head slightly in a silent thanks.

"One of the things we learned is this substance made its way through Asia, the Mediterranean, and Europe before ending up on your doorsteps." Looking at my mom and dads, he continued with a smirk. "We may have helped them out with a few situations here and there."

Riot's voice cut through, sounding skeptical. "How? How did you help them?"

Daddy Lex leaned forward, grinning before she finished her question. His hands waved in front of him like he was brushing away dust. "Oh, you know... like finding snitches, getting information, taking care of people trying to fuck with them, killing people—the good stuff. It's still vacation." All my parents were laughing, eyes twinkling with secrets.

Riot nodded once, dead serious, like she completely under-stood him. Ezra's mouth twitched, a hint of a smirk, but it was gone as soon as it appeared.

Dad Ax's voice growled like thunder, "While handling this, we tripped over some bodies in back alleys, ones that had green stuff coming out of their mouths or eyes. We found a couple of them alive, but they had to be put down after they tried to go on a rampage." His jaw flexed. "It was a little bit of the Wild West, but we kept it from getting out of hand."

The room went still, everyone taking in the weight of his words. If what he was saying was correct, this wasn't just an *us* attack. This was more of an attack on supes in general, and they were going for the strongest or the ones with the most power first.

Aniyah's arms folded tight across her chest, her nostrils flared. "And where were *their* people? Her eyes narrowed. "How come you guys were doing all the work?"

Five grown men, former bosses themselves, shifted under her glare. Red crept up their necks until they looked like schoolboys who'd been caught smoking behind the gym. All our lives, they'd had a big soft spot for Aniyah. She was the youngest daughter after all. *Eye roll.*

"I told you," my mom mumbled out the side of her mouth. "She's got you all wrapped around her little finger, and it's your fault for letting her."

Never one to resist a bad idea or a way to make everyone groan, Daddy Lex grinned. "She may have us wrapped around her finger, but you have us wrapped up in your pus—"

"Nope!" Calix's voice cracked through the air, sharp as a whip.

Aniyah doubled over with laughter, clutching her stomach. Mom's cheeks flushed a rosy hue against her pale skin, but she leaned closer to Daddy, lips curling with a promise only he heard. His face lit up like it was his birthday.

Father Falcon cleared his throat. "In doing all that..." His gaze cut across the room, silently reminding them to get back on track. "The data showed that the turned supes were able to last much longer and sustain their original forms better than born supes while on this substance. They eventually met the same end, but, in most cases, the time was doubled, if not tripled."

Calix's voice rose in a rush. "When Father told me his finds, I went to test the theory and found that he was right. The rate in which the substance would latch on and pump up the magic to consume was a much slower rate." He took a long exhale. "My thought is that, at the DNA level, there's a difference between borrowed magic and born magic."

That made sense considering we had a spike in missing turned supes. It wasn't just that they were poor or undesired; it was because he got more out of them. "That tracks with what we're experiencing." I nodded. "It's the turned supes that are disappearing."

I ran through what I had found in the cave, giving my parents this information for the first time. When I finished, my parents didn't have any questions, no, but their faces darkened.

Ezra's curiosity rang out. "What did these organizations do to get rid of the problem?"

Mom's lips thinned. "They didn't. Every time someone got close, the trail would vanish, whole labs emptied overnight, then the same pattern would start over somewhere new."

Ezra turned to Calix, her voice firm. "Can you make something to counter it? An antidote?"

Calix's cocky grin slid into place, smug and certain. "Already started on one." He looked at his watch. "Just give me another twenty-four hours and a consult with the bio team, and I'll have something to neutralize it." His gaze went over to something we couldn't see. "Then I'll look into that old fae blade that got Nova. See what's up with that ancient fae magic."

The moment Calix said the words, my parents immediately sat up straight.

"ANCIENT WHAT?!"

"What the fuck happened to Nova?"

"Fae magic knife?"

"Never heard of one."

EZRA RAISED BOTH HANDS, trying to keep the parents calm. "Nova ran into someone connected with all of this, and they had a magic knife that could stop a supe from healing." Before their voices grew louder, she followed with, "As you can see, Nova is fine."

As soon as the noise died down, Dad Ax thundered, "What the fuck? Since when do we have ancient fae magic?"

Papa Avery rubbed his chin, brows knitting. "Never heard of that kind of enchantment, and I'm like fae royalty."

Father Falcon's sharp eyes moved between us. "And how exactly do you know its ancient *fae* magic?"

Ezra didn't flinch. "A fae jaguar shifter identified it. From my research, he only left Faerie about five years ago. He said it carried the feel of old power, one that was locked away when the royal wars started in Faerie."

Daddy Lex leaned forward, smirking at me before licking his lips in excitement. "You talking about the fighter on the TV? The one bugging Nova?" His gaze swept toward the other dads. "I thought we'd agreed to kill him, no?"

The words "kill him" made my pulse stumble.

"No," I said a little too fast. Making myself talk slower, I added, "He's fine. We're, uh, bringing him on staff. He won't be a problem."

Five pairs of male parental eyes snapped to me, watching me intently, their skepticism loud enough to hum. *What is it with this family and giving people looks? Like, look somewhere else!* I tried to look away from their questioning stares, focusing on Ezra like I was waiting for her direction.

Mom shot up from her seat. "That's it. We're coming home." She was already motioning to the others. "Let's go. Pack your shit. They need us."

Ezra's tone came quickly, calm but unyielding. "Mom. No. You need to finish this last trip. We got everything handled at the home front."

Mom froze mid-step, head tilting like a lioness deciding whether or not to eat her cub. "Ezra," she said slowly, deadly, "I told you this *idea* of yours was not more important than our family."

457

Idea of hers? My eyes snapped toward Ezra. *What the hell is she plotting overseas?*

"I know," Ezra said softly, steady as a rock, "but I got this. We got this. We are the bosses, *remember?*"

Their eyes locked onto each other, waging that silent kind of argument only moms and daughters could have. Finally, Mom's eyes fluttered. She huffed, grumbling about her "stupid, stubborn kids," and dropped back into her seat.

Ezra smiled, her victory won.

"We've got this," she said again, firmer, loud enough for all of them to hear. "We're strong enough to handle it, so let us." She looked at the rest of us. "Right?"

We all chimed in, one after another.

"THIS IS NOTHING. Don't worry about it."

"We got this under control."

"No one's getting past my territory."

"The antidote is nearly done anyway. It's fine."

MOM CROSSED HER ARMS, still muttering under her breath, but she didn't stand again. That meant she was accepting our word. That had to be a win, right?

Always the one to try to bridge the gaps, Papa Avery took the high ground. "You know that we and your mom support you guys in everything you decide. We trust you." He winked at us and smiled. "Just know, we're always here. Ready to jump in if you need us."

The parents looked around at each of us before they got up, and the meeting adjourned. "And get that fucking knife examined," Papa Avery warned. "Contact your Papu Syris." He winced as he said it. "I know he's a handful, but he's the last survivor of the fae royal line. He might know something about this magic that we don't."

"We'll talk to him once I find him again." When Mom's brow lifted at that, Ezra huffed, "They found the tracking device."

Mom barked out a laugh, warning Ezra to find them because they were troublemakers even on their best behavior.

With the call winding down, the parents' holograms flickered like dying stars as they said their goodbyes. Ezra lifted a hand to scratch her nose, the movement too deliberate to be casual, and shot us a look over her fingers.

Her signal was clear. *Stay on the line.*

I folded my arms together. *Yeah, well, I have some questions for you, too, E.*

Once the parents blinked out, the silence stretched. Ezra turned to Calix. "Are you really that close to making that antidote?"

He nodded, rustling some papers again. "Yeah. The research Father sent from the other organizations helped fill in some odd gaps. I'm going to test it once we get off the line."

"Great," Ezra responded. "Send a batch to Nova first, then some to each of us just in case."

I leaned forward, brows furrowed. "Still doesn't explain why it landed here?" I asked, thinking over everything.

"It doesn't matter." Ezra's voice iced over. "We'll handle them. Same as every other infestation that crawls our way." Her gaze didn't waver. Judgment passed and sentence delivered, their fate sealed.

"So, E," Calix eased out, "when were you going to tell us about the parents meeting with other organizations?"

Ezra's jaw clenched, and the smallest tic trembled under her left eye, betraying the gears turning behind her calm exterior. She straightened, her words measured. "They were already traveling. I just... suggested they visit a few groups, see how things were done. Then if something came up, maybe lend a hand."

Aniyah's brows shot up. "A hand?" She knew that we never did anything for nothing in return. Out of the kindness of our hearts? *Ha! Yeah, right.*

Riot's voice followed, flat, suspicious. "Why?"

Ezra's smile didn't reach her eyes. "Because favors matter, especially the kind owed by leaders." Her tone softened, becoming much too smooth. "Just in case we ever need to call one in."

The room went quiet until Calix did a slow clap, cutting through like sarcasm wrapped in applause. "Of course," he said with a humorless laugh. "Our Ezra is always ten steps ahead."

Riot's frown deepened, the realization catching up to her before it did to the rest of us.

Ezra *never* made any moves without a plan. Power was her favorite language. I thought back over the last few years— planning this whole legitimate side of the business for us, making us so much money that I never knew what she planned to do with it all. Now she wanted to bank favors from overseas organizations. The picture was forming before I wanted to admit it.

"So," I said, trying for a laugh, "is the world the endgame?"

Ezra's eyes flicked across each of us, measuring our reactions. My heart skipped a beat.

She didn't deny it.

I almost wanted to ask her, *'The world, E? What the fuck are you going to do with the whole damn world?'*

When she finally spoke, her fingers flicked out like all of this wasn't that big of a deal. "We're years out from anything like that," she confirmed. "I'll bring it up when we're ready, then we can take a vote, of course. You all have a say, like always."

Good old Ezra. Not an outright lie, but she would set up the board so we were rigged to win. She was going to make it hard for us to refuse her when the time came.

Aniyah grinned, unbothered. "Sounds like fun. I've always wanted to have a second location in Paris."

Calix glared at Aniyah before turning back to Ezra with a groan. "E, taking on other organizations means we need intel, funds, and weaponry they don't know how to combat. We would also need to get some men on the inside." His fingers tapped on his desk in a steady, anxious rhythm. "That's a war plan."

Ezra nodded. "Which is why we're not there... yet. This is long-term, years-long." She glanced at her screen, feigning distraction. "I told you, Cal, I'll bring it to a vote when the time comes."

When he sputtered, not making coherent words, she folded her hands in front of herself, staring at all of us. "Until then, don't worry about it. When the time comes and I put it to a vote, if you don't think we're ready or the risk is too great, then you can always say no, and it will be squashed. Simple."

Thinking over the bomb she'd just dropped, none of us spoke.

Ezra sighed, breaking the silence. "For now, our focus stays on the home front and this substance. We need to find the source, the creator, and we need to eliminate them for good. Do you all agree?"

"Agreed," we said one by one, even though we all knew her plan wasn't over. It was just beginning.

Ezra was like that—a bulldozer when it came to what she wanted or thought was right. It was what made her such a great, effective leader.

We said our goodbyes. With my life the complicated mess it already was, the call had given me more to think about than I wanted, but she was right. I didn't have time to think of five to ten years down the future, but if I did...

I closed my eyes and let my mind wander.

I was at the same kitchen table, a small spoon clinking against the bowl. A child with turquoise eyes and ash-white hair looked up at me, pointing to the spoon for more. As the front door shut, a voice called out my name, making my heart race. Conrad. He was home.

Deslen padded into the room, a baby cradled on his shoulder. His laugh was soft as he kissed the crown of my head and settled down beside me.

A set of growls came from the backdoor. A large black wolf and a little white one padded through the door, tails sweeping against the floor before they came my way. The feelings of home and love took over my body.

I opened my eyes, knowing then and there that this was what I wanted.

Even if it led me to pain later. Even if I had to settle for less, I knew it would be worth it in the very end. That dream was worth the try.

Before all of that, I needed to fix this issue with this doctor now.

Fishing my phone from my pocket, I typed out a message for three. *We need to talk.*

My job was to keep my territory safe. That was my line in the sand to hold. I needed to be the arm of the Syndicate that stood forever strong, and I would be. I was Nova fucking Rossey, and our enemies would feel the wrath of my fists. That was my guarantee.

29

CONRAD

"Oh! Here you go, mate-broth—I mean, Conrad."

Deslen caught himself midword, flashing a sheepish grin that didn't fit a man of his size. He slid a thick contact folder across my desk, the paper whispering against the wood. Since he didn't know how long it was going to take Nova to officially recognize him as a mate, he wanted to solidify his presence in her life and make himself into an asset for her.

He rubbed the back of his neck, eyes darting anywhere but mine. "My manager's been on my ass about getting Nova to sign. Just... y'know, make it all legit."

I flipped open the folder, pretending to study the legalese instead of wondering why I hadn't thought of something like this first. Zeth, who was her second, had her loyalty. Deslen was quickly working up the fighter ranks, making it so he was a part of her world. And me? I was still trying to figure out where I fit.

"All right," I said, forcing my voice to steady. "I'll comb through this and flag anything shady."

"Thanks, man." His shoulders dropped like he'd been holding them tight for hours. "Just don't want to pile on more stress for her, ya know?" His arms got tight—probably twisting his fingers underneath the desk. A nervous habit, maybe?

I almost smiled. The big cat looked ready to shred someone one second yet could do nothing but wring his hands the next. I hadn't wanted to like him, not after I saw him and her covered in blood, leaning toward her, all easy smiles and familiar touches. When he'd reached out to shake my hand, calling us *mate-brothers*, I'd wanted to break that hand. We didn't need another rival for her attention, not when every part of me wanted to hoard her like treasure.

But things had shifted. All of us being her mates, Nick's betrayal, the chaos that followed… it gave even Zeth and me some common ground to bounce our anger off. That night, when he took us to Nova's place, we both spat out curses, agreeing that he needed to pay for his betrayal.

Deslen, on the other hand, barely looked at us that night. He'd been too focused on tearing through her kitchen then vanishing out the back door.

When Deslen finally came back from the forest, his arms were full of flowers and herbs, and dirt was smudged up his forearms.

"When she comes back from her run, I'll draw her a bath," Deslen said quietly, setting the handful of herbs and flowers on the counter. "The scents should help ground her."

That was the first time I saw him not as competition but as someone trying to keep her safe in his own quiet way.

Before either of us could answer, he was moving up the stairs, footsteps soft for a man his size.

Zeth and I just stood there, still fuming. Rage burned under my skin, raw and directionless. Nick's name sat on my tongue like acid, every thought circling back to what I wanted to do to him for breaking her heart.

Then I heard water running upstairs, along with the soft thud of movement, and it hit me. He wasn't thinking about revenge or how angry he was. He was thinking about *her.*

Why the hell wasn't I?

In my head, I'd built Nova up like some indestructible legend, our Syndicate boss, the woman who faced down enemies twice her size and walked away without a scratch. I forgot that power didn't make you immune to suffering. Under all that fire and command, she still *felt.*

A couple of hours later, the sound of the back door opening snapped me out of my head. She stepped through, barefoot, dirt streaking her skin. Blood was splattered on her arms and her hands. Her moonlit hair clung to her face, wild, tangled, like she'd fought the whole damn world and barely made it back.

Her rose gold eyes found us, their usual spark gone. What was left looked hollow, like something precious had been scooped out and replaced with silence.

Her lips twitched into a ghost of a smile, the kind people made when they were trying to keep you from worrying. It gutted me.

I'd wanted to be her protector, her partner, the one who could match her fire, but, in that moment, I saw how little that mattered. She didn't need another fighter. She needed someone who could hold her when the fight was over.

Upstairs, I heard the faint slosh of water, and the scent of wild flowers drifted down the hall. Deslen again, making space for her to breathe.

For the first time, I understood why fate had given her more than one mate. She carried worlds on her back, and she needed more than one set of hands to catch her when the weight got too heavy.

And I wanted—no, *needed*—to be one of them. Not just for me, not for the Syndicate. For *her.*

Deslen showed up at the top of the stairs, holding his hand out to her, beckoning her to meet him. She walked past Zeth and me without a word, only that hollow smile.

The moment Nova disappeared upstairs, Zeth moved.

"Kitchen," he said, jerking his chin toward it before looking up the stairs longingly.

We didn't need to talk about why. The air between us carried the same thought. *Comfort her.*

He rifled through cabinets, pulling out chips, fruit, chocolate, whatever he could find. I grabbed a tray and started arranging it like it was a damn peace offering. He tossed me a bag of popcorn and grunted, "Movie night."

"Yeah." We all needed to take a break for the night.

By the time Nova came back down, hair damp, eyes still swollen from everything she'd held in, the living room glowed a soft golden hue from the fireplace Zeth had turned on. Blankets. Snacks. A stack of movies that had nothing to do with heartbreak. We didn't mention Nick. None of us did.

That night was quiet. Sweet, even. No heat, no tension, no undercurrent of lust tugging at the bond between us. Just her soft laughter slipping through the silence like a spark in the dark. Every time her lips twitched into a real smile, my chest eased a little.

The golden thread that tied me to her pulsed stronger that night. I could feel it hum in my bones. But still, something inside her kept a wall up.

That was fine. I'd wait—forever if I had to. She was worth it.

The sound of my office door clicking open brought me back to the present, and I looked up to see Zeth stepping in, sunglasses pushed up into his hair. He nodded at me, then his gaze caught the stack of papers on my desk.

"What's that?"

"Contract," I said, tapping the folder. "Deslen's manager put it together. Thought I'd look it over before anyone starts throwing money around."

Zeth slid into the chair across from me, arms crossed, the hint of a smirk tugging at his mouth. "Good call. Better you than our lawyers. They'll try to bleed him dry. Plus, you got the head for that kind of shit."

For a second, I just stared at him. Compliments weren't exactly Zeth's language. The guy was all street edges and sarcasm, while I played the polished businessman. Oil and water, most days. Still, the respect in his voice felt real.

Or maybe he was still seething about Nick and was giving me a break. Could've gone either way.

He stretched, glancing toward the window. "Nova's got her boss meeting today. Gotta check in after, make sure things went smoothly."

Deslen grinned, bright and easy. "Good. Family's important right now."

At that, Zeth flinched. It wasn't much, but enough to notice. His jaw tightened, eyes flicking away like the word *family* carried too much weight.

"Yeah," he muttered. "Just... keep in mind, Nova's the sane one in that bunch. The rest of the bosses? Think 'genius' with a touch of homicidal. Or maybe the other way around."

He tried to make it sound like a joke, but the faint tremor in his voice said otherwise.

His words hung in the air like smoke because, hell, he wasn't wrong. The Syndicate ran on loyalty, blood, history, and shared violence. My own men? They'd sell me out the second a better deal came along, but that was the difference between running a business and belonging to a family.

Zeth leaned forward, elbows on his knees, eyes hard. "If you're gonna last in this family, listen close. Don't cross Ezra. *Ever.*"

Deslen straightened in his seat, taking his advice to heart. Zeth didn't blink. "You can negotiate with most of the bosses. They've all got their twisted sense of balance. Ezra doesn't. She'll burn a city to ash if it means protecting what's theirs." He scrubbed a hand through his hair, the movement tight, weary. "And she won't lose a wink of sleep over it."

Deslen frowned, a crease forming between his brows. "But... we're her sister's mates. She wouldn't—"

Zeth barked a laugh so sharp it cut through the tension. I smothered mine behind a stack of papers, keeping my eyes down to hide the grin tugging at my lips.

Everyone knew Ezra Desmond. Every fucking one. Even the ones who'd never met her had stories—friends who vanished overnight, rivals whose entire legacies were erased. She was a storm in heels, and you either moved with her wind or got torn apart.

"It's cute," Zeth said, wiping a tear from his eye. "You thinking that protects you."

Deslen's expression shifted from hope to confusion, then the slow, dawning dread of someone realizing he'd just stepped into deep water. He slumped in his chair, silent.

The buzz of three phones broke the moment. I glanced down.

Nova: *Can you come over? Found out some information and want to share.*

When I looked up, Zeth was already on his feet, jacket halfway on. "Let's go."

Who the hell made him alpha of this little pack? I shoved back my chair with a muttered "damn demon thinks he's Mister Perfect."

Zeth stopped mid-step, his profile half-lit by the desk lamp. "Perfect?" he echoed. His voice came low, even. "If it wasn't for Nick, I'd be the one who had hurt her the worst." His eyes pinched in pain, words coming out under his breath. "Didn't even realize it until too late."

He turned, eyes meeting mine. Dark, steady, stripped bare of the usual arrogance. "But I'm done being afraid. Done letting guilt run me. I'm stuck with you two, like it or not, because it's what *she* needs. I see that now."

A slow breath escaped him, and his shoulders dropped. "Right now, she needs to see that we're choosing her, all of us, no matter what. If putting up with you idiots helps her believe it, then fine. I'll take it. I'll do whatever needs to be done to make her happy, and you two, for some reason, make her happy."

And just like that, he was gone, the door swinging shut behind him.

I stared after him for a long moment, the room too quiet. Deslen shifted beside me, that big, gentle grin creeping along his face.

"Guess he's not wrong," I muttered, reaching for my coat. "You ready, Des?"

He nodded and followed me. I locked the office behind us, the two of us heading out after Zeth.

I hated that he was right. I could see the pieces they filled for Nova. I saw it when we were on the couch just lazing about. Deslen's soothing calmness and complete devotion, right from the jump. Zeth's steadfast loyalty and ability to anticipate her needs.

They were all-in on her, just like I was, but, for once, the thought of sharing her didn't burn quite as much.

NOVA WAS WAITING at the door before we even pulled up, her silhouette framed by the porch light. This time, her eyes weren't hollow. Those molten-pink irises burned again, fierce and alive, with the same fire I'd seen the night we met. Hope flickered in my chest. Maybe, just maybe, the three of us could be enough to stitch her heart back together.

She led us inside, straight to the dining table. The air was heavy with tension that rippled off her. Nova didn't waste time. She dove into everything—her meeting with the family, the news rippling across continents, why turned supes were being targeted by this madman, this "doctor."

"And this filth got into *my* territory." Her words lashed out, sharp enough to strike. The veins in her neck stood out as she slammed her fists against the table so hard it shook. "*Mine!*"

Zeth reached for her hand. "Nov, it's not—"

"No, Zeth. This is *my* job." She grabbed the edge of the table, exhaling before rolling her shoulders up, looking at each of us. "My family. My people. I protect them, or I don't deserve the title of Boss Rossey."

Her eyes went back to the table, narrowing as she searched the surface like it had answers. "I gotta find him." Her voice was half a promise, half a demand. "I have to do it quickly." Her hands turned into fists. "I need to make an example out of him."

Her whole body buzzed, her wolf waiting just beneath her skin, ready to shift, to unleash her power on the world. One wrong word, and she'd be gone, storming the streets, ready to draw blood.

We couldn't let her burn herself out like that.

Before I could think twice, I moved. The world blurred around me, and then I was in front of her. One hand slid behind her back, the other to the nape of her neck, steady but firm.

"Nova," I breathed.

She barely had time to blink before my mouth found hers.

She stiffened, shock flashing through her body, then melted. The tremor in her breath turned into a soft gasp against my lips as my fingers trailed lower, grounding her, reminding her to feel instead of fight.

Her lips parted, an invitation. Acceptance. Heat surged between us, wild and unrelenting, the world narrowing to just the two of us and the sound of our uneven breathing.

When we finally broke apart, her forehead rested on my shoulder, chest heaving.

Behind her, Zeth stood motionless, turquoise eyes sharp with jealousy that he didn't bother to hide. Deslen leaned back in his chair, eyes gleaming, watching like a man studying a storm.

I smiled at them, then let my lips brush the edge of Nova's throat. My voice dropped to a whisper meant for her alone.

"You know, the other day, I read that a stressful mind and body produce forty percent less than what they're capable of," I murmured, letting my hands roam her tight frame. "Let us help you, Boss."

A shiver rippled through her. Her fingers caught the bottom of my shirt and tugged it free before tracing those warm fingers along my stomach, slowly and deliberately.

It took everything in me not to groan.

Not one to waste time, I flicked the button of her pants and stuck my hand in, rubbing her clit just to watch her pupils dilate. The golden edge to her rosy irises caught the overhead lights like cut gemstones.

"Con—" she tried to get out, but I swooped in and captured her lips with mine, stopping her from talking. I swallowed the moan that worked its way out of her as I moved my fingers lower. The sticky wetness that pooled between my fingers had me aching for her, my tongue pressing against my fangs at the thought of tasting her and the image of her back arching off whatever surface I could pin her to.

"Con." She pulled away just enough to talk. "Seriously. We need to figure out—"

Using my vampire speed, I yanked her pants down and propped her on the table. Kneeling underneath her, I slowly peeled the pants down inch by inch, pressing my lips to newly exposed skin—the curve of her knee, the soft flesh of her calf—as I tugged them off completely.

"What was that, Boss? I don't think I can hear you." Her breath caught in her throat as I kissed my way up her leg, not paying much mind to the sound of a chair scraping against the floor.

Her chest rose and fell in rapid succession as she looked down, watching me suck hard on her inner thigh. These small noises escaped her throat as her hips thrust forward, seeking friction.

"I said—"

Zeth was at her side, grabbing her chin and yanking her face toward him before he devoured her. I couldn't help but watch as her spine curved under his touch, her shoulders rolling back. Where my kiss was controlled and methodical, coaxing her out, his was fast and all-consuming, demanding her attention.

I vaguely noticed the sound of another chair scraping, but all of that was shoved into the background as soon as that honeydew smell intensified. My eyes shifted down to her glistening pussy, and I licked my lips. That scent called to something primal in my soul. I could feel my heart beat in my ears as my focus zeroed in, and a rumble built in my chest. How wolfish of me.

Just as her noises took on a deeper edge, I slammed my fang into her thigh and slid two fingers inside of her, moving them in time with my long, deep pulls of her sweet blood. Her gasps were music to my ears. Her blood rushed through my body, heating up every inch of me until sweat beaded at my temples. My dick strained painfully, begging to be released from its fabric prison.

"I don't think we need this," I heard from the other side of her. A loud ripping sound caught my attention just in time to watch Deslen tear her shirt in half. "There…" His hand traveled up her taut stomach. She trembled, goosebumps rising in the wake of his touch. "Now, *that's* a thing of beauty." He cupped her breast, lips circling her nipple as he ran his other hand up and down his dick.

Feeling my fingers drenched in her sticky, hot pleasure, I drove a third finger in while licking at her clit. She tore away from Zeth, gasping for breath as she cried out, "Holy. Fuck. That feels good."

She looked down at Deslen, her teeth sinking into her bottom lip as her eyes found his cock bobbing for her attention. Her hand pushed his away, and he moaned against her breast as she began stroking him.

Zeth yanked her head back, using his thumb to press down on her tongue and open her mouth. His mouth was so close to hers you would think he was giving her the air she needed to breathe. "You're going to have to take all three of us, Nov. Can you handle that?" Somehow, all of his clothes were already off, his hips moving as he rubbed his fully erect cock on her thigh.

"Yes," she choked out.

He removed his thumb from her mouth and let go of her hair. She looked around at all three of us, and with the most beautiful, breathless words, she said, "I'll always be able to handle all of my mates, however you want me."

Those words sent heat flooding through my chest, and my muscles tensed, releasing in waves. My fingers tightened on her thigh, my other hand gripping the edge of the table hard enough that the wood groaned. The tightness that had lived in my shoulders for months suddenly released. Lungs expanded like I'd been holding my breath underwater and finally broke the surface. Her sweet scent intensified, making a round of growled moans circle her.

There was something so fucking beautiful about having this strong, powerful mate, her body honed like a weapon, smelling like a fresh wildflower dipped in honey. She was ready and simply waiting for us to pluck it.

When I shoved in a fourth finger, her eyes rolled into her head as her thighs trembled, then she began thrusting against my hand like all reason had abandoned her.

"Yes. Fuck. Yes," she cried.

Apparently, Zeth couldn't take it anymore because he hopped on the table and stood behind her, facing me. "This is for you, my Nova, my love." Power burst out of him, stronger than the power he'd used when we fought in the cave. This time, it flowed into me, racing up and down in a cycle, and my vision sharpened. Every color became more vivid, every sound amplified.

My heart raced too loudly, saliva flooding my mouth like a beast. Every thought, every inch, every cell of my body was consumed with the thought of making her come. My hands shook with it. My jaw clenched. My body ached for it, muscles coiled tight and eager.

Deslen moaned, kissing his way up her neck as her thumb rubbed over the head of his cock, smearing his pre-cum around.

Then Zeth's magic hit Nova. Her head flung back, her body convulsing as she screamed, "Yes. More. I want more. I want all of you."

"I'll give it to you, Nov," Zeth said with a smirk on his face. He positioned himself over her face, cradling the back of her neck before shoving his dick into her mouth.

"Oh, fuck, Nova. Fuck. You're so wet and warm. So fucking perfect." He moaned, pumping his dick in and out, and I was mesmerized by the rise and fall of the bulge in her throat. The erotic view had me craving more. I wanted more of her, all of her.

Standing up, I pulled my fingers out of her and tore my clothes off before adjusting her hips and positioning my pulsing cock right at her entrance. "You want it all, Boss? I'll give you everything." In one tight shove, I bottomed out, sinking into her so deeply I felt lost for a second.

Her screams were muffled on Zeth's cock, and he began to pump faster. Not wanting to miss out on the opportunity, I matched his pace, making it so she was fucked both ways at a steady pace. My eyes couldn't tear themselves away from where I thrust in and out of her, drinking in the sight of her pussy swallowing my cock. Those silky, soft walls turned into a vise grip, and she gushed all around me.

Zeth pulled back, giving her a moment to cry out her release and catch a breath before starting up again. "Fuck, Nova. I can't get enough of you." His breathless words continued as his head tipped back. "I want you all the time, every second of every day. I can't eat, sleep, or breathe without thinking about you."

Deslen's body moved next to me, lifting her leg up to give his frame some room as he positioned his cock closer to mine. "My heart and soul," he cooed, "I want to fill you, want to be inside you." His hand moved to her clit and rubbed it. "We're going to stretch you so wide you won't know where you begin and we end, then we'll claim your second orgasm together."

I was glaring at him for a second, about to tell him no, when Nova said, "I want to watch it." Her swollen, used lips and passion-filled eyes had me making room without thinking.

Wanting her to look at me, I thrust into her hard, and she released a long cry that worked me up even more. I wanted to fill her, fuck her, watch until her body couldn't take any more of what we were doing and gave in.

Deslen slowly worked his cock in next to mine. The sensation was odd at first, rubbing alongside his cock, but when her pussy tightened the further he got, my breath caught in my throat, and my abs clenched hard.

Getting the right position to fit us both took a little see-sawing, but once we did, we slowly pushed in together, stretching her as wide as she could go. Her eyes fluttered as her mouth fell open, but no sound came out. Her whole body was locked down so tight I hissed out a breath. *Fuck. She felt so amazing.*

We worked up a good, fast rhythm, fucking her at the same time, filling her up so completely that her arms could no longer hold her upright. Zeth was there to catch her, and he gently set her down as he knelt at her side.

Deslen shifted the leg in his hand, pushing it up and down toward the table, opening her hips up even further. "Fuuuc-cck! K-keep fucking m-me."

You couldn't make me stop even if you tore my heart out right here and now.

Her body jerked in motion with our thrusts, melting into a puddle for us, her muscles slack, head lolling to the side. That was until Zeth dove in for a kiss, taking her mouth as he gripped her throat.

He pulled away just an inch, whispering into her lips, "Let it all go. Let us in. Let us take care of you." His hand tightened, cutting off her airway. "Just feel."

His other hand snuck across her chest, plucking at her nipple then rolling it between his fingers as her body began to shake. Deslen and I had a firm grip on each leg, thrusting harder and harder.

Her thighs quivered underneath my grip before full-body tremors started, her pussy fluttering around my cock in rapid pulses. Her claws sliced out from her fingertips, digging into the table, knuckles white, tendons in her neck standing out as she strained against Zeth's grip.

Zeth must've noticed as well because he adjusted himself, moving his hand to his cock and pumping furiously, keeping their mouths locked. Deslen pulled out until just the tip of his cock was inside of her. Running his fingers up and down his soaked cock, he collected her pleasure before rubbing at her clit, then slamming back into her, causing both her and me to moan.

Her lips broke from Zeth's, gasping for breath, but her eyes stayed screwed shut until Deslen's calm voice coaxed, "Open your eyes, my mate." They slowly cracked open, and he gave her thigh a smack. They flew open after that.

"Watch how we love you. How you're everything to us. Our center. The connection to each other... it's all born from loving and desiring *you*."

Her breathing came short and clipped, her body locking down tight on us. With Deslen's cock rubbing up against mine, her soft, warm walls closing in around me, choking my cock, I couldn't stop myself. It just felt so good.

I gave one final thrust before my cum shot deep into her, filling her up. I wanted to stay locked together like this forever, to sink into her warmth and never leave.

Like a domino effect, Nova's toes curled, and her voice ripped from her throat. "I'm coming. I'm coming. Fuuucckkk!"

Deslen grunted, but I refused to move. I liked the spot I was in. He made do, gripping down on her leg for leverage as he fucked her harder. It didn't take long for him to pant, "My mate. My only—" His voice cut off as he moaned her name.

Her pussy was so full of us that our combined cum began to leak out of her, making a mess of us. I watched that cum drip, licking my lips, and my hips continued to move, my body demanding that I shove all that cum back inside her. I needed to mark her, claim her as ours.

Zeth was the last, moaning loudly as he shot his cum all over her chest, rubbing the head of his cock along her nipple as if he were painting her in himself.

For one blissful second, the only sound that echoed in the house was our panting. Deep, heavy and satisfied. That was the moment when the golden thread of our bond lit up. Nova's warmth flooded my chest, spreading outward through my veins like molten gold. The sensation was overwhelming but not painful. It was so intense my whole body stilled. I felt the door on her side of the bond open, accepting us in, and, suddenly, I could sense her completely.

A blissed-out haze radiated from her, but the flutter of anxiety was still present beneath the surface. There was also excitement thrumming like a second heartbeat. The deep ache for love—not just desire—and acceptance of every sharp edge of her shell and the soft curves of who she was inside. Underneath it all was a hollow space, a tender wound where Nick's ghost lingered even though she was trying to accept his vacancy.

Zeth rested his forehead on hers, smiling so wide it looked like it hurt. "I fucking love you so much, Nova. Thank you. Thank you for accepting an idiot like me. I promise I won't let you down. I'll be such a good mate. You'll never want for anything more."

She cupped his face, reaching up to give him a sweet, soft kiss. "I know, and I love you. I forgive you. Let's start over. Let's start this right."

Deslen pulled out first, carefully putting her leg down before coming up to her other side and tenderly kissing her neck.

"I've been searching for you for years, and now that I have you, I'll never leave. You're my whole world, the only thing keeping me tethered and whole."

She turned her head, pulling him by his chin and kissing his lips with a sigh. "We're your people now. Your family. Your shadow. You're my mate, for now and forever."

He buried his head into her neck, sucking down her scent like it was giving him life. Her blown-out, bliss-filled eyes turned to me as she lifted her hand and curled her finger, calling me to her.

I thrust into her one more time, making those pink eyes light up again, just for me, before pulling out. Her disappointed mewl had me wanting to rush back inside of her, but the bond tugged at my chest like a physical tether, and I moved around Deslen. Her head tipped back to look at me while the other two clung to her sides like they would never let go.

Her hand lifted, bringing my face down to hers, and she kissed me upside down. The pure shot of warmth that flooded through the bond wrapped around my heart like a fist. Breaking the kiss, she moved her lips over to the shell of my ear. "You deserve a mate, turned or not, and now that I have you, I won't be letting go."

How did she know? How did she know just what to say to make my throat tighten and my eyes burn? The spot in my chest where the bond had connected glowed and pulsed, and I realized it was a two-way communication. Just like I felt her concerns, fears, and happiness, she could feel mine.

"Come, mate." Deslen moved quickly, scooping up our mate. "Let's clean you up. I'll run a bath that will soothe any aches."

"Watch out," she giggled, looping her arms around his neck. "If you keep giving me the princess treatment, I'm going to get used to it and expect it all the time."

Leaning in close, he gave her a wolfish smile. "That's the goal. I don't want you knowing anything else but this princess treatment."

Watching them go up the stairs, my shoulders remained relaxed, my breathing even. I leaned back against the table, a small smile tugging at my lips. I was glad she had a mate like Deslen who put her bodily needs above all else.

Zeth sidled up next to me, pants already magically on, hands crossed over his chest as he watched them. "You know what we need to do, right?"

Remembering how she felt, the loss, the heartbreak, the void that even we couldn't fill, I growled. "Fucking Nick."

He sighed and nodded. "Fucking Nick."

While Deslen was the mate who would take care of her body, Zeth and I were the ones that would take care of her mind and heart. Our mate deserved to be whole, and this anger inside of me needed an outlet. It was time we paid Nick a visit.

NICK

The wolf mug stared back at me from my desk, its chipped grin mocking me. The guys thought it was funny, their little "welcome back" gift. Every time one of them walked past, I caught the smirk, the snicker under their breath, the muttered *good boy.* They laughed, but I could smell their fear beneath their cologne and sweat. That sour tang used to come from suspects, not my so-called friends and co-workers.

I used to be one of them—late-night takeout, card games between shifts, brothers-in-arms. Now, the air between us weighed heavy, full of sharp tension and foreign looks.

When did their jokes start to become annoying? When did the bullpen start smelling like something I wanted to escape?

The captain's gaze snagged mine from across the room, suspicion coiled behind his eyes just as it had the night I'd brought in the kid. His mouth had tightened then, too. *Did she do this? You get her? Can we finally kick out that bitch?*

His face fell with disappointment as I explained how she'd rescued the boy. The words had fallen from my lips without thinking. I remembered praising her for her fast action and leadership. I left out anything to do with the doctor or his experiments, making it sound like the boy was just in the wrong place at the wrong time. I couldn't make her his monster—not how he wanted me to.

After I was done, he yelled at me, ordering me off the case. Instead, I was to sit at my desk for beat cop work. According to him, I was a disappointment, but for some reason, that hurt less than I thought it would.

When I asked what he wanted me to do with the kid, he'd replied, "Do whatever you want with the supe's brat." With the way I felt when I heard those words, I'd expected a growl to come from my chest, but the wolf inside was silent.

Once he'd walked away, I grabbed the kid and got him a soda, a bag of chips, and some candy before taking him to one of the interview rooms for some privacy. His hands shook as I passed him the food, his eyes looking around like he knew he was in a place he shouldn't be.

"How did you know I was a cop?"

Shaking his head, the boy fingered the soda can before he whispered, "The other human kids. I overheard them talking at the gas station about an Officer Cordova being turned into a werewolf." He gulped hard, stuttering when he continued. "T-that the f-force l-lost a g-good one."

Stupid brats must've been some of the other officers' kids since the captain had been trying to keep my name out of the press. Only people at the precinct knew the details about my change, but it was bound to get out sooner or later.

After a smile to set him at ease and a few more minutes, I learned more about him. The boy's mother had just passed, and his dad was trying to find a way to support him. Dad had taken the job because it paid well. He thought his dad was a good guy, and he wanted to stay with him.

A deep rumble worked its way up my chest—the first sound the wolf had made since that night in the cave... since Nova turned away, eyes full of that quiet, final kind of hate.

I'd thought I wanted him gone. The beast. The instinct. But his silence had hollowed me out in ways I hadn't expected. Standing there in that fluorescent-lit office, I realized how lonely I felt once the thing inside me stopped talking to me.

It wasn't long before some lady came by looking for the boy. She was human, but she said that the Syndicate sent her to collect him and take him to a local safe house until his father was found. Since the captain didn't give a shit, it felt like the best option.

The next morning, my uniform fit wrong. Too tight at the throat, fabric scratching my skin like it was punishing me. I told myself it was just in my head. Undercover work messed people up, and I just needed to readjust. Breathe.

Except breathing felt impossible.

And I missed that damn fucking silk suit. The feel of it. The freedom. The space to move, to he.

A stack of paperwork was waiting on my desk, and I almost laughed at the sight. Paperwork. For a werewolf. My knuckles cracked against the edge of the desk so hard the mug rattled. I could chase down a perp in the dark with just a scent, run faster than any man in the precinct, and lift up a car with my bare hands, but I was stuck here with a stack of forms.

Maybe it was punishment. Maybe he just wanted to see if I'd break. If I'd wolf out on him so he could fire me.

I had to prove him wrong, so I filled out the fucking forms. One after another.

Keeping my head down, I drilled my way through the paperwork, but it didn't take long before I became the joke around the precinct. Dog puns thrown around left and right. Whistles to get my attention. Barking noises when I walked by. I refused to let them bother me, but when I didn't react, they just got bolder.

One morning, there were dog treats scattered across my desk. I looked up, saw the captain watching from his doorway, coffee in hand. When our eyes met, he just took another sip and turned away, his message clear. *This was acceptable. He wasn't going to stop it.*

The air in my throat burned, and that wolf inside of me bristled.

Even as a beast, a monster, I helped save those turned supes in the cave. I was there to help the human boy in a dangerous situation. Was on the hunt for a bad man doing bad things.

I've done more good as a criminal than I accomplished as a cop. That thought scared me more than the beast, the wolf, inside me.

Sleep didn't come easy that night. The sheets tangled around my legs, the pillow damp beneath my cheek. I could swear that I smelled her scent, soft, floral, maddening. It clung to my skin like a memory, drowning me with every breath.

I turned over again and pulled the pillow to my chest, pretending for half a second it was her, that her breath brushed against my throat, claws tracing fire down my back. My beast stirred, feeling restless, needy. He remembered, too.

But the bed stayed cold the rest of the night, and so did I.

When dawn bled through the blinds, I felt hollow, like something had been siphoned out of me. Even the light felt heavy on my skin.

I got up and tugged on that scratchy uniform, catching myself making a face in the mirror as I buttoned it up. I hated the way it felt on my body even more than yesterday. Every seam felt wrong, the fabric too rough, too human. I caught myself staring at my hands, the same ones that had been slick with blood in the dark, damp cave.

The vampire's snarl echoed in the hollow of my skull. I told the beast, *Rip him apart*, and he had obeyed. Our claws had torn through flesh like wet paper, ribs cracking beneath my palms, hot blood painting across my face. His heart pulsed in my mouth before my teeth chomped down, then it burst.

I didn't hesitate, didn't flinch at the act of hurting him, of tearing him apart with my own hands. When I transformed back into a man, looking at the damage I'd done, I hadn't felt disgust or regret. There'd been nothing but the high, savage and electric, coursing through me.

Even now, the ghost of that thrill spiked in my veins.

What if the true monster wasn't the beast underneath my skin but was really me at my core? What if it had always been there?

That thought haunted me through the day.

Somewhere between the reports and the whispered jokes, something shifted. I stopped calling him *the beast.* I called him *my wolf.*

He was mine. I was his. There was no going back. No tearing us apart. We were stuck together, forever.

The next morning, the uniform hung on the hanger like a lie. I tried to reach for it, but my arms wouldn't move. The stiff, starched collar, the badge, the neat lines, all of it felt foreign like a costume I'd outgrown.

The man who used to wear it followed rules, keeping his emotions buried under the weight of discipline and duty. He worked beside people who laughed in his face and called it camaraderie.

But *she*—she saw me. All of me.

Until she didn't want to anymore. Until I ruined it.

Her eyes, that night, drained of every trace of warmth. The way her breath caught before she turned away. My wolf had howled until my throat burned, begging me to chase after her, but I didn't move. I just let her walk away.

Standing in that cave, I'd told myself that I was just doing my job, but now I could admit the lie tasted bitter every time I thought about it.

If she'd wanted to kill me, she could've—even should've—but she didn't. That mercy cut deeper than any blade.

Being surrounded by the useless chatter and clicking of keyboards, I'd never felt more alone.

Each morning felt the same. The slow ache of a wolf mourning inside my ribs, his grief beating in time with mine.

The wounds never closed. They just kept bleeding quietly, a penance that seeped into everything.

The dark fabric of my untouched uniform caught in the window's light. Hand stretched out, brushing the sleeve carefully, half-expecting it to bite, I made my decision.

It wasn't born of guilt, nor was it because of the wolf whispering from the depths of my soul. This choice was mine, made by me.

Looking around my apartment, it slammed into me that I felt nothing. Nothing was holding me back, and nothing was calling me to stay. That was when I knew this life was no longer for me.

I didn't want my future to be built on pretending, on constantly being at war with myself, with my wolf. That was why I couldn't wear the badge anymore.

Initially, I joined to help people, to stand between good and evil, but years on the job had shown me it wasn't so cut and dry. The lines blurred until I couldn't tell which side I stood on anymore.

Whether they were a monster or a human, good people could do evil things and bad people could do good ones.

Sure, supes were violent in nature, but that was because they could handle it. Some of them had airs on, like they were better than humans, but others, especially the turned ones, just wanted to live a good life.

Same world. Different teeth.

Then there was the Syndicate.

Once, I'd thought they were nothing but criminals with crowns, but after Nova... after watching the way she moved through the chaos, protecting what was hers, I understood. She wasn't evil. She was *sure.*

Sure about her place in the world, sure about what she needed to accomplish. She was willing to give it her all, and I couldn't hate her for that. In fact, I was jealous of it.

Shoving the uniform into the garment bag, it was heavy and lifeless, like it was taking the weight from my shoulders. The badge followed with a dull clink. The gun came last—cold metal, no pulse, empty. The shedding of the weight felt great, even *right.*

Stepping into the station, I could feel all the stares, but I pushed past them to the captain's office. Knocking on the door, I waited until he called out, "Come in."

Burnt coffee and old resentment flooded my senses, and I almost covered my nose to keep from drowning in it. I needed to get out of here as quickly as possible. I dropped everything on his desk, the bag, the badge, the gun, the weight of the past years.

"I appreciate everything," I said, my voice steady, "but I don't think I'm a fit for the force anymore. I'm resigning."

His eyes flicked from the badge to my face. Anger flashed in his eyes, settling into contempt. "Is all this about the jokes?" he asked, scoffing as he folded his hands over his chest. "Christ, take a few days off. Grow a thicker hide." His head turned back to the computer, dismissing me like I was already gone.

That told me everything I needed to know.

I straightened, my jaw tight. "Thank you for the years, Captain." Then I turned and walked out.

His voice followed me. "Hey! Come get your shit!"

I didn't stop.

"Nick! Get your ass back over here!"

The echo of his chair scraping the floor chased me down the hall.

"I had plans for a cop like you!" he shouted from his door. "Don't you ruin this for me!"

That was when it hit me, and the sharp truth almost made me laugh. Nova Rossey might've been a criminal, her family a nest of killers and crooks, but she'd never say something like that. She didn't need anyone to make her plans work.

She stood on her own power, ruling with her blood, claws, and strength of will.

A leader who lived by the same code she demanded of her people…. There was something almost *pure* in that. Something worth following.

Pushing through the double doors, I walked out into the sun and closed my eyes, taking a deep breath. The air burned my lungs like a purifying flame. Clean, raw, *real.*

For the first time in years, the world felt light and honest. I felt free.

Danger.

My wolf's voice ripped through my mind, low and primal. I stopped mid-step, breath stalled, right before a blur shot out of the shadows.

White-hot pain tore across my cheek, slicing down my neck like fire under my skin. Instinct took over. My palms hit the ground before my face could, my body twisting into a crouch. Gravel bit into my hands, and my wolf surged forward, ready to fight.

"Fuck. His face is fucking solid."

That voice. That arrogant tone. I knew it.

Blinking through the pain, the shape in front of me sharpened. Golden-brown hair, smug grin, fangs flashing. *Conrad.*

Relief flickered for a split second, but it vanished as arms locked around my chest and hurled me into the wall. Bricks met my spine with a sickening crack, and the air got caught in my lungs. The force itself should've killed me, but I could already feel my body knitting itself back together, bones humming as they realigned.

My eyes snagged on the scuffed black boots in front of me, and I lifted my head as a familiar growl filled the alley.

"Now, Nicky," Zeth snarled as he crouched down, those green-blue eyes glowing in my face. "There are rules in this world. You hurt my mate, so now I hurt you. The vamp," he threw his thumb toward Conrad, "felt the same way, so he came along for the ride."

Conrad rolled his eyes, sighing under his breath. "Or it was *my* idea to catch him at the station, and *you* followed, but who cares? I just *came along for the ride.*"

Zeth surged up, turning to Conrad, and grumbled through clenched teeth, "What the fuck is your problem now?"

Seeing them here, my wolf backed down. The adrenaline drained right out of me, and I dropped back to the ground. I sat there with my head tilted up toward the two of them as they continued bickering in front of me.

For a heartbeat, the tension broke in my chest. My wolf peeked out.

Pack. Our pack.

Conrad shifted, nodding his head at me. "Look. Let's just finish this."

Zeth jabbed a finger at him. "Nah. You got something to say, say it, then we can get back to beating the shit out of him. Don't worry about him."

Conrad's eyes slid to me, and before I could blink, he was in front of me. His kick drove into my gut, folding me in half. The impact rattled my ribs, the sharp bloom of pain swallowing my body whole.

"My problem," he said, turning to Zeth, "is that ever since we mated with Nova, you act like you're the leader."

The words hit harder than his kick.

Mated.

My wolf whimpered, a guttural sound, inside my chest. Nova. My mate. *Their* mate now.

Zeth and Conrad's fight became background noise as my mind reeled from the fact that she'd completed this... mating thing with them. I thought that because of the tattoo on her forearm, they couldn't...

Conrad's voice broke through my haze. "Fuck that. I don't care if you've known her the longest. That just makes you the *dumbest*."

A hollow laugh slipped out before I could stop it. My head thunked back against the wall. Of course. She didn't need me, not when she had *them*. Not when Deslen could heal her, when Zeth could stand next to her in her world, when Conrad could keep up with the business side of things.

I was nothing but a ghost in her story now.

Throwing his hands up, Zeth glared down at me. "Great. Now he's laughing at us. Real intimidating, Conrad." His palm dragged down his face before a fist lashed out, unexpected and quick, its impact ringing through my jaw. Blood filled my mouth, warm and metallic, but I didn't fight back.

Didn't deserve to.

"Let's just do what we came here to do," Zeth said, flexing his knuckles. "Beat him down, make him pay, maybe bring her a souvenir to cheer her up. A hand, a tongue…" He shrugged. "Whatever takes the longest to grow back."

The words barely registered, but my brain snagged on one line: *Make her forget all about him.*

She still thought about me?

"Is she…" My voice broke. "Is she really upset?"

They froze. Conrad's brows pulled together, and Zeth's face twisted, fury sparking to life again.

"What the fuck do you think, pissant?!" Zeth roared. The next blows came fast. Fist after fist, my vision clouded, but I just sat there and took it. I welcomed the pain, finding it grounding.

When he finally stopped, chest heaving, he jerked his chin toward Conrad. "Your turn."

I braced for the next hit, but it never came.

---

* Its Not Over by Naughty

When I dared to open my eyes, Conrad was crouched in front of me, those deep forest green eyes studying me like he could see through the wreckage of my face to something deeper.

"Why do you ask?" he asked coolly.

Zeth's boots scuffed the pavement behind me, his pacing sharp, restless. Muscles trembled under his jacket like he could barely keep from lunging.

"Looking to sell us out some more, huh? Hand the Syndicate over for a cushy desk and a pat on the head from your human cop boss?" His voice cracked with fury that was sharp enough to cut. "Well, we won't let—"

"I didn't." Both of them narrowed their eyes on me. "In fact, my boss was pissed that I didn't give him what he wanted, so..."

"I quit," I rasped, spitting blood onto the ground. I winced when my ribs groaned, the broken bones snapping back into place. "Today, actually."

The sound of footsteps stopped me cold. I looked up through one good eye to find Zeth frozen mid-step and Conrad leaning back on his heels, one brow raised.

Neither spoke. They just waited.

I shrugged, though the movement caused more pain. "Didn't belong there anymore."

Zeth huffed out a bitter laugh. "Yeah, no shit. You're a fucking *werewolf.*" He jabbed two fingers against his temple. "Apparently, your skull's too damn thick to accept that."

Pressing my palms into the brick wall, I forced myself upright to stand. "That's not what I meant." My voice came out steadily despite the dull throbbing throughout my body as it healed. "It's just... I see clearer now. That badge, that job... it isn't me anymore."

The two shared a look, a silent language of raised brows and subtle shifts I didn't need to translate. I cut in before they could say anything.

"I just wanted to know how the search was going. I know she's got you three now, her *true mates.*" The words scraped out of me, each one heavier than the next. "Not trying to step on anyone's toes."

Lie. The taste of it seared my tongue. I didn't want her to be happy without me. I wanted her to ache, to miss me like I missed her. Even if I couldn't be her mate, I needed a way to stay close—as a guard dog, a grunt, anything. If letting them beat me bloody bought that chance, so be it.

"Are you stupid?!" Zeth threw his hands in the air like he was done with me.

Conrad tilted his head, his expression curious instead of furious. "You really don't know how mates work, do you?"

I looked at him, my breathing shallow. "You're mated to her, so, what, you're married now, right? She's married to all of you?"

Zeth dragged his hands down his face with a groan. "We don't have time for this shit. We need to get back before the search starts."

Search? My pulse jumped. *They're hunting that doctor? The one torturing turned supes?*

Conrad's sigh cut through the tension. "It's not like marriage," he said, eyes fixed on mine. "A mate bond is... fate.

Your soul's other half. Not all supes get a mate, and those who do usually only get one, but if you're lucky, fate might bless you with more."

A feeling of hope that I thought was lost bloomed deep in my gut.

"Each species does it differently," Conrad went on, tapping his chest. "Vamps bite. Share blood. A mark shows up on their mate's body. It's to warn other vamps to back off. Demons—" he jerked his chin toward Zeth—"grow horns. The only two times they show are under extreme anger or when they find their mate."

Zeth's lip curled as he crinkled his nose at Conrad, but he didn't argue.

Then Conrad pointed to me. "Werewolves, on the other hand, are a little different. Your wolf, in essence, picks your mate, and it's for life. In fact, I think that's how most shifter-based beings are, but we would have to ask Deslen since he's both fae and a shifter. It's not like he has wings that can change colors like fairies do."

His eyes locked on mine, steady, unflinching. "Anyone can reject a mate bond by just ignoring it and dealing with the longing that eventually turns into physical pain, but there have only been one or two known cases of that. Mates are normally treated like a gift from fate, so no one wants to turn that away." His eyes drilled into mine, saying, *'Except for you.'* At least he had the class not to say it out loud.

The thing that my mind snagged on was the longing and pain, but I wasn't thinking about me.

The words lodged in my throat. "Does that mean…" My breath hitched. "She's in pain because of me?"

Zeth groaned, his shaking hands balling into fists. "I'm done. He ruined the fun of… all of this. I'll be waiting in the damn car." He started off, then paused halfway to the street, glaring over his shoulder. "Fuck you, man. I hated you at first. Thought you'd steal her from me. Then somewhere along the way, I… hated you a little less." His jaw flexed. "You're still a major dick." With that, he stomped off.

Conrad's lips twitched, barely holding back a smirk as he watched Zeth yank the door open and slam it shut. The demon sat there with his arms folded, waiting.

After a few seconds, he sighed and slowly stood up before brushing his coat clean from invisible dirt. His fury had cooled into something worse—disappointment and maybe even pity.

"Get your head straight," he barked. "She's missing a part of her soul. That part is you. We'll hold things down, but if you're not all in, if there's even a shred of doubt, don't come back. Just disappear from here. Get as far away from us as you can. Any pain she feels will be replaced with pleasure. Every stray thought of you will be turned into sweet or dirty thoughts of us. We'll make her soul whole by giving her all of ours because we're her mates."

Leaving me with that, he strode away. Once he got into the car, I could see Zeth shouting about something, but Conrad didn't take his eyes off me until he turned the wheel and drove off.

"Got off light," I muttered to myself, letting out a shaky laugh. Zeth could've broken more than bones tonight. Conrad's restraint was the real wound.

They'd done it all for Nova. Even their mercy was for her.

That tiny spark of hope flickered again despite everything. She *did* miss me. That meant something. Everything. It had to.

Having decided what I wanted, I dusted my hands off and made my way over to the truck. My mind was already spinning through the details—gear, routes, supplies. If they were going after that doctor, I wasn't staying behind.

I had started this fight, and I was damn sure going to finish it.

31

NOVA

"Boss, we've hit every lake, every stream with a bank big enough to hide something. Every rock formation, landmark, and…" Robert swallowed. "Nothing."

My palm cracked against the table. The holographic map flickered in and out. I didn't bother turning toward him as heat crawled up my neck, my words coming out like I'd swallowed gravel. "So, we tore through half the damn wilderness, and not a single thing looked off to you?"

Silence. A hollow, guilty silence that only fed the fiery rage in my chest.

I turned on my heel and closed in, the air between us tightening with quiet menace. "You're a werewolf," I hissed, jabbing a finger at his chest. "One of my best trackers. Supes are getting snatched and turned into walking time bombs, and you're standing here telling me you can't sniff out one damn clue?"

His gaze hit the floor. At least he had that much sense.

I turned away and stalked back to the table before I did something regrettable. The map hovered above it, blue and gold layers twisting in slow rotation, showing mountain ranges etched in sharp, bright light. I touched the marker in the region he claimed to have checked, and the surface flashed before it became grey.

What the fuck am I missing!?

The door opened, and Zeth's voice rang out with authority. "Rob, *out*."

Robert hesitated for a heartbeat, looking at me, and when I gave a curt nod, he retreated as fast as he could. One set of footsteps faded down the hall as two sets of footsteps came up from behind.

Deslen was in the room with me, lingering by the window with his arms folded, eyes combing the forest like he expected something to pop out. An earthy grapefruit scent wafted from close by, and Conrad sat next to me, jaw tight, his glare firmly fixed on the glowing terrain.

Tattooed arms slid around my waist, that familiar cherry almond scent wrapping around me.

My first instinct was to shrug him off. Couldn't have my men thinking I'd grown soft. That I wasn't some weakling that couldn't handle the pressure.

I closed my eyes and took a breath, but Zeth tightened his grip before I could move. "Shhhh," he murmured against the shell of my ear. "No one's watching. I waited 'til he left."

My shoulders unclenched as my worry melted away. He was right. It was just us.

I leaned back into him, letting his quiet sway pull the tension out of me. It was so... gentle. So un-Zeth that I almost doubted it was him for a second.

The Zeth I'd known for five years? Jokes, lingering glances, hesitant to do anything that might step over the line.

The Zeth holding me now? Pushy. Intense. A spark of heat licking under every word. And, damn it, I liked this version just as much.

"We'll get him, Nova," he whispered, an angry heat that matched my own threading through the promise. "We'll make him pay."

A soft laugh escaped me, breathier than I meant it to be. His voice lit something low in my spine, but the reminder of the mission dragged me back. Even if I wanted this moment to stretch on, I couldn't. That was what bosses did—the hard thing.

I'd like some hard things right now.

That very Aniyah thought slipped through my mind, and I almost laughed out loud. Instead, I pressed a kiss under his jaw, squeezing my thighs together when I felt the small, involuntary groan rumble out of him. *Focus, Nova. Boss work. Not mate work.*

Even though mate work sounded *way* better.

My wolf howled her agreement in the back of my mind, but my damn Desmond pride shoved everything else aside. I tapped his arm, and he let me go even though neither of us wanted that.

With the heat in my chest cooled, I faced the map again. The cave guy's words replayed in my head. *Lake* and *bank.* I'd assumed he meant the bank of a lake, which made perfect sense for someone running a hidden operation or a lab. Easy access to water meant free power. A homemade hydro set-up wasn't exactly rocket science.

I'd already sent teams to comb through every possible spot, but all of them had come back empty.

Which meant I was missing something. I needed a new angle. A different interpretation.

If he isn't drawing power from water, then what the hell is he using?

I yanked out my phone and punched in Gil's number. If my brother wanted to pretend his little pet techie was *my* IT guy, then fine—I'd use him like one.

As soon as the phone clicked over, I said, "Gil, it's Nova."

A crash echoed on the other end, metal hitting tile, a yelp, then the muffled scrape of someone scrambling to grab their phone. When he finally spoke, his voice wobbled. "Y-yes, Boss Rossey?"

"I need you to hack into the power company and check for any spikes. Anyone pulling more energy than usual, I need that information now."

A breath, followed by a dry swallow I could practically hear. "Um... I—I don't know—"

"That's the wrong answer, Gilly." My jaw locked, every word sliding out like a warning. A familiar tingling pricked my fingertips, claws itching to break the surface and remind him what failure cost around here. "I'm calling back in ten minutes. I expect answers."

I hung up and slammed the phone onto the table. A crack split the silence. I winced. *Great. I broke another one!*

"So, you don't think he's near a lake anymore?" Conrad asked.

My eyes drifted back to the shimmering map. "I'm not ruling it out. I'm just not betting everything on it. The only thing I know is that he needs power. A hydroelectric source makes the most sense, especially when you put it with 'lake' and 'bank,' but we've got nothing to show for it, so I'm widening the search."

I tapped a button on the side of the table. The terrain dissolved, replaced by a holographic layout of the city. Another tap, and patches of red flared across the display.

"If they're hiding in plain sight," I said, pointing at the glowing sectors, "these are the areas my men patrol the most. Easy to blend in. Easy to disappear."

I dropped into a chair, lacing my fingers together before I broke something else. "If they're in the city, it's a smaller crew. Easier movement. I'm betting he's got a mage—probably an air mage—handling transport for the captured supes. Quiet. Efficient. Off my radar."

Zeth stepped beside me and hit another switch. A constellation of green dots blinked to life. "Our properties," he said. "You can eliminate those."

Conrad leaned forward, studying the map like it had insulted him. "Underground," he muttered. "If I wanted to keep something from you, that's where I'd put it." His chair scraped as he rose, arms folded as he paced. "And with an air mage, they could dig silently and filter debris right into the wind. You'd never see it."

I nodded and fired off a message to my men. *Sewer scans. Full sweep. Anything weird, notify me immediately.*

"We'll have a map of the underground system in twenty minutes."

I'd barely set my phone back down when Gil's name flashed across the screen. I hit the speaker and dropped my voice into something that left no room for hesitation.

"Talk."

"U-um… s-so—" Gil's voice trembled like it was trying to escape his throat. "I c-cross-referenced l-last year's usage with th-this year's, and there's a… a pretty big jump at the c-city's hydropower plant."

Deslen turned from the window at the same time all three of us snapped our attention toward the map. My fingers flew across the controls, zooming in on the section he mentioned. The hydropower plant sat right on the outskirts of town, hugging our biggest lake.

My heart stuttered against my ribs, adrenaline humming through me. "What buildings are around it?" The question came out sharp, but the edge was pure anticipation.

Rapid, panicked taps sounded through the speaker. The room held its breath, every one of us leaning forward as if we could somehow will him to go faster.

"Looks like they b-bought up the surrounding buildings a f-few years ago… planned to expand but…" He hesitated. "But the project was stopped due to funding."

My words snapped tight. "What buildings?"

More clacking. "Uh… a strip mall with a coffee shop, a thrift store, and a massage parlor. And—"

He paused again. "Oh. And a local bank."

My chair scraped the floor as I shot upright. Conrad moved at the same time. Zeth already had his phone to his ear, barking orders until I threw out a hand.

"Wait. Tell them to stage a few miles out."

He relayed the order without question.

Deslen drifted to my side, brows pulled together. His strawberry and peppercorn scent had me licking my lips. "Why not roll in and take the place now?"

I shook my head, mind already moving ahead of him. "We don't know what the hell we're stepping into. A full assault could spook them or give them enough time to slip out a back tunnel. A small, quiet team gets in cleaner. We gather intel and grab the doctor for answers before getting rid of him."

Zeth hung up and faced me, jaw set. "They'll get into position and wait for our signal."

A feral smile slowly curled across my face, one I hadn't felt in a long while. The thought of the doctor's blood covering my hands, his screams traveling through the air as I beat the truth out of him, sent delicious tremors down my hands.

I looked at my men, my mates. Smart. Fast. Precise. The perfect blend.

Still could use a scrappy black wolf with good instincts. Shaking that thought off, I made sure to keep my smile in place. I didn't want them to know who I was thinking about.

"Looks like I've got my go team," I said, letting my gaze drag over each of them. The energy in the room spiked, all of us needing some kind of action after the week we'd had. "Ten minutes to get ready, boys. Gear up."

THEY WERE ready faster than I expected, already lined up by the door. Black shirts clung to muscle, cargo pants fitted sharp, boots planted. A dark, menacing, lethal wall of men. My men.

My wolf slammed against my skull.

Mates. Ours. Take them. Now.

For once, I didn't force her back. I let her rise up and press against the edge of my skin, her hunger entwining with mine. Heat licked up my spine as I dragged my gaze over all three of them. Every instinct screamed to pin them to the nearest surface and ride out this lust.

Conrad smirked, his voice light with mischief. "We should probably wear these outfits again. Preferably when we're... not in a time crunch."

A ridiculous laugh nearly slipped out of me, but I caught it in time. That was too soft for someone who planned to spill blood tonight. I took one more heartbeat to indulge in the sight of them, in the ache pooling low in my stomach.

Then, like flipping a switch, I closed my eyes, inhaled, and opened them again with rage and violence simmering right beneath my skin.

"After," I said, my voice all wolf. "Right now, I want that man's blood coating my claws. His bones cracking between my fangs as he screams every secret he's been hiding. Tonight, he learns what trespassing in my territory costs."

The shift in the room was instantaneous. Focus sharpened. Hunger redirected.

We left the house and headed to my Jeep since it could fit all of us, but something prickled at the back of my neck. Eyes on me, watching. The sensation stalked me all the way to the vehicle. While the guys climbed in, I scanned the tree line, nostrils flaring, senses stretching to catch the watcher hiding in the shadows of the forest.

"Nova?" Deslen stood beside the open door, hand extended.

It took me a second to understand the gesture. He was trying to help me in, which was cute. Sweet. Ridiculous, even. My immediate reaction was to tell him I didn't need it. That I'd climbed in and out of cars long before he learned to shave, but instead, I slipped my hand into his and let him steady me. Let myself enjoy it. A girl like me only got so many chances to be treated like this.

Zeth drove us out to meet my men, and once I got there, I met with the lieutenants and gave them the rundown in clipped, direct orders. Spread out, stay low, and wait for my signal. I had a magical device that could ping my men within a five-mile radius. As soon as they felt the ping, that meant: *tear the place apart.*

I couldn't have any slip-ups—not this time. I'd be damned before I let this bastard embarrass me in front of my siblings. I'd become the laughingstock of the family, and I could never let that happen... ever.

The low rumble of an engine approached, too fast, too close. I tensed, ready to shred whoever thought about ruining this op. An off-road motorbike skidded to a stop in front of me.

He killed the engine and removed his helmet to show off a Syndicate tattoo on his neck before pulling a thin box from his backpack. "Delivery to Boss Rossey from Boss Winstale."

I snatched it the second it was offered. Inside laid a syringe filled with yellowish liquid and a folded note showing familiar handwriting.

> *Had to rush this to you. Use it wisely. Only have one for now.*
> *- From your amazing, gorgeous big bro*

A sharp puff of laughter escaped me. *Gorgeous? Gods, Cal has a big head.*

Looking down at my skin-tight gear, I searched for a place to stash it without the risk of cracking or losing it. I only had fucking one.

"Here." Zeth held out a gloved hand, palm open, steady. "I've got a pocket."

I handed it over, watching him slide it into his right pocket, carefully, deliberately, while praying we wouldn't need it.

Leaving the Rossey men behind, the four of us moved on foot through the forest shadows. This fucker was a slippery one, so I didn't put it past this 'Doc' to have speed triggers setup, leading up to the bank. That way if any one supe used their super speed to try and catch them off guard, they'd be warned and could make a quick escape.

"Did Gil send the layout yet?" Conrad asked.

I thumbed my phone, checking for incoming messages. I'd texted Gil earlier for the old bank's schematics. Normally, I'd just walk near the building and tap my watch. It could pull up a full magical layout showing us the walls, rooms, and holo-people drifting inside with their species tagged like floating labels, but that tech ran on air and rune magic. If they had an air mage inside, and I was betting they did, we'd lose the element of surprise the second I used it.

An email pinged. "Hold up," I murmured, stopping as I opened the file. "Got it."

The guys closed in around me, heads lowering in unison to examine the building plans glowing on my screen.

Deslen surprised me by speaking first. "Don't think the front will work." His finger hovered over the image. "Wall of glass. Too exposed. Even vampire speed can't outrun that many sightlines."

"Even if we made it through the door," Conrad added, raking a hand through his hair, "the floor plan's wide open. First step inside, and we're lit up like targets."

Zeth let out a rough, irritated rumble and threw up his hands. "Great. There goes our element of surprise."

I studied the layout, deep in thought. *Front was suicide. Back wasn't much better, with blind entry into who-knows-what. Unless...*

"What about the ceiling?"

Three heads snapped toward me.

I pointed to the blueprint. "Here. Large exhaust vent on the roof. Big enough to crawl through."

Zeth and Conrad immediately turned to stare at Deslen like he was the hinge this whole plan rested on. He plucked the phone from my hand, studying the image before shrugging. "My jaguar form might fit."

"That works." I looked at the other two. Conrad gave a slow nod. Zeth rolled his eyes like he wanted to object but didn't. I put my phone into my boot again. "Then that's the plan."

As we neared the building, I saw exactly what Deslen meant. The entire front was a glass showcase. No way in hell that would've worked, but the sides and back were brick walls that led up to the roof. Ceiling it was.

The boys followed my lead as we slipped around to the rear, moving silently and keeping low as we checked for traps. My watch pinged faintly, showing tiny mines tucked into weeds and shadows around the building. Zeth crouched to disable each one in our path, his fingers quick and sure.

When we reached the wall, we scaled it in silence. Using claws and fingers to find grip holes in the brick, we pulled ourselves onto the roof. The vent sat near the back corner, the opening wide enough for a person if the individual wasn't too broad.

I used a claw to loosen the screws on the grate. Metal gave with a soft groan. I pulled out the filter, revealing the dark drop within. One look told me Deslen's human shoulders weren't making it through.

"Yep. You're going to have to—"

I didn't even finish before his body blurred, shifting in a smooth cascade of magic. Midnight fur rippled into existence. Pale yellow eyes lifted to mine, the same calm, steady gaze I'd come to lean on. Fae sigils shimmered down his sides like liquid starlight.

He padded forward and lowered his massive jaguar head to me. My hand rose without thinking. Fingers slid behind his ears and down the back of his skull. His body melted into the touch, a deep purr vibrating through him.

Behind me, Zeth muttered, "How's he making me jealous in his damn cat form?"

The comment snapped me back to the mission. I let my hand fall and gave Deslen a wink before kneeling at the vent's edge.

"Order's simple," I whispered. "I'm first. Then Zeth. Conrad. Deslen last. Stay tight. Stay silent."

Conrad shot Zeth a glare, and the demon's grin stretched wide. I frowned at them until Zeth leaned in, murmuring against my cheek, "I get the best view."

I resisted the urge to smack him.

"Listen up." I tapped the metal rim. "Short drop, then a flat crawl. Go in headfirst. Press your hands and feet against the sides so you don't slide down like a sack of rocks and give us away. Clear?"

All three nodded. Predators, primed and ready.

The metal groaned softly under my palms as I crawled through the vent, inching forward until the shaft leveled out beneath me. Behind me, the guys followed, controlled, careful, bodies pressing into the sides to keep from dropping too fast.

I slid forward, scanning for my first vantage point. The nearest vent slats opened into a dark office. Empty, still, untouched. I kept going.

The second vent showed a werewolf leaning against a wall below, his thumb lazily flicking across the screen of his phone. Every few seconds, he lifted his head, eyes sweeping the hall before dropping back to the glowing screen.

I kept moving, keeping my breath quiet and even.

The next vent revealed a pink-haired fairy pacing the teller area. She muttered to herself, soft, frantic syllables, wings twitching in restless agitation. Her nerves sparked through the air, and even from up here, I could feel the tension rolling off her. I took extra care not to let the vent creak.

Then, further down, I reached the last grate and froze.

A demon lounged outside a massive vault door, one leg crossed over the other. He tossed knives toward a wall, each blade sinking with casual yet precise flicks. A familiar shimmer rippled along the metal. Fae magic. Enchanted blades. One wrong move, and those things could make us bleed out.

Yeah. He'd be a problem.

The vent looped back around, and when I returned to the drop point, all three of my men were silently waiting, steady, eyes sharp.

I whispered my findings. "Fairy at the front, frantic but alert. Werewolf in the hall, phone scrolling, bored. Demon by the vault with fae blades and ready to use them." My finger tapped the empty office vent. "Entry point. Quiet and clean."

They nodded, and we moved as if a single mind guided four bodies. Not a scrape. Not a breath too loud. Down the vent into the darkness, we entered into enemy territory.

It only took a second to get to the right opening. Lifting up the vent grate, we silently dropped onto solid ground inside the empty office. Pride filled my chest as I saw how effortlessly they matched my movements.

Once we were in position, I pointed at Conrad then the hall where the werewolf was patrolling. I mimed sinking my teeth into a person's neck, trying to tell him what I wanted him to do. Conrad's mouth twitched with a suppressed laugh, but he gave a thumbs-up. Target understood.

Next was Zeth. I wiggled my fingers in a slow swirling motion, then fluttered my hands behind me like wings. He looked confused for a second before a grin split across his lips as he winked at me. Jerk.

Finally, I turned to Deslen. I curved my fingers over my head like horns, then pointed to myself, telling him the demon was mine. His massive jaw dropped open in a silent protest, his head shaking so hard his ears flopped around. Too bad. I was the fucking boss.

I wasn't about to have any of them go up against someone with fae-magicked blades, so they didn't need to know that little detail.

I switched over to miming a giant vault door, using two fingers to show a person walking through it, then pointed at him. His job wasn't the demon. His job was what laid behind that vault once I created the distraction.

He still shook his head in rigid refusal, so I flicked his nose.

His pale yellow cat eyes went huge, betrayal, outrage, and disbelief filtering through them as he took a startled step back. I just crossed my arms and waited.

Eventually, after he looked to the others for backup, and they gave him none, he dipped his head in surrender. *Good boy.*

Now that everyone knew their roles, it was time. I pointed to Conrad and mouthed *'go.'*

He silently slipped through the door with a feral smile.

We'd see how good these boys really were at following directions. One wrong move could get us into deep shit.

32

NOVA

Once I heard a soft shuffle of feet sliding across the floor, I inched my head past the doorway just in time to see Conrad lower the werewolf's body with careful precision, an empty cavity where the heart had once been. His fangs glistened with crimson drops.

Then he blurred. Suddenly, he was in front of me, the werewolf's phone dangling from his hand. Despite the blood still dripping from his mouth, his smile was surprisingly clean. Smug satisfaction oozed off him.

Perfect. I opened the bond between us, letting him feel both my pleasure and pride at his quick, efficient work. His eyelids fluttered, and his response pulsed in my chest, a warm ripple of feeling.

Biting my lip, I tore my gaze away from him, afraid I was seconds away from shoving him into the nearest wall and devouring his mouth loudly enough to wake the dead.

Zeth brushed his shoulder against mine, catching my attention with those bright, jeweled Caribbean eyes. They were sharp and commanding, wanting my attention.

He winked at me before closing his eyes and taking a deep breath. Power slid off him in a subtle wave, smooth as silk. It was almost invisible—unless you were trained to detect mind-altering magic. He moved down the hallway, ignoring the crumpled werewolf on the floor, and stopped before heading into the room with the pink-haired fairy girl.

Her voice carried before we saw her.

"Precious work. Must protect. Must. Can't fail. No. No. No."

Her pacing sounded frantic, wings flicking, hands rubbing together. A cult-follower's cadence on her lips.

My skin crawled. Greed, I understood. Power, money, desperation, I could break those, but blind devotion? That kind of madness had no edges to hold on to. No way to easily get through.

I could tell when Zeth's influence touched her because her muttering sharpened into something violent.

"No! No!" A slap cracked through the room. "It's them. They hold us down—"

They hold us down? What the fuck was she talking about? Wasn't she part of the 'them'?

"His work… revolutionary. Change the world! Renew—" Another slap.

A snarl echoed from the other side of the room. "Val! Get your crazy under control before I do it for you! I can't listen to that shit for the whole shift. I won't!"

Breathlessly waiting for the heavy footsteps that meant discovery, we froze, but all that followed was silence. Then nothing.

Zeth gave me a look—*going in deeper*—and shut his eyes, pushing more of his power into her mind. I could hear her breathing hitch and her heartbeat fluttering like a trapped bird.

A weak sob broke through. "I'm wrong. I'm like them. Not enough. *Never* enough."

It seemed like he had a good grasp on her now. My curiosity pulled me forward, and I peeked around the corner.

The fairy was kneeling in front of the teller counter, staring at the ceiling with hollow, reverent eyes. Her wings had calmed. One hand pressed a blade, shimmering with that same fae magic, against her heart.

"I'll never betray him. His vision. Our god." A broken pause. "I g-give my life to you."

She slid the knife into her chest with silent devotion. No scream. No hesitation. Her hands lifted skyward as she took her last breath. Blood bubbled out in quiet gurgles, soaking her shirt. Her final bloody whisper drifted in the space around her.

"Only for you... my only god." Her body collapsed with a soft thud.

Zeth stood inches behind me. His eyes were locked on the body, expression carved from stone. No remorse. No guilt. Just cold, righteous satisfaction.

I slipped my fingers into his, and he looked down at the contact. His eyes didn't soften, not even a fraction, but he reverently traced a finger along my cheek in a way that made my pulse skip.

"Don't make me your goddess," I murmured, using the teasing to cut the tension.

His eyes narrowed, and his hand grew hotter in mine. Leaning in close to me, he whispered along my neck, "Too late."

My knees grew weak, and I leaned against the doorway to keep me upright. I searched his eyes for the joke, a twitch of his lips, some hint of a grin, but I found nothing. Just absolute, terrifying certainty.

Footsteps echoed from the hallway on the opposite side of the room.

"Val, I need a drink," the same voice from before called out, moving closer.

I gave Zeth one look before I dove behind a desk while the guys melted back behind the wall, out of sight. Good. I didn't want them tangling with this bastard yet.

"Can you watch the—"

He stopped mid-sentence, and I knew that was my window of opportunity.

When I burst from my cover, the demon's hollow eyes narrowed on me just as the first knife sailed through the air. I dodged to the side, and the knife hit the wall, missing my skull by inches.

Before the next knife could be thrown, I sprinted toward him, then dropped to my knees, sliding across the floor as the next blade whistled overhead. My hands shifted mid-slide, claws ripping free, ready.

Two more knives appeared in his grip.

"Go, Des! Now!" I roared.

Deslen's jaguar shot out from the hallway like a shadow unlatching from the wall, slipping between the teller stations and streaking toward the vault, bypassing its demon guard.

The demon's gaze flicked toward him, one heartbeat of distraction. He hurled a knife that hit a glass divider. The glass crumbled to the floor with a loud smash.

That was all the opening I needed.

Sliding right up to him, I swiped my claws up, tearing his thighs with deep slices. His mouth dropped open in a silent, agonized O, then I yanked my claws down, shredding all the way to the bone.

Torn fabric fell to the floor, exposing the open, oozing flesh beneath. Blood sprayed as I flicked my wrist and ripped through his crotch, the scent of ruptured skin and terror exploding into the air. He staggered back, barely managing to stay upright, but he couldn't shake me. I carved my way down his chest, opening him from clavicle to belly.

He slashed at me with another knife, but the desperate move was too slow. I ducked beneath it, swatting the blade from his hand. Metal clattered to the floor, useless.

A cruel smile crossed my lips as I looked down at him. He was a long-range fighter. Not good at close combat. Perfect for me.

Letting my jaw morph into my wolf's muzzle, I snapped my teeth at him before latching onto his shoulder and dragging him to the ground, using my weight to pin him down.

"No—no—get off!" he shrieked, but my jaws only tightened, fangs digging in deep.

Plunging my claws into his chest, I ripped at his flesh and bones like an animal at a feasting session. Wet clumps of muscle, skin, and organs splattered the floor beneath me. Fresh blood covered my face, rolled down my throat, and soaked the front of my clothes in a thick, metallic heat. I drank in the scent. It was rich, primal, intoxicating.

Pain. My wolf was practically vibrating in my skull. *Give him pain.*

Not this one, I reminded her. *The doctor suffers until death. This one dies fast.*

His heart thudded wildly against my palm, its beating panicked, frantic. I drew a claw down its center. The organ spasmed, flesh splitting open. He whimpered, the sound collapsing into a wet rattle as blood filled his lungs.

I let my jaw revert back to human form, breath steadying as I stared down at the twitching muscle. Blood pumped out hot and fast for a few seconds until it slowed then finally stopped. His immortal life was extinguished.

Just to make sure, I ripped the sliced heart free and tossed it across the room. It hit the far wall with a satisfying smack before falling onto the floor with a splat.

A pale hand appeared beside me, reaching to help me up.

Conrad.

Sliding my blood-slick hand into his, I let him pull me to my feet. I expected to see hesitation, maybe even fear, but instead, his dark, awe-filled eyes burned with hunger, directed solely at me.

"The control you have over your body…" His voice was almost reverent as he whispered, "Incredible." He glanced down at the demon's ruined corpse, his lip curling up in a sneer. "And he deserved worse."

When his palm cupped my cheek, I leaned into it, only for a second, before his mouth crashed into mine. His tongue dragged across my lips, cleaning me in the slowest, filthiest, most intoxicating way possible.

We would've kept going, maybe for too long, if Deslen's voice hadn't echoed from the vault.

"You need to see this."

I pulled away, wiping at my mouth as he grinned down at me. Zeth stepped up to my other side, muttering, "Copycat."

Conrad's reply came smooth as sin. "Jealousy is an *ugly* emotion."

Zeth's angry inhale and laser-burning eyes almost made me laugh.

Heading through the doorway first, I led them down a short hallway and slid around the large vault door until I saw Deslen standing atop a gaping hole in the floor. His worried eyes flicked to me then down at the hole, but all I saw was miles of smooth, dark skin I wanted to lick. When my eyes traveled down, my heart stopped for a beat.

"Is my mate having trouble focusing?"

His deep, soothing voice woke me from my lust-filled stupor, so I tore my attention away from him and down to the hole in the ground. "Did you go down?"

The wild, loose strands around his face moved as he shook his head. "Not yet. Waited for you first."

Zeth walked up to it, crouching beside the hole. "What's the plan?"

"We still haven't met the air mage," I said, "so no magic tech. No watch. We move slowly. Check every corner."

I had stepped to the edge, about to jump down, when I realized Deslen didn't offer his hand to me. His gaze was fixed behind us, body tight as he looked down the hallway.

"Des?" I asked. "What is it?"

He didn't answer. Instead, he shook his head and forced a smile as he extended his hand. "Sorry. Here. Let me help you."

Suspicion prickled. Annoyance, too. I didn't have time to argue about it, so I ignored the hand and dropped down alone, landing in a crouch.

The others followed one by one. Deslen shifted midair, landing in his jaguar form, dark fur glistening like wet ink. He padded to my side and nudged his huge head beneath my hand. Feeling petty, I resisted, but he nudged again and again until I finally slid my fingers through his fur. All forgiven. *Boy, am I turning into a pushover.*

We moved down the carved, underground pathway in a silent formation, each step measured. Ears tuned. Breath slow.

A soft hum bled through the tunnel as a low, steady vibration began to pulse under our feet. At the far end, a hazy green glow seeped from the left-hand corridor, casting the stone across it in an eerie tinge. The closer we crept, the louder the room sounded—liquid bubbling, machines chirping, a wet churn like something alive being fed.

Just as I was about to turn the corner and head in, Conrad's hand landed on my shoulder, his grip firm but careful. "Let me check it."

Before I could answer, he vanished in a blur and reappeared an instant later. "Empty."

We all walked into the room, still moving cautiously despite Conrad's go ahead—because you never knew. My eyes grew wide as I looked at everything before me.

The lab sprawled out before us. Tubes twisted across the table like veins. A bead of bright green fluid floated through a clear line, burbling as it traveled into beakers, then vapor chambers, and finally emerging as a syrup-thick mixture that dripped into a vat at the end of the table.

So, *this* was where he birthed the substance.

My legs moved without permission, drawn to the grotesque beauty of the set-up. Each step followed the absurd path of the formula, from liquid to vapor to liquid again, like he was coaxing life from poison.

Pulling out my phone from my boots, I took pictures and sent them to Calix. I didn't know what the fuck all this was, but he would have the best idea. This was definitely not in my wheel house.

Past the vat at the end of the table, a desk waited with a laptop and a large warped notebook. I flipped the notebook open as the guys looked around the room. Pages were packed with equations and jargon I couldn't decode. This was another Calix job, so I swiped the book and tucked it into the back of my pants.

Once this was over, I'd have my team confiscate everything,

but I had a feeling this book needed to stay away from the wrong hands.

I didn't sense movement behind me until the notebook was snatched clean from my waistband. I spun, claws out, ready to take on whoever dared to take what I had fucking stolen, only to find Zeth looking at it with a critical eye. He casually lobbed it over to Conrad, who caught it with ease. *When did they start working together?*

"Keep it for her," Zeth said dryly. Before I could get a word in, he followed with "She forgets that sometimes she doesn't go home with clothes."

Conrad slid it into a cargo pocket on his pants, giving me a conspiratorial wink. I wanted to smack both of them... mostly because they were right. If I shifted, that thing would've hit the floor and probably disappeared, which would just piss me off.

All our heads snapped to the entrance when a cry tore down the tunnel, raw and panicked, followed by a heavy smack. We could come back to the lab. What laid ahead of us might be even better.

We quickly moved out of the room and went further down the pathway, staying tight to the shadows until we reached another brightly lit entrance. Pulling my back to the dirt wall, I peeked around the corner, making sure I did so at a glacial pace.

A grey-haired man in a white lab coat was leaning over a metal table where a supe was secured with chains. The captive's voice cracked as they begged. "P-please... don't... I don't want to be... l-like them..."

A roar exploded from a dark corner, and the chained down supe flinched, whimpering. Focusing on the captive, I realized he looked like the picture Ezra had sent me of Jeremy Delton. The kid's father was still alive... for now.

"Oh, don't worry," the old man cooed, smoothing his hair. "I'm going to make you better. Faster. Just like you wanted." He called over his shoulder, "Nyx!"

A syringe floated toward him, green liquid swirling inside. Air mage. Of course.

Before he could inject the supe, another voice cut through the room, soft, velvety, and colder than metal left in snow.

"Doc. We've got company."

Shit.

Holding my hand out to the guys, I signaled for them to stay put. Maybe I could buy us enough time to wait for the right moment to strike, but I had to know what I was dealing with first.

Stepping into the doorway with a feral grin, I lifted my hands toward him. "Doctor! I've been dying to get an appointment."

He turned slowly, tucking the syringe into his coat pocket as he faced me like an old friend. "Nova Rossey! If I'd known, I might have made the place more... presentable." He made a show of looking around before laughing hard.

He looked normal enough, but the magic clinging to him was wrong, twisted. His eyes glowed neon purple, and the corrupted air around him shivered.

"Nyx," he purred, "welcome our guest."

A cloaked figure slid out of the shadows. A slim hand lifted. Fingers flicked. The air tightened, sucked inward, forming a spear of compressed wind that shot toward me.

The magic was fast. Sharp. Clean. But Riot had trained me better.

I waited for a heartbeat, a single breath, letting it get danger-ously close so she wouldn't be able to redirect it, then I dropped and rolled. The spear sliced the air where my ribs had been.

By the time I rose, the mage was staring at me, the hood thrown back. Her cherry red hair spilled onto her shoulders, and her face was contorted with pure disgust.

"That should've obliterated you," she hissed.

I licked my teeth and smiled, slow and wicked. "Yeah, well… I'm Syndicate. I'm not that easy to kill."

Frustration rolling off her in hot waves, the air mage exhaled hard through her nose, a dragon ready to blow fire. It was the doctor who spoke first, his voice syrup-sweet and filled with delusion.

"You know it's futile to try to stop us."

He lifted his phone, eyes swirling with manic purpose. "Even if you kill us all today, I can send the corrected formula to him. He'll make more doses. *Thousands.* When the time's right… Boom!"

He dragged his tongue around his lips in one long, gross circle. My stomach clenched, not from fear, but from disgust. I'd lived with psychos. Been raised by psychos. But this guy? This guy made my skin want to crawl off my bones just to get away from the way he *looked* at me.

"Come with us," he whispered.

Nyx, the air mage, jerked her head toward him, eyes wide, mouth half open in protest, but he ignored her. His attention was locked on me like I was the final piece to his fucked-up puzzle.

"We could use your strength," he coaxed, stepping closer. "Join the winning side. Our master seeks a partner... someone worthy to stand with him. To carry his seed. To birth a superior race."

My smile didn't reach my eyes. "Is that what he's doing? And who is *he*, exactly?"

A feverish gleam spread across his face as I stepped closer. "Why tell you," he purred, "when we can take you to him? Much clearer when seen up close."

He grabbed my arm and yanked me closer, which was exactly what I wanted.

I softened everything—my eyes, jaw, the tension in my shoulders—trying to make myself look harmless. Curious. "Is he like you?" I asked, my voice feather-soft.

His gaze swept over me, that oily magic that was and wasn't his caressing my skin like a sticky hand, touching everything it could. His pupils dilated, greedy and bright. "You're already a perfect specimen," he murmured, "but I can improve you. Strengthen your limbs. Enhance you beyond imagination."

My hands slid up his cheeks and cupped his face, looking deep into those bright lavender eyes. "I hoped," I said, sweet as poison, "for eyes like these."

He laughed arrogantly. "Not everyone can have these. They were hand-picked for me."

"Then…" I batted my eyes before letting my smile drop. "I suppose I'll have these ones."

My fingers elongated into claws mid-sentence, and I drove them straight into his eye and ripped it out.

His scream rippled through the lab as he shoved me backward. "YOU BITCH!" Blood streamed down his face. I blinked at my claws, one hooked around a bright purple eyeball.

Got one.

"Nyx! Kill her!" he screamed.

*"Boys," I yelled, "let's tear them to shreds."

Conrad flashed into existence beside the doctor, his hand snapping around the man's throat. Rage vibrated off him like static. "You laid your hands on her?! You die today."

The air shifted for a split-second before a spear of compressed wind shot toward him, and instinct took over. I kicked his leg out, knocking him off balance. The look he gave me was one of disbelief, but when his arm began dripping blood instead of his heart, he let it go real quick.

"Nova!" Zeth appeared at my side, hauling me up by the arms.

Across the room, a blur of midnight fur and iridescent streaks slammed into Nyx, pinning her to the ground with a jaguar's snarl.

---

* Fangs by Neoni

The doctor crabwalked away on his hands, panting. "Let's see how you face *these*." Giggling, he slapped a red button on the wall.

Chains rattled onto the ground. That guttural growl from earlier echoed again—closer. Angrier.

"Tear them apart," he shrieked. "Make them bleed!"

Something lurched out of the shadows, a twisted mass forced into a body it didn't want.

Fluorescent light illuminated all the bumps and deformities of this creature. A hunched spine, patches of fur fighting for territory along with bare flesh. One side of its head bulged grotesquely, pulsing with green fluid, and a single long fang emerged from its mouth. Its fists were two slabs, meaty hammers forged to crush bone.

We all stepped back, catching our breath.

"Zeth," I murmured, "can you control it?"

He closed his eyes and hurled his power at the creature. When the blast hit, the thing staggered, then shook it off like rain. Zeth strained harder, face contorting and body trembling with the force he was pushing into it.

"I… can't…" he gasped, chest heaving, sweat along his brow. "I can't take over."

The monster took a step toward us, and I knew all hell was about to break loose.

Zeth pulled the magical guns from the back of his waistband —one for each hand—and snapped them open to load each with a glowing round. His voice was steady, focused. "I think the heart is the core. That's where the magic's concentrated."

Before I could answer, a sharp whine sliced through the air.

I snapped my head back just in time to see Nyx fling Deslen across the jagged wall like a discarded toy. His body smacked into the stone wall with a crack that tore a cry from my throat. He slid down. Didn't move.

No—

She lifted herself with air currents, gliding across the room until she hovered above him. Air spear forming. Arm raised. All her power aimed at the man I—

No. No, no, no—

I lunged forward even though I knew I wouldn't make it in time. If I couldn't save him, I'd at least bring her down with me.

A feral growl split the air, and she paused.

Midnight fur tore past me, a blur of fangs and raw fury. The wolf hit her midair, driving her into the ground. Claws and teeth ripped into her throat before she could scream properly. Blood painted the wall as her body convulsed beneath him.

Deslen's jaguar shook his head as if waking from a nightmare and leapt toward the black wolf's side just as she tried to kick him off.

Nick.

The wolf was Nick. He was here.

He'd saved Deslen. He'd saved *my mate*.

Something cracked open inside, panic, relief, joy, confusion, all knotted together so tightly I couldn't pick them apart. No time to try. I pushed it all down and focused on the monster in front of us.

"We can take this bitch." I gave a humorless laugh, ready to take on the world.

Claws burst from my fingertips with a satisfying sting. "I'm Nova Rossey. I don't need help killing my enemies." Glancing back at Zeth and Conrad with a wink, I added, "But I'm a generous boss, so I'll let you two assist."

Their matching grins erased any lingering doubt.

"Whatever you say, Boss," they chimed in unison, then their heads snapped in each other's direction to glare at one another.

"Help me! Help me, p-please! It's Donnie. That's Donnie!" Jeremy thrashed and wailed on the stretcher. Annoyed at the sound of his screams, I kicked the stretcher aside, rolling him out of our way. He had a kid to get back to, so he should be out of immediate danger.

The creature roared, making the earth tremble beneath us, and I looked back at it, realizing what he'd meant. This thing was *Donnie*. Examining his form, I realized he was too far gone to help. The best I could do was end his suffering and make it quick.

So, I charged.

The beast was focused on me, and when one meaty hand swiped out at me, I ducked under its swing, extending my claws as I carved deep gashes into its side. Hot blood sprayed across my face, and I made sure to keep my mouth closed. I did not want to look like this by morning.

Zeth fired two sharp pops. Each bullet slammed into the thing's chest, making it stagger.

Conrad vaulted onto its arm and scrambled up by digging his claws into its hide. Its other arm rose to swat him off, but I buried my claws into its thigh, wrenching it downward.

The monster collapsed onto its knees with a roar that shook the lights. Conrad tore into its neck, ripping flesh in handfuls. Zeth emptied every shot straight into the center of its chest, and I saw his head loll.

We were winning.

Looking back, Deslen and Nick were tearing the mage apart while Conrad, Zeth, and I had this monstrosity on its knees. Victory was seconds away. All I needed now was the doctor—

A scream ripped through the space—"Watch out!—then everything flipped.

My body slammed to the ground, skull cracking against the floor so hard I was swamped by blurred vision and dizziness. Something heavy crushed me, pinning me in place.

"You're going to pay for that," the doctor snarled above me. Spittle hit my cheek. "For ruining *everything.*"

My head slowly knit itself back together, my vision clearing just in time to see his raised hand holding a syringe glinting with green liquid, aimed toward me.

"Noooo!" a voice roared out from behind, one I knew even if it hurt to admit it.

A body jumped onto me, acting as a shield. Nick.

My chest thumped, warm hope spreading, then time fractured. Moments passed before my eyes like hours.

The doctor's face took on a crazed look. His hand plunged the needle down, sinking the syringe into Nick's back.

My eyes flew open, a scream caught in my throat as cold dread took over.

The green substance surged into him. His body jerked on top of me violently. His head snapped back in an unnatural arc, eyes rolling up until only white showed, then the gold color I loved so damn much bled into a sickly, glowing green.

His pupils drowned in a neon glow. The spark behind them dimmed, swallowed whole, and the flickering bond—our bond—twisted. Tightened. Like it was trying to rip itself free from me.

A massive black paw swiped out, backhanding the laughing doctor across the room. The sound of his head cracking against the ground woke me up.

Scrambling up, my hands shook as I pulled Nick into my arms. His body was still convulsing violently, muscles seizing, breath stuttering against me.

"Nick! Nick!" I tapped his cheek. "Stay with me—"

The only answer was the tremor of his body and the sick green glow rising through his veins. The terrifying thought that I might have already lost him hit me.

"No. No. NO!"

Sharp, cracking, wild, the scream tore out of me before I even knew I'd made the sound. I could hear the others fighting the doctor behind me, the sound of bodies slamming, bones breaking, but it all blurred into the background.

The world shrank until all that existed was the man collapsed in my arms.

My hands flew over him in frantic, useless movements, searching for the puncture as if I could somehow steal the venom from his veins if I were just fast enough.

I knew it wouldn't work, but I didn't care. I had to try.

He saved me.

Nick saved me.

My fingers trembled, and his eyelids cracked open. Unnatural neon green eyes blinked up at me. His breathing stuttered into pained hisses, then his hand found mine, weak, shaking, fighting like hell to lift.

"I'm a wolf, Nova..." His voice broke, and my heart stopped. Did he just admit that he was a werewolf?! The man who didn't want to be anything but human finally admitted the truth!

"A-and I f-found my mate. You."

My world tilted.

Those words, the words I'd dreamt of, feared, and wanted from him were spoken into existence, but instead of filling me with joy, they split me open. They carved their way into my ribs until my heart felt flayed and exposed.

No. No, please. Not now. Not like this.

I couldn't lose him, not when he finally saw me. Not when he finally accepted himself. Not when he finally accepted *us*.

His eyes slipped shut as a groan of pure agony ripped out of him. Panic detonated in my chest. I looked up and saw Zeth, Conrad, Deslen, staring with terrified eyes.

I didn't care about fate. I didn't care about "forever." Love, rejection, staying, leaving, none of it mattered.

I just had to keep him alive. He had to *live.*

My gaze snapped to Zeth's dark cargo pocket where a thin, familiar outline was sticking out.

The antidote.

"Zeth!" I choked, my arm shooting out. "Give me the antidote! *Now!*"

His turquoise eyes locked on mine. For half a heartbeat, I saw the hesitation, the conflict. His lips pressed together, gaze flicking to Nick.

"Please—" My voice fractured into splinters. "Please."

I didn't need to say the rest. My eyes said everything.

I can't lose him. He's mine. He's my mate. I won't survive losing him. Not like this.

Zeth exhaled, and the syringe was suddenly in my hand.

I tore the cap off with my teeth, spit it on the floor, and drove the needle into Nick's chest, shoving the antidote into him as fast as I could.

His eyes and mouth flew open.

His back arched off the ground as a scream ripped out of him, the raw, guttural sound piercing the air. The bond between us snapped tight, vibrating like a wire about to break, but I refused to let it go.

His eyes rolled back, body taut, then he collapsed into my lap, going limp as a ragdoll.

My wolf howled inside me, a keening, broken sound.

I shoved my fingers to his neck, searching for his pulse. I closed my eyes and listened, feeling the slight tremor in his veins. It was weak but there. The bond flickered as I held onto it tight, then it slowly stopped trying to tear itself loose from me, settling into a calmer state. Relief punched the air from my lungs.

A wet, choked laugh echoed across the room, grabbing everyone's attention. The doctor. Bloodied, broken, yet still smiling.

This was his fault.

All of it.

He tried to beat me. He tried to take one of my men from me. He tried to rip my mate from me in the most agonizing way possible.

If he thought death was the worst thing I could have planned for him, he had no idea what real suffering looked like.

He would learn today.

33

NOVA

I lowered Nick's head to the floor as if he were made of glass, my hands refusing to let go until the very last second. Slowly, I rose to my feet, keeping the glacial pace to make sure my fury didn't get out of hand, thanks to the new cavern of hate that had unlocked inside me.

Cold fury filled my limbs. My breath came steadily and strong. I was locked in the kind of stillness that only existed right before something terrible happened.

The others must have felt it too because they stepped back without a word.

Every muscle in my body loosened, ready to strike, as my gaze locked onto the doctor. He trembled beneath Deslen's jaguar form. A computer cord bound his wrists, cutting into his skin.

"You're going to pay for that," I whispered menacingly.

My finger twitched as I weighed my options. Rip out his tongue, shift, then tear him open, one slice at a time, making it so his silence drew him mad? Or take out all of this aggression, all this need for pain and vengeance, on his body, then slice him into pieces and hang them in the woods as a warning?

Answers first, Nova, my mind tutted.

Fine. I'll do it the right way.

I jerked my chin toward the stretcher, never taking my eyes off the doctor. "Get him on it. Strap him down."

Zeth and Conrad moved in an instant, their sharp, clipped motions betraying the barely leashed violence burning under their skin. They wanted blood as badly as I did.

I could hear them letting Jeremy loose, telling him how to get out. Jeremy thanked them, then a set of running steps echoed down the passageway until it was silent again.

In seconds, the doctor was on the stretcher, thrashing uselessly as my mates cinched the restraints tight enough to bruise bone.

Once they backed away, I grabbed the straps and yanked them even tighter under the guise of checking their work. What I *really* wanted was for him to feel me taking away the last millimeter of freedom he had left.

"You know how this goes," I murmured as I leaned over him, my body pressing him further into the table. "The warnings. The pain. The lessons. Rinse and repeat until you get what you want, right?"

My hand slid up his throat. I squeezed lightly, using just enough force to steal a breath. His left eye flicked toward me, wide and frantic.

"But unlike the others I've interrogated," I whispered, my tongue running over my elongated fang, "you're not making it out alive."

"You know nothing," he snapped, his breath hitching as he tried to build up a mental wall of resistance. "He'll come, and when you're begging for death by my hands, you'll see the error of your judgment."

I rolled my eyes hard enough to see stars. "Really? *That's* the line you're using?"

My fingers closed around his collar and pressed down hard enough for his mouth to open and close, gasping for air. "Every time you idiots mention *him,* I grow bored. If he's sending you as scouts, then he's already losing."

His whole face started to shake as he truly realized that he wasn't going to live past this night. I squeezed harder, savoring the panic building under my palm.

"I don't give a damn about your shadow puppet master." My voice dropped to a growl. "He's sending pawns. Pawns who keep dying at our feet."

His eyes bulged as he rasped, "Pawns...."

A hollowed acceptance settled in his gaze as he nodded. "Yes... we're all pawns in his game. You and your siblings... you're the final pieces. His summit. His endgame. And once he's on top..."

A deranged smile split his lips.

"...revolution begins."

He was just as crazy as that fairy girl upstairs. I wasn't going to get anything out of him, not in the way I wanted, so at least I still had this lab and that book.

I ran my claws down, scoring the side of his face. His screams matched the excited thumps in my chest. His blood splattered on the table and floor, and I finally found a small amount of release from that well of anger.

"I'll destroy your little lab here and take all your notes so we can make sure this never happens again."

This time, he laughed. Blood bubbled out of his mouth as his one crazy eye looked to the ceiling. "You can do that. I've already sent it to him. He has all my notes, including the step-by-step procedure, and he will make them perfect. He will finish what I started."

He became lost in manic giggles as my mind raced. How did he send those files? His computer was in the other room.

I looked around, my eyes catching on the corner where he had scooted. On the ground was a black square object, his phone. As I was staring over there, it lit up and beeped. He must've sent it via his phone. *Fuck!*

That rage inside of me decided this was the moment. All I saw was red, and I didn't hesitate.

I drove my hand straight into his chest, shattering bones with a wet crack. His scream ripped through the room, raw, guttural, desperate. *Good.*

Twisting my fingers, I snapped his ribs one by one like brittle twigs, carving a brutal path to the hot, slick muscle of his heart. It beat against my palm, steady, arrogant, and I squeezed.

His breath hitched, a choked silence replacing his defiance. In that silence, I finally saw it. Real fear.

"I won't be the last," he whispered, his one eye glazed. "More will come. Morte doesn't let us go... not until everything burns, and we begin again."

Of course. He wasn't just unhinged. A mindless worshipper kneeling to his false god was useless to me.

I ripped my hand free, and he sucked in air again, choking on relief. I ignored him entirely, scanning the room for something better. Something fitting to be his end.

My gaze locked on a briefcase by the dead air mage.

"Conrad," I said, smiling down at the doctor as I pointed to it, "bring me that."

He vanished and reappeared in the span of a single exhale. The case was already open, the four vials of neon green toxin inside gleaming like wicked little stars.

The doctor laughed when he saw them, a broken, giddy sound. "Go on," he taunted. "Bet you don't know what it does to human bodies."

His joy scraped against my nerves, but I swallowed the urge to tear his throat out. I forced a smirk instead, the kind that made monsters nervous.

"Oh, I know *exactly* what it does."

I plunged the needle into his arm and pushed the poison in, watching his eyes widen, locked on the glowing liquid disappearing under his skin. His pulse hammered under my fingers, frantic.

"I wanted to test a theory," I murmured. "Thought you might... help me with that. Be an experiment for the cause."

Terror flickered, sweet and sharp. Leaning down, I dragged my blood-soaked fingers across his cheek, making him shiver as I left behind a streak of crimson.

"You stole those magic eyes," I whispered. "And that got me thinking."

I picked up the second syringe and slowly slid it into another vein.

He tried to jerk away. "You're not supposed—"

Another tremble, then his mouth screwed shut as I roughly shoved the needle around.

With a smile, I grabbed the third syringe and slammed it into his forearm hard enough to draw fresh blood. "That's the experiment."

By the time I held up the fourth one, his whole body was trembling, sweat mixing with blood on his terrified face. I tapped the syringe just inches from his eyes, letting the green glow reflect back at him.

"You see," I said softly, almost tenderly, "the dosage is different for you. You're not a supe. Your body doesn't run off magic." I carved a circle around his remaining eye. "But you *did* steal those magical eyes."

I pressed the needle to his skin—slow, deliberate.

"Let's see how long your stolen power can last."

I slammed the fourth syringe into his arm, burying the needle to the hilt.

"Let's see if your precious little virus is a starving dog," I purred in his face. "Will it claw its way straight to the only magic you have on you? I wonder how fast it will eat away at that."

The reaction was instant.

His remaining eye snapped wide open, the bright purple flaring in panic, before his whole body seized, his tendons standing out like steel cords beneath his skin. The green neon light tore through his veins, making them bulge as it searched for something to hold onto, something to devour. Ignoring his useless human genetics, the veins leading up to his face lit up, flaring as the substance sensed the magic.

His last precious eye.

It ballooned grotesquely, swelling against the socket like it was going to burst. Veins spiderwebbed neon green, then crimson, finally turning black. The skin around it blistered, rotted, and caved in.

He writhed hard enough to rattle the stretcher, shrieking as half his face liquefied beneath the skin. Flesh sloughed off in wet chunks, sliding down his cheek in strips. The smell of burnt ozone and rot hit the air.

And, gods, it was *beautiful.*

Watching the magic he'd stolen get devoured, watching the horror close in on his one good eye... it was a justice I could practically taste.

The virus quickly finished its feast. His eye imploded with a wet pop. His screaming cut off mid-breath. The twitching in his body slowed, then finally stopped entirely.

His death, exactly as I had promised.

Exhaling slowly, I let the warm, dark satisfaction melt through my chest. One less monster. One less threat. The cherry on the top was that bastard died in agony, his own creation eating him alive. It was poetic.

Gazing at the carnage that laid before me, I tapped my watch, sending out the signal to the men I had waiting. On my phone, I typed out a longer message to the one in charge. *Collect anything valuable or dangerous, then call the Devils for clean-up.*

With that done, I pivoted sharply and strode back to Nick's side.

Some color had returned to his cheeks. I dropped to my knees beside him, my heart tightening as I grabbed for him.

"Here." Zeth motioned to Deslen, and they carefully lifted Nick, each taking a side. "I got the little fucker." He looked at me, trying to ease my worry. "He's not dying on our watch, Nov. We got you."

I swallowed hard and nodded, the relief so fierce it almost hurt.

For the first time, I prayed. I didn't give a shit who listened to me, but if some higher power could help Nick pull through this, I would do anything they asked.

When it was all boiled down and this was what I was left with, I found the pain of potentially losing a mate was worse than being rejected by one.

ONCE WE GOT Nick settled in my room, I refused to leave his side. I sat on the edge of the bed, elbows on my knees, eyes glued to the rise and fall of his chest, waiting for the antidote to do its job, waiting for *anything* that hinted he'd still be mine when he woke up.

My phone buzzed again.

Cal: *Anything new?*

Cal: *Anything weird?*

I'd told him that I had to administer the antidote to one of my men. He kept asking for an update every few minutes.

Groaning in frustration, I turned my phone to silent for the first time in five years and tossed it onto the far pillow. I didn't have the energy to deal with Calix's constant "updates" and "vital checks." Not when my heart was suspended between beats, too terrified to hope.

Hours crawled by, and time laughed at me, enjoying its torment until the whole world stopped when Nick's eyelids fluttered.

I leaned forward just as he blinked up at the ceiling, confused but alive. A breath left me, so long and heavy it dragged the fear out of my bones. His head turned at the sound, eyes landing on me before he spoke.

"Have I been out long?" he asked weakly, scanning the room for a clock that didn't exist.

I shook my head. "Just a few hours. A... troubling few hours."

He nodded, his gaze falling as though he couldn't bear to meet mine. I watched him take a deep breath, shift in the bed. His hands clenched and unclenched, moving his lips like he wanted to say something but didn't know how, and yet, even after everything, he was drawing me in.

"You heard me earlier, right?" he asked, his tone shy but steady. He was trying to play it off, but the words were too big to ignore.

"Yeah." Staring at the sheets I was playing with between my fingers, I kept my voice casual, even though my heart thumped harder.

The silence that followed was thick and awkward, charged with something that made the air warm and the floor feel too thin beneath us.

His throat bobbed before he whispered, "A-am I too late?"

My brows knit. "Too late? For what?"

"To be… your mate." He sucked in a sharp breath, wincing at his own words.

I froze. Not because I didn't know the answer but because hearing him say it made something in my chest break open.

His cheeks flushed at the admission. "I mean—if you still want me. If… I still have a place by your side."

When the silence stretched, he panicked.

"I—I mean, I get it if I did." His jaw ground together. "If I could just stay somewhere nearby, I think—"

His face fell, and the insecurity I saw there punched me right in the ribs.

"No," I said softly, wringing my hands together. "But I want you to think, really think, about it. I'm not accepting a mate who doesn't choose me or someone who's only here because his body told him to be."

I hated saying it. Hated how my voice dipped. Hated how

raw it felt... but I hated seeing him in this bed even more. Hated the feeling of losing him.

His next words hit like a wrecking ball.

"I quit the force." The words were solid and sure. "I never told them a thing about you or your operation." Words continued to tumble from his lips in a rush. "And I've... been watching you these past few days. Wanting... no, *needing* to help."

I blinked. Hard. *He quit?* I'd read his file after I learned who he was. He'd been on the force for five years, an exemplary cop, and he'd even got turned into a werewolf after saving a young kid from drifting too far into the wrong woods. He was on track for a promotion. The perfect law-abiding cop. He had everything going for him. *And he left it.*

He reached for my hands and gently, reverently, lifted them to his lips, pressing soft kisses to each fingertip. My breath hitched at the tenderness.

"I didn't know how to handle my life turning upside down," he murmured. "The grief. The confusion. Then you came in. You demanded I choose. You pushed me. You lit something inside me."

His voice trembled. "You made me want to find myself again." His fingers laced with mine, warm and hesitant.

"Say something," he whispered, eyes refusing to lift, his shoulders trembling.

I didn't say a damn word.

I climbed onto the bed, onto *him*, and crushed my mouth to his, answering in the only way my heart could speak. His lips parted on a shocked inhale, melting beneath mine like they'd been waiting for me since the day we met.

The bond between us ignited, lighting up so fiercely, so bright, I gasped into the kiss. Every muscle locked up as that golden thread slid into place. My heart giddy and ablaze, the feeling of completeness engulfed me.

His hands traveled up my arms, slow but desperate, as if savoring every inch of me before he took in a ragged breath. "Do you want to stop?" I could hear his hesitation, but hope threaded through every syllable.

Sliding my hand behind his head to weave my fingers through his raven locks, I tugged his head back until we were nose-to-nose.

"No," I growled softly. "But I want you to know something."

His breath stuttered, his eyes flicking between mine.

"My body has wanted this for a long time."

I reached down, my claws cutting at the seam of my pants. The sound of fabric tearing was loud in the quiet room. His pupils blew wide.

"I'm going to want it hard and rough," I murmured, letting him hear the promise in it. "Do you understand?"

He kicked the blanket off, leaving him naked, his eyes locked on mine. "Then do with me what you want." His palm slowly dragged against his length, working himself harder. His nostrils flared with each inhale, chest rising and falling, gaze burning into me like he was carving this moment into memory.

I positioned myself above him, took the head of his cock, and dragged that velvety tip against my clit. My breath hitched. Lungs seized.

No more waiting.

I slammed down on his length. His fullness stretched through me, creating that perfect blend of a pleasurable ache. My hips rocked, and we both groaned. A deep rumble came from his chest, mine breaking from my throat.

His hands cupped my breasts, thumbs circling the stiff peaks before his mouth followed, tongue flicking, teeth grazing. I kept my rhythm steady, hips rolling in waves, until his fingers found my clit and rubbed tight circles. He thrust up hard, bucking beneath me.

My head fell back, spine arching as I let myself feel all of him. Gulping down his scent, I gripped his chest and rode his cock like it was both our last and first night.

His hands carved into my hips, grabbing onto me like he was never letting go. This raw, desperate thing between us had always simmered just beneath the surface. Now, it was ablaze, ready to consume us.

Heat coiled low in my belly, tightening, spinning faster. I needed more. Needed to shatter.

I shifted my leg up and around. His hands hovered, steadying but never stopping his thrusts. I pivoted until my ass faced him, feet planted under his thighs. I felt every muscle flex as he drove up into me. One hand gripped my hip, fingers digging crescents into skin. The other wrapped itself in my hair, tugging my head back as he pounded up like something had been unleashed.

"That's what you want, my mate? You want to be fucked dirty? You want to be so blissed out you can't walk?"

"Yes." The word came out breathless, broken by each snap of his hips. "More. Yes. All."

A growl tore from his throat, feral, possessive. In the blink of an eye, he picked me up and slammed me face-down into the bed. His palm cracked against my ass. The pain had my eyes crossing before he drove into me so hard white spots burst across my vision.

Thrust.

Thrust.

Thrust.

Relentless. Demanding. All-consuming. His hips slammed into me over and over. The slapping of our skin echoing against the walls. I kept wanting to hear the addictive sound louder, faster, harder.

His forehead pressed to the back of my neck, shaky lips trailing kisses across my shoulders as he fucked me exactly how I craved.

My toes curled against the sheets while that coil in my abdomen wound tighter, tighter. His teeth sank into my shoulder, and I broke. "Fuck! I'm coming, Nick!"

He kept thrusting through every aftershock, every tremor. Relentlessly. Then he turned me onto my back, dragged my body to the edge of the bed, and re-entered me slowly and deliberately. A hand drifted between my breasts, fingers trailing up the valley.

"I've wanted to do this for so long." His voice dropped, rough and low. Fingers curved around my throat, not tight, just there, possessive. "It feels like I've wanted you my entire life and never realized it." A thumb traced my pulse, making it leap. "I didn't know then... but I do now."

He bent down and sealed those words with a hot, wet kiss, something that consumed me entirely. His tongue swept into my mouth, and his thrusts grew erratic, more forceful.

His lips never left mine, but his body became rougher, more demanding. His grip was bruising, but I arched into it, wanting every mark as proof of this hunger.

"Take me," I whispered against his mouth. "Take it all."

A groan ripped from him. "Oh, fuck. Shit." His forehead balanced on my collarbone, his voice breaking into a quiet, desperate confession. "I think... I think I'm addicted to you."

He thrust into me harder, hitting that spot inside that made me see stars. "I can't stop thinking about you. What you're doing. Who you're with." Finally, he whispered, "If you need me."

His hips snapped as he croaked, "Fuck... I fucking love you."

His golden eyes caught mine, shining brightly with his true confession. I basked in the attention for a moment before his face screwed up tight, and he groaned my name over and over. His warm cum shot up into me, and I clenched down hard on his cock, milking it for all I could get.

That golden thread pulled taut between us, humming with certainty, and something clicked into place. His desperation to make this work, to prove that he wanted this, flooded our connection. My lips curved up.

I wrapped my legs around him, trapping him to me. He grunted against my skin. Over his shoulder, three sets of eyes watched from the doorway. Heat darkened their gazes, second by second. Waiting.

Their thoughts rang as clearly as if they'd spoken. *He had his moment. Now it's time for ours.*

I nipped at his lobe, feeling him grow hard again inside me. I got close enough to whisper in his ear, "I hope you're ready for the full mate experience."

He pulled back to look at me, hesitation written on his face. The door smacked open with a thud, and his eyes went wide before he peeked over his shoulder.

Wholeness settled in my chest, and four bonds blazed bright in unison, pulsing their agreement.

"I hope you're ready for round two."

34

NOVA

Looking at the clock, my pulse kicked hard. One beat, then another, then the oh-shit frantic rhythm that meant Ezra was going to skin me alive.

I swept the hair out of my face and flung the covers off, but before I could escape, an arm tightened around my waist and reeled me back to a cool chest that smelled of warm spices and grapefruit.

"Where you going?" Conrad mumbled, his voice thick and raspy, the kind that almost made me melt straight back into bed with him.

"I have to go," I whispered, already sliding my leg out of Deslen's loose hold and easing it up and over Nick's stomach. Four bodies in one bed was comfortable last night, but it made for a hazardous morning.

Conrad let out a soft, needy whine. "Come back. Work will still be there later."

His fingers curled around my torso, but I peeled them off one by one, pressing a kiss to each of his knuckles. His sleepy smile loosened, head dropping back to the pillow. Good. Perfect. Now I just needed to—

I attempted one heroic leap over Nick, but one foot got snagged by the sheet. My arms windmilled. Disaster loomed with me crashing down on a pile of supernaturals, or worse, kicking Nick into oblivion.

A familiar tattooed arm shot out and caught me, setting me upright with surprising gentleness. A coffee cup appeared in my hand like a peace offering, and I stared into a set of green-blue eyes I'd lost myself in a time or two.

Zeth.

My thumb brushed against the ink on his forearm—the Syndicate mark. A memory of the day he'd gotten it tugged at me, the way he'd gritted his teeth and sworn it didn't hurt. Swore his loyalty to my family… and me.

"She has a meeting," he murmured for the benefit of those groaning in bed. I caught the smirk on his face before he dipped his nose into the crook of my neck and inhaled deep, his hands already flirting with the waistband of my shorts. The tobacco and cherry scent of him slid right under my skin, and I leaned into it without thinking. Wanting more of him, all of him, now that he was mine.

Before I could put the mug down and jump his bones, he smacked my ass sharply enough to jolt my brain back online.

"Ezra hates it when anyone is late," he reminded me. "Remember when Aniyah was two minutes behind because her dancer went missing?"

I winced. Ezra's lecture had lasted longer than the dancer's entire contract. Unity. Control. Punctuality. Respect. I didn't want to hear that again, let alone have it directed at me. I launched myself out of the room and toward my office.

"Nova!" Zeth called from my bedroom door.

I turned just in time for a shirt to hit my face. "Probably don't wanna show up like that."

I looked down at a set of bare tits.

...Right. No shirt. Oops.

Trying to keep my coffee steady, I yanked the shirt on with one hand before sprinting down the hallway. An urge hit me, sharp and impossible to ignore, as I saw him leaning against the doorway, smiling at me.

I didn't have time. I shouldn't. But...

He's my mate. I get to want him. For once in your life... live a little, Nova.

Setting the coffee down, I crossed the hallway in three quick bounds, hooked one arm around his neck, and gave him the kiss I'd been wanting to for over six years.

He responded immediately. Groaning into my mouth, his hands explored my body, touching as much as he could as he slid them beneath the shirt. I hitched a leg around him, and his hand cupped my breast, playing with my nipple in a way that made my breath stumble.

The sudden pinch of his fingers made me gasp, then melt. His eyes drank me in. Every flinch, every breath, guided me without a word, pulling me along for the head-spinning ride.

When his other hand went into my shorts, his thumb circling my clit, the world snapped white. I bit off a cry that still escaped as a shaky, breathless prayer of his name.

I sagged into him, my forehead on his, a plea just a breath away. Zeth lifted his fingers to his mouth and tasted me with slow, deliberate swipes of his tongue. I watched helplessly, entranced and greedy enough to consider risking Ezra's wrath.

"You're already gonna be late," he teased against my lips, his voice edged with a real warning.

He was right. Damn him for being good at his job.

I tore myself away before my self-control combusted, sprinted to my office, dropped into my chair, and flicked on the receiver.

My siblings' faces blinked into focus.

"Ooooh, Nova is…" Aniyah checked her watch with theatrical horror. "Three minutes late! Shame corner! Shame corner!" She pointed somewhere off screen like a game-show host.

"Aniyah." Ezra's voice sliced cleanly through her laughter. "I'm sure Nova has a perfectly good reason for being late to a meeting that has been the same time for five years. The meeting in which we discuss the Syndicate's stability. Where we meet as equals with respect and loyalty. The meeting that strengthens our unified front. Correct, Nova?"

Her words were a sugar-coated blade, and the hit made me flinch. I'd seen it coming. Still hurt.

"I'm sorry," I said, my breath still uneven. "Last night wrecked me. But I'm ready. I'll walk you through everything."

Ezra didn't speak. She didn't have to. Her glare was a scalpel, and I was the flesh waiting to be carved into, but she gave one sharp nod. My chest rose and fell with relief that she wasn't grilling me now... but that didn't mean I was safe from later.

I proceeded to lay out the night piece by piece: the bank, the cultish fairy girl with pupils too wide to be sane, the demon carving air with fae-forged blades, the underground lab that smelled like fear and chemicals. The doctor. His words, his experiments, the way he'd broken when I finally ended him.

With every detail, a shadow crawled deeper across my siblings' faces. Their projections flickered in the air, but the static heat rising off them felt real, like the first exhale before a wildfire.

"Supe eyes on a human." Aniyah's upper lip curled. "Wannabe trash."

Calix leaned forward, brain already in gear. "Interesting," he muttered, rubbing his chin. "The one at Aniyah's place was like a sleeper agent—mixed bloodline, probably meant to pass unnoticed. But the one Nova fought?" He tapped a pen hard against the desk. "Almost like a soldier class. Powered up by that substance. Created to hit hard but not sustain over time."

His gaze snapped downward, and he started scribbling like a man possessed.

Ezra's smirk was small, eyes glinting in thought. "Revolution, hmm?" She reclined in her chair, unbothered in the way only someone who thrived on war could be. The others looked ready to hunt someone down; she looked ready to play chess with their bones.

Riot tilted her head. "You said the doctor mentioned something—Morte?"

I nodded. "He said, '*Morte doesn't let us go... not until everything burns, and we begin again.*'"

Aniyah's eyes narrowed, fox-sharp. "Leader? Group? Anyone heard the name?"

We shook our heads in a silent, unified admission. We were staring at a ghost of a person with a grudge.

"One thing's clear," I said. "We're the finale. Whoever they are, they want everyone else handled before they come for us. I just don't know who *everyone else* is."

"Then we have time," Ezra cut in, eyes bright with something almost predatory. "Calix. Weapons. New ones. Ones no one's ever seen."

Calix pointed at his temple, grinning wild. "Already got blueprints screaming in here."

"Good." Ezra's tone became iron. "Stay alert. Someone around us is feeding them information. Inside eyes are always the first move in war. Keep everything quiet. People know we're strong, but I won't have them knowing how strong."

The humor slipped away. Her gaze swept across all of us, and, for a moment, the room felt smaller than the threat.

"We *are* going to war," she said, her voice cold enough to sharpen steel. "Not if—when. Fortify your territories. Train your people. Build your strike teams. It will get bloody before it gets clean."

A smile tugged at my mouth. There she was. The monster we needed. The one who didn't believe in losing, not because she was arrogant, but because she'd never even entertain the idea. We were Syndicate, and we'd never back down to an enemy.

"Whatever you say, E. We've got you," Calix said without looking up, his pen still dancing over his page.

Riot nodded once. Silent, deadly, absolute.

Aniyah's grin was practically feral. "Let's paint the streets with their blood."

"My people are yours," I said, and I meant it.

My thoughts drifted to those men still in my bed, my mates, and my chest ached. They'd never let me walk into fire alone. I couldn't help wanting this war to leave them untouched, but it also didn't matter what I wanted. If they were Syndicate, they would be in the fight, just like me, and they were my mates, which meant they were undeniably Syndicate.

Ezra's attention shifted. "Calix. Progress on the fae blade?"

Calix dragged a hand through his hair, the universal sign of nearing burnout. "Yes and no. The blade's powerful. Testing confirms it. But the power source? How the enchantment binds? Not sure yet. Similar to rune work… but not exactly." He sighed. "Avery had no idea, but that was also him trying to examine it over the phone. Papu Syris is coming to see it in person."

"Good," Ezra said. "We need that edge. It's their trump card. If they pair it with something worse, we're facing a disaster before the first wave even hits."

"I'll crack it," Calix said, and he meant it. The fire in his eyes could melt metal.

Ezra nodded once. "With the antidote Calix made and Nova's person as proof of its effectiveness, we now have a counter-agent for their other advantage. Even if the doctor managed to send the formula to someone else, we have a way to neutralize it. Thank you both."

Calix and I exhaled together. A small victory. Still, it felt like running blindfolded through a maze while someone else turned the walls.

We were moving in the right direction, but the enemy was moving with us.

Ezra tone snapped out, "Aniyah, Riot—start asking around about this 'Morte.' *Quietly.*" Her gaze locked onto Aniyah. "Have your British mate check his circles. I'm not crossing any names, international or state side, off the suspect list just yet."

She turned and began typing on her keyboard, the meeting winding down, and pressure gathered in my chest. *Now. Say it. Stop stalling.*

"I have something to tell you."

Four pairs of eyes slowly turned to me in unison, and the sudden weight of their attention made my pulse stumble. I forced myself to sit up straighter. *Just. Say. It.*

"I…" My gaze flicked to Aniyah. For once, she wasn't smirking. She sat there quietly, almost stunned, until that slow, wicked grin unfurled across her face. Like she knew before I even said a word. Weirdly enough, it steadied me.

"I have four mates," I blurted. "And I want you all to come meet them." I kept my face as neutral as possible, but my knee was bouncing underneath my desk.

The silence was so sharp I swore I could hear the static hum of the receiver. Riot blinked. Calix froze mid-scribble. Ezra's jaw actually dropped. And of course...

Aniyah exploded into laughter.

"I *knew* it!" She leaned in towards me conspiratorially. "You got yourself a pretty little... well, maybe not so little kitty, huh?" She lifted her hands and began to spread them wider... and wider... and *wider* until her hands froze at the twelve-inch mark. Giving me a knowing look, she whispered in awe with a smidge of jealousy, "Birthday dick? You got birthday dick on tap?"

My lips pressed together, trying and failing not to laugh. *Why does she have to be so outrageous?* I can't help but find it funny.

"I *knew it!*" she shrieked, slapping her desk and pointed at me. "I *knew* that kitty was packing!"

"Aniyah! Stop!" Calix snapped, then he rounded on me, horrified. "Please. Please tell me it's not that Zeth bastard. I warned him! I told him he—"

My eyes flew open. "You did *what*?!" Heat blasted through me as I glared at his guilty, shifting eyes.

"Enough." Ezra's voice cut through everything. She inhaled, steadying herself, then fully turned to me with full focus. A shiver crawled down my spine.

"Nova," her voice tightened. "Tell us what is going on."

Giving Calix a final glare, I took a breath and answered her as honestly as I could. "I've known Zeth was my mate for a while. We just... had some miscommunication... for a while." I winced. Understatement of the century.

Ezra's expression didn't move.

"It wasn't until I met Conrad Mecariee and Nick Cordova that my tattoo reacted. I was already neck-deep in this substance mess, so I put all of them off. Then Deslen arrived... and the tattoo became visible."

I lifted my arm and showed them the wolfsbane blooms. All four of them went still.

"I know it's strange," I rushed out. "Trust me, I thought I'd lost my opportunity for a mate bond a long time ago, but life... changed." I didn't explain the pain or the guilt or the quiet hope. They didn't need to know that part.

"This won't affect my work," I continued, readjusting in my seat, folding my hands in front of me. "The Syndicate has always come first. They know that and respect it. Conrad even offered me his turned-supe fighting ring, but I told him to keep running it. I'm focused on other ventures." I hoped that would let them know my mates were ready to be a part of and pull their weight in the Syndicate.

"Good," Calix muttered, slumping in his seat. "If they weren't worshipping the ground you walk on, I'd kill them myself then find you new ones. Better ones."

The threat was real. So was the warmth behind it. Gods, my siblings were feral, and I shouldn't encourage it, but the edges of my mouth creeped up into a smile.

"I want to announce it to the Rossey clan," I said. Their eyebrows shot up, but I pushed through. "But, first, I want you all to meet them..." I looked away as heat rose up my neck, "get your approval of sorts."

"Of *course,* we're meeting them!" Aniyah squealed, clapping like she'd been handed front-row tickets to a murder-circus.

Calix punched his fist into his palm. "Yeah. I need to look these guys in the eyes and set the law down."

Riot nodded slowly, a rock of reassurance. "Anything you need."

Ezra… didn't answer. Her mouth tightened, eyes drifting sideways like she was weighing something heavy. The quiet stretched until Calix, brave fool that he was, ventured, "Uh… E? You coming to Montana with us?"

Her head snapped back to me. Something flickered in her eyes, too fast for me to catch, before her expression smoothed into something soft and unreadable.

"Yes. Of course I want to meet Nova's mates. I'll arrange the transportation."

Her fingers flew across her keyboard, already commanding Arion through her speaker to prepare the planes and solidify times with everyone while they were on the line.

And suddenly, my stomach dipped. Hard.

What if they don't like my mates?

What if Zeth and Calix go for each other's throats?

What if this all explodes before it even starts?

A small tug came from the bond, a reminder of who was on the other side and I shook those thoughts off. Overthinking had already cost me enough.

Whatever happened next, I'd handle it—hopefully without too much blood.

But with my family? That was never a guarantee.

EPILOGUE - DESLEN

"I'm beginning to think Aniyah did that on purpose." Conrad collapsed onto the sofa, huffing like a man who just came back from a battlefield.

I didn't blame him. I'd watched Nova's little sister Aniyah and her grandfather corner him. She kept firing off explicit questions with enthusiasm as Syris nodded solemnly, urging him to "speak freely, boy," while giving him a look that promised judgment if he did and judgment if he didn't. Conrad tried to keep his cool and remain unflustered, but the red on his neck was a dead giveaway.

I'd been too nervous to jump in those waters. If anyone could wade through that shark tank with all limbs intact, it was Conrad. He had a way of smiling through awkwardness, so I left him to it.

Zeth snorted and cracked open a Hellscape beer, chugging half before dropping onto the armchair.

"Count your blessings," he muttered. "You got the fun pair. Meanwhile, *I* had Ezra breathing down my goddamn neck about how I let all of this happen, then Calix breathing down my neck, chewing me out or contradicting every goddamn thing I said." He shuddered. "I can handle Calix's temper. But Ezra's death stare?" His shoulders trembled. "Feels like she's peeling your soul open with a serrated knife while deciding what parts she wants to keep."

He wasn't wrong. I was much bigger, more physically intimidating than Ezra, but when her eyes met mine, it felt like the room darkened. Like something with claws and smoke, a deadly hunger that pressed in close, sniffing at my thoughts. I hadn't felt fear like that since I was a cub.

That woman had the same coloring as my mate's eyes, but the souls that looked back were completely different.

The one thing I could say for sure about Ezra was that her loyalty to her siblings was unmatched. The way she always kept her eyes on them, her ear turned to whatever they were saying and doing, cataloging it all. It was both awe inspiring and terrifying. She was a woman who'd go on a war path, destroying anyone in her way, for those that she loved. I was just glad my mate was one of them.

Nick wandered in, drying his hands on a towel, jaw tight. "Okay," he growled, bracing his hands on his hips. "Are they always that... intense?"

"Yes," Zeth said instantly, taking another swig.

He pointed the mouth of his beer at us. "I told you, Nova's the most grounded. The rest? Absolute chaos gremlins."

"Riot seemed nice," Conrad offered with a shrug.

Zeth barked a laugh. "Sure. Until the air blades come out and she needs a moving target. She doesn't blink when she cuts someone apart. She *enjoys* it. They don't call her the Red Artist because she paints sunsets."

The Red Artist? I was going to need to read up on her siblings so I didn't embarrass my mate.

A question itched across my skull, finally pushing its way out. "What about her parents?"

Zeth's grin widened, softening with old admiration. "Her parents—all six of them—are cool in their own way." Then he snorted, lost in some memory, before jabbing a finger at me. "But don't *ever* turn your back on Lex. If he's feeling froggy, he'll knock you out just to play a game of 'find your limbs.' Says it's a bonding exercise."

He chuckled as he took another long swig. "The only one who can shut him down is Rayla, Nova's mom. If she snaps her fingers, he falls to his knees and begs for more."

I couldn't help the smile tugging at my mouth. Hearing about her parents reminded me of my old shadow, the pack I'd grown up with. The men were brutal, fierce males who fought tooth and claw for territory and pride, but they crumbled in adoration of their mate with equal ferocity. Savage and loyal. Deadly and soft in the ways only family could see. Safe and protected with each other.

Zeth stretched out. "They should be back from their world travels soon."

Warmth bloomed through my chest. I'd known Nova came from a big family, but I hadn't realized how tightly they clung to each other. How close this family really was. It echoed something old inside me, memories of my youth, of my own people before the war tore us apart. So many voices.

So much love, even among the violence and duty to the royals.

It was comforting to know that if fate ever took us from her, she wouldn't be alone. She'd have a small army of blood and loyalty to hold her together. That thought let something in my chest unclench, my worry softening into the wind.

In Brazil, I'd heard whispers about the Syndicate family, rulers of the supernatural world in America. They were to be feared and respected, or else you'd meet a painful doom. Seeing them now... I understood it. Knowing Nova belonged to them only made my pride burn brighter. Fate had paired me with a perfect mate, a warrior queen.

The door swung open, and all of us turned as if pulled by the same string.

Nova stepped in, hair wild, except for the braid sweeping one side. Her silhouette was as sharp as a blade, but those sunset-pink eyes held the soft vulnerability she showed only to us since that night in that cave.

My heart sang at the sight.

"Wow," she said, blowing out an exaggerated breath. "Didn't think it'd take that long to get them to the hangar and say goodbye. It's not like we won't talk again in a few days." She shook her head before looking at us, wincing like she was sorry for what we'd endured.

"Okay, first of all, I'm sorry Calix was such an asshole." She rolled her eyes and threw up both hands as she moved toward us, blowing out a frustrated breath. "I get that he's my big brother and that gives him some cosmic right to act like an asshole guard dog, but did he have to be such an asshole?"

Nova dropped onto the couch beside Conrad, exhaustion rolling off her in waves. His hands instinctively slid to her shoulders, kneading into the knots. Her eyes fluttered shut, and a soft, satisfied sound slipped from her lips, one that made my tongue swipe across my own without thinking.

"Aniyah was…" she started, then gave up with a helpless laugh. "I mean—Riot is nice, right?"

"Sure," Zeth chuckled, giving all of us a look before he passed his beer to her. She grabbed it greedily and drained it in two long gulps. "She only spent twenty minutes describing how long it takes to torture someone with a metal rod, then casually switched over to which tools make prettier blood splatter. Totally nice."

Nova groaned into her hands, laughing at herself. "They're not that bad. I swear."

"Ezra scared the hell out of me," Nick piped up earnestly as he came up behind her.

Every single one of us nodded. Even Nova.

"Yeah. She scares me sometimes, too." Nova shrugged, then rolled her shoulders back into Conrad's hands. "But you get used to it. And the fact that you all survived?" She smiled wide. "Means they approve."

Conrad worked his thumb into a spot under her shoulder blade. Nova arched, a sound caught between relief and pleasure slipping from her.

"And they don't mind that two of your mates are turned?" he asked quietly. His face was crafted into a calm mask, but his eyes showed just a sliver of hesitation. Of fear.

Her head tipped back, a small smile stretching across her lips. "The Syndicate does value power and strength, but we already have that. What's more important to us now is trust and loyalty. That is priceless." Her expression softened. She leaned forward and pressed a gentle kiss to his lips. "As long as you are dedicated to me and the Syndicate, everything will be fine."

Zeth snorted. "What she means is that you won't end up in the Syndicate dungeon with her family taking turns showing you every flavor of pain until you're halfway to madness then dragging you back to life to do it all over again."

He grinned around the rim of his bottle. "You know, *that* kind of fine."

Honestly? That felt perfectly reasonable given what was at stake and who they were.

I turned my attention back to Nova, who was currently biting the inside of her lip, which meant Conrad had hit the spot. His hands worked the muscles lower on her back, and she melted under his touch. Her mouth parted, soft and inviting, and heat rolled through me so fast my pulse stumbled. *Everything she does makes me want her.*

Her eyes snapped open and locked onto mine, hot and knowing. That golden thread between us tugged, and I knew she felt my sentiment through the bond.

I gave her a slow and deliberate smile. If my mate wanted more, I'd give her everything.

*Rising from my spot near the wall, I crossed the room toward her. Her gaze tracked me with the focus of a predator

---

* Better by Khalid

watching something it wanted to devour. When I knelt in front of her, her breath stuttered. My palms slid up her thighs, coaxing rather than claiming.

"So, my mate… my soul…" I murmured against her thigh, feeling her quiver at my fingertips. "Now that your family's given their blessing, I feel like we should prove our worth."

Her hips shifted, and her tongue swept across her bottom lip. A silent invitation.

"If that's what you want," she breathed.

My hands stilled, grip tightening just enough to stop her squirming. "Oh, no, meu amor. That's not how this works."

My jeans grew tight, constraining, but I ignored it. This wasn't about me. This was about her.

"You see," I said, leaning closer, my voice dropping to a low rumble, "we're always going to want you."

The air shifted as the others moved in, surrounding her with their heated presence. "Always craving this strong, irresistible body." Sliding my hands up her thighs and around her waist, I teased the skin there. "Wanting to keep you here, locked away with us until the days and nights blur together. Knowing nothing but our bodies and pleasure. Nothing but what we can make together."

A chorus of soft, primal sounds rumbled from the men around her, agreement, devotion, hunger, all threading together to make our song of want and desire.

When I dragged my thumb over the seam of her jeans, her breath hitched, eyes growing hungry. Even through the denim, I felt her wetness spread. Her scent, that intoxicatingly sweet, honeyed flavor that I couldn't get enough of, rose between us, making my pulse hammer.

"But *you*," I whispered, lowering my forehead to her knee, "are the one in control. We exist to satisfy you. Again and again. As much as this body can handle. That's our role as your mates at home."

I stayed there, waiting, showing her that she was the one to make the choice, not us. No one touched her without her word. Not even her mates.

"And outside the home?" she asked. Her finger twirled a dark strand of my hair around it, and her voice was slightly dazed.

Zeth was the first to answer. "Outside, you're still the boss. The only difference is I've got more help." Those turquoise eyes flared with heat as his voice became something dangerous. "Now we're your inner circle. The ones you trust when everyone else falls short. The only ones allowed at your side."

Conrad slid his lips close to her ear. "The ones you come to when you need to strategize or need someone to listen."

Nick reached over the back of the couch, fingers catching her chin, tilting her face up. His lips stayed in a thin line, but his eyes were filled with that stark honesty.

"And the ones you can be your whole self with. The killer. The queen. And the woman who wants her body to be fucked as hard at it fights."

Her eyes fluttered. I could hear her pulse throbbing against her throat, and a rosy flush was rising to her cheeks.

Nick had taken far too long to get his act together, and the other guys weren't done punishing him for it, but, in this moment, it was obvious.

He had earned a place in her heart.

We all had.

I watched him step in front of Nova without hesitation, his instincts cutting through whatever arguments or tension still lingered between them. That was what a mate was supposed to do. Show up when it mattered. Stand between danger and the woman we all swore ourselves to. The woman fate told us we needed with all of our being.

After that moment, I trusted him. Not because he said the right things, but because his body moved before his mind told him to.

Before Nova could tease or sidestep our attention, I slid my hands under her thighs and lifted. She let out a startled cry as I hoisted her over my shoulder.

"Nope," I said, heading up the stairs. "If we're doing this, it's happening in that big bed of yours. The couch won't survive us."

Her laughter warmed the back of my neck as the others trailed close behind. "Well, the couch thanks you. Calix gave me that as a housewarming gift."

"Perfect reason to break it in!" Zeth called wickedly at my back.

I didn't slow, just shrugged. "Next time." We would be having a lot of next times with this woman.

Tonight wasn't about chaos or competition. This was about showing her that the four of us could move in sync when it mattered.

In her room, I eased her off my shoulder and caught her head in my hand, lowering her onto the bed with more care than

I'd used in carrying her. Her breath hitched, soft and warm, and her pink-jeweled eyes followed my every motion.

"Let me show you," I murmured, leaning over her, "how your mates can take care of you."

Her fingers curled into my shirt, and the fabric tightened, giving me a small tug as an answer.

She didn't have to tell me twice. I crushed my mouth against hers, savoring the sweetness of her lips like it was the first time. Her body surrendered, shoulders dropping as a soft exhale escaped into the kiss.

Her fingertips grazed up my spine, light enough to raise goosebumps. Fingers tangled in my hair, yanking me closer, while her legs hooked around my waist. She ground her hips forward, slick heat pressing along my hardening cock.

A low groan rumbled from my throat into her mouth. The pull of her grip sent a spark through me, urging me to yield to her. I changed my breath to match hers, my rhythm bending to whatever she set.

She wrenched my head back by the hair. My scalp burned in perfection, causing a delicious ripple of pleasure to travel straight to my dick. My balls tightened, and my cock pulsed against her thigh, rigid and ready.

"I like tasting your lips, but I think I want to see what we taste like together." Her lips curved slowly, eyes darkening as my pulse leapt at her words. Desperately trying to control myself, my fingers hooked into her waistband. I intended to take off her clothes slowly, but my hands were too rough. Seeing her bend up toward me, I lost all reason and ripped the fabric off her with one firm tug.

She gasped, a quick inhale of shock, but I didn't let that expression stay on her face for long. I buried my face between her thighs, tongue lashing over her swollen clit flat and fast. Her sweet and intoxicating musk slid down my tongue as I licked every inch of her.

My eyes rolled into the back of my head as I moaned against her pussy, making sure she felt every vibration. The small gasps and whimpers she made were driving me wild, making me want to spend all night between her thighs like this.

Her chest heaved, head tipping back against the pillows. A muffled moan vibrated as Nick's hand clamped around her throat. He sealed his lips over hers, swallowing her sounds like he owned them. The noises grew louder, and her flavor intensified, flooding my mouth with her mesmerizing taste. My cock jerked upward, skin stretching tight around my throbbing length.

Her thighs shook under my palms, muscles clenching. The mattress shifted to the side with a creak.

"You look so beautiful, Nova." Zeth crawled onto the bed, bare skin gleaming, his palm sliding under her shirt to cup her breast. He dragged his mouth along her neck, grazing it with his teeth. "Lying down, spread out wide like this." His tongue flicked out, tracing her pulse. "You look like a damn feast, Nov, and I'm famished."

Her hands reached out, wrapping around Nick and Zeth's cocks, palms stroking from base to tip in firm pulls. Nick's mouth stayed locked on hers, devouring her cries, while Zeth kept his lips on her chest. Conrad kneeled, pressing in beside me, and I shifted to give him room as his lips brushed kisses up her right leg.

His breath ghosted over her inner thigh. "I want to make you scream, Nova. I want to hear that voice of yours choke." Then his teeth sank in, fangs piercing flesh, and he growled like a beast. Her mouth broke free from Nick's with a sharp cry, balancing herself on her elbows.

"Oh, fuck!" She looked down at him and thrust her hips upward. "Suck on me hard and deep. Take it all." She bit her bottom lip as she watched him feast on her. I seized the moment, thrusting two fingers deep into her soaking pussy, knuckles curling against her walls to get that right spot.

"Aaahhhh." The sound tore from her, raw and wordless, hips bucking hard against me as her grunts spilled out. Zeth's mouth trailed to her chest, and his fingers pinched her nipples hard while his tongue lapped against her stiff peaks. Her body jerked, spine arching off the bed.

As she got wetter, I tried to catch all of her in my mouth, but it was getting harder and harder to not take this further. To fill myself with her. It was just my luck that Conrad slid his fangs out, his tongue sealing the punctures with slow, sensual swipes.

Getting up, I grabbed her hips and turned them to the side, hoisting one leg high over my shoulder. My cockhead nudged her entrance, slick with her wetness. Her eyes, glazed with need, met mine. "I'm going to take you, mate," I rumbled. "I'm going to show you what being claimed feels like."

I pressed in slowly, the tight ring of her pussy stretching around my girth, inch by thick inch. Her eyes widened, breath hitching as she adjusted to the fullness. Zeth and Nick groaned as her fists clenched tighter around their shafts, veins bulging under her grip.

Seated to the hilt, her inner muscles fluttered around me, making it hard to stay still. Conrad's fangs sliced his wrist open, blood welling crimson. He smeared it over her toned ass, the red streaks glistening against her taut skin. Dipping his fingers into the flow at his wrist, he coated his cock in a thick layer before letting the cut knit itself shut.

Conrad lined his cock up against her curved rear entrance, a low chuckle rumbling from his chest. "I love when you scream. Will you do that for me, Boss?"

Her teeth sank so far into her lower lip that a bead of red appeared and dripped down the side of her mouth. The vision of her bleeding at the mouth, her gaze full of lust as she watched him position himself, was irresistible. Nick moved close to her face, his swaying cock inches from her mouth, and caught her attention. Her tongue darted out to wet her lips.

"Be a good girl and scream for him, Nova," Nick said.

Conrad thrust forward on those words, burying his cock deep into her ass in one brutal push. Her mouth flew open, and a raw scream tore out. "Coooonnrrraaddd!"

Nick wasted no time shoving his cock past her lips to fill her mouth. His head tipped back, a deep groan escaping. "Fucking shit, Nova. Your mouth is so hot and wet. Fuck. You feel so fucking good."

"So fucking good," Conrad growled, and her pussy walls clamped down around my shaft, stealing my breath in a sharp gasp.

Zeth leaned in, pressing her breasts together with his hands, and slid his cock between the soft mounds. "Nov, fuck. This body is fucking perfect. There's nothing about this body we don't fucking love."

A muffled garble vibrated from her throat around Nick's length in response.

Our rhythms synced without a word, and we all drove forward at once, cocks plunging deep, stretching her pussy, ass, mouth, and cleavage to the brink. Her athletic frame radiated power, and, god, it was intoxicating. The way her thighs flexed, the way her back arched, the way she held you like she knew exactly what she could do to you. Like she knew she could take it.

Wet slaps of flesh echoed off the walls, mixing with our grunts and her choked whimpers, the sounds twisting into a raw rhythm that pulsed through me. An addictive melody I could listen to forever.

The bond flared hot in my core, and I shoved waves of pleasure straight into her. The others must have too because she became downright feral. Her hips bucked hard against Conrad and me, one hand clamping onto Nick's ass, fingers pushing him deeper down her throat. Her other hand wrapped around Zeth's hip, two fingers thrusting into his ass in time with his thrusts.

Zeth snarled, his hips snapping faster, cock pistoning between her tits until his body seized. Thick ropes of cum spurted across her stretched neck, his face screwed up tight as he cooed. "Fucking hell, baby," he rasped, slumping onto the bed beside her. "You look so good in that necklace I made you." His hand trailed up her chest and circled around her neck, rubbing his cum into her skin as he tightened his grip when Nick went deep into her throat.

Her muscles down below contracted, tightening around me and Conrad, to which we both moaned.

"I fucking love you, Nova Rossey," he whispered against her skin. His mouth trailed soft kisses down her chest and belly, continuing further until his tongue flicked out, licking at her clit while I slammed into her soaked pussy.

Nick's grip tightened on her neck, his voice rough, desperate. "Drink it down, sweetheart. Take me inside you nice and deep." She stretched her mouth wider, tongue extending out flat. His thrusts turned wild, hips jerking unevenly, as the wet noises of her deepthroating him echoed in the room.

Soon, a guttural moan ripped from him. "Oh, fuck. Fuck! Nova."

His moan turned into a soft, choking gasp. "Oh, Nova. Fuck." Fully seated in her mouth, her throat working to swallow and lick every last drop, he growled, "You're fucking mine."

He slowly pulled out of her mouth, chest heaving, rubbing the head of his cock against her lips before his lips crashed against hers, his tongue plunging deep. He slumped right beside her, cupping her face as they broke apart. "Nova," he gasped, voice full of awe and reverence. His forehead rested against hers, his fingers trembling as they traced her jaw.

I was going to let them have their sweet moment until Conrad's hand clamped around her wrist, jerking her up and out of his grasp. Her legs wrapped around my hips, leaving her sandwiched between us. He twisted her arms above her shoulders, bending them back until they met his hair when he leaned forward and whispered, "Hold on, Boss. Me and the big guy are going to fuck you into oblivion."

"Mmmmm." Her moan vibrated through her body, low and needy. My guilt over ruining the moment with Nick melted away as her fingers tangled in Conrad's hair, yanking him toward her. One arm let go to hook around my neck, nails digging crescents into my skin. "Yes," she panted, eyes fluttering shut. "Harder. Faster. Make me pass out from the pleasure."

My hands holding her up flexed, getting a better grip, as I bent forward, my lips bouncing against hers. "Whatever you want, my soul."

Locking my hands onto her thighs, I slammed my cock into her pussy with brutal force, just as she demanded. Zeth's cum trailed down the curve between her breasts, glistening under the dim light, spurring me to go deeper before it traveled past her belly button.

My thrusts grew savage as my jaguar rose to the surface, wanting to fuck its mate. Each thrust burrowed to the hilt, driven by the urge to fill her, to coat every inch inside her with my claim. I wanted to leave her wrecked and spent beyond comprehension. Once she was boneless, eyes glazed, and shaking in pleasure, I'd draw her a bath. Washing her in warm aromatics, I'd clean and soothe her body with my diligent and careful hands.

I almost came right there at just the thought of it.

Her pussy clenched around my cock, muscles squeezing like a vise, reluctant to release my cock, but I drove through the resistance, hips snapping forward at a punishing pace. Her breasts jumped with every impact, head lolling back against Conrad's head, hands still in his hair, gripping him for dear life. Her breath came in sharp, ragged bursts. Sweat beaded on her skin, all the signals pointing to her being close to the edge.

Conrad pounded into her just as hard as I was, kissing along her neck, but as soon as he looked at me and winked, I knew he was going to push her into oblivion.

He slammed his teeth into her neck, making loud slurping noises that curled her toes and had her crying out, "I'm coming. Fuck! I'm coming."

Her release gushed around my cock, hot and slick. The obscene squelch of her cum mixed with my thrusts had my whole body tightening, a spring ready to burst. I bit my tongue to stifle a groan, hips pistoning faster until my climax erupted through me. I buried myself deep, cock pulsing as my cum shot up into her core, leaving her so full it ran out the sides.

I gave her a few more deep thrusts, shoving that cum back inside her before I slowly withdrew. Dragging my still-hard cock along her inner thighs, I smeared the mess on my cock over her swollen pussy and clit. Compelled by the sight of her covered in me, I claimed her mouth, my tongue delving in with a desperate hunger, pouring every ounce of my devotion and claim into the kiss. She was my world, and every rough thrust and tender touch was hers alone.

She softened against my chest with a sigh, lips parting under mine for a single moment before she was yanked away. I growled on instinct. Conrad's lip curled up, his fingers desperately digging into her skin. His eyes were glazed over in so much hunger and lust that I knew he would fight me if I tried to take her.

Nova moaned, her hands digging into his hair as she bent back and nibbled on his ear. I backed down, knowing that she wanted to please him, too. He flung her onto the bed, and her back bounced once before he seized her leg and yanked her over to him, putting both legs over his shoulders.

"Make me come." His voice was rougher than I'd ever heard it before. "Command me to come for you."

He thrust back into her ass, the force bowing her spine, stretching her wide. Her hands went to his chest, and her fingers flexed before her nails lengthened into sharp points that pierced his skin, drawing thin lines of blood that trickled down his pecs in crimson rivulets.

Her gaze locked on his, eyes blazing with feral hunger, lips curling back in a snarl. "Fuck my ass, Conrad," she demanded, voice laced with command. "Don't stop until I say."

Conrad's moan tore from his throat, raw and strained, like each breath was scraped against broken glass. His gaze locked on hers, unblinking, as he hooked his arms under her knees and shoved her legs flat against the mattress, pinning her body beneath his. His hips snapped forward, cock plunging into her ass with relentless fury, skin slapping against skin in a frantic rhythm that shook the bedframe.

Sweat slicked his brow, muscles bulging in his neck as he ground out, "P-please. Nova." The choked words pushed past his lips, desperate and fractured.

Her fingers went up to his neck and tightened. Her nails bit deeper into his flesh, squeezing until his chest stilled, no air rasping in or out. Still, his thrusts didn't falter—hips bucking wildly, cock stretching her wide, even as his eyelids fluttered and his eyes rolled back, whites flashing in the dim light.

"Come, Conrad," she rasped, her voice like a cracked whip. "Fill me up until I can't breathe."

A guttural roar ripped from him once his cock was fully seated inside her. His hands clamped down on her thighs, fingers digging bruises into her skin. They began blooming purple under the pressure while he did just what she said and filled her until her breath stopped.

Giving them their moment, I slipped into the bathroom, twisting the faucet until steam rose as the tub filled up. I scanned the bundle of herbs I'd been collecting from the forest on the counter and plucked out the witch hazel sprigs, crushing them between my fingers before sprinkling the leaves into the water. The sharp, clean scent cut through the humid air, promising relief for her aching body.

I returned to the room to find her yanking Conrad down by the throat, smashing her lips against his in a fierce, devouring kiss. Tongues tangled, breath mingling until her strength ebbed, and she sagged back onto the sheets, limbs heavy and limp.

Conrad's mouth trailed feather-light kisses along her arm, from wrist to elbow, drawing soft, breathy whimpers from her, tiny sounds like contented purrs. Her eyelids stayed sealed, chest rising and falling in shallow waves, every muscle slackened to exhaustion. As her head lolled to the side, I smiled at the others and nodded. *Job well done, mate-brothers.*

I tapped Conrad's shoulder. A low snarl curled his lip, fangs peeking out, until recognition dawned in his eyes. They darted to the bathroom door, then back, and the fog cleared. He dipped his head in a sharp nod, releasing her with reluctant, shaky hands.

Gathering her into my arms and cradling her against my chest, I carried her to the tub and lowered her into the warm water inch by inch. As I watched the water lap at her skin, soothing the red welts and tender spots, my soul settled in contentment.

I moved my hands with care, lathering soap over her whole body, rinsing away the stickiness of sweat and cum. Her lashes fluttered now and then, eyes cracking open to meet mine. "Thank you," she murmured, her voice a sleepy thread, before her head lolled to the side, and she sank deeper into the heat of the tub.

"Come," I whispered, "before you get all pruny."

She turned her head toward me, blinking slowly in recognition, and managed to lift one arm to loop around my neck so I could get her out of the tub. Taking my time, I dried her off and slipped a robe onto her arms, tying it loose around her waist. My fingers combed through her damp hair, parting it into sections to weave a simple braid down her back, keeping the strands from knotting in her sleep.

This right here, taking care of her, seeing to her, made my chest light and my soul sing. I gently let her feel how incredibly happy I was in this moment, and she leaned back, letting me wrap my arms around her and just hold her.

"I love you, Nova. My mate. My everything." Kissing her damp hair, I tightened my arms around her, giving her my heart. "I promise to be a good mate, from now until forever. You'll never be left wanting. You'll never feel alone. We're here for you and only you."

Turning her head, her lips found mine in such a sweet, soft kiss that I almost fell to the ground, wanting to be on my knees before my warrior goddess.

"I love you, Deslen. Your quick and fierce devotion might've scared me at first, but I see now that I need your soft strength more than ever." She cupped my cheek, pushing her love and appreciation into the bond. "Thank you for finding me."

I sat there for a second, holding her in my arms, memorizing the way she felt against me. The way she smelled, the soft, even rhythm of her breathing. How her body surrendered to me. This was what heaven felt like.

Knowing that I needed to share this moment with my mate-brothers, I picked her up and took her back into the room, lowering her onto the mattress with care.

The rest of her mates, freshly showered and wearing loose pants, clustered around her. They propped her up gently, pressing bites of meat to her lips, tipping a glass of water so she could sip. Hands brushed her cheeks while lips grazed her forehead, temple, and jaw, each man taking his moment to lean closer and whisper words of devotion and love to her.

My mouth curved as a quiet warmth bloomed in my chest at the thought of my grandmother. I had felt like she abandoned me by kicking me out of my home, but, standing here now, I knew she did me the biggest blessing of my life by forcing me out of Faerie. I sent out a silent thank you and I love you to her, hoping she was doing well.

Nova was nestled atop Zeth's chest, body curling into his warmth, while Conrad stretched out on her right, his arm draping her waist. Nick mirrored him on her left, fingers tracing idle patterns on her hip. I let the towel I was wearing fall off as I shifted. Bones cracked and fur rippled along my body as my jaguar emerged. Padding up onto the bed, I curled around her feet, chasing away the chill from her toes.

No part of my mate should be cold, not when she had her mates surrounding her.

Murmuring in her sleep, she said, "In the morning, I'm going to tell the whole clan that you four are my mates, and if they have anything bad to say to me or you, I'm just going to fucking kill them. I deserve to be happy."

Zeth's eyes softened, a grin splitting his face as he pressed his lips to her crown. "Yeah, you do, Nov. You deserve that and so much more."

The words hung in the air, solid as stone. Whatever storms brewed ahead of us, we'd weather them together. We had her, and she had us. Whoever thought they could cross her wouldn't live past her Syndicate fists.

Continue the story in Syndicate Prince....

AFTERWORD

Alright…. We're getting somewhere now. LOL Slowly but surly we will find out who is trying to take on the Syndicate… and what those damn parents have been doing overseas!

For those of you who might think that this was little more fluffy… I will tell you, you're right. Nova's story was not about her growing in power or showing people she's the boss. She has already done that.

What she needed to do was learn to love the pieces of herself she didn't think fit the "Rossey Boss" standards. Standards that she made.

She let others opinions affect her. She let self inducing pressure build up until she deprived herself of what mattered most, what she craved with all her heart: someone to love her soft feminine side.

Someone who didn't mind her hard body and grueling life. Someone who could bring her into her feminine space.

Someone to see that side of her and not think it was a weakness but a privilege.

It just so happened to take a smooth talking business man, a surly cop, a devoted jaguar and the unconditional love of her best friend to get her there.

I will warn you that none of these stories are going to be a carbon copy of Syndicate Princess. Each kid is different. Their struggles are different. The way they see themselves is different. The people they accept in their hearts are different.

Some of the stories are going to be more sexy and some are going to be more emotional, but the thing that all of these books will have is a family that loves hard... in their own psychotic way.

Thank you to those that have been reading these as they come out. It means the word to me.

-Kira

ABOUT AUTHOR

Kira Stanley lives in Arizona with her husband and two little monster children. She graduated ASU with a degree in Fine Arts, and has always been interested in anything that people create with their hands or minds. Which lead her to write about the characters swarming around in her head, putting them on paper for readers to enjoy.

When she is not taking care of life and all it has to throw her way, she is enjoying trashy TV and comedy movies to the fullest. Quoting every funny line that can fit into her daily life.

She is passionate about strong woman, funny characters and psychotically devoted men who fill her mind with all the things they want to do to their woman, their world.

Want to keep up with what Kira is doing?? Follow Her!

Check out all the pretties at
Kira's IG Page

Chat with others about her books in
<u>Kira's Facebook Group</u>

Find funny stuff and Book Videos at
<u>Kira's Booktok</u>

Want to be the first to know? Sign up for her newsletter at
<u>Kira Stanley Website</u>

ALSO BY KIRA STANLEY

My Alpha Series(Contemporary Spy RH)

Crazy People

Agent People

Us People

Assassin of Onisea(Dark Fantasy)

Assassin's Refusal

Assassin's Quest

Assassin's Capture

Assassin's Kingdom (TBD)

Reluctant Queen (Standalone) (Paranormal RH)

Celine (Standalone)(Paranormal MC RH)

Syndicate Mafia (Paranormal Mafia RH)

Syndicate Princess

Syndicate Queen

Syndicate Mayhem

Syndicate Next Generation (Paranormal Mafia RH)

Syndicate Flower

Syndicate Fists

Syndicate Prince (March 24th)

Syndicate Psycho (TBD)

Syndicate CEO (TBD)

Ambros Brothers Duet (Dark Stalker RH Romance)

Obsessions of the Heart

Fixation of the Mind